IT MEANS MISCHIEF

IT MEANS MISCHIEF

Kate Thompson

BANTAM BOOKS

LONDON • NEW YORK • TORONTO • SYDNEY • AUCKLAND

IT MEANS MISCHIEF
A BANTAM BOOK : 0553 812459

First publication in Great Britain

PRINTING HISTORY
Bantam Books edition published 1999

Set in 11/13pt Baskerville by
Phoenix Typesetting, Ilkley, West Yorkshire.

Bantam Books are published by Transworld Publishers Ltd,
61–63 Uxbridge Road, London W5 5SA,
in Australia by Transworld Publishers,
c/o Random House Australia Pty Ltd,
20 Alfred Street, Milsons Point, NSW 2061,
and in New Zealand by Transworld Publishers,
c/o Random House New Zealand,
18 Poland Road, Glenfield, Auckland.

Reproduced, printed and bound in Great Britain by
Cox & Wyman Ltd, Reading, Berks.

Acknowledgements

Thanks are due to: Monica Frawley, Ruth Hegarty, Maureen McGlynn and my sister Pat for reading early drafts without sniggering and telling me to trash it; Emmet Bergin for making me laugh; Eunice McMenamin and Seamus Walsh for being computer gurus to a complete Luddite; Ciaran Hinds for the fax from Australia; Abby Oppermann for the equestrian advice; Wesley Burrowes for the phone calls; James Hickey for translating all the legalese; Marie-Louise Roden for the first aid; Hazel Douglas for the Garden of Eden. All at Brookside: my editor, Frances O'Rourke, as diplomatic as she is perceptive; Edwin Higel, Dermot Bolger and Tony Glavin, who saw potential. All the real-life people who allowed me to use their names and wished me luck; all at Transworld who worked so hard to make sure I didn't feel too much like Norma New Girl; Sarah Lutyens and Felicity Rubenstein for the brilliant chats and the birthday faxes. Finally, the book would not have been written without the support of three people. Deirdre Purcell, whose unfailing encouragement and astonishingly positive attitude carried me through; my husband Malcolm, who believed in me when all I saw was ashes, and my daughter Clara, the light at the end of the tunnel.

For my mother,
Hilary Beaufoy Thompson

Chapter One

The sound of a phone ringing twice woke her, and then there was silence. Deirdre O'Dare squinted at the display on the digital clock beside her bed. It read eight-fifteen. Shit! The alarm wasn't set to go off until a quarter to nine. She rolled on to her other side and curled herself into a foetal position. Perhaps if she pretended she had never woken up she could fool her brain into going back to sleep for another half hour.

'Deirdre? Deirdre, are you there? Can you hear me?'

Deirdre sat bolt upright. There was a voice coming from the entrance hall of her apartment.

'Deirdre, it's Nick McCarthy here. I need to talk to you.'

Nick McCarthy? What was her stage director doing in her flat? Befuddled with sleep and not sure that she wasn't dreaming all this, Deirdre scrambled out of bed and stood there hesitantly for a minute before teetering towards the door and poking her head cautiously round it. There was no one there, which was just as well because she was stark naked.

The green 'in use' light was glowing on the answering machine. Deirdre's early morning brain finally copped on to the fact that Nick's voice had been coming from the speaker of the machine which sat on the floor of the tiny hallway.

'Where are you? We've an emergency scenario here, Deirdre.' Nick's voice was urgent. 'I need to talk to you ASAP. Will you call me on my mobile when you–'

Deirdre grabbed the receiver. 'Nick? Hi – it's me.'

'Deirdre? Well, thanks for finally picking up.'

'Sorry. You took me a bit by surprise, that's all. I didn't expect to hear a disembodied voice calling me to the phone so early in the day.'

'Sorry to disturb your beauty sleep. You were on the skite with the birthday girl last night, weren't you?'

'Yeah. 'Fraid so.'

'Hungover?'

'Mm. A bit.'

'Then you're not going to like me. I'm ringing to ask you to come into rehearsal half an hour earlier this morning.'

'Oh? What's up?'

'David wants a word with you.'

Deirdre was wide awake now. 'David? What on earth for, Nick? Am I in trouble or something?'

'No. He left a message on your answering machine yesterday evening, but obviously you didn't get it.'

'Oh God, Nick. It was late when I got back. I didn't bother to check messages when I got in.' She was starting to feel a bit panicky.

'Don't worry about it, Deirdre – just try and get your ass into the rehearsal room early. He wants to see you before the rest of the cast get in. In private.' Private! Deirdre's heart started to go a bit jumpy.

'Say nine-thirty?'

'Sure.' Deirdre would have complied if he'd asked her to get there in five minutes.

'Good. Nine-fifteen would be even better.'

'OK.' She was suddenly uneasy. 'Nick? Can you fill me in on any of this?'

'Sorry. That's not my brief. I can't pre-empt the main man on this. Just let me reassure you that he's not going to chew you out. Catch you later.'

'OK. And I'm sorry I didn't get the–' she began, and then stopped as the connection was cut.

She put the receiver down and looked at the answering machine which squatted like a small black beast at her feet. The green 'in use' indicator had gone out and had been replaced by a flashing red light. It looked ominous, somehow. She hesitated fractionally before pressing playback. There was the usual sequence of answering machine noises before a dark chocolate voice slid over the speaker. Deirdre dropped to a sitting position on the carpet and leant against the wall, listening with her eyes closed and her lips curved in a smile. How pathetic, she thought. Even the sound of his voice makes me go weak.

'Deirdre. David Lawless here. Please phone me the minute you get this message. I'd be obliged.' He concluded by leaving a telephone number which Deirdre repeated to herself like a mantra so that she wouldn't forget it. Resisting the temptation to replay the message, she turned off the machine before Nick McCarthy's voice could come on again and then scribbled the number down at once on the dog-eared Post-It pad by the phone. She drew a big heart shape around it to distinguish it from all the other hieroglyphics on the page.

As she added an arrow through the heart, a terrible thought struck her. For all she knew, today might be the last time she would ever hear his voice! She'd only have those few words on the answering machine as a kind of memento. Maybe he was going to tell her that he'd made a mistake in casting her – that she couldn't hack it as an actress and that she should think about doing something else. The prospect filled her with cold dread. Maybe she'd have to waitress or chamber-maid again. Those were the only other ways of earning a living that she had any experience of. If she was to be completely honest with herself, she'd have to admit that she didn't even have that much experience of acting. Although she'd spent three years doing a degree in Theatre Studies at Trinity College, this show with Lawless Productions was her very first professional engagement.

She took one last look at his phone number on the pad and hauled herself off the floor. Whatever was going on, she needed to get started. As she flew through her routine in the bathroom she cast her mind back to the first day of rehearsal, remembering David's introductory speech to the company. '*A Midsummer Night's Dream* isn't just a play about magic and fairies,' he'd said. 'It's one of Shakespeare's most complex plays and we're going to have to work hard. Fairies have had a bad press. But in this play magic is a primal force and fairies aren't ethereal, other-worldly beings. They're rooted in the earth, they're dangerous, and they're very, very sexy.' Oh God. Maybe *that* was it. Maybe she just wasn't sexy enough. She decided she'd wear her Wonderbra today. She didn't usually bother with a bra, but it might be advisable to try to look a bit sexier this morning. When she'd finished dressing she studied herself in the mirror. Even thrusting her chest out like a Page Three girl didn't seem to help. She was the only person she knew for whom a Wonderbra did nothing.

In the kitchen she gulped back Gold Blend and went through the contents of her backpack to make sure she had everything she needed. Script, pencil, jazz pumps (she made a face at the dilapidated state of them as she forced them to the bottom of her bag), leggings and T-shirt for the pre-rehearsal warm-up. Bicycle keys. Rescue remedy. She was sorted and ready to go, but the time check on the radio told her she was ahead of herself for once.

She poured herself another mug of coffee and stuck her last Pop Tart in the toaster, making a mental note to buy some more. Her flatmate Sarah, who had been two years above her in college, was the kind of enviably organized person who always kept a shopping list stuck on the fridge door. But Sarah had landed a year's contract with the RSC and had gone off to Stratford a week ago, and Deirdre didn't bother with a shopping list any more. There didn't seem much point when she was living on her own.

When the Pop Tart popped she cut it into bite-size pieces and waited for it to cool. Timesaver Traffic droned on 98FM. She was calmer now, and something told her that the worst-case scenario she'd tortured herself with after she'd put down the phone to her stage director didn't ring true.

Her gut feeling was that she wasn't a bad actress. Her college tutors told her she had talent and had encouraged her every step of the way during the three years she'd spent studying there. Anyway, why would a hot-shit director like David Lawless bother to cast her if she was no good? She had only been in rehearsal for a couple of weeks, and her role as First Fairy in *A Midsummer Night's Dream* was of the 'don't-blink-or-you'll-miss-me' variety, but she couldn't help feeling she'd made an impression. She was having fun with the little part, and really looked forward to going into work every day. She stuffed the last of the Pop Tart into her mouth and looked at her watch. Time to go.

As she undid the security chain on the front door she caught a glimpse of herself in the mirror in the hallway. She wished she'd had time to wash her hair. On an impulse she ran back to the bedroom and sprayed herself with the Diorissimo her mother had given her for Christmas, and which she allowed herself to wear only on special occasions. As far as she was concerned, this *was* a special occasion. She was on her way to meet the sexiest man in the world.

* * *

She chained her bike to a parking meter around the corner from the dance studio which had been requisitioned as the company's rehearsal space and sprinted through the door, sending a breathless 'Hi!' to the girl at reception before taking the stairs two at a time. Fluffing her hair with nervy fingers, she swung through the rehearsal room door and let it fall shut behind her with a thud. David Lawless was standing talking to Nick McCarthy at the other end of the room. He looked up at the sound of the door closing. 'Deirdre. Hi. Thanks for making the effort to get in here early – I appreciate it. Can you give me a minute? I need to sort something with Nick.'

Deirdre returned his smile rather nervously. 'No problem,' she said. She retrieved her backpack from the chair where she'd left it and got out her script. She needed something to do to cover her awkwardness while David and Nick finished their business.

The margins of the book were covered in doodles and sketches – most of them little thumbnail portraits of members of the company. David Lawless featured prominently, and she had another twinge of anxiety. Maybe *that* was why he wanted to talk to her! Maybe he was fazed by the way she watched him so intently as he worked. Because she was hungry to learn all she could on her first professional show, she had made a point of studying David and the more experienced actors every time they took to the rehearsal-room floor. She had come into work even when scenes she wasn't involved in were being rehearsed just so that she could observe from the sidelines.

She looked at him covertly now as he stood talking in low tones with Nick McCarthy, and allowed herself the indulgence of admiring him for the first time that day. On a normal day she'd make sure to sneak at least half-a-dozen opportunities to admire him.

He was too old for her, she knew that – probably somewhere in his early forties. He was married, too, to an actress – Ann Fitzroy, who played a Queen Bitch in the soap opera *Ardmore Grove.* She was rumoured to be a bit of a diva, and it was common knowledge amongst theatre people that the marriage wasn't a happy one. It was certainly obvious to Deirdre. You could see it in his eyes. His eyes sometimes reminded her of a wounded panther she'd seen on David Attenborough. She often wondered why he'd stuck the marriage for so long, especially now that Ireland had finally heaved itself into the twentieth century and divorce was on the statute books at last. If Ann Fitzroy was anything like her screen character, the Lawless's domestic life must be pretty grim.

She had already given up all pretence of studying her script and was studying him openly now. She could see that he was too involved in his discussion with Nick to notice. She was almost tempted to get her pencil out and start sketching him. He wasn't a particularly handsome man, she had to admit, in spite of being tall and dark. There certainly wasn't anything conventionally good-looking about him. He had what she supposed could best be described as a Byronic attraction. *That* was what was sexy about him! He had the high cheekbones and olive complexion of a Slav, and a lean, athletic body. His black hair was worn shoulder-length. It had been ponytailed the first time she'd met him.

As she watched him now his eyes met hers again without warning, and, as usual, nothing prepared her for the impact. Thrown into confusion by his glance, she sent him an imbecilic grin. He had the good grace to acknowledge it with a vague nod before handing Nick a manila envelope and unclipping a shrilling mobile from his belt. 'Hello?' he said into the phone. He sounded uncharacteristically curt. 'Yeah. That's right. Remind her to change the cast names on the press release, won't you?' Deirdre dug her nails into her palms. Oh God. Her first reaction had been right – he was recasting her. She felt like crying with humiliation. 'Please. Thanks.' He put a hand over the mouthpiece and muttered something urgent to Nick McCarthy before resuming his phone conversation. As Nick walked past her towards the door of the rehearsal room he gave her a smile which could only be described as sympathetic.

She dug her nails in even harder. 'As soon as possible,' David Lawless was saying now. 'Thanks. I appreciate it. Bye.' He clipped the mobile back on his belt and then strolled across the floor in her direction.

'I'm sorry I didn't get back to you last night, David,' she said immediately.

'That's OK. I understand you were out celebrating Jessica's birthday. Good time?'

'Yes, thanks.'

Her heart was ricocheting against her ribcage as he took a chair and set it down opposite her, sitting astride it and letting his arms rest on the back. With a casual hand he pushed back the wing of glossy dark hair which fell over his forehead and smiled at her. The smile softened the intelligent, rather guarded expression of his amber-coloured eyes. 'There's something I want to put to you, Deirdre,' he said in a serious voice. 'And I'm afraid I'm not going to allow you a great deal of time to think it over. Suki Hayes has – *chosen* to leave the company. I would like you to replace her.'

Deirdre didn't say anything because she couldn't. She sat there frozen in an attitude of disbelief, horror scrawled across her face in block capitals.

'I'm very sorry to spring this on you without warning, but I can't afford to waste any more time now that we're a full two weeks into rehearsal.'

She found her voice. 'You're joking, David.'

'I'm not joking, Deirdre. I've been watching you carefully for the past few days with this proposition in mind, and I'm confident you can bring it off. I know you're inexperienced, but you're a hard worker and a quick study and you have a terrific, vibrant quality. I don't foresee any problems with Equity, and it goes without saying that we'll hike up your salary. Will you do it?'

Of course she would do it. There was no question about it. At this moment she was actually living a scenario most aspiring actresses only experience in their dreams. But this was real life, not make-believe, and she was suddenly scared to death. Her mouth felt as if it was full of cornflour, and she had difficulty in articulating the words when they finally left her mouth. 'Yes. Yes I will,' she managed. 'I'd be honoured, actually.' She meant it.

David Lawless smiled again. 'Hermia's feisty, Deirdre, and I've a suspicion you are too. Of course, I could have recast from outside the company, but that would have meant starting from scratch. I've seen the way you've been observing rehearsals from the sidelines. You'll know the blocking inside-out, and it wouldn't surprise me if you had the dialogue down, too. By casting you I'll be saving myself and the rest of the company time and energy, and that's imperative. It'll be tough, but I know you're able for it.' He laid a reassuring hand on her arm and Deirdre felt her nerve endings flare. Then he swung himself off his chair and looked at his watch. 'We've time to grab a coffee before the rest of the cast arrive. Once everyone's here I'll make a quick announcement and then we can get started.'

Just then his mobile sounded again. 'Excuse me,' he said with a resigned sigh as he reached for it. 'I should have turned this thing off.'

Deirdre veered in the direction of the coffee room, still feeling gobsmacked. She couldn't believe that it had taken a matter of only a few minutes to completely change her life around.

'Deirdre?'

She turned back to him. 'Yes?'

'Thanks.' And he sent her a heart-stopping smile before pressing pick-up.

* * *

In the coffee room which adjoined the studio she filled the kettle and sat up on the draining board while she waited for the water to boil, leafing through her script for Hermia's bits. Hermia was a dream role for an actress just out of college. It was of juve lead proportions, and a brilliant showcase. The character was winsome and devious at the same time, and although Suki Hayes, the actress who'd originally been cast in the role, certainly *looked* the part of a girl who has men falling over themselves to bed her, she hadn't managed the winsome and devious bit. In fact, Suki Hayes's embarrassingly wooden performance had been much discussed in low tones in the coffee room when she wasn't around. She remembered how careful David had sounded when he'd told her that Suki had walked. 'Suki Hayes has *chosen* to leave the company,' he'd said. Deirdre had a sneaking suspicion that Suki actually hadn't had much choice in the matter at all, and that she'd been paid off.

She was starting to feel excited now. She mentally replayed the conversation she'd just had. Feisty. That's how David Lawless had described her. She'd do right by him and inject some of that feistiness into her portrayal of Hermia. She'd go through hoops for him!

Just then the door to the coffee room opened and Jessica Young, the Assistant Stage Manager, stepped through backwards. She was balancing several packets of biscuits, a big jar of instant coffee and a carton of polystyrene cups.

'Hi, Deirdre,' she said. 'I hate that fucking corner shop. They never have any carrier bags. How's your hangover?'

Deirdre realized that the mild hangover she'd been nursing since she'd been woken up by Nick McCarthy's phone call was gone. 'Not too bad.' She smiled happily at Jessica. 'Deadly evening, wasn't it?'

'Yep. I slept right through the alarm this morning.' Jessica dumped the groceries on the counter. 'What are you doing in so early?'

Deirdre suddenly laughed out loud in incredulous delight. She couldn't help it.

Jessica looked at her with curious eyes. 'What's the big joke?' she asked.

'Suki's out. David's asked me to play Hermia.'

Even as she articulated the words she could hardly believe them.

Jessica whooped. 'Yes! I'd a funny feeling that was on the cards. Wow! You must be feeling pretty bloody smug, girl!' She gave Deirdre a big hug.

'I am,' Deirdre admitted, hugging Jessica back. 'But I'm feeling a bit scared too, Jessica. I'm just a New Girl. Suki Hayes may have been crap, but she's a lot more experienced than me.'

'In more ways than one.' Jessica raised a cynical eyebrow. 'Come on, Deirdre. She may look gorgeous, but she's a brutal actress. She's flavour of the month, that's all.'

'She's been flavour of the month for the past three years.'

'So what's she got that we don't have?'

Deirdre shrugged her shoulders. 'Svengali appeal?'

Jessica laughed. 'Maybe. But have you *ever* seen her deliver the goods? David was practically directing her by numbers and she still couldn't get it right.'

'She was good in that shampoo ad.'

'The one where she didn't have to say anything?'

'Yeah. Her hair was really shiny, though, Jessica.'

'And she pouted quite well.' They shared a smile.

Then Deirdre had a sudden thought. 'I wonder how the rest of the cast are going to feel about it?' she said anxiously. 'Having a total unknown suddenly take over.'

'Jesus, Deirdre – they'll all be delighted. Suki was threatening to scupper the show – everybody knew that. And Rory was going bonkers playing Lysander. He said that snogging Suki was like snogging Lassie.'

The realization that she was going to have to do love scenes with Rory McDonagh made Deirdre feel even more nervous. She didn't really know him that well. He was good-looking, she supposed, in a kind of dissolute, rangy way. But there was something about him that she was uncomfortable with. A kind of recklessness. She knew that Kate O'Connor, another of the fairies, was crazy about him. 'His hair's *not* dirty-blond,' she'd insisted once, when Deirdre had observed that Rory badly needed a hair-cut. 'It's *sun-kissed.* He's just come back from Morocco.' And her eyes had gone all swoony.

'Here – have a Bourbon Cream to celebrate,' said Jessica, handing her a biscuit.

'Thanks.' Deirdre took the biscuit and bit into it without tasting it. She still had that cornfloury feeling in her mouth.

'I wonder who's going to replace you as First Fairy?' said Jessica.

'First Fairy's going to be Sophie Burke.' Nick McCarthy answered Jessica's question for her as he came through the door. 'And you, Jessica, are going to take over as Moth. You're being promoted to *Acting* Assistant Stage Manager –'

'Yes!'

'– from just plain old Assistant. Congratulations, Deirdre.' He plonked a kiss on her cheek and then made for the biscuits.

'You're not to touch the Jammie Dodgers, Nick,' warned Jessica. 'They only had one packet left in that stinking corner shop, and it's got Eva's name on. They're her favourites.'

There was the sound of banging doors and chattering voices from the rehearsal hall. The cast was beginning to arrive. Deirdre started to stew again. She was anticipating with a kind of excited dread the moment when David Lawless would make his announcement. She hoped that one cast member in particular would be happy with the news. If Eva Lavery approved of David's casting decision then all would be right with Deirdre O'Dare's world.

*   *   *

Nobody was brazen enough to actually cheer after David announced the change in casting, although Rory McDonagh let out a kind of strangulated sob which sounded a bit like 'thank you God'. Most of the actors wore rather relieved expressions as they strolled towards the coffee room, congratulating Deirdre as they passed her, although both Adrian Pierce and Maeve Kirwan, who were playing the other pair of lovers in the show, had a slightly guarded look about them. Deirdre didn't blame them – they'd have a lot of scenes to re-rehearse now that she was playing Hermia, and she was an unknown quantity as far as they were concerned. Deirdre looked around for Eva, to see if she could gauge her reaction to the news, but there was no sign of the leading lady.

Sophie Burke looked as if her smile was stapled to her face when she eventually got round to congratulating Deirdre. 'Well done, Deirdre. I'm sure you'll make a very – um – *unusual* Hermia. I'm delighted for you.'

'Thanks, Sophie.' She's really a crap actress, thought Deirdre – she might have made an effort to sound more convincing. Sophie, like Deirdre, had just graduated from the Theatre Studies course at Trinity. There was history there. Deirdre could never, ever, ever forgive Sophie Burke for robbing her of Beautiful Ben – her first truly important boyfriend – and Sophie could never forgive Deirdre for landing all the parts *she* wanted to play in college productions.

Sophie tucked a strand of her expensively streaked hair behind one ear. 'You'll be in for a rise now, I suppose.'

Deirdre knew that whatever salary she took home would be like pocket money to Sophie, who made frequent reference to the Gold credit card her father had given her for her twenty-first. 'Well, I'll be working my ass off for it,' she replied a tad tersely. Then she relented. She knew she'd be feeling pretty pissed off if *Sophie* had got the part. There was no point in continuing hostilities. 'Congratulations on your promotion to First Fairy, by the way, Sophie,' she added with an attempt at an encouraging smile.

Sophie's eyes narrowed. 'Well, it's not a terribly challenging role, is it, Deirdre? But I'll try to make something of it. You don't mind if I'm perfectly frank, do you? I wasn't that keen on your interpretation. I might try and put a different slant on it.'

Deirdre could hardly believe what she was hearing. She couldn't let Sophie get away with such an unprovoked attack without swiping back. She smiled at the other actress. 'Well, if your performance as Moth was anything to go by I'm sure you'll have the audience in stitches,' she said pleasantly.

'Very droll, Deirdre.' Hostilities resumed. Looking as if she was sucking on a lemon, Sophie turned and walked away.

'Put your claws back in, sweetheart.' Deirdre turned to find Rory McDonagh at her side.

'Oh, hi, Rory,' she said, colouring slightly. She wished he hadn't overheard her.

He smiled at her. 'I hope you enjoy a good snog. We've a lot of raunchy scenes together.'

'Yes, I suppose we have.' Something about the look in his eyes made her feel horribly inadequate. She tried hard to be cool. 'I don't think I'll have too many problems identifying with Hermia on an emotional level,' she said, remembering the kind of jargon a visiting lecturer at college had used. 'I really feel I can relate to her, you know? I think maybe I'll go out to the zoo to see if there's some animal there that might hold the key to my emotional identification.' God. What a load of crap, she thought.

Rory smiled politely and inclined his head.

'Have you ever done that, Rory?' she asked.

'No,' he said, adopting an expression of extreme interest. 'Tell me about it.'

'Well, when I was cast as Cecily in the third-year production of *The Importance of Being Earnest* at college the director advised me to go to the zoo and find Cecily's animal equivalent. I decided on an ibex – you know those elegant little goats?'

'I thought they were a kind of sheep,' said Rory.

'Oh no – they're definitely goats,' replied Deirdre firmly. 'Anyway, I drew on the image of this little ibex during rehearsal, and I'm convinced it really helped to inform my interpretation. What do you think I should decide on for Hermia?'

Rory looked her up and down with interest. Deirdre squirmed. It seemed to take him ages to make up his mind. 'A vixen,' he said finally.

'Oh – good idea! Thanks, Rory.' He was actually spot on. A vixen was perfect for Hermia. 'And what sort of animal do you see Lysander as?'

Rory furrowed his brow. 'Mm. That's a tough one. A gerbil, maybe?'

'A *gerbil*?' For a millisecond she was completely taken aback. Then she started to smile. He was quite right to take the piss out of her Theatre-Studies-Speak. That was the kind of guff Sophie Burke came out with.

She was wondering how she could backtrack and make Rory see that she didn't take herself *that* seriously, when she realized that his attention had been diverted elsewhere. 'Dear Jesus,' he said.

'What's wrong?'

'Lavery's just arrived and she's wearing those leather trousers again.'

Deirdre followed Rory's eyeline to where Eva Lavery stood. She had just shut the door of the rehearsal room behind her and was now leaning against it, talking to David Lawless. She was wearing silver hoops in her ears, a faded black T-shirt tucked into black leather trousers, and she was toying with the frayed edge of a flame silk chiffon scarf which hung over her shoulders. She looked as if she hadn't made an effort. She looked sensational.

'It's not like our leading lady to be late,' Rory remarked. 'But then, she's got a rather post-coital look about her, hasn't she, Deirdre? Maybe that accounts for it.' He looked down at her and gave her a lazy smile. 'Let me get you a coffee.' He was gone before she could think of anything to say.

She wished she hadn't come out with all that stupid psychobabble. Emotional identification! Oh, God! He must be dreading working with her now. She wondered if she'd ever figure out how to handle Rory McDonagh. She'd heard that he'd had a pretty chequered career. Kate O'Connor had told her that he'd got into the acting business by default several years ago, when he'd been working as a horse wrangler on a movie during the summer break from college. He'd been studying veterinary science in Galway, but had given it up when the acting bug had bitten.

Eva Lavery's familiar laugh drew Deirdre's attention back to her. Deirdre wondered if David had filled her in on the new casting yet. She desperately wanted her leading lady's blessing. She had been Deirdre's role model and heroine for years.

Eva was one of a very small and prestigious number of actors who had managed to establish a highly successful acting career on both sides of the Irish Sea. She had also starred in a rash of critically-acclaimed Hollywood features, but had resisted the temptation to settle in Tinseltown. When Deirdre had heard that Eva was to double as Titania and Hippolyta in David Lawless's *Midsummer Night's*

Dream she'd been a bit taken aback. She must be hitting her early forties now, and Deirdre had always visualized both characters in *Dream* as being much younger – especially Titania. But when she had seen Eva in the flesh at the first read-through of the play two weeks ago, she had had to acknowledge that the casting had been inspired. When an actress possessed the kind of charisma Eva had, age just wasn't an issue.

She had been surprised to find that in real life the actress was actually quite petite. She appeared curvier on screen, somehow. But the camera hadn't lied about her bone structure. Her strong chiselled cheek bones lent her an aristocratic air and redeemed her from being just ordinarily pretty. There was an aristocratic set to her head, too, which she assumed now as she listened to David. When he finished speaking she threw back her head and gave a deep, throaty, utterly infectious laugh. Deirdre found herself smiling. It had to be the filthiest laugh she had ever heard. Eva turned suddenly and met her eye, and Deirdre felt a bit embarrassed that she'd been caught staring. But Eva was unfazed. Blowing David a kiss, she moved straight across the rehearsal room in Deirdre's direction.

'Shrewd move of David's, darling, to cast you. You'll cakewalk it,' she said with authority.

Deirdre's smile was heartfelt. 'What a kind thing to say, Eva! Though I'm not so sure. I've a lot of hard work ahead of me.'

'Feel free to come to me for help any time. I

played Hermia once aeons ago at the RSC.'

'Thanks a lot, Eva. I'll do that.'

'Don't tell David, though. He hates the idea of people tampering with his work.'

'Oh?' Deirdre looked uncertain. After all, her primary allegiance was to David, not Eva.

Eva gave her a level look. 'Don't worry. I never tamper. We're on exactly the same wavelength, David and I. It's just that he doesn't speak girltalk. D'you know what I mean?'

Deirdre laughed. 'Yes, I do. I don't think there's a man on the planet who speaks girltalk, Eva.'

Just then Rory rolled up with a dripping polystyrene cup and a Jammie Dodger which he presented to Eva as if she were a goddess. His worshipful stance was belied by a distinct glint in his slanting green eyes. 'What made you so late this morning, beautiful?' he said. 'You looked as if you'd just fallen out of bed.'

'I had.'

The actors shared a smile, and Deirdre felt awkward again as Rory turned his wicked eyes on her.

'Oh – sorry, Deirdre,' he said, not sounding sorry at all. 'I forgot your coffee.'

'That's OK, Rory.'

Rory moved closer to Eva and ran an experimental hand over her bum.

'Well, thank you, angel,' she said, with a feline smile. 'That feels quite delightful.'

'It's just as well you enjoy it, you gorgeous

creature. You shouldn't wear lethal trousers like that if you don't.'

'Not many people would get away with putting a hand on my bum you know, Rory. I only allow you to do it because you're sexy. And special.'

'And you're the cat's pyjamas.' Rory trailed his index finger up Eva's spine. 'Correction. You're the *glamour*-puss's pyjamas.'

'I never bother with pyjamas.'

'I didn't think you would. What do you wear in bed, Deirdre?' he asked in a throwaway manner, taking her quite off guard.

She was saved the necessity of a reply by Nick McCarthy clapping his hands for attention and calling the cast on to the floor to give them their revised rehearsal schedule.

Eva turned to Deirdre. 'Welcome to the world of working actresses,' she said cheerfully. 'You'll find there are some wonderful fringe benefits. Actors like Rory, for instance.' Then she linked Rory's arm and drew him over to where Jessica was setting out a circle of chairs, sending a radiant smile to David Lawless as she drifted past him.

Deirdre smiled at her retreating back and moved towards the chair where she'd dumped her back-pack. Working actress! She was a working actress! It made her feel very grown-up. As she pulled on her battered jazz shoes she felt a kind of frisson. What a prestigious production to mark her professional debut! She'd seen a rough for the poster advertising David Lawless's Shakespeare season at the Phoenix Theatre. David and Eva's names featured prominently, while hers had been in very small print. She wondered if they'd have to make it bigger now. Lost in reverie, she didn't see the malevolent look that came her way as Sophie Burke shimmied past to strike a pose on the rehearsal room floor.

Chapter Two

She was up against it. The dress rehearsal was nearly on top of them, and Deirdre was in despair. Up till now things had gone unbelievably smoothly. Everything had been sorted with the actors' union, Equity; she was word perfect and hadn't needed a prompt for over a week; and most of the cast had been really helpful. Rory McDonagh had surprised her by turning out to be an incredibly generous and supportive actor, even though she still found it hard to make out where he was coming from. There was a word for what he was. Disconcerting, she supposed. He had an uncanny knack of making her feel idiotic, even though there didn't seem to be anything deliberate about it. Maeve Kirwan had been kind, too, and had given Deirdre hints about how best to handle Adrian Pierce. Adrian's intense approach owed a lot to the Stanislavski Method style of acting. Robert de Niro was his hero, and he liked to think that he actually *became* his character on stage. This could be a bit hard to take at times. 'There's madness in his Method,' Maeve had remarked after the stage punch he'd aimed at Rory had hit the mark one day. Nick McCarthy had to intervene like lightning in order to prevent Rory from knocking Adrian sideways.

She'd also learned a lot from watching Eva Lavery. She and David Lawless had an extraordinary rapport. There was an air of complicity about the two of them, almost as if they had a secret language in common. More often than not, David didn't even need to say anything to Eva when they worked on her scenes. He would stop her in her tracks from time to time and before he could speak she would laugh and say: 'I know! You don't have to tell me!' and then launch into the scene again.

Deirdre remembered one morning in particular when Eva had taken the floor to rehearse with Finbar de Rossa, the company's leading man. Finbar was cast in the dual roles of Theseus and Oberon. As Eva adopted the prostitute's swagger she used as Titania, Deirdre's gaze had wandered automatically to where David Lawless was sitting. She was still smitten, and while she could do nothing to stop feeling scorched every time he laid a casual hand on her arm or shoulder in the course of his direction, at least she had stopped burning up every time he looked at her. He had been lounging back in his chair with his long, denim-clad legs stretched out in front of him and his hands clasped loosely behind his head as he watched the actors go through their paces. But his relaxed posture was at complete variance with the look on his face. He wore an expression of rapt concentration, with something fierce about it, and his narrowed eyes were fixed unswervingly on Eva Lavery.

Eva had just started into one of Titania's long speeches in her inimitable husky voice, contriving to look enviably lazy and confident at the same time, when her eyes had suddenly met David's and she had stopped dead. Her head had assumed its imperious little tilt as she looked at him with one eyebrow raised, and then she nodded in his direction in an oddly formal manner. The gesture was elegant – gracious, even – but there had been a hint of a challenge there, too. Deirdre had been more aware than ever of a strange sense of collusion. It was almost as if the air between them was shimmering with a kind of electric tension. What secret did they share? she wondered. There had to be history there somewhere. Then she had caught herself on, realizing how rudely she was staring, and she had quickly returned her attention to the script in her lap.

That very afternoon David had come to her at the end of rehearsal and kissed her on the cheek, and she'd blushed when he'd told her what splendid progress she was making. She'd felt so buoyed up that she'd even offered Sophie a stick of chewing gum as they'd left the hall with the other fairies and headed towards the pub.

But now the dress rehearsal was only two days away, and she was in the pits. Something strange had happened to her performance – she felt that an edge was gone from it somehow, and she just couldn't work out where she was going wrong.

David had noticed it too, for at the notes session which wound up the day's rehearsal he warned her about her concentration level before giving her a long look of frank appraisal. 'Otherwise I'm very pleased with your work. Thank you, Deirdre.' And then he turned his attention elsewhere.

Deirdre sighed and dug her fingers into the nape of her neck where she could feel a knot of tension beginning to form. She was feeling very tired and a headache was threatening. The 'No Smoking' sign was being totally ignored as usual, and the cigarette smoke was beginning to make her eyes smart. It was unbearably stuffy in the rehearsal hall, and very warm. A heat wave had begun the previous week and the cast had taken to spending their lunch-breaks in the nearby park. They were all tanned now, in various shades ranging from bright pink to dark copper. Sophie was the only one who refused to leave the confines of the hall, saying that it was deeply untrendy to have a tan these days and she had no intention of ending up with skin cancer. The fairies had been sent off to rehearse their song at the far end of the hall, and Sophie was posing by the piano, trying to look like one of the Corrs, and singing in a rather squawky voice. The only one of the fairies who really sounded good was Kate O'Connor, but she was doing a Dolores O'Riordan on the song, and it was making Deirdre's headache worse. A trickle of sweat was meandering down her ribcage.

Over by the door to the coffee room Rory McDonagh and Jonathan Hughes, the actor playing Puck, were messing around with poly-styrene cups, poking holes in them for nostrils and pretending they were pigs' snouts. Nick McCarthy shot them a warning look, whereupon Rory said something in an undertone to Jonathan and the pair creased up. It was weird to see two grown men behaving in such a juvenile manner. She'd heard that Jonathan Hughes was meant to be a member of MENSA. Hard to believe, she thought, after the behaviour she had just witnessed. She sighed as she returned her attention to David Lawless, hoping to be soothed by his gentle, authoritative tones.

Deirdre cherished a pet fantasy – a very private one. She would have died rather than reveal it to another living soul. It involved David finally seeing the light, dumping his wife and discovering that Deirdre O'Dare was actually a more fascinating and complex creature than he'd realized. Sometimes she embroidered the plot with a darker thread. She had a suspicion that divorcing Ann Fitzroy might prove a bit difficult for David. No woman in her right mind would let go of a man like David Lawless without a struggle, especially since the woman in question was approaching her best-before date. So she'd have the soap opera actress conveniently die of something unspecific in her fantasy. ('She died instantly, David. She didn't feel any pain. You mustn't blame yourself,' she could hear herself saying when he turned to her for support.) Then she'd immediately mutter the little prayer she always used when she saw a single magpie, to ward off ill luck in case anything awful actually happened to Ann Fitzroy in real life. After a suitable period of mourning David would be free to choose another partner. He'd go for someone younger – they always did – and she would be waiting. The only snag was that she'd heard he had a daughter who was somewhere in her teens. It was a bit weird having a teenage stepdaughter in her fantasy, so she resolved it by having David send her away to boarding school. That was much more satisfactory – she'd really prefer to have her dream lover all to herself.

She was replaying this fantasy now, and had just got to the bit where David was looking at her with an awed expression, as if seeing her for the first time, when she realized that the notes session had finally come to an end. The actors were getting to their feet, stretching and yawning, and those who weren't putting out a cigarette were lighting them up.

On the other side of the room, Rory and Jonathan had been joined by Eva, who was scribbling something down in her diary. 'Wonderful sandals, darling,' she said as Kate O'Connor walked by. 'Where did you get them?'

'Oh, thanks Eva. I got them in Penney's last week. They were dead cheap – only nine ninety-five.'

'What stunningly good value!' Eva ran a hand through her messy straw-coloured bob as if to smooth it, but succeeded only in making it look even more wrecked. 'You wouldn't mind if I copied you and got a pair, would you?' she asked Kate.

'Not at all.' Kate actually looked extremely flattered, and had gone pink with pleasure. 'I'd offer to let you try them on, but they'd be too big for you. You've got the daintiest feet of anyone I know.'

Deirdre snuck a look at Eva's tiny, elegant feet, and then glanced down at her own. They looked like boats in comparison. She'd always hated her feet. Stuffing her script into her backpack, she stood up, feeling stiff. The pre-rehearsal warm-up had been particularly vigorous that day.

Across the room, she saw Rory wink at Kate O'Connor, who went pinker still and mumbled something about having to make a phone call before scurrying away. Rory's eyes studied her retreating rear with interest, and then made contact with Deirdre's. He raised his eyebrows at her, and she busied herself immediately with the buckle on her backpack.

Most days Deirdre hit the pub with Kate and Jessica after rehearsal, and Sophie sometimes came along as well if there was nothing more socially desirable to do. There she was now, announcing to Jessica that she was 'goin' down the pub for a bevvy' in an embarrassing Cockney accent. Deirdre decided she'd just go home. Anyway, she needed time to herself to go over her part and try to figure out exactly where she was going wrong.

She trailed down the stairs, wished the receptionist an abstracted 'enjoy your weekend', and stepped out into the blazing sunshine. The prospect of the cycle home was grim. It was uphill nearly all the way. Deirdre stepped out on to the footpath. A filthy pigeon with a stump where its left claw had once been scrabbled morosely for crumbs among the litter at her feet, looking as dejected as she felt.

She rounded the corner, rummaging in her backpack for the keys to her bicycle chain, and then stopped in dismay. Her bike had gone from the parking meter where she always left it. She looked further down the street to check she hadn't chained it to another meter, but the only bicycle in sight was the sleek racer owned by Sophie Burke, restrained by a gleaming Kryptonite padlock.

'Shit,' she said, and burst into angry tears.

'What's the problem, darling?' came a voice from behind her. She turned to discover Eva Lavery.

'Oh – hello Eva.' Deirdre was mortified. She was glad to find that she had a tissue in her pocket for once, to wipe away the evidence of her childishness. 'It's stupid really – it's just that my bike's been stolen.'

'Oh no – how awful. That's the second bicycle to be nicked from around here this week. Adrian's disappeared yesterday, didn't it?' Eva squinted at her through the darkest sunglasses Deirdre had ever seen. 'You poor thing. Let me give you a lift. Where do you live?'

'I'm near St Patrick's Cathedral,' said Deirdre. 'But please don't let me take you out of your way.'

'It's not out of my way at all, darling. I'm just around the corner, off the South Circular.' And as she moved off at a brisk pace she indicated a white car parked half way up the pavement. It was an unusual-looking car, and looked as though it had been several months since it had been through a car wash. Deirdre had difficulty in working out what make it was. As she waited for Eva to unlock the door she could just decipher the words 'Karmann Ghia' beneath the grime in which someone had written: 'Please wash me. I'm so pretty.'

Eva plucked a parking ticket from under the windscreen wiper and screwed it into a ball. Then she lobbed it deftly into a litter-bin where it narrowly missed the hapless one-legged pigeon which was teetering on the rim.

'Excuse the mess.' Getting into the car, Eva stretched across the passenger seat to open the door for Deirdre. As she did so, she swept a pile of scripts, books, out-of-date newspapers, banana skins, cassette boxes, parking tickets and half-empty bottles of Ballygowan on to the floor. She turned the key in the ignition and loud rock blasted from the stereo.

'Oops. Let's have something a little more relaxing, shall we?' Ejecting the cassette, she ransacked the glove compartment and produced another. 'Here – stick that in, will you? I'll reverse us out of here.'

As Eva gunned the engine and manoeuvred the car out of its cramped parking space, the pure, celestial voice of kd lang soared through the speakers. Marginally less rattled, Deirdre sat back in the passenger seat. It felt weird to be sitting in a car beside the person she admired most in the world. Apart from David Lawless, of course – but that was a different kind of admiration. She realized she was a bit shy.

'The Cathedral. Isn't that where you said you lived?' asked Eva.

'Yes.'

'One of those big apartment blocks, is it?'

'Yes. I've only been there a few weeks. Just since rehearsals started.'

'Are you on your own or sharing?'

'Sharing. Well, actually I'm on my own at the moment. My flatmate's just gone off to work with the RSC.'

'London or Stratford?'

'Stratford.'

'Lucky girl. I love it there. When's she due back?'

'Not for ages. She's rehearsing *King Lear* at the moment, and once that's up she's straight into rehearsal for *The Winter's Tale.* She'll be back to visit when they go into rep. I kind of miss her.'

'Why don't you get someone else in? Sophie told me she's looking for a flat at the moment.'

Deirdre slid a look at Eva. There was a tiny smile playing round the actress's mouth.

Deirdre smiled back. She was feeling much better now. 'Sarah doesn't want anyone else staying there while she's away. She wants to be able to come back to see her boyfriend once she starts getting time off. Anyway, it's her uncle's flat. We're caretaking it for him and he's a bit picky about who has the keys. I'm very lucky. If it weren't for him I'd still be out with my mum and dad in Kilmacanogue and having to trail in by bus every day.'

'What do your parents do?'

'Dad's a potter. He does all right – Kilkenny

Design stock a lot of his stuff. My mum paints. She used to be an actress but she gave it up when she had me.'

'What's her name?'

'Rosaleen O'Dare.'

'So O'Dare's your real name?' Eva sounded surprised. 'You know, it's such a perfect stage name that I just took it for granted that you'd assumed it.'

'Oh, no – it's real all right. I've always thought that Deirdre O'Dare sounds so much like someone out of *Bunty* that I'm sure *most* people think it's a stage name. I've always felt a bit self-conscious about it. I wonder if I shouldn't change it, Eva?'

'Don't you dare!' Eva made throwing-up noises at the unintentional pun. 'It's a perfect name for an actress – it's compact and it's memorable. You mustn't dream of changing it.'

As Eva put the car into gear the engine suddenly stalled, provoking a concerto of horn blasts from the traffic behind her. Seemingly oblivious of the surrounding road rage, she took her time getting the engine going again, and Deirdre suspected that she was taking perverse delight in frustrating the other drivers. As the car started up again, she turned to give them a disconcerting smile and a gracious wave of her hand. Squirming in the passenger seat, Deirdre was amazed at the actress's complete unselfconsciousness.

'What was your mother's maiden name?' Eva asked.

'Whelan.'

'Whelan. Rosaleen Whelan. Oh, yes!' said Eva.

'She was at the Abbey school, wasn't she? I was there for a short time too, you know – a lifetime ago.' Eva pushed back her hair and frowned, as if trying to remember something. 'She was good, your mother. You take after her.'

'It's very kind of you to say that, but–'

'I mean it. I knew from the very first day of rehearsal that you had what it takes, when I saw how closely you scrutinized every individual in the rehearsal room. You looked as if you wanted to learn them all by heart. Any actor worth his salt knows how important it is to study the way people behave.' Eva gave a cheerful wave to someone in the street. 'There's Marianne. I must give her a ring.' Deirdre caught a glimpse of Marianne Faithfull getting into a car. She was madly impressed. 'Some actors think that their job is all about being observed, you know, Deirdre,' continued Eva. 'They're wrong – they have to learn to be observers, too. Oh – I love this track!' She turned up the volume on the tape deck and gave Deirdre a big smile.

While they were stopped at traffic lights next to a building site, a shirtless construction worker with a lean, bronzed torso and over-familiar eyes recognized her.

'Hey, Eva – you're gorgeous!' he yelled.

'So are you! God – aren't you just!' She grinned and blew him a kiss as the lights turned green and the car accelerated away amid a chorus of wolf whistles and obscene suggestions from the leering gangers. 'Nice bit of rough,' she said in a growly voice, turning to Deirdre with a wicked smile. 'What *is* it about hard hats?'

Deirdre laughed, but she couldn't help feeling a sense of mild shock at seeing her heroine flirting with such abandon. With complete strangers, too.

'There's something wrong, isn't there, darling?' Eva said, quite out of the blue. 'I don't just mean having your bike stolen. Something upset you in rehearsal today. Was it David's note to you?'

Deirdre bit her lip. 'Not really. He was absolutely right to say what he did. I don't have a problem with that, Eva – I just don't know how to put his note to good effect. I was extremely *bad* today – there's no other word for it – and I can't understand why!' She spread her hands in a gesture of bewilderment. 'I'd gone through the whole week thinking I was making some progress, and then it all just kind of evaporated and I got an awful fright. What am I going to do? David's probably regretting that he hadn't asked Sophie to play Hermia instead of me. Her First Fairy was brilliant today.' Deirdre suddenly felt like crying again. 'Finbar de Rossa must have noticed how crap I am, too. He volunteered to give me some help.'

'Finbar offered to help? Private tuition, I bet. Tell him where to get off, Deirdre. He has a shocking reputation, as I'm sure you've heard. He tries it on with everyone. Except me. He's scared of me.'

Deirdre had noticed that the two leading actors had very little time for each other, although they were both professional enough not to let it get in the way of their on-stage relationship. In rehearsal, their scenes together crackled with electricity.

'Why do you sometimes call Finbar "Iggy", by the way, Eva?' asked Deirdre, with sudden curiosity. 'I've been meaning to ask you that for ages.'

Eva smiled cheerfully. 'Because de Rossa's only his stage name, darling. He was christened Ignatius Looney.'

Deirdre gave a delighted laugh, and then Eva said, 'Tell you what. Why don't you come back to my place and we'll open a bottle of wine? *I* might be able to give you some help. We can't have you going through the weekend in a state of self-doubt, especially with the previews coming up. Asshole!' And she blared the horn at the driver who'd swung into her lane without indicating.

'Oh – would you do that, Eva? I'd really appreciate it.' Deirdre found herself breathing a sigh of pure relief. She suddenly felt that everything was going to turn out all right.

After negotiating the rush hour traffic with much grinding of gears and graphic gestures at kamikaze couriers – which had Deirdre furtively checking to make sure her seat-belt was properly fastened – Eva finally pulled up outside a terrace of redbrick Victorian villas.

A riot of pink clematis grew like a child's scribble around the front door of number twenty-two, and the narrow railed-in patch which fronted the house was more jungle than garden.

Humming a little tune, Eva produced a key from her floppy leather bag, unlocked the door and preceded Deirdre into the house. Deirdre shut the door behind her and studied the hallway with interest. It was painted in vivid and violently contrasting shades of blood red, shocking pink and purple. The combination shouldn't have worked, but somehow it did, to outlandish effect. A Turkish runner stretched the length of the polished floorboards, and enormous framed prints of theatre designs by David Hockney faced each other on the walls above the dado rail. Two doors led to what Deirdre presumed were reception rooms on the right, and between them was a small gateleg table in oak, heaped with correspondence and flanked by a pair of ancient-looking ladderback chairs.

Ignoring a belligerently flashing answering machine, Eva scooped up the pile of letters on her way past and led the way down to the basement. As she descended the stairs she sorted through the sheaf of mail, making little noises of irritation every time she came across any brown envelopes or any that had windows, and flinging them to the ground as if they were some kind of particularly offensive litter.

Having already witnessed Eva's total disregard for order, Deirdre was surprised to discover that the basement was extremely tidy. What had obviously once been a warren of small rooms had been knocked into a large single space comprising kitchen, dining and sitting areas and extended out into the back garden. The ceiling of the extension was of glass, which meant that the basement, instead of being gloomy, was full of light and air.

Eva's walls were washed in a warm shade of coral and covered with original paintings by Irish artists. Two great big squashy sofas upholstered in amber-coloured velvet stood on either side of a cast-iron fireplace which had pretty art nouveau tiles inset. There were alcoves on both sides of the chimney breast with shelves built in, accommodating a bewildering quantity of books and curious artefacts.

Deirdre longed to poke about. She was thrilled when she recognized some of the artists whose work lined the walls, especially when she noticed a beautiful domestic interior by Eithne Jordan, who was a friend of her mum and a sister of Neil Jordan, the film-maker. She'd heard that Eva had been cast as the lead in a forthcoming film of Neil's which was to begin shooting in the Wicklow mountains some time later in the year, and wondered if there'd be a part in it for her.

'Make yourself comfortable, darling,' instructed Eva, flinging the pile of mail into an empty fruit bowl on the long welsh dresser which segregated dining and kitchen areas. Deirdre sat down on one of the chairs ranged around a refectory table so massive it took up most of the floor space in the dining area. She counted twelve chairs, all worn smooth with age and gleaming with beeswax, and none of them matching.

'Red or white?'

Deirdre took her cue from the sound of a fridge door being opened on the other side of the dresser, which was laden with a random assortment of cheerful blue and white patterned china. 'White, please, Eva,' she said.

The actress rounded the dresser with a bottle in one hand, two enormous long-stemmed glasses in the other, and a wooden corkscrew tucked under her chin. 'We're in luck. I'm clean out of plonk, and this stuff is special. I'd put a couple of bottles in the fridge last night because some friends were meant to come round to have supper, but they had to go to Holles Street to have a baby instead. Anyway, you deserve a treat, you poor little miserable thing.' Eva deftly stripped the foil from the neck of the bottle, pulled the cork and filled the glasses. 'Cheers!' she said, raising the glass to her lips. Deirdre followed suit, savouring the first sips of the cold, clean-tasting wine. Although she wasn't an expert, she could tell that this stuff was infinitely superior to the wine they served up in the pub.

'What a gorgeous house,' said Deirdre. 'You've two homes, haven't you Eva? I read in some magazine article that you'd kept on your house in Dublin, even though most of your work's in London now.'

'That's right. I have a flat in London, but my heart is firmly rooted here. And home, as they say, is where the heart is. I always think of this city as my real home, no matter where I'm working.' Eva had started rummaging in her bag. 'I bought this house years ago with the proceeds from my first film. I love it. Oh – where are my blasted cigarettes?' Eva upended the bag on to the bleached surface of the table and proceeded to hunt among the contents, finally locating a pack of Marlboro Lights under a rather grubby lace-edged handkerchief.

Without warning, the glass doors leading to the garden slid open. A tiny, elderly woman marched into the room with an air of alarming efficiency. A peg-bag dangled from the waistband of her flowery apron.

Eva started to her feet. 'Oh – Mrs O'Toole! You're not still here, are you? I thought you would have been gone *ages* ago.'

The mystery of the uncharacteristically neat state of Eva's house was solved for Deirdre by the arrival of this person called Mrs O'Toole. She had to be Eva's housekeeper.

'So I should be gone,' Mrs O'Toole sounded cross. 'But it took me a whole two hours longer this week.' She paused and gazed mutely for a moment or two at the cigarette pack in Eva's hand with an expression of such infinite reproach that the actress let it drop like a stone to the table. 'It's always the same when you're up to ninety, Eva,' she resumed. 'The harder you work, the more like a pigsty this place becomes. I'd say there's been no laundry done since I was here last, and I saw from the bin full of cartons that you've been having take-aways again.' Mrs O'Toole's mouth was so pursed up with disapproval that it resembled a full stop.

Eva looked genuinely contrite. 'I'm really sorry, Mrs O'Toole.' She made her smile more obsequious. 'I'll try my best to keep it tidier next week, honest.'

'Hmph.' Mrs O'Toole gave her a cynical look. 'Well, I'll be off, so.' The bird-like woman divested herself of her apron, folded it and put it away in a drawer of the dresser along with the peg bag. 'You look after yourself, now, you bold thing.' And she stomped off up the stairs, making tutting noises as she stooped at several intervals to pick up Eva's discarded bills.

'Oops,' Eva said ruefully when she heard the front door shut. 'I promised her I'd given up.' She retrieved the packet from the table, extracted a cigarette and lit up, inhaling the smoke with relish. 'Well, I have, sort of. I only ever smoke in the last few days coming up to an opening, and once it's out of the way I give up again, easy as anything. Now, Deirdre,' she said, taking another sip of her wine and leaning her elbows on the table. 'Tell me what's bugging you?'

Deirdre was encouraged by the note of concern in the actress's voice. She found herself launching into a non-stop torrent of words, trying hard to articulate the reasons behind her despair. It was difficult to convey exactly how she felt, but she was reassured to see that Eva was nodding her head as she listened, and observing her with unwavering concentration. She let her speak without interruption, drawing speculatively on her cigarette. The phone rang twice during the disjointed monologue, but Eva just let the answering machine pick up. When Deirdre had finished, the actress extinguished the long stub of her second cigarette and refilled their wine glasses.

'I know exactly what's going on, darling – and believe me, there's no reason for you to be so worried.' Thoughtfully she ran a finger around the rim of her glass. 'What's happened is this. You've reached a kind of plateau stage in rehearsal. You're marking time now, and putting some distance between yourself and your performance so that you can sit back and look at it in a more objective light. Do you understand me?'

Deirdre nodded. 'I think so,' she said.

'It seems horribly artificial and uninspired, but that's only temporary, believe me.' Eva cocked her head. 'Do you sometimes feel as if you're up on the ceiling looking down at yourself on the rehearsal room floor and wondering what the hell you're doing?'

'Yes! That's it exactly!'

Eva smiled, piling her hair up on to her head and securing it with a jaws which was lying amongst the debris that had spilled out of her bag. Most of her hair fell down again. Deirdre thought she was a bit like the White Queen in *Through the Looking Glass* – though much wiser, and infinitely more beautiful, of course.

'You mustn't fret about it, darling. Treading water may feel unproductive, but it's very, very necessary sometimes.' She took a swig of her wine. 'Hermia's alive and well, you know, Deirdre. You just can't feel her at the moment. But she's right around the corner, waiting for you to catch up with her.'

Deirdre believed her. It was the best reassurance she could have got. She was just about to jump up and give the actress a kiss when Eva exclaimed: 'Oh, my goodness! Look at the time!'

The hour hand of the old meeting-house clock on the wall above the dresser was pointing to eight.

'I'd better go.' Deirdre was reluctant to leave the contented, comfortable ambience of Eva's house. Sarah's uncle's apartment was convenient and well-equipped, but it was really more a space for living than a home.

'Phooey. Don't go yet,' said Eva. 'I'm absolutely ravenous – let's send out for a take-away.'

'Oh – what a lovely idea!' Deirdre was delighted by the prospect of eating take-away food with her heroine. A month ago she wouldn't have dreamed that such a thing could be possible. She laughed suddenly. 'You'd better remember to hide the cartons from Mrs O'Toole.'

'Good thinking. Maybe I should fill that bowl with fruit and dig out the wok so that it looks as if I've been eating apples and healthy stir-fries and stuff next time she comes. Devious, aren't I?' Eva poured the remains of the wine into their glasses and dumped the empty bottle on the floor. 'We might think about opening another one of these. We may as well push the boat out tonight. Next week's going to be an absolute *nightmare*.'

Deirdre was already dreading it. Next week's

schedule was the schedule from hell. There was to be a technical rehearsal followed by a dress rehearsal on Monday, and more rehearsals on Tuesday and Wednesday as well as previews in the evening. On Thursday night Deirdre would walk on to the stage of the Phoenix Theatre and deliver her first ever professional performance. The thought of it made her insides feel as if they were slowly unravelling.

Eva picked up a cordless phone and punched in a number from memory. Without consulting a menu she machine-gunned off a list of dishes. 'Two onion bhajees, one chicken bhuna, one alloo saag, one chana pilau, some raita – oh, and lots of poppadoms, please.' Putting her hand over the receiver she mouthed: 'Is that OK for you?' Deirdre smiled at Eva and nodded enthusiastically. She suddenly felt very happy.

A couple of hours later, sated with food and feeling pretty pissed, Deirdre asked Eva why she thought David Lawless had cast Suki Hayes as Hermia in the first place. It was a question that had been niggling at her for ages.

The actress raised an eyebrow and shot her a sceptical look. 'Don't tell me you can't guess?'

'Oh! You mean they were sleeping together?' Deirdre was aghast. She'd heard all the rumours about casting couch syndrome, but she was convinced that such behaviour was beneath David Lawless.

Eva looked down at the ashtray where the cigarette she'd just lit was burning and then stubbed it out, taking her time. 'Suki's a very sexy girl, of course, and I'm sure David was flattered to know that she would have jumped into his bed. Whether or not they shagged is anybody's guess.' The actress shrugged her shoulders. 'But David isn't immune to flattery, Deirdre. No one is.'

Eva raised her eyes. Her mood seemed to have changed. She drained the rest of the wine in her glass and got up from the table with a smile that appeared artificially bright. 'Now I'm going to hunt you out of here. It's getting late, and I want you to go over your part before you go to bed. If you do that you'll be better equipped to do some homework tomorrow. Sweet dreams, darling.'

And giving her a quick peck on the cheek, Eva sent Deirdre out into the balmy Dublin night.

Chapter Three

Eva had been right. The following morning Deirdre awoke feeling as panic free as a mother whose lost child had just been restored to her. On Sunday night she fell asleep with a smile on her face as she re-read the playscript. It lay on her chest like a security blanket as she slept, undisturbed by dreams.

She walked into the theatre at 10.00 on Monday morning to find the place a scene of mayhem. The crew had been working all day Sunday through into the small hours of the morning constructing the set, rigging up the sound system, and hanging and focusing lamps. The theatre was festooned with cable. It was draped across the rows of red plush seating in the auditorium, looped from lighting bars, and coiled like cobras in the aisles. The riggers were already hard at work. Deirdre watched with trepidation as they hoisted lamps up unsteady ladders and sauntered along treacherous-looking gantries with macho carelessness. The sound of hammering filled the theatre.

Feeling a little lost, Deirdre scanned the auditorium until she found a familiar face. Jenny Cummings, the designer, was sitting slumped in the stalls, nursing a takeaway coffee with her legs slung over the seat-back in front of her. She was alternately squinting through the gloom at the barely visible set and scribbling madly in a notebook. Deirdre set off down the aisle in Jenny's direction, manoeuvring herself between the rows of seats and taking care not to trip over the cable.

Suddenly a command rang out from somewhere to the rear of the stalls and the stage was flooded with light. 'Wow,' said Deirdre, dropping open-mouthed into the nearest seat.

The set was a magical construction of muslin columns that swayed in the draught from the wings. One minute they were birches, bathed in a pale silver shimmer and silhouetted against a midnight blue sky. The next minute the lighting operator's deft manipulation of the controls on the console transformed them into a palace whose fluid golden pillars rose into an azure heaven. A succession of coloured gels were brought into play, washing over the columns and finally transforming them into vines of dark jungle green. 'Shit, Jenny! It's out of this world,' exclaimed Deirdre.

Jenny, who was sitting a little further down the row, turned and smiled. 'Hi, Deirdre. You like it?'

'It's stunning. Oh God – I can't wait to get on to the stage!'

'Thanks, Deirdre. You say all the right things.' The designer was obviously chuffed.

'There's something really sensual about it, isn't there?'

'I'm glad you said that. That's exactly the effect I wanted to achieve. That's why you lot are wearing real silk next to your skin.' Jenny rubbed her eyes and yawned. 'The backers made noises at the added strain on the budget, but I asked them how they'd like to try acting sexy if they had to wear some horrific cheapo fabric under hot lights every night.' She swigged back her coffee, scrunched up the polystyrene cup and let it drop to the floor.

The stage was plunged into darkness again, and Deirdre got to her feet. 'D'you know where I'm meant to be, Jenny?'

'Yeah. They're running a line-call in the green room until we're ready for you out here.'

Deirdre looked dubiously at the surrounding chaos.

'Don't worry,' said Jenny. 'The mess is superficial. We're actually a lot more organized than we look. And we're pretty well running to schedule, which is kind of unusual. Some might say miraculous.' The designer yawned again and stretched in her seat. 'You might even have time to fit in a meal break before the dress.' A deafening crash and a chorus of obscenities came from the flies, and Jenny returned her attention to the stage.

After the line-call, Nick McCarthy told them to take fifteen, and Deirdre disappeared to the dressing-room, curious to recce the space she was to share with Maeve Kirwan and the three fairies for the next four months. It was up three flights of concrete steps at the very top of the building – a long barrack-like space inadequately illuminated by neon strips. The only natural light came through a glass dome in the low ceiling, the surface of which was covered in wire netting and thick with pigeon droppings. The furnishing was basic, consisting of a number of institutional-looking chairs, and an ancient and extremely tatty chaise longue which looked as if it had somehow crawled by itself into the middle of the floor and then suddenly collapsed. Three sides of the room were lined with long counters which served as dressing-tables, with make-up mirrors screwed to the walls at intervals above them. Deirdre noticed that several of the light-bulbs round the mirrors were missing, and that only one had its full quota.

The space below this particular mirror had already been appropriated. A cream-coloured towel had been spread over the countertop, and an artillery of cosmetics had been lined up on top of it. Numerous good-luck charms in the shape of stuffed teddies and ceramic animals were arranged along the top of the mirror, a smart black leather make-up case was stowed under the counter, and a terry-towelling wrap with a price tag still attached hung from the back of the chair. Deirdre snuck a look at the price tag and felt sick.

Sophie Burke swanned into the room. 'Isn't it a kip?' She hauled her make-up case out from under the counter and began to extract more toiletries. Deirdre noticed some very expensive logos. 'It's absolutely filthy, you know. I arrived at nine o'clock this morning and had to spend at least ten minutes scrubbing down my place before I could unpack.'

'I'm surprised you didn't ask someone to do it for you.'

Deirdre had forgotten that irony was wasted on Sophie.

'I did,' she replied. 'I asked Jessica to do it.'

'Jesus, Sophie! You've some bloody neck.'

'Pardon me, Deirdre – you might remember that assistant stage manager is still her brief even though she's recently acquired an "Acting" tag.'

'What did she say when you asked her?'

'I'm sorry to say she refused to do it. But I decided not to report her to Nick.'

Deirdre suspected that if Sophie had reported Jessica, Nick would just have told her where to get off.

'I'm not going to let a relatively minor incident like that stand in the way of our friendship,' continued Sophie. 'We'll be spending a lot of time cooped up together in this hell-hole.'

Put that way, the future looked less than rosy. Deirdre decided to find a mirror as far away from her enemy as possible.

'Wasn't I lucky to bag the best place,' said Sophie, with an unconvincing giggle. 'My mirror's even got its full allocation of bulbs!'

As she unpacked her stuff, Deirdre speculated whether this stroke of luck was due to happy coincidence, or the purloining of bulbs from other mirrors. She watched as Sophie produced several phials of vitamin supplements from her case and set about knocking back the contents with Aqua Libra. 'I'm surprised you didn't bring in a cappuccino machine, Sophie,' she said.

'Oh – that's a good idea! I must remember to do that tomorrow.'

Other cast members arrived. Maeve drifted in and shared an oblique smile with Deirdre as she registered Sophie's rapacious take-over bid. Deirdre and Maeve had become quite good friends since Deirdre had replaced Suki Hayes, and she knew that Maeve shared her mistrust of Sophie. Maeve had so much going for her it was almost unfair. As well as possessing buckets of talent, she was elegant, clever and an Uma Thurman look-alike. Sophie was so blindly jealous of the actress that she'd been unwise enough to make a snide remark about her sexual preferences once. She hadn't done it again. Nobody with an ounce of cop-on made jokes about the fact that Maeve was a lesbian.

Choosing a place next to Deirdre at the far end of the room, Maeve proceeded to empty a battered leather backpack with the kind of method born of routine. All her things bore the hallmark of frequent use, and it amused Deirdre to compare them with Sophie's sparkling new acquisitions. As Maeve draped a threadbare silk kimono over the back of her chair, Sophie snuck a look at it and then stroked the fluffy cream sleeve of her own dressing-gown with a smug little smile.

A rattling noise of approaching wheels outside on the corridor announced the arrival of the wardrobe mistress. She bowled through the door, pushing a costume rail arrayed with billowing silk. Deirdre had only had one fitting, during which it had been agreed that the costume originally intended for Suki Hayes needed no alterations. She was dying to try on the gown again – to slide her hands over the smooth, saffron-coloured silk, to do big twirls in it and feel the feather-light touch of the fabric against her skin. Jenny had been right. Silk was one of the sexiest fabrics there was.

Ten minutes later, Deirdre wandered down to the wings with Maeve to start on the technical rehearsal. 'I hate technicals,' said Maeve. 'I've been through some that have lasted until the early hours of the morning. But I've a feeling this one'll be easy-going.' She sank on to her heels, adopting the relaxed sitting posture of a Red Indian, and rocked gently from side to side.

'How come?' asked Deirdre, sitting down on the dusty floor beside the other actress, and wrapping her arms around her knees.

'David's surrounded himself with the most efficient – and the most expensive – people in the business. He's got a lot of money tied up in this season. So has Eva.'

'I didn't know that. So that makes her management as well?'

'Yeah. You can be sure there'll be no penny-pinching on this show. We're working with real class, Deirdre. And David Lawless has got something else going for him that most people in this game wouldn't know how to spell.'

'Oh? What's that?'

'Integrity. In the moral as well as the artistic sense.'

Craning her neck, Deirdre peered out past the black drapes which masked the wings from the audience. In the darkness of the auditorium she could just make out the silhouette of David Lawless where he was sitting in the stalls between Jenny Cummings and the lighting designer.

'Go to state two, please.' David Lawless told the lighting operator, and Deirdre felt the familiar somersault of her heart at the sound of his voice. Then she rose to her feet and prepared herself to walk out on to the stage.

* * *

As anticipated, the technical rehearsal went without too many hitches. There were several delayed sound cues due to a gremlin in the works, a couple of lamps needed tweaking, and Finbar de Rossa went into a sulk when he discovered that Eva's spotlight was marginally upstage of his, but by five o'clock they were finished, and free to do as they wanted till the optional pre-show warm-up. Nick McCarthy took pains to remind them all that the half-hour call was twenty-five past seven, and not a minute later.

Most of the cast chose to leave the building for the duration of the break. Deirdre needed space to herself. She decided to take advantage of the fact that the dressing-room would be empty, and she made her way towards the backstage stairs.

As she passed the prompt corner, Deirdre overheard Eva asking Jessica if she'd be an angel and fetch her a sandwich from the local deli. Deirdre hovered, glad of an opportunity to thank the actress for being so kind to her on Saturday evening.

'Eva?'

'Oh, hi honey.' Eva put an arm round Deirdre's waist and led her further back into the wings, away from the gang of stagehands who had reappropriated the stage now that the actors had finished with it. The crew was in overdrive now, under pressure to put the necessary finishing touches to the set before eight o'clock, when the dress rehearsal was due to start.

'How are you feeling today?' asked Eva.

'Oh – *much* better, thank you, Eva!' said Deirdre earnestly. 'You were spot on. Everything came back to me like magic. It's weird, isn't it?'

'So you and Hermia are reacquainted? I won't say I told you so.' There was a smile in the actress's voice.

'I hope I'm not speaking too soon.' Deirdre leaned across to touch the wooden frame of a nearby flat. 'And thanks so much for your hospitality the other night,' she added. 'The food was brilliant. I'll definitely use that take-away in future.'

'For nothing, sweetheart. I enjoyed your company. And make sure you have fun tonight.' Eva glanced to her right where David Lawless was standing centre-stage, surveying the set. 'That's what it's all about, when it comes down to it,' she added over her shoulder to Deirdre as she strolled towards her director, linking his arm in a gesture of easy familiarity and drawing him aside.

Deirdre was once again struck by the conspiratorial dynamic between them. She experienced the tiniest stab of jealousy and suppressed it immediately, telling herself not to be so ridiculous. After all, it was only a fantasy life that granted Deirdre O'Dare exclusive rights to David Lawless.

The dressing-room was, as she'd hoped, unoccupied. She ate the tuna sandwich she'd made for herself before setting out that morning and perused her script for the millionth time, curling herself up on the lumpy chaise longue. Studying the script at this stage wasn't doing her any good. It was only making her wonder how well she knew her lines. They were suddenly looking very alien to her.

She picked up a stack of old theatre programmes and tried to distract herself by leafing through them. There was one for a production of *Saint Joan* which Deirdre had seen last year, with Suki Hayes in the title role. She ran her eyes over the potted biography provided. It was impressive reading. How *had* she managed to do it? How had she managed to hoodwink every director she met into believing that she was right for some of the juiciest parts going?

Deirdre looked at the head-and-shoulders photograph next to the actress's biog. She was looking sideways at the camera and wearing a sultry expression. There was an orchid tucked into the mane of hair which tumbled over her bare shoulders, her pouting lips were slightly apart and there was invitation in her eyes. Deirdre examined the pout and then tried it out for herself. It felt stupid, and she knew that she'd never fool anyone.

She cast the programme aside and got to her feet. It was very hot and airless, and as there was no way of opening the skylight she opened the door in the vain hope of inviting in a draught. Her T-shirt was beginning to stick to her, and as she pulled at it in an attempt to make herself more comfortable her eyes fell on the costume-rail where her saffron-yellow robe floated enticingly on its hanger. She couldn't resist the call of the gossamer gown. She pulled off T-shirt and jeans and slid the filmy fabric over her head. It shimmered down over her bare breasts, its myriad folds whispering as they enveloped her, and at last she felt the air move as she twirled round and round in the centre of the room, arms outstretched, hair flying. Deirdre hadn't done anything like this since she was about ten years old. She knew she must look like a total eejit – she'd never excelled in the movement classes in college – but she didn't give a damn because there was no one around to see her.

Common sense finally told her to stop. She should be conserving her energy for the show, not wasting it prancing around her dressing-room. Reluctantly, she surrendered to the heat once more, settling down on the part of the chaise which had the fewest broken springs.

She lay there for a while in a pleasant torpor, knowing that she should change into her warm-up gear, but feeling too lazy to make the effort. The heat was making her drowsy, and she wondered idly if stage management would think about installing fans in the dressing-rooms, and why she wasn't feeling scared shitless by the fact that the dress rehearsal was only a couple of hours away, and why someone didn't do something about the awful snot green paint on the walls. Curling one leg over the other to make herself more comfortable, she closed her eyes, made a pillow of her left arm, and rested her head on it.

'Flaming June.'

Deirdre shot up as if one of the springs in the bockety chaise beneath her had just snapped.

David Lawless was leaning against the lintel of the open door, studying her.

'I beg your pardon?' stammered Deirdre. Her hand fluttered to her face to push back the strands of hair that were clinging there and she hurriedly adopted a more modest position, sitting up ramrod straight and clamping her knees together. Her costume was in a bit of a mess after all her prancing about. To her horror, she realized that the silk had slipped down off one shoulder, half exposing her right breast. Deirdre cringed inwardly and debated whether or not to adjust it. She knew that to do so might only draw attention to the bare flesh, so she left it as it was and pretended that she simply hadn't noticed.

'I wish I hadn't disturbed you.' David Lawless smiled lazily and brushed his hair back from his face with the relaxed gesture she had grown to know so well, and which always made her heart clench like a fist. She blinked and cleared her throat unnecessarily in a pathetic attempt to cover her confusion, feeling increasingly conscious of her dishevelled clothing, tousled hair and foolish expression. 'You were, just now, the living embodiment of the Frederick Leighton painting,' he continued. 'The one called "Flaming June". Do you know it?'

'Um, no – I don't think so,' she mumbled. Her voice sounded like that of an adolescent schoolgirl hauled up in front of the headmaster.

'I used to admire it, in an academic way, until countless reproductions drained it of its sensuousness. It's rather commonplace now. Go into any card shop and you'll find it. You'll recognize yourself at once.'

Deirdre tried to arrange her features into an attitude of polite interest, but she knew that her eyes betrayed her, and that David Lawless must be able to see that the thumping of her heart was making the silk over her left breast tremble visibly. He could not fail to be aware of the sexual tension in the air.

He straightened himself suddenly and moved towards her. When he spoke, his voice had taken on a new timbre. 'You're very gifted, you know, Deirdre,' he said, reaching out a hand until his fingers touched the sheer fabric of her gown where it had tumbled over her shoulder. 'And you're very, very young. I envy you all those years you have ahead of you. If I had my youth back, I suspect I'd do things very differently.'

She could not read the expression in his eyes because his back was to the light, but there was something regretful about the way he gently slid the silk back up her arm to cover her nakedness.

'Maybe it's not too late,' he said, as if to himself. Then suddenly his demeanour changed. 'Don't let me down, Deirdre,' he warned, in a more jocular tone. 'Be good tonight. Be excellent.' He smiled into her eyes, turned, and walked with an unhurried tread back out through the door.

Where his touch had lingered, Deirdre's skin was electric.

Chapter Four

It was opening night. Deirdre was on stage, and things were starting to go terribly wrong. She couldn't understand why Maeve and Adrian Pierce had walked right into the middle of a scene where they had no business to be. She tried to ignore the pair of them and started ad-libbing like mad in a kind of makey-up Shakespearean language, using lots of 'thou's' and 'shouldsts', and trying to stick to iambic pentameter, but Maeve and Adrian still wouldn't go away. She had never been in a situation on stage like this before, and she hadn't a clue how to handle it.

She wished Rory would do something to help. After all, he was the one with more experience. She was playing the balcony scene with him, and he was being really uncooperative. He was muttering something urgently under his breath, something that she couldn't make out. She tried as hard as she could to decipher what he was saying, but she was becoming increasingly anxious and confused, and Rory fazed her further by grabbing both her hands and pinioning them to her sides. She struggled, but was powerless to break free. Looking into his face she saw his mouth move, and although she couldn't hear the words, she realized that she was lip-reading. 'You're in the wrong play,' Rory was saying. *'The wrong play.* We're not doing *Romeo and Juliet*, Deirdre. You're not Juliet – you're Hermia. *Hermia.* It's *A Midsummer Night's Dream.*'

Over Rory's shoulder she became aware of David Lawless. He was standing watching her from a distance, and his eyes were very narrow. He let his gaze travel down her body until she knew that he was looking at her breasts, and she was horrified to discover as she followed his eyeline that she was completely naked. A hand brushed against her nipple and it hardened instantly. She felt sure that it had been David Lawless who had touched her, but when she looked up she saw that it was Rory who was caressing her. He trailed a finger lightly over her left breast, and there was something speculative about the way he was looking at her as he repeated: *A Midsummer Night's Dream. A Midsummer Night's Dream.*

In the blackness beyond the stage, an invisible audience took up the refrain. *A Midsummer Night's Dream. Midsummer Night's Dream.*

She struggled to make sense of what was happening, but the intensely pleasurable sensation produced in her by Rory McDonagh's sure fingers as they grazed her nipple over and over again was depriving her of all reason. *Midsummer Night's Dream.* The mesmeric chanting of the audience continued, increasing in volume until it felt as if it was inside her skull. *Night's Dream. Night's Dream. Dream. Dream.*

Dream.

Deirdre awoke with the rhythm of her heart like a drum in her head. Her breathing was rapid and shallow, she was drenched with sweat and something was curling and uncurling in the pit of her stomach.

Gradually she forced her conscious mind to assert itself until the black cloud of her nightmare receded. She adjusted the pace of her breathing with an effort, and after a while her pulse slowed correspondingly. She lay there for a while with her eyes wide open until she had chased all traces of the dream from her head. But try as she might, one image remained stubbornly fixed in her mind. She could not forget the sensation of Rory McDonagh's hand on her breast, and the intensely erotic thrill it had elicited in her.

Suddenly the thing in her stomach lurched. It *was* opening night. No wonder she was feeling peculiar. No wonder she'd been visited by a classic actor's nightmare. Her mind floundered as she slid out of the bed. She sat on the edge for a while, observing herself curiously in the wardrobe mirror, as if seeing her naked reflection for the first time. What on earth had all that sex stuff been about? It was the first time in her experience that a nightmare had been tinged with eroticism. And why Rory McDonagh? Why hadn't David Lawless been the one to caress her breast? After all, he had been near enough to it in real life. It didn't make sense.

With a bemused air she ran her hand experimentally up over her belly to her breast. Her nipple hardened immediately, and she let her hand drop. How stupid. How could she think that a *dream* should make sense? She stood up, and gave the duvet a vigorous shake before heading towards the bathroom. It was amazing how quickly dreams faded away, she thought as she turned on the shower. Her recollection of the details were already more than a little hazy. Perhaps it hadn't been Rory's hand on her breast after all.

By the time she had finished showering she had decided quite firmly that the caress in her dream had come from David Lawless.

* * *

The atmosphere in the theatre, when she arrived later in the day for a line-run, was one of controlled panic, with people rushing about doing a hundred last-minute things. Because Jenny Cummings had requisitioned the green room as an extra workshop the place reeked of paint and glue, so the line-call and notes session were held in the auditorium, where the cleaning staff were buzzing up and down aisles with vacuum cleaners.

The line-run was faultless. Afterwards Nick McCarthy told them to take ten before the notes session, when they all reassembled in the auditorium with cups of coffee. Nobody had really wanted to take ten, and nobody really wanted coffee. They just wanted to get on with it.

When David Lawless arrived, his exhausted eyes were the colour of dark honey. He betrayed his fatigue by no other sign, however, and his notes were delivered with his usual consideration and diplomacy. As he reached the end of the session he looked up from his notepad at Eva and made an observation.

'Eva. I can say nothing to you because I honestly feel your performance cannot be bettered. One word of warning only. Be careful of your emotional level in your battle with Oberon over who should win custody of the changeling boy – especially on the line: "The fairy land buys not the child of me." It's reached a precarious high. You might try pulling back a little.'

Deirdre noticed that, as rehearsals had progressed, Eva had been investing that particular speech with increasing intensity. Maeve had remarked on it, too. Deirdre personally thought that Eva's delivery was flawless. The lines were imbued with anguish and regret, and when she referred to her "changeling child" there was a spine-chilling catch in the actress's achingly beautiful voice. She couldn't understand why David Lawless was asking Eva to hold back – unless he was simply concerned for her emotional well-being. It was, after all, an extremely tough scene for her.

There was a long pause. 'Eva? What do you think?' asked David. 'Will you try reining in a little?'

Deirdre looked at Eva. She had lowered her eyes and was plucking at a loose button on her cuff. Then she raised her head, looked directly at David, and gave him such an odd, haunting smile that Deirdre felt the hairs rise on the back of her neck. 'I can't,' she said simply. Then she stood up and left the auditorium.

Deirdre was astonished. She hadn't suspected that the word 'can't' was in Eva Lavery's vocabulary. An embarrassed silence fell over the cast. Even David seemed fazed by Eva's behaviour. Deirdre had never seen him lose his cool before. He recovered himself with what seemed like an effort.

'I'd like to thank you all for your hard work. It's been tough going, especially in the last few days, but you've all coped admirably and without complaint.'

Deirdre stole a look at Sophie who was looking insufferably smug. Then her eyes met Maeve's, and, as the pair of actresses realized that they were thinking mutual thoughts, they had to bow their heads to hide their smiles. They'd heard nothing *but* complaints from Sophie since they'd moved into the theatre.

'I'd particularly like to thank Deirdre O'Dare for stepping in at such short notice.'

Deirdre's smile disappeared as, startled, she looked up at her director. He paused and held her gaze for a second or two, which seemed to her to stretch into infinity.

Then he stood up. 'This is going to be an extraordinary evening. I have a feeling in my bones. Be good, all of you, and enjoy it.'

Deirdre went backstage with the rest of the cast and proceeded to do the rounds of the dressing-rooms, delivering posies of flowers she'd made up earlier in the day. Most of the other actors had also observed the opening-night present-giving tradition, and all the dressing-tables were littered with envelopes and tokens of good luck.

Rory McDonagh had distributed the kind of plastic farmyard animals you find in toy-shops, telling the girls in the communal dressing-room that they were for playing with during the interval. The sheep he'd given Deirdre had a tag attached saying: 'Let's try and make it "short as any dream tonight", D.Well, maybe not the snog. Love, R.' Sophie had got a cat, Maeve a sheepdog, and Jessica a little donkey. Kate O'Connor was clearly delighted with the kitten that Rory had presented to her with a cavalier's flourish. Hers was the only animal that was made of plush instead of plastic.

Maeve gave Deirdre a slim volume of Walt Whitman's poetry. Ironically, the title poem was 'I Sing the Body Electric', and Deirdre thought wistfully of the charge she had felt when David's hand had made contact with her skin the other evening. Sophie got a copy of Rimbaud's *A Season in Hell.*

Sarah had sent her a card from Stratford wishing her luck and telling her that she'd dumped her boyfriend in Dublin because she'd fallen in love with one of the scenic artists at Stratford. She'd added a PS in her big swirly writing. 'What on earth made me think of you when I saw this card?' It was a reproduction of Edvard Münch's 'The Scream'.

There were snipes of champagne from Eva waiting for them on their places after the warm-up. The instructions on the accompanying cards warned that they were not to be cracked before the performance otherwise she'd get into trouble with David.

Deirdre opened the note attached to the bottle and read, in violet ink and block capitals: 'TWINKLE, TWINKLE . . . LOVE, EVA'. She suddenly realized with horror that she had unaccountably forgotten to include Eva when she'd done her Interflora act earlier on. She took the stairs down to the leading lady's dressing-room three at a time, knowing that to disturb her much later than the half-hour call would be to commit a serious professional blunder. Giving a gentle rap she waited for the actress's invitation to enter before pushing the door open.

The dressing-room was like a florist's shop and the air was heady with scent. Bouquets and baskets of flowers were everywhere, with riotous bright bunches crammed haphazardly into every available container. Even the plastic wastepaper basket had been commandeered as a vase. A sheaf of enormous, tousle-headed white chrysanthemums protruded from it.

Eva was wearing a long robe of finely embroidered white cotton, and was standing on one leg in the middle of the room. Her left foot was tucked up high against her right thigh with the knee angled outward and her arms curved up above her head. She looked like a golden Shiva.

'Hi, honey,' she said lightly.

'Oh, Eva – I *am* sorry to disturb you,' Deirdre said awkwardly. 'I just wanted to say thank you for the champagne.' Deirdre laid the flowers on Eva's dressing table, feeling acutely conscious of how insignificant her gift was compared to the other spectacular floral arrangements which jostled for attention in the room. She noticed a small plastic fox on top of the mirror, and for some reason she was slightly taken aback. Rory had compared *her* character of Hermia to a fox. Why had he chosen to give Eva that particular animal? Deirdre would much rather have had a fox than a sheep.

'Oh, sweetheart, thank you!' said Eva, as Deirdre deposited the flowers on her dressing-table. The actress had taken hold of her left foot and was stretching her leg in the manner of a dancer limbering up. Her robe had fallen open, and the inside of her thigh was displayed. Deirdre couldn't help noticing a thin silver scar which ran just above her knee for a couple of inches. She averted her eyes and made for the door. 'Aren't they pretty!' Eva lowered her leg and shook it out, and then moved to the dressing-table to pick up the flowers, burying her nose in them. 'Oh – they smell utterly divine, Deirdre! Did they come all the way from your garden in Wicklow?'

Deirdre paused by the door and nodded, feeling herself going as pink as the sweetpea at the actress's obvious pleasure. 'Yes. My mum had to come into town yesterday so I asked her to bring me in some flowers from the garden. I even got some roses, but I kept them for the men. Sweetpea didn't seem suitable for them, somehow.'

'What a lovely idea! So thoughtful of you! And

how refreshing to have flowers from a real live garden instead of these ostentatious hothouse confections. Look at that.' And she crinkled up her nose with contempt as she gestured towards an elaborate arrangement of florid gladioli, tiger-lilies and waxen-looking roses. Deirdre actually thought the flowers were rather impressive. She wished she were glamorous enough to get bouquets like that delivered to *her* dressing-room.

'Nervous, darling?' Eva took an egg from a bowl on the countertop and broke it into a glass.

'Mm – I'm feeling a bit shaky all right.'

'Good. There's nothing like a shot of adrenalin to add an edge to your performance. I'm positively quivering with fright.'

Astonished, Deirdre watched as Eva calmly sprinkled the raw egg with an alarming measure of Lea and Perrins. Then she tilted back her head and swallowed the contents of the glass in one gulp.

'Oh, Eva – yeuch!' she couldn't help herself from exclaiming. 'How can you *do* that?'

'Sets me up, darling. Instant energy and protein in the most convenient possible package. The secret is buckets of Lea and Perrins. When you think you've put in too much, add another lash. You should try it. This and a couple of bananas and I'll be raring to go. Here – have one.' And she tore a ripe banana from a bunch in a basket and handed it to Deirdre.

Dutifully eating her banana, Deirdre returned to her dressing-room. There was a new, unopened envelope on top of the pile of discarded ones on her place, and her heart contracted as she recognized David Lawless's bold black italic hand. Trying hard to look casual, she slid out the card. Her whole being was flooded with pleasure as she made instant connection with the image on the front. It was a reproduction of the painting he'd compared her to – Frederick Leighton's 'Flaming June'. She studied it, feeling gobsmacked. He'd been right. The position of the sleeping figure was virtually identical to the one Deirdre had adopted that evening she'd curled up on the chaise longue in her dressing-room. Only this gorgeous creature was a lot more voluptuous than Deirdre. The curves of her body were draped with flowing, saffron-coloured silk chiffon and the nipples of her softly rounded breasts were clearly discernible under the diaphanous fabric. There was something profoundly warm and sensuous about the painting, and Deirdre felt almost faint as she realized that David Lawless had seen her as this glorious, erotic figure.

He *was* tempted to touch my breast! she thought triumphantly. He *does* find me desirable! And she found it difficult to govern the arousal that the idea produced in her. *Maybe he wants me as much as I want him . . .* She remembered what he'd said to her that same evening as he'd slid the sleeve of her gown back up her shoulder. 'If I had my youth back I'd do things very differently.' It was obviously a reference to his ruined marriage. Maybe he was finally ready to turn his back on the past and embrace his future.

She gazed at the image on the card for a while

longer before opening it. Inside was the legend: 'To Deirdre, who embodies "the simplicity of Venus' doves". Rise and shine. David.'

'The simplicity of Venus' doves'! The words were from a speech of Hermia's in which she agrees to a secret tryst with her lover. It was the proof she needed. David Lawless wanted her!

Chapter Five

'Act One beginners, please.' Nick McCarthy's voice crackled over the tannoy. Deirdre descended the stairs to the wings feeling as if she was in freeze-frame.

The atmosphere backstage was electric with a tension which the noise coming from beyond the fire curtain did nothing to alleviate. Deirdre was quite unprepared for the decibel level from the auditorium. The pre-show murmurings from the preview audiences had been sedate compared to the near-clamour coming from the opening night crowd.

The strain showed in the behaviour of all the actors involved in the first scene, although they handled it in very different ways. Maeve adopted her Red Indian posture, hugging herself as she squatted, swaying to some internal rhythm and worrying a nail with her teeth. Rory's expression was inscrutable as he paced the floor, but Deirdre could see the muscles working in his jaw, and as the long minutes wore on and there was still no let-up from the braying in the audience she heard him muttering: 'Come on, come on, come *on*!' Adrian Pierce was as skittish as a racehorse under starter's orders, and Deirdre kept well clear of him in case his feverishness was contagious. Eva Lavery and Finbar de Rossa were standing a little apart from each other in the wings opposite them, waiting to go on. Eva was standing perfectly erect and absolutely motionless, her countenance trance-like.

As the curtain finally rose and the noise from the audience died down, an almost tangible air of anticipation deluged the stage. Across from her, Eva shut her eyes, and Deirdre could see the actress's chest rise under the deep intake of breath. She allowed herself a beat or two, and then she focused her attention on Finbar. Suddenly smiling and totally relaxed, they strolled on to the stage together arm-in-arm, and Finbar launched into the opening dialogue.

Deirdre felt a snake of fear writhe in her stomach as her cue sounded in her ears like a death knell, but somehow she found herself on stage without really knowing how she had got there, and the snake was banished as suddenly and miraculously as if the patron saint of Ireland had been responsible. The show was up and running.

Deirdre worked her way through the evening with such astonishing effortlessness that she felt as though she were gliding. Nothing went wrong, and she was aware of an uncanny sense of fusion between the actors as they delivered the performances that had been so finely tuned by David Lawless.

The sense of enjoyment from the cast was so powerful that it couldn't but communicate itself to the audience. Deirdre knew that a first night audience was a dangerous animal – notoriously difficult to please and often determined to remain unimpressed – but by the end of the evening everyone on stage sensed that they had established a terrific rapport with the crowd out front. The dangerous animal was eating out of the palms of their hands.

When Jonathan Hughes walked downstage as Puck and delivered the final lines of the play the hackles rose on Deirdre's neck.

Give me your hand if we be friends,
And Robin shall restore amends.

There was a brief hiatus, like a collective intake of breath, before thunderous applause descended like a wave upon the stage. Deirdre was overwhelmed. Nothing could have prepared her for this sort of reaction. She looked around at the other cast members and saw her own totally confounded expression mirrored in their faces.

As they lined up to take their curtain call the realization of what they had achieved was beginning to dawn, and Deirdre found that a beaming smile had spread itself across her face. Maeve looked catatonic, Rory euphoric, and Eva Lavery was laughing in open delight as she made her deep curtsies. Instead of his customary intense curtain-call frown, Adrian Pierce was wearing the broadest smile Deirdre had ever seen him give.

Over and over again the actors were called back to take their bows, and as the audience rose cheering to their feet, hands clapping high in the air, the stunned cast clapped them back. It was obvious to everyone that the show wasn't just a success – it was a total triumph.

The atmosphere backstage afterwards was exuberant. Raucous laughter punctuated by the sound of champagne corks popping rang through the corridors, and the walls echoed to the congratulatory clucking noises of the first-nighters as they mobbed the dressing-rooms, shrieking endearments.

Maeve and Deirdre cracked open their snipes of champagne and set about cleaning the heavy theatrical make-up from their faces. Their friends had enough cop-on not to come backstage on an opening night. They'd meet up with them in the pub later. Lots of the people milling around were connected to the theatre world by the most tenuous of links. Maeve's smile didn't always reach her eyes as she said 'Thanks. Thanks a lot,' over and over again, but Deirdre couldn't but feel a little flutter of delight every time a compliment came her way. All her 'thank yous' were uncoolly enthusiastic. When the hubbub died down Maeve leant back in her chair and assessed her face critically in the mirror. She took a swipe at her lipsticked mouth with a cotton-wool pad and then drained what remained of her snipe into a polystyrene cup. 'Kinda sums this whole acting lark up, doesn't it?' she said with an air of pensive cynicism. 'Drinking champagne from a plastic cup smeared with Make-up Forever's TO4.'

* * *

Meagher's – or Meagre Meagher's, as Rory McDonagh had christened their local because he'd once been served a short measure – was crowded, but the atmosphere was marginally less frenetic than it had been backstage. Management had reserved the function room for the opening night shindig and had organized live music and a bar extension. There was a tab at the bar, though it looked as though it would run out at a fairly early stage of the proceedings if the rapacious behaviour of the liggers and the more laddish members of the company was anything to go by. Michael Meagher, the proprietor, was lining up an infinite row of pints and expertly avoiding all eye contact with the punters who were waving their arms in a desperate bid to attract his attention.

Deirdre's eyes roamed the party, seeking out her mum and dad. She spotted them at last on the other side of the room and headed in their direction. So many flattering remarks were coming her way that she didn't really know how to handle them. As she navigated the crowd she focused on her parents, quite unable to keep from smiling. Her mother still looked amazingly young, Deirdre thought, and very beautiful.

Both her parents were glowing with unconcealed pride. Her mother put her arms round Deirdre and kept them there for a long time. Her father, always more reticent when it came to displays of emotion, laid his hand on her shoulder. 'Well done, Deirdre,' he said in his gentle voice.

Then Rosaleen held her daughter at arm's length,

and the look in her eyes made Deirdre feel that she was infinitely precious. 'I know I'm partisan,' she said, and her voice was flooded with love. 'But you were utterly, utterly perfect. If I had had a thousandth of your talent I would never have dreamed of giving up the business. You're better than I ever was, my darling girl.'

Suddenly and quite unexpectedly Deirdre started to cry. Rosaleen hugged her again and stroked her hair, making little reassuring noises. It felt as if someone had pulled the plug on the reservoir of tension which had been filling up inside her for the past few weeks, and now it was all draining out of her. Laughing and crying at the same time, she made a concerted effort to pull herself together. 'Bloody hell, Mum,' she said, wiping the stupid tears from her eyes with a tissue which Rosaleen had produced for her. 'That's the second time I've had a crying jag recently. I'm turning into a real cry-baby. Oh God, how embarrassing! I hope nobody saw me.' She blew her nose and stole a covert look around the room.

'Don't worry, my love. They're all too busy talking about themselves. New dress?'

'Yes.' Deirdre had splurged on her opening night outfit. She'd chosen a short, sleeveless dress of plain black satin by Marc O'Neill, telling herself it was investment dressing as she'd recklessly scribbled the cheque.

'Very sexy.'

'Thanks. Hey – you don't have a drink, either of you. What can I get you?' Deirdre noticed that her father was still wearing his jacket and was rather red in the face. 'Why don't you take off your jacket, Dad, and I'll see if I can find somewhere for us to sit. I can't believe this place has filled up so fast – I don't even *recognize* half the people here.'

'Nothing for us, thanks. You're very sweet to offer, but it's getting late.' Her mother took the damp tissue from Deirdre and dropped it into her bag. 'We only stayed on to tell you how wonderful we thought you were – we never intended staying so long.'

'Oh, don't go yet! The party's only just starting. Please – let me get you both a glass of wine and introduce you to some of the cast? Eva Lavery would love to meet you, Mum – I'm sure she would. She remembers you from the old days at the Abbey school.'

But Rosaleen was adamant. 'It's a long drive home, Deirdre, and you know that Jack hates these kind of occasions.'

Her father had become increasingly uncomfortable-looking as the room became more crowded and the chattering got louder. 'I'm sorry I'm such an anti-social bugger,' he said. 'I always dreaded your mother's opening nights, but I never told her until after she quit the business. I used to suffer them in silent agony.'

'Deirdre! Well done!' A friend from college aimed a kiss at Deirdre's cheek on his way past to the bar. 'What'll you have to drink?'

'Oh – thanks, Conor. I'm OK for the moment – I'll catch you later?'

'Sure. The show's fan-fucking-tastic, you know – and you looked amazing!' added Conor as he disappeared into the sea of people.

Rosaleen turned to Deirdre with a smile. 'You really don't want your parents hanging around cramping your style on a night like this,' she said.

Her father plonked a kiss on her forehead. 'Good night, love,' he said. 'Well done again. Come out and visit us some weekend. I miss you around the house.'

'Good night, Dad.' She kissed him back. 'I'll come out for Sunday lunch some time soon, will I?'

'Do that. I'll do a big roast.'

Rosaleen leaned forward to give her daughter a final embrace. 'Give me a ring in the morning if you're up to it and let me know how the party went.' And as her parents moved away through the gesticulating crowd with her father's arm wrapped protectively round Rosaleen's shoulders, Deirdre felt something tug at her heart.

'You were pretty good tonight. Hell, you *look* pretty good tonight.'

Deirdre turned to find Rory McDonagh at her side. She tried to ignore the fact that he was looking down her cleavage. 'Oh, thanks, Rory. So were you.' Suddenly remembering her dream of the previous night, she found to her horror that she was blushing, and she looked wildly round the room, anxious to find some topic of conversation that might cover her embarrassment. Surrounded by satellites, an incandescent Eva Lavery was holding court over by the buffet table, managing to scoff sausage rolls and look scintillating at the same time. Rory's eyes followed Deirdre's gaze.

'She walks in the sun, that lady,' he said with a warm smile in his voice. 'She's a real live star.'

Deirdre nodded. 'Yeah. What exactly *is* it about her?'

Rory looked speculative. 'Her kind of stardom is hard to define. People just gravitate towards her. She's magnetic.' His eyes slid towards the leading lady again. 'And the fact that she's extremely foxy doesn't exactly detract from her class act.'

Deirdre remembered the little fox she'd seen on Eva's dressing table, and was astonished to find when she opened her mouth that there was a slightly petulant tone to her voice. 'You fancy her then? I would have thought that she was too old for you, Rory.'

Rory smiled. 'Part of the attraction, sweetheart. You've heard of the fascination that the older – or should I say more mature – woman exerts over the younger man? It's a syndrome thing. My own inamorata has a few years on me, you know.' He nodded his head in the direction of a woman whom Deirdre recognized as Rory's partner. She was sitting at a nearby table with a group of people who were all talking away earnestly. 'I don't know anyone who wouldn't want to fuck Eva Lavery,' Rory continued. He looked at Deirdre with wicked, piratical eyes, as if to assess her reaction. She refused to let him faze her, and met his gaze unwaveringly.

'Who's Eva's male counterpart, then?' she asked

archly, trying to sound a lot more sophisticated than she felt. She was actually finding the sexual nature of their conversation slightly unnerving.

'Lawless, of course,' he said, looking directly at her. A slow smile curved his mouth as he registered her abrupt discomfort. Laughing, he reached out his hand and stroked her hot cheek. '*You* know that, don't you?'

Deirdre broke contact with his eyes. The maddeningly knowing expression they held had finally defeated her.

'Just another show-biz hussy,' he said, with a sigh of mock reproval. 'They all fall for him in the end.' His eyes travelled downwards. 'Oh, yes. That dress is *sexy*, O'Dare. I suppose a ride'd be out of the question?'

'I imagine your girlfriend might raise some objections, Rory.'

'Marian? I'd say she'd probably be grateful to you for the pleasant respite.'

Just then Eva drifted by. 'Hi, gorgeous,' she called to Rory. 'I met you on the astral plain last night. You do a very nice line in dirty talk en français.'

The dream image of Rory McDonagh's hand on her breast rose again before Deirdre's mind's eye. 'Hey,' she found herself blurting out. 'He certainly got around last night.' She suppressed a smile at her own joke and then caught herself blushing again as the two actors shot looks at her, eyebrows like question marks.

'Ah – that explains why I was so knackered this

morning,' replied Rory, re-diverting his attention to Eva with a grin.

'I really don't know why you should be,' came Eva's airy riposte. '*I* did all the work.' And her laugh was flagrantly sexy as she sashayed past them in the direction of David Lawless, trailing admiring glances like a scarf.

Deirdre wondered ruefully if she would ever be able for the kind of banter that Eva and Rory constantly engaged in. She felt that life would be easier somehow, if she possessed an ounce of the wonderful insouciance that radiated from her leading lady. And Eva was looking particularly radiant tonight, Deirdre thought, swathed in softest Lainey Keogh from head to foot, the moss green gossamer of the gown complementing her golden beauty.

'Let me get you a drink, Deirdre. What'll you have?'

'Oh, thanks, Rory. A glass of white wine, please.'

Rory winced. 'Domaine de Monsieur Meagher? You're an intrepid girl. I'll be back in a minute.'

'It'll take you longer than that to get served. This place is heaving.'

'Mister Meagher likes me, Deirdre. As I said, I'll be back in a minute.'

Deirdre pulled a sceptical face at his cocksure attitude. As he headed in the direction of the bar, she checked her watch. Some childish impulse made her want to be able to puncture his arrogance by saying: 'So Mister Meagher likes you does he, Rory?' when he showed up with her wine ten minutes later. She leaned against a pillar, studying Rory's girlfriend with interest. Marian, he'd said her name was. She'd heard him complaining once about the antisocial hours she worked, and she'd asked Maeve what she did. She was a freelance journalist, apparently. Deirdre had seen her with Rory in Meagher's a couple of times before. She had an intelligent face which had a kind of Renaissance beauty about it, and she was madly sophisticated-looking which Deirdre found surprising given that she chose to live with someone like Rory.

Without warning he was back again with her drink, and Deirdre snuck a look at her watch. It had taken him fifty-eight seconds. 'Thanks very much, Rory,' she said.

* * *

As the evening wore on, things became more riotous. Meagre Meagher and the bar staff were run off their feet, and the crew had a rowdy sing-song going on in one corner of the room, trying to outdo the band in the opposite corner. Having consumed several glasses of very mediocre white wine, Deirdre wandered around the party feeling absolutely no pain. The air in the room had become fetid and heavy with cigarette smoke and Sophie Burke, in whose company she had inexplicably happened to find herself, had been far too liberal with Gucci's 'Envy'. She and Beautiful Ben were posing together trying to look like something out of a Calvin Klein ad, and Deirdre was appalled to think that she could ever have been interested in Ben. He'd been talking about himself non-stop for the past fifteen minutes, and hadn't once asked her how she was, or even mentioned her performance as Hermia. She should have given him to Sophie gift-wrapped.

Deirdre decided she needed a breather. She floated out on to the terrace which adjoined Meagher's rather tatty function room.

The pub was making a serious effort to clean up its act, knowing that there would be a lot of competition from nearby rival establishments for the lucrative post-theatre crowd. They were in the process of building a beer garden to accommodate the late-night summer drinkers. It was only half-finished, and looked a bit tacky with its plastic 'wrought iron effect' garden furniture and fussy brickwork, but at least the flowers in the hanging baskets were real. Deirdre wondered when they'd start getting round to doing up the inside of the pub. Rory McDonagh had sworn that if they turned it into one of those formula 'Irish' pubs he'd transfer his allegiance to O'Riordan's down the road.

There weren't many people around. The party had spilled out on to the terrace an hour or so earlier and then spilled back inside again as the sing-song got underway. Two crew members were having a meaningful drunken discussion at a nearby table and there was a couple snogging behind a stack of beer kegs. Deirdre wondered idly who they were, and whether their liason was licit or not. Brief affairs seemed to flourish and die within the company every other week.

The pub's cat, Growler, who had been snoozing on a beer keg, stretched himself luxuriously and rubbed against her shins on its way past to go night-hunting for an obliging female. Deirdre stroked him with a leisurely hand and then watched as he slunk off into the darkness. The hanging baskets were suddenly sent swinging by a little breeze. The heady fragrance of summer lilies wafted across her senses as she leant further over the newly-constructed balustrade, trying to follow the meandering progress of the cat. The breeze had disturbed the warm night air, and she gave a slight shiver.

'Are you cold?'

Deirdre did not need to turn to know the identity of the speaker. He had sought her out as she had known he would. This had to be the preamble to the tryst he'd hinted at in his opening-night card. 'Not really, David,' she said dreamily. She trailed languid fingers over her bare arm and then lifted her hand to the neckline of her dress and undid the top button, slowly pivoting her hips against the balustrade so that she faced him at last. She was aware that her body language was provocative, but that was her intention. She shifted a little against the stone wall in a way that would draw attention to her legs, and took a sip of wine.

'I didn't get a chance to thank you for the card,' she said with meaning, dropping her eyes to her feet in their high, strappy sandals.

'You're welcome,' said David. 'Thank you for your rose – and for your terrific performance this evening.' He inclined his head and smiled at her. She smiled back, trying to replicate Suki Hayes's pouting look of invitation and wondering how he could hold back from kissing her. She didn't realize that she looked a bit like a surprised trout.

'I wanted to talk to you in private, Deirdre, which is why I followed you out here where we can hear ourselves talk. It would be impossible in there.' He indicated the turmoil beyond the patio doors. 'Let's sit down, shall we?' Yes! Deirdre whooped inwardly as he motioned her towards a table on the far side of the terrace, guiding her by the elbow. She was sure that he too was aware of the static as his fingers touched her skin. He drew out a chair and invited her to sit, and she descended on it rather unsteadily.

'Oh, these stupid shoes,' she giggled. 'They're impossible to walk in!' She noticed that David Lawless's face had taken on a slightly uncertain expression, and she felt that she should explain. 'It's the high heels, you see. They take a bit of getting used to after Docs, as you can imagine!' The inflection in her voice made her sound as if she was delivering the punch-line of a hilarious joke.

'I see,' responded David, and his voice now held the trace of a smile. 'Look, Deirdre – maybe I should talk to you some other time.'

'Oh, no!' She was appalled. 'I'd much rather talk to you now – I mean, when will I get a chance to see you again? I'm very busy these days, you see.'

Oh God. What a pathetic excuse. 'Of course, I know you are too,' she added hastily.

'Are you sure you'll be able to follow me?' His tone lacked conviction. 'I've something rather important to tell you.'

Something important! 'Oh, yes. Of course I'll be able to follow you. Please do go on, David.'

He was looking at her with his head on one side and rather narrow, speculative eyes. Deirdre had never seen him look sexier. 'Listen carefully, Deirdre,' he said in his come-to-bed voice. 'First of all I want to find out whether or not you have an agent.'

'Not yet.' She leant forward in an attitude of rapt attention and vaguely wondered why her elbow immediately slipped off the table.

'Right. Sally Ruane was in at the show tonight, and we talked about you. She was impressed, and she's prepared to take you on her books on my recommendation. On a trial basis, you understand.' David Lawless looked at her blank face. 'You have heard of Sally Ruane, haven't you?' he queried, in the manner of someone trying to communicate with a small child.

'Oh, yes!' Her face lit up as she suddenly made the connection. 'She's one of the top theatrical agents in Dublin, isn't she?'

'That's right. Here's her business card. Get in touch with her tomorrow – she'll be expecting to hear from you.' He handed her a matt card which bore the discreet logo of Sally Ruane Management and Deirdre launched into an excited torrent of ‘thank-you-Davids’. He interrupted her at once.

‘Next item. I don’t know if you’ve heard any rumours about the proposed changes to our season at the Phoenix?’

‘No.’ Deirdre indicated interest by opening her eyes very wide. In the dusk his hair looked as if it was streaked with midnight blue.

‘I’m surprised. Everyone else at this party seems to know – even though they shouldn’t. It’s not official yet. Let me run something by you, Deirdre.’ He fixed serious eyes on her. ‘You’re already cast as First Witch in the next show, as you know, but I’d like you to double as Lady Macbeth’s waiting woman. You’ve proved to me over the course of the last weeks that you’re extremely able, and you could do with more experience. The part is small, but you know what they say–’

‘There are no small parts, only small actors,’ Deirdre intoned like a parrot.

‘Exactly. And I’m confident that you’ll be able to do something with it.’

Again David Lawless was obliged to interrupt her fervent expressions of gratitude. ‘Listen to me, Deirdre. This is where it gets complicated.’

‘Oh?’ She rather laboriously uncrossed her legs and then crossed them again at what she hoped was a more flattering angle. Her dress was now riding precariously high on her thighs.

‘There’s a problem with our final production. You may have heard that Eva’s involved in Neil Jordan’s latest project. It’s gone into production earlier than originally scheduled, and she’s foreseeing serious clashes. She won't be able to do both the play and the film, and the film company has contractual priority. It's unfortunate, but we've lost our Cleopatra.'

Deirdre's jaw dropped. David Lawless was offering *her* the role of Cleopatra! There was a beat as she tried to overcome her amazement, and then she managed to blurt out 'Oh, David – what can I say? Thank you! I can hardly believe it!'

'Sorry? I'm not with you.'

'I can hardly believe you're asking me to replace Eva! Cleopatra! It's to die for!'

David Lawless bowed his head, and Deirdre wondered why the muscles around his mouth seemed to be somehow contorted. As she squinted at him he regained control of his expression and looked her in the eyes. 'I'm sorry, Deirdre – you've got the wrong end of the stick. You've got to shut up and listen. I'm *not* offering you Cleopatra.'

Her sudden injured expression made Deirdre look so vulnerable that he reached out and laid a reassuring hand on her arm. She was so numb with embarrassment that this time the contact barely registered.

'You mustn't anticipate me. You may not be playing Cleopatra, but the news is still good. Because of all the rescheduling, we decided on the simplest option possible. I won't go into details now because I've a suspicion that you might have some difficulty taking them all in.' He gave her an enquiring smile and she nodded in solemn, almost tearful agreement. 'In a nutshell, we've decided on

Hamlet as an alternative. I approached Maeve Kirwan about playing Ophelia, but she's tied up in soap opera in September. I'm telling you straight up that you're not my first choice because if *I* don't someone else will, and they'll stick the knife in while they're doing it.'

'I'm not your first choice for what?' asked Deirdre, uncertainly.

'For Ophelia, of course.' David Lawless threw back his head and laughed. 'You're a little confused this evening, aren't you, Deirdre?' She found his smile dangerously seductive. 'I trust that you'll be happy with that? It's some measure of compensation for not playing Cleopatra, don't you think?'

She was gobsmacked. 'Oh, yes! Yes! Ophelia! Oh, thank you, thank you, David, oh tha–' She was so obviously on a loop that David Lawless made an immediate move to stop her in her tracks. He leaned over the table and placed two fingers on her lips. The effect was magical. Deirdre shut up instantly. Then David took her face between his hands. She held her breath.

'Shh, Deirdre. You take time out to think about everything I've said, OK? We'll talk again soon. Take care of yourself and enjoy the rest of the party.'

As he rose from the table and moved in the direction of the patio doors, Deirdre panicked. What about their tryst? This wasn't working out properly. 'Don't go! Don't go just yet! Please, David.'

He turned and gave her a long look, and then

returned slowly to the table. This time he didn't sit down, but remained standing by her chair. 'What's the problem?' He shot a glance at his watch. His body language was relaxed, but Deirdre was aware that a barely perceptible note of impatience had crept into his voice. She stood up with an effort, holding on to the back of her chair for support. There was concern on his face as he looked down at her.

'Are you all right, Deirdre?'

Her eyes were trapped in amber. He was so close that she felt faint. 'Yes, I'm all right. Thank you.' To her own amazement she found herself raising a hand and sliding it round the back of his neck, drawing his face closer to hers. Then she closed her eyes and raised her mouth for a kiss. Her lips brushed his, and she very gently touched the tip of her tongue to his mouth, inviting him to respond. She was aware that his body had gone tense, and instinct told her to move against him.

'Stop it.' Her eyes fluttered open and she felt drenched with shock. David Lawless had put his hands on her shoulders and was holding her firmly at arm's length. She sobered instantly. His eyes were very serious, and his high Slavic cheekbones seemed more pronounced than ever, accentuated as they were by the shadows cast on the contours of his face. 'You are extremely desirable,' he said in a gentle voice. 'But let's not do anything to compromise our working relationship. That would be very, very messy.'

He put a hand to his lips and held it there for a

second before transferring on to Deirdre's mouth the kiss he'd planted on his index finger. To her shame, she felt her lips part spontaneously under his touch. 'Take care of yourself,' he said for the second time that evening. And he was gone.

Deirdre was in agony. Humiliation flooded her, and washed away the last vestiges of alcohol-induced haze. She was suddenly conscious of only one over-riding need – to get out of there. All she craved now was oblivion. To get home, to get into bed and to pull the duvet over her head. Sleep was the only way of obliterating the horrific realization of what she had just done.

Reeling with painful embarrassment, she made her way along the terrace trying to remember where she had left her bag. Who was the last person she'd talked to in the function room? Sophie. Deirdre teetered on the threshold, raking the room with her eyes. The party was thinning out now, and all but the most stalwart drinkers in the cast were preparing to leave. She was vaguely aware of Finbar de Rossa leaning too closely in towards Kate O'Connor where he had pinioned her against the far wall, and of Rory and Jonathan Hughes lolling against the bar, roaring with juvenile laughter. There was no sign of Marian. She was relieved to see Sophie still sitting at the same table where she'd left her, looking like a salamander in expensive, skin-tight satin. Deirdre took a deep breath and steered herself across the room.

'Hi, Sophie.' She was surprised to find that her voice sounded quite normal. 'Is my bag still here?'

'Good God, what's wrong with you? You look frightful.' Sophie's expression had surprise written all over it and was genuine for once.

'Thanks.'

'Sit down, Deirdre. Take it easy. Your bag's OK.'

Deirdre felt so drained that she suspected that if she didn't sit down she might fall down instead, and she found herself doing as Sophie suggested.

'I need to get home.'

'If you want, you can share a cab with me and Ben,' said Sophie with uncharacteristic amiability. She must have had too much to drink, Deirdre thought. 'He's just gone to hail one.'

The ignominy of sharing a cab with Sophie and her ex seemed a fitting enough way to end the evening.

'God, he's such a babe,' said Sophie, gazing across the room with a dreamy expression on her face.

'Who?' asked Deirdre without interest. She had surreptitiously done up the top button on her dress again, and was twisting a strand of hair with listless fingers.

'David. Look at him – over there. That shirt he's wearing is gorgeous, isn't it? It really sets off the colour of his eyes.'

Deirdre obeyed the awful compulsion that seized her and followed the line of Sophie's gaze. David Lawless was standing by the door. He had his jacket slung over his shoulder, and was clearly taking his leave of the party. An elegant, ice-cool blonde, the epitome of poise, stood by his side. She had a vaguely familiar look.

Deirdre was curious suddenly. 'Who's that woman?' she asked Sophie.

'D'you mean to say you don't *know*?' Sophie was incredulous. 'It's Ann Fitzroy, of course – the soap opera star.'

Deirdre's failure to make the connection was understandable. The actress was a lot more sophisticated and beautiful in the flesh than she was on the telly.

'Ann Fitzroy. His wife?'

She saw the woman laugh at something David was saying and then lay her hand on his arm in a proprietorial fashion as Eva Lavery walked past them. Ann acknowledged the smile Eva flashed them with a vague inclination of her head.

'Mm hm.' Sophie's tone was full of admiration. 'Of course, I've been a fan of hers for years. I suppose you could call her my role model. Just look at her. You can tell she's the perfect society wife as well as being a deadly actress.'

Deirdre stole another look at Ann Fitzroy. She was wearing a long, backless sheath which had a metallic sheen to it. She looked as if she were encased in liquid silver. Deirdre pictured herself standing in her place at David's side, and if she hadn't felt so gutted with misery she would have guffawed. How could she ever have dreamt that David Lawless could be interested in someone like her? She cringed when she remembered how she'd actually fantasized about marrying the man! Sophie was still droning on in her ear and she forced herself to return her attention to the other actress.

'She has amazing business acumen, apparently, and of course she's incredibly well-connected. My grandfather told me that David would never have got where he is today without her.'

'Your grandfather?' What on earth had Sophie Burke's grandfather got to do with anything?

'You haven't been listening to a word I said, have you?' Sophie sounded put out. 'I just told you. My grandfather is a member of the same golf club as Ann Fitzroy's father.' Across the room they could hear Ann Fitzroy's tinkling laugh. 'They make a terrific couple, don't they?' observed Sophie.

'I thought their marriage was supposed to be on the rocks?'

'Don't believe everything you hear, Deirdre. Golf club gossip is a lot more reliable than theatre gossip, you know. Ann is a valuable asset to David.'

Over by the door, Ann Fitzroy was nodding in a knowledgeable way at one of the season's backers, who was helping her into her coat. She thanked him with a smile which displayed pearly little teeth. Deirdre slid further down into her seat, feeling even more wretched. Even Ann Fitzroy's teeth were perfect.

Just then Ben came through the door and waved at Sophie – 'The taxi's here, angel,' he called across the room.

David and Ann Fitzroy were making their exit. Meagre Meagher himself was holding the door open for them, nodding in the ingratiating manner he reserved for David Lawless and Rory McDonagh and emphatically not one other human being on the face of the planet. As the luminous couple strolled from the room, David looked back over his shoulder. His eyes met Deirdre's and he smiled. She rose from her seat, swaying a little, and managed to lob a bright smile back at him. It was the best performance of her life to date.

Inside, Deirdre O'Dare just wanted to die.

Chapter Six

Deirdre's hangover was colossal. As soon as she woke, scraps of remembered details from the previous night began to invade her brain and each fresh one made her cringe more abjectly than the one before. She desperately tried to force herself back into the sanctuary of sleep so that she could blot out the horrible thoughts, but as the trickle of memory gradually became a flood, she abandoned all hope of regaining unconsciousness.

Gingerly she slid out of bed and veered towards the bathroom, following a trail of discarded clothes and fighting a creeping nausea. Her mouth tasted like a rat's nest and her brain felt as though it had swollen during the night and was now being constricted by the helmet of her skull. She knocked back a couple of paracetamol, and, scrubbing her teeth with as much vigour as she could muster, shambled into the kitchen to put on the kettle. She badly needed a hit of caffeine. Sitting at the kitchen counter nursing her mug, she made herself confront her situation.

She searched for extenuating circumstances. There were none. She had made a complete fool of herself in front of the one person in the world whose respect she was desperate to win. Any credibility she may have had with David Lawless was now totally, irretrievably blown. OK. So she'd been pissed. But that didn't excuse her behaviour. It had been mind-bogglingly arrogant of her to assume that he would be interested in her just because she was young and available. She'd been very lucky. Most men wouldn't have hesitated to wolf her straight off the plate on which she'd presented herself to her director last night. It had taken an incident of monumental crassness to finally wake her up to the fact that David Lawless wasn't like most men.

Her panic mounted when she thought of the knock-on effect the incident could have on her career. David was probably even now regretting offering her the role of Ophelia, and she wouldn't blame him if he decided to change his mind. She deserved everything that was coming to her.

She'd have to do something to try and repair the damage she'd done. She was tempted to just stick her head in the sand and hope for the best, but she knew that ignoring her dilemma wouldn't make it go away. Should she write to him to say how sorry she was? An apology was the very least he deserved. But writing a letter was a coward's way out. And it wouldn't get around the fact that she would still have to face up to him at some stage. No. She would have to talk directly to him – and the sooner the better. She would telephone him at once.

Feeling slightly less wretched now that she had come to some decision, Deirdre reached for her battered faux-leather Filofax and practically ran to the phone, flicking through the pages as she went. E F G H I J K L. Oh God. What should she say? Shouldn't she rehearse something before picking up the phone to him? No, no – she'd lose her nerve if she did that. She would just have to bite the bullet: admit she'd made a total eejit of herself and ask him to forgive her.

Trying to breathe the way her voice coach in college had taught her, she picked up the phone and punched in the number correctly at the third attempt. The hiatus after the fourth ring alerted her that she would be connected to an answering machine. Shit, shit, *shit.* Deirdre floundered again. She had braced herself for a personal contact – what kind of message could she possibly leave on a machine? Something along the lines of: 'Oh, hi, David, this is Deirdre O'Dare here. Sorry for getting pissed and trying to snog you last night'?

'Hello. We are presently unable to take your call,' came the recorded voice. It wasn't David Lawless's voice – it was Ann Fitzroy's. Deirdre recognized it immediately. It was already familiar to her from hearing it countless times on TV and radio commercials, usually advertising stuff like body lotions or shampoo. The actress's voice was beautifully modulated and resonant with class. Deirdre's initial instinct to put down the phone was usurped by a kind of fascination as Ann Fitzroy continued to purr over the line.

'Perhaps you'd be kind enough to leave your message or send a fax after the tone. Or you may contact me on my mobile on the following number: 087–'

She got a sudden shock as the recorded message was abruptly cut off and the phone was picked up.

'Ann Fitzroy.' This voice held little of the honeyed tones of the recorded one. Deirdre overcame a second impulse to drop the receiver.

'Oh, hello. Could I – um – may I speak to Mr Lawless, please?'

'May I ask who's calling?' There was no inflection in the question. It was more of a command than an inquiry.

'It's Deirdre O'Dare here.' The silence which followed invited elaboration. 'I'm – I'm in Mr Lawless's *Midsummer Night's Dream*.'

There was another pause. 'You need to consult him on some detail of your – performance?'

Deirdre tried not to gulp. 'Yes, I do.' She wasn't lying. She *did* need to talk to him about her performance, although it wasn't her stage performance she was concerned about, it was her performance as a drunken slapper.

'I see,' said Ann Fitzroy. 'Hold on.' Her voice held ice.

The interval before David came to the phone was agonizingly long, and as the seconds ticked by Deirdre's tension mounted. Had she imagined it, or had Ann Fitzroy put subtle emphasis on the word 'performance'? Oh God. Was she referring obliquely to Deirdre's behaviour last night? What if someone had told her that they'd seen Deirdre O'Dare making a pass at her husband? No. She was pretty sure there'd been no-one around to witness her lunacy. She'd vaguely noticed the two crew members staggering back into the pub, and it would appear that the snogging couple had passed out because they'd never emerged from behind the beer kegs. At least she had managed to avoid *public* humiliation.

Maybe David had mentioned the incident to his wife? That could account for Ann Fitzroy's frosty manner. Oh God, oh God. Maybe she should just drop the receiver. But all of a sudden David Lawless's voice was in her ear, and she was struck by the unexpectedly intimate sensation of it.

'Deirdre.'

'Oh – hi, David,' she managed.

'I thought that I might hear from you this morning.' She deduced a trace of a smile, and once again shame engulfed her.

'I'm so sorry. I'm so, so sorry,' she heard herself saying, unable to control the tell-tale quaver of her vocal cords. David Lawless's response was instantaneous.

'It's OK, Deirdre,' he reassured her. 'Don't upset yourself. As far as I'm concerned, last night never happened. All right?'

'I – I'm sorry, David,' she said again. 'I don't know what made me do it. It was unforgivable of me to put you in a compromising situation like that.' She took a deep breath. 'Your wife doesn't – you didn't–'

'My wife knows nothing. I don't deem it necessary to acquaint her with every detail of my private life. Please let me assure you, Deirdre, that absolutely no-one knows or is ever likely to know what happened last night.' His pitch was low now, and very gentle, and Deirdre began to feel the first stirrings of relief.

'Thank you for being so – so understanding,' she stammered. 'And I promise it'll never happen again.'

'I'm almost sorry to hear that.' His voice was like velvet in her ear. 'Desirable young women don't attempt to seduce me every night of the week.'

'Oh, they do, you know – all the time – except you don't notice it,' said Deirdre earnestly, and then kicked herself. 'Their technique is a bit subtler than mine, that's all.'

David Lawless laughed his wonderful laugh, and Deirdre suddenly felt OK again.

'Thank you for calling, Deirdre. It can't have been an easy thing to do. You've got guts as well as charm. I'll see you later. And remember to set up an appointment with Sally Ruane. I've a feeling you could do with an agent on your case as soon as possible.'

'Yes, David.'

'And get out your *Complete Works*. You're going to want to re-read *Hamlet*. Bye, Deirdre.'

'Good-bye, David – and thanks again.'

Deirdre put the phone down and let out a massive sigh. David Lawless was the best hangover cure she'd ever had.

She remained sitting on the floor of her hallway for a while, idly plaiting strands of her hair. Her curiosity had been tickled by Ann Fitzroy. If David hadn't filled her in on Deirdre's clumsy attempt to seduce him last night, why had she been so cool towards her during their brief exchange on the phone? She'd noticed that David sounded distinctly offhand when he'd referred to his wife. What had he said? 'I don't deem it necessary to acquaint her with every detail of my private life'? There was something odd about that. What private life? Maybe David was having an affair with someone? She'd often imagined that he might be in love with Eva Lavery, but if they were having an affair it was an extremely well-kept secret. And she knew it wasn't easy to keep things secret in the theatre world.

Maybe she'd try picking Sophie Burke's brains this evening. Being a dedicated gossip, Sophie would easily be persuaded to spill a few beans. She decided that a temporary cease-fire might be in order. She did up the popper on her Filofax with a decisive air. That's what she'd do. She'd offer to buy Sophie a drink in Meagher's after the show and extract information from her. Now that she thought of it, Maeve might know something about the Lawless/Fitzroy set-up, too. Maeve had worked on *Ardmore Grove* – the soap opera that Ann Fitzroy was in – and she was sure to have had dealings with the actress.

She picked herself up and headed towards the bedroom to locate her *Complete Works* of Shakespeare. Then something struck her for the first time. She hadn't a clue who'd be playing opposite her. Who, she wondered, did David Lawless have in mind for Hamlet?

* * *

The atmosphere in the theatre that evening was euphoric.

In spite of the massive collective hangover, the morale of the company was sky-high after the success of the opening night. Photocopies of the reviews – which were unanimous raves – were pinned up on the notice board in the green room, and Nick McCarthy announced over the tannoy that the advance booking had gone into orbit.

There was a lot of gossip about the substitution of *Hamlet* for *Anthony and Cleopatra*. It was common knowledge that Cleopatra was a role that Eva Lavery had been longing to play all her life. It must have been devastating for her to have to relinquish it, but there was no way round it. The change in the planned schedule for the Neil Jordan film would make it impossible for Eva to take on any additional burdens. What with filming, performing her next role as Lady Macbeth and simultaneously rehearsing the exacting role of Cleopatra, she'd be under inhuman pressure.

But Eva's contribution was essential. Her celebrity was the linchpin on which the success of the entire season had been hung, and a lot of money had been invested in it. Lawless Productions simply wouldn't attract the audience figures they needed to stay afloat without the pulling power of a major star like Eva. So she and David had cast around for a less demanding vehicle for her and come up with *Hamlet.* Eva had already played the part of Gertrude, Hamlet's mother, in a production in New York not so long ago, and this way she could remain involved in the season in a less pivotal capacity.

As the cast assembled for the pre-show preparation, speculation was rife as to who would be playing what in *Hamlet.* The subject of most of the speculation was, naturally enough, that of the identity of the actor who was to play the prince.

The warm-up was a shambles. Most of the actors were too hungover and giddy to take it seriously, with the exception of Sophie, who threw shapes left, right and centre and shot cross looks at anyone who disturbed her concentration. Deirdre had been avoiding Sophie assiduously, and intended doing so until she could corner her in the pub later to worm out the information she wanted. She didn't want to run the risk of getting into a discussion about the casting of Hamlet with Sophie. She had a suspicion that Sophie would be less inclined towards social intercourse if she heard that her arch-rival Deirdre O'Dare had been cast as Ophelia.

Rory McDonagh had positioned himself behind Sophie, and was doing a perfect imitation of her rapt expression when they got round to doing their vocal exercises. 'Me, me, my, my, moo, mooo, moooo,' they intoned in unison, and Deirdre almost had to leave the stage. Jonathan Hughes actually did leave the stage with a hand clapped over his mouth, but the expression on his face indicated that he was going to throw up from hungover nausea rather than laughter.

Nick McCarthy was not amused. 'Let's please try and avoid the pitfalls of second night syndrome,' he reprimanded them. 'I know you're all relieved that we've got through the opening, but that's no reason for complacency. Just keep it in mind that the people out there this evening have paid a lot of money for their tickets. They don't want to watch a shower of lazy, hungover bastards strolling through the show – they want to be entertained, and it looks like you lot will have to work pretty damn hard if they're going to get their money's worth tonight.'

Deirdre felt guilty about giggling. She determined that she'd work her ass off to deliver the goods this evening, and she forced herself to stand tall and focused in the wings before making her first entrance, just as she had seen Eva do last night. She shut her eyes and took deep breaths and then she had a brilliant idea. If she gathered the folds of her dress up behind her back she could let go of the silk just as she walked out on to the stage, and it would all flow out behind her in a glorious billowing mass. What an entrance! She was delighted with herself, and wished she'd thought of doing it before. She saw Rory giving her a curious look as she grabbed the fabric of her gown and bunched it up around her bum just as her cue was coming up.

As she wafted on in front of him she stumbled over a stage weight and caught the hem of her gown on the wooden frame of a flat. She hovered for a moment or two at a complete loss, and with an expression of chronic dismay on her face. Then she tugged surreptitiously at her skirt. Nothing happened. She tugged again, a bit harder this time. Still nothing happened. In desperation she bent down and pulled with great force. As she heard a ripping sound, her eyes met Rory's. The actor gave her a wicked, sideways glance, and then he averted his face from the audience so that only Deirdre could see the smirk playing around his mouth. Deirdre suddenly felt hot and then cold, and was horrified when a great snort of laughter escaped her quite involuntarily. Rory's back was now firmly to the audience and she could see his shoulders shaking and a muscle going in his cheek.

On the other side of the stage she was aware of a growing tension in her fellow actors, and there was sudden consternation in the wings. Adrian Pierce actually stepped out of character for a beat or two, and Eva and Finbar were trying hard not to look too watchful. Then Finbar took action. He strode across the stage in an unplotted move and, taking Deirdre by the arm in a deceptively casual manner, steered her upstage and away from Rory.

Deirdre blanched, and spent the rest of Finbar's speech trying to regain her composure. She could not bring herself to meet her colleagues' eyes, and though she fought it, the image of her undignified entrance and Rory's diabolical smile kept swimming perniciously in front of her mind's eye, provoking sudden awful hiccups of uncontrollable laughter. She had never 'corpsed' before, and she was finding it really frightening. The spasmodic snuffles which seized her at intervals left her panicky and in a cold sweat.

The cue for her first speech was coming up. She took a deep gulp of air and fixed her gaze firmly on the middle distance. Miraculously, the dialogue with Finbar went smoothly enough. She was conscious of Eva's look of concern and of Finbar's eyes boring into her own, willing her to concentrate. She was agonizingly aware, too, of Rory McDonagh's presence downstage right, but she could not steel herself to send him Hermia's usual inviting looks. She was dreading the moment when the rest of the cast would leave the stage and they'd be alone together. She would have to meet his eyes then.

The comic aspect of her dilemma quickly faded and she felt a touch of cold fear when she suddenly thought of the possible repercussions of her extremely unprofessional behaviour. She couldn't allow herself to let that worry her now, though – she'd think about that after she'd got through the rest of the scene.

The moment of their meeting arrived. Thankfully, Rory seemed to have sobered also, although Deirdre noticed that, rather than making direct eye contact, he seemed to be focusing on her left eyebrow. By the time Maeve walked out on stage they were both in control of things, though Deirdre found it difficult not to deliver the final lines of the scene with a sense of real relief rather than with the air of excitement they'd rehearsed:

Keep word, Lysander: we must starve our sight
From lovers' food till morrow deep midnight.

She was seriously scared as she made her way to the green room to apologize to the other actors. Rory had got there before her and was doing likewise. Finbar accepted her apology coolly, while Eva was generous. 'It can happen to anyone, darling – especially on a second night when everyone's feeling a bit dizzy. Massage my shoulders for me, will you, angel? There's an awful knot of tension – just there, that's right. Oh, heaven!'

Deirdre started to knead her fingers into Eva's shoulders. 'But I ruined the scene, Eva!'

'No you didn't, Deirdre. I know you felt as if the entire audience was staring at you, but I doubt very much if anyone other than ourselves was aware of what was going on – especially when Finbar came to the rescue. Further up the spine, please, darling. Now, dig your fingers into the back of my neck as hard as you can.'

As Deirdre parted the switch of false hair and started to rub vigorously at the muscles on the nape of Eva's neck, she noticed for the first time a small tattoo on the skin immediately below her natural hairline. It was in the form of a tiny, jewel-coloured Siamese Fighting Fish. She knew it was a Siamese Fighter because her father kept tropical fish in a tank at home. He could only ever allow one Fighter in the tank – if two were introduced they would kill each other. Deirdre didn't comment on it. There was something private about a tattoo in such a secret place.

'Onstage incidents like that are always magnified out of all proportion in an actor's mind,' Eva went on. 'I've seen dozens of actors corpse a million times worse than you did tonight and the audience didn't bat an eyelid. You must apologize to Nick, though, otherwise he might feel that he'd have to report it back to David.'

'Oh God!' Deirdre's hands flew to her mouth.

'Oh, Deirdre, you mustn't overreact! Corpsing is a notorious leveller amongst actors. D'you know how John Gielgud once described it? He called it "exquisite agony", which wouldn't be a bad way of describing your massage technique. Oops – let me go. I'll be late for my entrance.'

Across the room Deirdre saw Rory mimicking her pratfall and the stunned expression she'd had on her face as she had fumbled with the folds of her gown on stage. He blew her a kiss when he saw her watching and she had to laugh at the glint in his eye. But it was a rather guilty laugh.

She joined Maeve, who was sitting cross-legged on the floor, poring over the property section of the previous day's *Irish Times.*

'You're not thinking of moving, are you, Maeve?' Deirdre asked, sitting down beside her.

'Nah – I can't afford to. The market's gone bananas. But it's nice to dream. Someday maybe I'll have a mansion on the Vico Road.'

Deirdre sat down beside the other actress and together they perused the pages. On the front there was a feature about a Georgian manor house complete with tennis court and stables for £695,000. An island with two cottages was for sale in Clew Bay. Inside the paper the advertised property was more modest, but still fantasy-island stuff as far as the two actresses were concerned.

'Oh, look,' said Maeve with sudden interest. 'There's a house for sale on the road where David lives. Christ, they're expensive. They've just rocketed in the past few years in that area.'

Deirdre took in the upmarket address. It was on a road of very beautiful detached Victorian houses in Dublin 6.

'Well, Ann must be feeling pretty smug.' Something in Maeve's tone made Deirdre curious.

'Ann Fitzroy?'

'Yeah. She's really into home improvement – decorating, entertaining, all that side of life. Keeping up appearances, basically.'

'You've worked with her in *Ardmore Grove,* haven't you, Maeve?'

'Yup. I've had that pleasure.'

'What's she like?'

Maeve looked careful. 'Do you want the official version or the truth?'

'The truth, please. I promise I won't repeat it.'

Maeve turned the page of the paper and continued to run her eyes over the photographs of the houses advertised for sale. 'Well,' she said with deliberation. 'She's got this incredibly sophisticated aura about her, but I've seen her behave really badly. She can go totally ballistic over the smallest upset. Maybe she's very insecure underneath it all, but that's no excuse for the way she treats people. She gets jealous if anyone else gets any attention whatsoever, and she really takes it out on them. Wow – look at that conservatory! And–' Maeve lowered her voice fractionally '– she really gets off on the fact that she's a soap opera diva. Though I reckon she'd secretly love to do more work in the theatre–' Maeve articulated each syllable of the word, pronouncing it 'thee-ah-tah' '– you know, the really classy kind of stuff that Eva does? I bet she's fuming that David didn't ask her to step in as Cleopatra when Eva had to let him down. I've a sneaking suspicion that there's no love lost between her and Eva Lavery.'

'Oh?' Deirdre was more curious than ever. This was gripping stuff, especially coming from Maeve, who was normally the soul of discretion.

'Mm. She'd see Eva as an arch-rival.' Maeve paused in her examination of the *Property Times* and looked thoughtful. 'You know, I'd say Ann Fitzroy was cracked actually – she's nothing but sharps and flats. There's no middle C there at all.' She sounded quite matter-of-fact.

'Wow.' Deirdre was intrigued by the idea of David Lawless having an unstable wife. Maeve had once described him as a man of integrity. Maybe *that* was why he stayed married to her! He felt he had to protect her – a bit like Mr Rochester with his mad wife in the attic.

Maeve looked over her shoulder to check that nobody had wandered into earshot. 'You'd never believe it from her public persona, though. She's always got this incredible veneer of composure, and looks so – shit – what's the word I'm looking for? French word – begins with an "S"?'

'Soignée?' suggested Deirdre.

'Spot on, Deirdre. Soignée. Like an Ice Queen.'

Maeve started worrying a cuticle with her teeth. 'Most people who don't know her are in awe of her. Most people who do know her are scared of her. I just steer clear of her.'

'I saw her for the first time in the flesh last night. She's much more beautiful than she looks on the telly.'

'Yeah – most soap actors are better looking in real life. Skinnier as well – the camera makes you look at least half a stone heavier than you really are.'

'David said something last night about you going back into the soap in the autumn?'

'That's right.' Maeve had succeeded in detaching the loose skin from her cuticle, and was sucking the raw flesh. 'Shit. I really wish I could stop biting my nails. That hurt.'

'It's the only bad habit you have, Maeve.'

'Thanks, Deirdre.'

'Will you have much to do with Ann Fitzroy when you go back?'

'I dunno. I haven't a clue what the story-lines are this season. I hope not. That woman can trail misery in her wake like a cloak. "Tragedi-Ann", Rory calls her.'

From the tannoy, Deirdre could hear that it was time for her to be moving into the wings again. She rose to her feet and stretched herself. 'Oh – Deirdre!' Maeve dashed her hand against her forehead. 'I completely forgot that congratulations are in order! I heard you've been offered Ophelia!'

'That's right, Maeve. Thanks.' Deirdre almost squirmed with pleasure. She'd been dying to mention it earlier, but didn't want to look as if she was crowing about the fact that she'd landed the part that Maeve had had to turn down. It was typical of Maeve to make no mention of the fact that she herself had been the original casting. 'And guess what else? David Lawless spoke to Sally Ruane about me. I rang her secretary today, and I've got an appointment to see her on Monday morning!'

'Excellent! I'm sure Sophie will be delighted at the news,' remarked the older actress. Then she grinned. 'Does she know yet?'

'No.' Deirdre returned the smile. 'I think I'll put off telling Sophie for a while.'

* * *

In Meagher's after the show Deirdre sought out Sophie's company for the second night in a row. She was sitting with the other fairies, gossiping about the casting of *Hamlet*, and Deirdre decided it might be wise to keep schtum and listen for a while.

'It's a really weird choice,' Sophie was saying. 'Why *Hamlet*?'

'Eva's preference, apparently,' answered Jessica.

'They decided to opt for something that would be showy but not too taxing for her. Anyway, she's a shareholder in the company. She can do what she likes, within reason.'

Sophie's lip curled. 'God! She thinks she's great!'

Kate O'Connor looked at her in a rather perplexed way. 'Why shouldn't she, Sophie? She *is* great.'

'But Hamlet *is Hamlet* – you cast the prince first and *then* the secondary characters. I don't know how she gets away with it – she has Lawless wrapped round her little finger, that's plain enough to see. I think it's really selfish of her.' The look of outrage on Sophie's face was almost comical. Please let her not speculate on who's playing Ophelia, prayed Deirdre.

'I think they *have* a Hamlet.' Jessica spoke with exaggerated caution, like a supergrass anxious not to be overheard – even though it would have been virtually impossible to eavesdrop in the pub, given the level of the din. Deirdre's ears pricked up.

'Oh? Who?' The actresses leaned forward simultaneously.

'Jonathan Hughes probably,' hazarded Kate. 'Or Adrian Pierce. He'd be the obvious choice, wouldn't he? He's so introspective.' She rubbed at her cheekbone where a patch of residual glitter from her fairy make-up still lingered. 'But of course David wouldn't *take* the obvious route. I bet it's Rory McDonagh!' Deirdre noticed that Kate's eyes took on an excited gleam when she mentioned Rory's name.

'Oh, God – neither of *them*, I hope. Their pulling power couldn't attract a single punter between them.'

That was unfair of Sophie, thought Deirdre. In fact, Rory had quite a following after appearing in sizeable cameos in a spate of recent movies, and she had already noticed an accumulation of mail for him on the green room notice board. So far he was either ignorant of its existence or he simply hadn't bothered to pick it up. That was pretty cool, Deirdre thought, to be so laid-back about fan mail. If by a long shot anything ever arrived at the theatre for her she decided she'd let it hang around on the notice board for a couple of days to show that she could be nonchalant about such things too.

Jessica was enjoying being the centre of attention. She toyed with their curiosity for a while longer, taking a long swig from her bottle of Sol before gratifying them with an answer. 'Not Adrian, no. As far as I know he's playing Horatio. And both Rory and Jonathan are too old to be cast as Eva's son.' The confidential tone dropped to a stage whisper. 'Hamlet's been offered to Mark Llewellyn.'

'Mark Llewellyn!' Kate bounced up and down with gleeful excitement, and even Sophie seemed impressed. 'You mean Mark Llewellyn from *Yeats Country*?'

'Of course she does, Kate,' said Sophie scathingly. 'There are hardly two Mark Llewellyns in British Actors' Equity, are there?'

'Oh God, he's so *gorgeous*,' said Kate in a swoony

voice. 'He's kind of got the look of a younger Rory McDonagh, hasn't he?'

'Well let's hope he doesn't behave like Rory. One joker in the company is more than enough, thank you,' said Sophie primly. Then she made a sudden connection. 'I've just remembered something. Eva played Gertrude in some production in New York a couple of years ago. *That's* why they've decided on *Hamlet*! It's something she's done already, so she'll know the part inside-out. God! How lazy can you get – she might as well *phone* in her performance.'

Deirdre suspected that Sophie's fierce resentment of the leading lady was because Eva had no time for her. Sophie had spent the first fortnight of rehearsal sucking up to Eva like mad and had only succeeded in alienating the actress further and further. She'd been livid when Deirdre had casually let drop that she'd been round to Eva's for dinner one night (she'd made reference to the 'wonderful Meursault' they'd drunk, but had omitted to tell Sophie that the meal had actually been an Indian take-away). Since then, Sophie had taken to referring to Eva in sarcastic tones as 'Deirdre's new pal'.

'It makes sense, you know, Sophie,' said Jessica authoritatively. 'I heard David say that this way Eva'll be able to deliver the goods as economically as possible without compromising the integrity of the season.'

'How do you know all this, Jessica?' asked Kate.

'I overheard him talking to one of the backers at the party last night.'

'Why Mark Llewellyn instead of someone in the company?' This was Deirdre's first contribution to the conversation so far.

'*Yeats Country* did so well in the TAMS when it was transmitted on RTE at Easter that they reckon he'll be big at the box office.'

'They're lucky he was available,' said Kate.

'Eva was the carrot, apparently. I heard David say that Mark Llewellyn jumped at the chance of working with her.'

'The entire planet must be teeming with Eva Lavery's admirers,' Sophie remarked caustically. 'But I have to say that Mark Llewellyn's not really my type. I prefer more sophisticated men. Like David Lawless. Or Finbar de Rossa.' Finbar de Rossa! Deirdre was appalled, but kept her mouth shut. How could Sophie possibly mention David Lawless and Finbar de Rossa in the same breath? 'Finbar has such class, hasn't he? And d'you know what? I think he fancies me!' she added in a kittenish voice, curling her legs up on to her seat to show off rose-pink suede pumps.

Jessica and Deirdre both averted their eyes, but Kate fell for it. 'Oh, Sophie – your shoes are lovely! Are they new?'

'These old things? No – I've had them for ages. Got them in Harvey Nicks about six weeks ago,' she said casually. 'I wonder who's playing Ophelia?' Her green eyes roamed the room until they settled on Maeve where she stood with her arm draped loosely around the waist of Jacqueline Moynihan, her partner. They were both nursing bottles of

Rolling Rock and talking with relaxed intimacy. Sophie's mouth curled into a little smile of pleasure. 'It's probably Maeve. Ha! Poor Mark Llewellyn will have a bit of a surprise in store for him when he finds out his Ophelia is gay!'

'Actually, I'm pretty sure it's *not* Maeve,' said Jessica. 'As far as I know she's going back into *Ardmore Grove* in the autumn.'

Deirdre suddenly jumped to her feet. 'Can I buy anyone a drink?' she asked. The three actresses looked at her in astonishment. They never bought each other rounds of drinks.

'Sophie – what will you have?'

'Well, thanks, Deirdre – I'll have another one of these.'

'Jessica? Kate?'

'Are you sure, Deirdre?' asked Kate, doubtfully.

'Absolutely.' The price of a round would be worth it if she could distract Sophie from speculating about the casting of Ophelia. 'I had a bit of a windfall today.' Actually it was true. When she'd phoned her mother earlier in the day, Rosaleen had told her that she'd just sold five of her paintings to some corporate business firm and that she was going to make a lodgement to Deirdre's account. She hadn't mentioned a figure, but from her excessively jolly tone Deirdre guessed that it might be in the region of a hundred pounds or so. Deirdre had practically sung hymns to her down the phone. It meant that the cheque she'd written for her opening night frock wouldn't bounce after all.

As she waited for the barman to get the drinks she

wondered how poor Mark Llewellyn would feel when he discovered that they'd cast a nobody as Ophelia. She suspected that she was out of her depth, and found herself wondering if she shouldn't get out while the going was good. Handing money over the counter she suddenly caught sight of her reflection in the mirror behind the bar. Come on, Deirdre – stop being such a wimp, she told herself. Everyone has to start somewhere, and if a young actor like Mark Llewellyn could blaze a trail, why couldn't she?

It was really just a question of confidence, after all. If she thought positive from now on, maybe she'd develop a more sophisticated attitude to life. She could start by making an effort to be a bit more dignified.

Adopting a slightly superior expression and sucking in her cheeks to make her cheekbones look more prominent, she accepted her change with a gracious smile at the sullen barman and headed back towards Sophie's corner. She discovered that it wasn't that easy to move elegantly through a crowd with a rake of bottles clutched to her chest, and she tried to make her frustration look more like world-weariness.

'What's wrong with you, Deirdre? You look as if you've got something stuck up your bum.'

She registered Rory's irritating grin as he slid round her to take up residency at the bar.

'Oh, Rory – you're so jejune,' she sighed, delighted at last to have the opportunity to use the word. She'd come across it in an article she'd been reading in her mother's *Vanity Fair* and had found it so intriguing that she'd looked it up in the dictionary. She loved good words. She'd found that it meant 'wanting in substance' or 'puerile', and she reckoned it would be way above Rory's head. She smiled at him in a pitying way.

'I'm not at all insubstantial, sweetheart,' said Rory with a laugh which dripped innuendo. Dammit. Rory obviously loved good words too. 'On the contrary. Would you care to find out, Deirdre? You could start by taking me to a very private place . . .' His voice in her ear was silky, and she could tell that he was taking great delight in her discomfort. Why did the bastard always succeed in nettling her? She felt about ten years old instead of twenty-one. She gave a little sigh to indicate ennui, and winced inwardly when it somehow came out sounding more like a rather priggish 'tisk'. His exasperating laugh pursued her as, cheeks blazing, she worked her way back towards her friends. Rory McDonagh was the most politically incorrect person she had ever met.

Kate and Jessica had been joined by a couple of students from the Gaiety School of Acting who'd been at the show. Sophie must consider it terminally uncool to be seen talking to mere students now that she was a professional actress, because she had angled her chair away from the body of the group and was studiously ignoring them. Delighted with the chance to get Sophie on her own at last, Deirdre pulled up a chair beside her.

'Cheers.'

'Cheers.' From the delicate way Sophie sipped at the mouth of her bottle of Sol, Deirdre reckoned that the other actress probably didn't really like drinking from the neck, and that she only did it to be hip. She wondered how she could steer the conversation in the direction she wanted it to go without it seeming too obvious. As it turned out, Sophie's opening gambit couldn't have been more auspicious.

'What did you think of Ann Fitzroy's outfit last night? I must say I thought your pal Eva Lavery's was rather drab by comparison.'

Deirdre had thought that Eva's dress had had real class, but she refrained from contradicting Sophie and just made a noncommittal hmming noise.

'Ann looked absolutely stunning, I thought. Far too elegant for this kip. Pretty sad bash really, wasn't it? Sing-songs and sausage rolls for Christ's sake. They might at least have run to sushi.' She took another genteel swig from her bottle. 'I wonder where Ann got that dress? It had a real French couture look.'

'She must be very wealthy. Is she, Sophie?' Deirdre's opportunity had arisen without any difficulty at all, and she seized on it like a terrier.

'Oh yes. She's pretty well-loaded, you know.'

Deirdre knew that what constituted Sophie Burke's idea of wealth would be a million times in excess of her own. Ann Fitzroy must really be stacked. 'I didn't think soap opera paid *that* well.'

'Oh, Ann's *independently* wealthy. Her father died two years ago and left her a fortune. Rumour has it that she's a millionaire. My grandfather plays golf with the solicitor who drew up the will.'

Deirdre hugged herself inwardly. This was even better than she'd hoped for. She was finding Sophie uncharacteristically riveting this evening, and she knew she'd have no difficulty in persuading her to tell all. 'Do you know her personally, Sophie?'

'Well, no – not *personally.*' Sophie obviously hated to admit it. 'But I know quite a lot about her family from golf club gossip,' she added brightly.

'It must be fascinating,' Deirdre hazarded. 'I've heard she's a very – complex individual.'

'Yes. She's had a lot of tragedy in her life. I always think that suffering makes you a more complex person.'

No wonder Sophie was one of the most one-dimensional people Deirdre had ever met. 'What happened, Sophie?'

'Oh – it seems she had a series of miscarriages and women's problems early on in her marriage.'

'Wow – that's really tragic.' There was a beat. 'But she did have a child in the end, didn't she?'

'Oh yes – one. A girl called Aoife.' Sophie was clearly delighted to be able to impress Deirdre with her insider knowledge of the Fitzroy/Lawless union. 'She's about eighteen now. I've heard that David absolutely dotes on her.'

Deirdre smiled at Sophie. She didn't find it very easy. 'How long have Ann and David been married?' she asked, as if she was just trying to make idle conversation.

'Let me see.' Sophie did some mental arithmetic.

It took ages. 'Well, it must be more than two decades,' she said finally.

'Wow – she's incredibly well-preserved.'

'Well, they were married when they were really young, not even out of their teens.' Sophie leaned forward slightly. 'Actually, my grandfather told me they *had* to get married.'

'You mean Ann was pregnant?' Sophie nodded in an irritatingly confidential manner. Deirdre shrugged her shoulders. 'What's the big deal about that?'

'Well, I know it wouldn't be an issue now. But it was back then. Especially for people like the Lawlesses and the Fitzroys. Oh – hi, Finbar!' Sophie dimpled and waved her fingers at Finbar de Rossa who was passing by on his way to the bar. Deirdre thought for one awful minute that he was going to halt in his tracks, but to her relief he just sent Sophie the kind of smile he probably practised in the mirror and sauntered on by. She didn't want anyone cramping Sophie's style at this crucial juncture.

To Deirdre's delight Sophie continued without missing a beat. 'You see, they were both from top-notch families, and it was essential to keep up appearances.'

'David's from a wealthy family too?'

'Oh yes. He's from the Westmeath Lawlesses, you know – the Brewing Family.' Deirdre registered the block capitals in Sophie's voice. This was getting more and more intriguing. 'Although David's not as wealthy as Ann, of course,' continued Sophie. 'His father didn't approve of him going into theatre. He settled the bulk of the money on David's younger sister.'

'You're a mine of information, Sophie.'

Sophie gave a smug smile. 'It gets better – I *told* you it was a tragic story.'

'Go on,' Deirdre encouraged her. 'This is spell-binding stuff.'

'Well, David's sister was the only one in the family who had any sense, as far as David's father was concerned. He thought the two boys–'

'So there's a brother as well?'

Sophie gave Deirdre a meaningful look. '*Was* a brother.'

'He's dead?'

'More than twenty years ago,' said Sophie in a faraway voice. Then she sighed. She was in her element. 'Anyway,' she resumed, in the manner of someone shaking themselves out of a sad reverie, 'as I was saying, David's father thought the two boys were completely irresponsible, and not to be trusted with the Family Fortune.'

Deirdre wished she'd stop talking in capital letters like that. It was obvious that Sophie was enjoying herself too much, now. She'd have to hurry her along a bit. 'But the father was proved wrong,' she prompted.

'Yes. David's was a real success story, as we all know – unlike his older brother Richard. I heard only recently that his father finally acknowledged in an announcement to the *entire* golf club that his second son was a genius and a man of integrity, and that there had been no real shame in getting a young girl pregnant out of wedlock because he'd done the right thing by Ann and stayed married to her for all those years. And produced a beautiful granddaughter for him. Of course, it would have been a *total* tragedy if David had taken the other course.'

Deirdre had noticed that Sophie's Dun Laoghaire accent became even more pronounced when she was having fun. 'You mean there's even more tragedy?'

Sophie leant back in her chair and adopted an enigmatic expression. Deirdre resisted an impulse to shake her. 'What happened, Sophie?'

Sophie gave a little smile and she narrowed her green eyes at Deirdre. 'You know, I shouldn't really be telling you this, Deirdre. You see, it involves someone I know you have great respect for. I'd hate to be the one to point out to you that this person has feet of clay, after all. Still, I suppose it's reasonably common knowledge – although it happened so long ago that people may have forgotten all about it by now.' Sophie pursed her lips and took another ladylike sip of her Sol.

The decibel level in the pub had been rising steadily during their conversation and Deirdre was finding it increasingly difficult to hear what Sophie was saying. 'Who are you talking about, Sophie?' she half-shouted. The other actress looked demure. She obviously intended to keep Deirdre guessing. 'Oh, come on, Sophie – don't be so bloody mysterious.'

Sophie widened her eyes and threw Deirdre an injured look. 'Well, pardon me, Deirdre. I always thought you considered yourself to be a bit above dressing-room gossip. You've never been a great one to bother about it until now.'

Deirdre backtracked rapidly. 'Well – I *am* a great fan of Ann Fitzroy.'

'You are?' Sophie looked sceptical. 'You didn't even recognize her at the party last night.'

'That's because the lighting was crap. And because she looks so different in real life.' Over Sophie's shoulder Deirdre could see Finbar heading in their direction with his drink. This time he looked as if he intended joining them. She wanted to shoo him away, but he was bearing down on them with an air of calm inevitability. She no longer bothered to disguise her urgency. 'Anyway, Sophie – who *were* you talking about?' she said in a rush. 'Were you hinting that David might have married someone else if he hadn't got Ann Fitzroy pregnant?'

'That's right.'

'Who? Who was it?'

Sophie was smirking. 'It was your new pal, Deirdre. It was Eva Lavery.'

That explained a lot. Deirdre sensed there'd been history there.

Finbar sat down beside Sophie, and she leaned over and whispered something in Deirdre's ear before turning to give him her undivided attention. At the same time someone turned up the volume of the football match on the television. Almost demented with frustration, Deirdre had to ask Sophie to repeat herself.

'I *said,*' Sophie hissed the word at her, like a snake, 'I *said,* Deirdre, that Eva Lavery was responsible for the death of David Lawless's brother Richard. He'd still be alive today if it hadn't been for her, you know.'

Deirdre was taken aback momentarily. Then she adopted a cynical expression. 'Oh, yeah, Sophie?'

Sophie arranged her features into the expression she assumed when talking to members of the opposite sex. 'Oh yes indeed, Deirdre,' she returned, and she turned her back squarely on the other actress.

Deirdre stood up slowly. She was glad that Sophie couldn't see her face. She was totally confused.

'Deirdre!' Kate O'Connor was manoeuvring her way towards her through the crowd. 'Deirdre! Why didn't you tell us earlier? I just found out from Maeve that you're playing Ophelia!'

'Oh, yes. That's right, Kate, I am. David approached me about it last night.'

Out of the corner of her eye, Deirdre saw Sophie Burke's back stiffen like a bowstring.

Chapter Seven

The first thing Deirdre did the next morning was phone her mother.

'Mum? You know I said to you the other night about Eva Lavery remembering you from the old days when you were at the Abbey school? Well, I'm sure you remember *her*, don't you?'

'Of course I do. Nobody could forget Eva. But I didn't know her that long. She joined later than me, and didn't stay the course.'

'I wonder could you fill me in on something?'

'I'll try. What, exactly?'

'Well, Sophie was telling me this amazing story about Eva last night. She didn't have time to finish it and I'm dying of curiosity to find out how everything turned out.'

'Why don't you just phone her?'

'Eva?'

'No, you dingbat. Sophie.'

'Oh, Mum – I just couldn't. I'd have to grovel, and she'd be so bloody smug I couldn't bear it. Anyway, now she knows I'm playing Ophelia she's not going to be in the mood to do me any favours.'

'Don't tell me you two are still worst enemies?'

'Sort of. You know we've had a rocky history, Mum.'

'Don't you think you're being a bit childish, Deirdre? That thing with Beautiful Ben must have happened at least two years ago. It's silly to bear a grudge for so long.'

'It's not just the Ben thing, Mum. Sophie can be a real pain in the ass.'

Her mother sighed, but there was a trace of amusement in her voice. 'OK. What is it you want to know?'

'Well, Sophie said that–'

'Hang on a sec, Deirdre,' Rosaleen put in. 'I've an idea. Why don't you get the DART out here? Ring me when you get to Bray station and I'll pick you up and treat you to lunch in Avoca Handweavers. I'm reasonably flush at the moment, and I haven't had a proper chat with you for ages.'

'Oh – thanks, Mum. You rock. I'd love a decent lunch. I've been living off convenience foods for the last while.'

'I can imagine,' said Rosaleen drily. 'And you don't mean convenience, Deirdre. I'd say junk is the more appropriate word, knowing you. Come out around three. Avoca'll be less crowded then.'

'OK. You know something, Mum? This may sound really uncool, but I love my life. Bye.'

'Bye, Deirdre.' Deirdre could tell that her mother was smiling down the phone.

She put down the receiver and went into the bedroom to do her yoga. She'd decided to take it up after seeing Eva doing yoga in her dressing-room on the opening night, and had bought herself a 'How-to' book in a second-hand book shop on her way in to work the previous evening. Unfortunately, it wasn't as easy as it looked in the pictures. In spite of the fact that her body was contorted into uncomfortable-looking knots, the girl in the book wore a permanent happy smile. Deirdre also found it impossible to focus her mind once she had managed to wrangle her limbs into a vague approximation of the pose in the photograph. Instead of it becoming serenely blank as the book recommended, she was besieged by uninvited thoughts which jostled for her attention – most of them rather frivolous. She stuck a Portishead tape on in an attempt to create more *gravitas.*

Stretching her legs as far apart as they would go – the girl in the picture was practically doing the splits – she twisted her left arm behind her back and her right arm over her shoulder and tried to clasp her hands together while straining to bend her torso down towards her right leg. To take her mind off the pain, she found herself wondering what kind of music David Lawless listened to. Not Portishead, anyway. Mozart, probably. Definitely something classical. The image swam before her mind's eye of the two of them in bed together, with Mozart playing softly in the background. There'd be white linen sheets tumbled tempestuously all over the place, and sunlight filtering through filmy white curtains. They'd be lying with their limbs intertwined, satiated with sex, and her hair would be spread out all over the pillow. What would he be saying to her? The word 'adore' would feature a lot in their post-coital musings. Maybe she could recite some of Shakespeare's sonnets to him? No. She'd be too self-conscious. Maybe he could recite them to her? She had a feeling that David Lawless was the kind of man who could get away with being sexy and reciting sonnets at the same time. After all, he was unique. She was just picturing exactly how his languid fingers might caress her bare shoulder as he read to her when she was seized by a violent attack of cramp in her right foot. 'Ow!' she yelped, laboriously trying to extricate herself from the cat's cradle of her own limbs. Leaning cross-legged against the bed, she worked her fingers into the muscles of her instep. What was she at – still indulging in fantasies about a man who'd made it perfectly plain he wasn't interested in her? She mentally replayed the evening of the dress rehearsal, when he'd hooked the sleeve of her gown back up over her shoulder. She'd convinced herself then that David had been consumed with desire for her, but hindsight told her that it hadn't been the action of a man motivated by sexual interest. In fact – if she was to be totally honest with herself – there'd been something paternal about the gesture.

Deirdre turned up the volume on Portishead and hummed along loudly to try and blot out the agony of embarrassment she felt at having got it so wrong. The complacent face of the contortionist in the photograph smiled up at her, as if she knew exactly what she was thinking. She sent the stupid yoga book skimming under the bed.

* * *

Even at three o'clock in the afternoon the self-service restaurant in Avoca Handweavers was packed. Busloads of tourists had descended on it, and Deirdre and Rosaleen had to wait nearly fifteen minutes in a queue listening to someone grumbling in German behind them. They finally made it on to the cash register with laden trays. Deirdre's included an indecently calorific strawberry pavlova.

It was another glorious day. The heatwave was in its second week, and the paved area outside was crowded with relaxed, good humoured people. The surrounding gardens were blooming and the terrace was kaleidoscopic with hanging baskets. They located a table near the steps which led down on to the lawn where an ancient cypress tree grew, its branches trailing on the grass like Rapunzel's hair.

Rosaleen had filled her daughter in on all the family news while they'd been waiting in the queue, and now it was time for Deirdre to check out the Eva Lavery story.

'I was wondering when you were going to bring that up,' Rosaleen remarked as Deirdre laid into her pasta. 'I suppose gossip is an occupational hazard for you now. You never used to be interested in that kind of stuff. You'll be reading *Hello!* magazine next.' Deirdre didn't mention that she *did* spend a lot of her time off-stage reading *Hello!* in the green room.

Rosaleen picked up her bag and took out a brown A4 envelope. She passed it across the table to Deirdre. 'Here. Have a look.'

Deirdre opened the envelope and drew out three rather battered-looking black and white photographs. 'Wow,' she said. 'Where did you get these?'

'They were stowed away in a box in the attic, along with some old theatre programmes.'

'These are amazing, Mum.'

The first photograph showed a handful of people standing around a half-finished stage set. For a minute Deirdre thought one of them was her until she realized it was her mother as she had been around two decades earlier. 'Oh, Mum! Look at you! You're so young! You look beautiful!' Her mother was standing slightly apart from the group, wearing jeans and a big white shirt, pre-Raphaelite hair tumbling down her back.

Rosaleen leaned back and smiled at her daughter. 'I wasn't much younger than you are now,' she said. 'Take another look.'

Deirdre returned her attention to the photgraph. There was a small figure in the foreground standing in a defiant posture with her hands on her hips, laughing at the camera. She was wearing tight satin pants, a halter-necked top and high, ankle-strapped shoes with polka-dots. She had long blond hair and huge eyes rimmed with black kohl which Deirdre could just make out under the unkempt fringe. She looked about twelve.

'It's Eva!'

'David took that photograph one day in rehearsal. I can't even remember what play we were doing.' Rosaleen took a sip of her wine. 'Do you recognize the person in the background, on the right there?'

Deirdre scrutinized the photograph and made out the figure of Ann Fitzroy standing slightly to the right behind Eva. She was giving the actress what looked like a venomous, sideways look. She hadn't changed at all.

'So all three of them were at the Abbey school at the same time? What an amazing photograph!'

'Have a look at the other ones. You can keep them, if you like.'

'Thanks, Mum. It's like a piece of theatrical history.' Deirdre set the rehearsal shot down on the table. The next photograph was of David Lawless. He was sitting on the ground leaning against the wall, loose-limbed and relaxed as ever. His hair was a little longer then, and he was almost too thin. He was looking away from the camera with that intense look about the eyes that Deirdre knew so well, and she could hazard a guess from his expression as to who he had been looking at.

The third photograph was a close-up of Eva. It looked as if it had been taken on a beach on a windy day. Her coat-collar was turned up and long strands of hair lashed about her face. She wasn't looking at the camera this time, and she wasn't smiling. Her grey eyes looked almost black and she was wearing no make-up. She looked immeasurably sad, but very, very beautiful.

'What show was this photograph for, Mum?'

'I honestly couldn't tell you, Deirdre.'

Deirdre stared at the photograph for a little while

longer and then put it on top of the others before attacking her plate of food again. 'Sophie Burke hinted last night that David had had a fling with Eva.'

'She was right.' Rosaleen moved the salt cellar to the other end of the table. 'You shouldn't use so much salt, Deirdre.'

'Sorry, Mum. Go on.'

'Let me see. I remember Eva exploded on the scene about six months after David and Ann had got together. Ann was very put out. She looked on David as being something of a trophy. I suppose he was.'

Deirdre found that pretty understandable. 'Sophie told me he's from the Westmeath Lawlesses.'

'Yes – but the trophy-hunting wasn't just a class thing, Deirdre. David was incredibly glamorous. He was dynamic, stylish, good-looking – he had it all. I fancied him myself, to tell you the truth, but I don't imagine he even knew I existed.'

'Of course he did, Mum. You looked fabulous in that photograph.'

Rosaleen smiled. 'Thank you, my love. Anyway, he and Ann made a stunning couple. Ann knew that, of course.'

'What was *she* like?'

'Brittle. Selfish. Difficult – but in demand socially. I can't say I ever really bothered to get to know her. I remember she had absolutely no sense of humour.' Rosaleen poured more water into Deirdre's glass and then added some to her wine.

'Everybody wondered why David put up with her, but she was very sophisticated and very beautiful, and we were all very young and impressionable and set store by that kind of stuff in those days. God, you must be starving, Deirdre – you're demolishing that pasta. I suppose you're not looking after yourself properly?'

'I do try to, Mum. I take a vitamin supplement every day.'

Rosaleen sighed. 'That's not the way to stay healthy, Deirdre – I've told you that before. I *knew* that once you started living on your own you wouldn't bother with a proper diet. The weight's fallen off you. I'm going to take you home before I run you to the DART and fill up a bag with decent, wholesome grub for you.'

'Thanks, Mum.' Deirdre broke off some wholemeal bread and stuffed it into her mouth. 'So what happened when Eva showed up at the Abbey school?'

'She outclassed the rest of us at once.' Rosaleen furrowed her brow, casting her mind back again. 'Somebody had spotted her at an amateur production of *Pygmalion* and encouraged her to join. I'm not surprised. She was a natural.'

'Even when she first started out?'

'Oh yeah. And she was stunning to look at. They would have made a terrific couple. I don't blame David for falling for her. She was warm and clever and funny. She was some piece of work, Eva.'

'She still is.'

'I can imagine.'

'What happened, Mum?' Deirdre forked the last of the pasta into her mouth and started on her salad.

'What did Sophie tell you last night?'

'Well, she said that she thought David had only married Ann Fitzroy because he'd got her pregnant.'

Rosaleen nodded.

'And she said something really awful about Eva.'

'I suppose she mentioned David's brother?'

Deirdre's eyes opened wide in disbelief. 'It's not true, is it?'

Rosaleen adopted a slightly careful expression. 'What's not true?'

'That Eva Lavery was responsible for his death?'

Rosaleen's laugh was dismissive. 'Is *that* what Sophie told you? In that case I'm glad I'm able to set the record straight.'

'Oh, good.' Deirdre speared a cherry tomato with her fork, and juice spurted out on to her white T-shirt right on to the spot where her nipple jutted. 'Shit,' she said, ineffectually rubbing it with a paper napkin. 'Go on, Mum.'

'Let's see. I remember Ann announced that she was pregnant not long after David and Eva started their affair. They'd tried to keep it secret for a time but it was patently obvious to everyone that they were crazy about each other. They couldn't look at each other and pretend otherwise – the best actors in the world couldn't disguise that kind of body language.' Rosaleen gave a little smile of regret. 'It was such a bloody shame, really. They were so perfect for each other, like two halves of the same soul. She was his lost anima.'

'What's an anima?'

'The female half of a man's psyche. They say that we are all created with a part of our soul missing – for men it's their female side, for women it's the reverse – and we spend our lives trying to find the missing half. Some of us are lucky enough to find it. I was.'

Mother and daughter smiled at each other. Then Deirdre pushed away her salad plate and started on her pavlova.

'But David felt he had to do the honourable thing by Ann Fitzroy?'

'Yes. He was a very honourable man. I imagine he still is.'

'He is,' said Deirdre, with a twinge of regret.

'I know he was also under serious pressure from both sets of parents to get married. His mother was very ill with cancer at the time, so that would have affected his decision. She died shortly after he and Ann were married, so he did the honourable thing by his mother, too.'

'Poor David.'

'And poor Eva. It practically unhinged *her*.'

'Really?'

'Yes. That's when David's brother got involved. Shall I get us some coffee?'

'Oh, no, thanks, Mum – this is too exciting. Don't stop now.'

'OK. But give me some of your pudding. It looks delicious.'

Deirdre spooned a big dollop of pavlova into her mother's mouth.

'Mmm. I think they do the best pavlova I've ever tasted here. Anyway,' Rosaleen wiped a blob of cream from her chin with her napkin. 'Eva went off the deep end. She disappeared to London, and it seems the only contact she had there was David's older brother, Richard. He was a hell-raiser and an absolute bastard – he'd been practically disinherited by his father.'

'Sophie said something about that. Did you know him at all?'

'I saw him at a party in Dublin once, out of his head. He was quite like David to look at, except he was gaunter. Wasted-looking. He wasn't unattractive, I suppose. He had the look of a young Keith Richards.'

'And Eva went off with him?'

'Yeah. It was a classic case of rebound, and Rick did her no good at all. He was into everything. Sex, drugs and – yes – even rock and roll. He fronted some band over there – what did they call themselves? "Mephisto Ritz" – that was it. It was around the time of glam rock.'

'Glam rock? You mean people like David Bowie and Roxy Music and that whole *Velvet Goldmine* vibe?'

'Yeah. I was mad into Steve Harley. I probably still have some of his records in the attic. More pavlova, please.'

'You can have the rest, Mum. I'm stuffed.' Deirdre pushed her plate across the table.

'Anyway, Eva dived in and went with the flow. She started doing serious drugs. I heard she was permanently strung-out in her first few months in London.'

A staff member stopped by to clear away plates, and Rosaleen stopped talking.

'Was everything all right for you?' asked the girl with a smile.

'Lovely, thank you. I'd give anything for the pavlova recipe,' Rosaleen replied.

'Oh – that's classified information, I'm afraid!' The girl continued to pile plates and glasses on to a tray. 'Beautiful day, isn't it? I love the way everybody's always in such good form when the weather's like this. It certainly makes my life a lot easier. Wouldn't it be wonderful if we could have this kind of weather every summer?'

The girl was being perfectly pleasant, but Deirdre wished she'd go away. At this rate she'd *never* get to hear the end of the story. It was beginning to acquire a Scheherazade-like quality.

'I read something in the paper about it being all to do with global warming.' Oh, God – now even her *mother* was at it. 'Apparently the hole in the ozone layer above Ireland . . .'

With a resigned 'Excuse me a moment,' Deirdre decided she might as well go and get coffees after all. The queue had dwindled, and by the time she arrived back, their table had been cleared and the chatty staff member had disappeared.

She put the coffee down in front of her mother and resumed her seat. 'Thanks,' said Rosaleen, looking at her watch. 'God – is that the time? I'd better get a move on with the Eva saga if I'm going to sort you out with some decent food to take back to town. You'll need to get to the station soon. Where was I?'

'Eva's gone off with the bad brother.'

'Oh, yes. Well, apparently she and Rick were flying on some lethal combination of illegal substances one night on their way to a gig outside London. There was an accident and Rick was killed instantly. No-one really knows who was to blame.'

For a second Deirdre was speechless with horror. 'Jesus Christ, Mum – I don't believe you.'

'Sad, isn't it?'

Deirdre was silent for a while, and then she said: 'What happened to Eva?'

'She wasn't too badly injured, apparently. But of course you don't walk away from something like that emotionally unscathed.'

Deirdre remembered the silver seam of scar tissue on the actress's inner thigh.

'How did she cope? What did she do after the accident?'

'She disappeared for a while. Then she just wised up. She gave up drugs, cleaned up her act, and went back to London. That's when she won the scholarship to RADA. And the rest, as they say, is history.' Rosaleen stood up from the table. 'Come on, Deirdre, we'd better go.'

'Mum?'

'Yes?'

'Sophie told me Ann Fitzroy had a miscarriage

just after she married David. Is that true? Or do you think that maybe she wasn't even pregnant when she married him? Maybe she thought that claiming to be pregnant was the best way of getting him back from Eva?'

Rosaleen shrugged her shoulders with a little smile. 'I suppose that's something only Ann could tell us. You know I went through two miscarriages after you were born and I wouldn't wish one on anyone. But they can be convenient things for some people. And you wouldn't be the first person in the world to have speculated about it, Deirdre. She never struck me as the maternal type, I must admit, and I would have thought that she was an unlikely candidate for an accidental pregnancy. She was determined to get whatever she wanted. And at that stage all she wanted out of life was success as an actress.'

And David Lawless, thought Deirdre as she followed her mother to where the car was parked. She definitely wanted him.

* * *

She arrived at the theatre that evening laden with carrier bags containing fresh produce from the organic farm that supplied her mother. There were lettuces and tomatoes, bunches of spring onions and radishes, purple-flowering broccoli, asparagus, potatoes and free-range eggs. Rosaleen had insisted that she take it all away with her, even though Deirdre knew she'd never get round to eating half of it, and that most of it would end up mouldering in the fridge. She was crap at cooking real food, and had absolutely no interest in it. She and Sarah had tried to organize a kitchen routine during the first few weeks of rehearsal just after Deirdre had moved into the flat, but it had foundered pretty quickly, and in the end Sarah did most of the cooking. In return, Deirdre did most of the other household chores, like hoovering and cleaning the bath. She'd rather do that kind of stuff than try to make sense of recipes, and Sarah would rather do almost anything than be subjected to Deirdre's culinary efforts.

As she struggled up the stairs to her dressing-room she had a bright idea. She'd offload some of the stuff. Maeve would be glad of it, she knew – her partner Jacqueline was a caterer by profession, and a demon cook. Maybe Rory would take some too, although she couldn't imagine that he ever bothered to cook, or that Marian ever found the time. She knew that Eva wouldn't know what to do with it. Didn't *other* people cook and then serve it up to your table, or package it all up nicely for you to bung in the microwave? Then she remembered how Eva liked to knock back an egg before the show. Maybe she could use half-a-dozen.

Dumping her bags on the landing she unearthed a carton of eggs with a picture of a happy-looking hen pecking around the top, and went back down the stairs. There was no response to her knock, so she tried a second, less discreet one. The actress had obviously not arrived in to work yet, which was not surprising, because when Deirdre checked the clock in the scene dock, she found that it was much earlier than she'd thought. Even Eva, who always allowed herself plenty of time to prepare before a show, didn't come in at ten-to-six. Deirdre decided that she'd just leave the eggs on the actress's dressing table.

She opened the door and nearly let the carton fall to the floor. David Lawless was emerging from the shower stall at the opposite side of the room. He was dripping wet and stark naked. For a moment he didn't register the fact that there was anyone there, and Deirdre held her breath in the ludicrous hope that maybe he would go back into the shower without noticing her. She stood there for a moment, frozen like a rabbit in the headlights of a car, before he became aware of her presence. He wasn't remotely fazed. In contrast to Deirdre's expression of agonized confusion, he seemed totally unperturbed, and his attitude was almost resigned as he stretched out a relaxed hand for a towel.

'Oh, Deirdre, it *would* have to be you, wouldn't it?' he said, shaking his head with a vaguely amused air as he wrapped the towel around his lean hips. 'Please don't say "sorry" again. At this rate you'll spend the rest of your life apologizing to me.' He yawned and rubbed a hand over his unshaven jaw.

She wished he *had* let her apologize. Now she wasn't able to explain what she was doing by letting herself into Eva Lavery's dressing-room, and she felt even sillier than ever. Still clutching the box of eggs to her chest, she made an inarticulate sound in her throat and turned towards the door where Eva was standing with an expression of mild reproach on her face.

'David. You've been using my shower without my permission again. I know it's the only power shower in the theatre, but I had hardly any shower gel left and I bet you've used it all.' She floated into the room and kicked off her sandals before acknowledging Deirdre with a dazzling smile. 'Hi, honey.'

Eva gave absolutely no indication that she found anything unusual about discovering Deirdre O'Dare standing in the middle of her dressing-room with a half-naked David Lawless, and Deirdre was even more confounded. She felt that she should attempt to say something by way of explanation, but her dilemma had rendered her speechless. Instead she stumbled towards the actress and thrust the egg carton into her hands before turning and bolting for the door.

'For me? How kind,' she heard Eva say in a puzzled voice as Deirdre fled up the stairs to her dressing-room, hoping fervently that there'd be no-one else in yet. She needed time to herself to let her embarrassment subside and to let the significance of what she'd seen in Eva Lavery's dressing-room dawn on her. As David Lawless had reached for the towel her eye had been drawn to something unusual on the tanned skin of his abdomen, not far from the line of his pubic hair. Fearful that he might misinterpret her gaze she had taken care not to let it linger, but there was no mistaking the mark for what it was. After all, she'd seen it before on the nape of Eva Lavery's neck. It was a tattoo of a Siamese Fighting Fish so fresh that his flesh was still raw.

* * *

There was hardly anyone from the cast in Meagher's that evening. Kate and Jessica had headed off to The Kitchen in search of male company, and Maeve was going to a late-night film in the IFC that Deirdre had already seen. She'd decided against joining the others in The Kitchen because she was anxious to explain herself to Eva after the appalling incident in the actress's dressing-room. To her disappointment there was no sign of her leading lady in the pub.

As she paid for her glass of wine, she looked around for a friendly face. Adrian Pierce was sitting by himself in the corner immersed in *Men are from Mars, Women are from Venus.* He might as well have been wearing a "Do Not Disturb" sign. Finbar de Rossa was immersed in conversation with an Asian looker, and Deirdre didn't imagine he'd welcome company. There were a few members of the crew congregated around the pool table, but Deirdre wasn't much of a pool player, and Joe, the stage carpenter, was one of their number. He fancied her, and she didn't fancy him back at all.

She gave the boys a friendly wave and sat down at a far table. Someone had thoughtfully left behind an *Evening Herald* and she picked it up, trying not to look too much like Norma No-Friends and cursing her stupidity at having bought a drink before checking out the social aspect of things. She wished she'd just gone home to the telly. She leafed through the *Herald* for the telly page and drank her wine in a succession of quick sips. She didn't bother to finish it. After a decent interval spent studying the paper, she grabbed her backpack and headed for the door, feeling Joe's eyes on her as she passed the pool table. As she swung through the door, Rory McDonagh swung through in the opposite direction and collided into her.

'Leaving so soon, gorgeous?'

'Oh, hi, Rory. Yeah, there's no-one in tonight.'

'I'm here, aren't I? Let me buy you a drink.'

Deirdre quickly weighed up the pros and cons of Rory's company versus sitting through *Terminator Two* or yet another chat show. Rory won. 'OK. Thanks, Rory.'

'A glass of that foul white wine for you, I suppose? Don't know how you can stomach the stuff. You'll never be an oenophile, will you Deirdre?'

Deirdre made a mental note of the word so that she could look it up later. She wasn't going to give Rory the satisfaction of asking him what it meant. Knowing him, it was probably just a big word for something smutty. She made her way back to the table she'd just left and resumed her perusal of the *Evening Herald*. Across the room Finbar de Rossa had draped an elaborately casual arm across the back of the banquette behind the smooth shoulders of the beautiful Asian, who was looking at him with an increasingly bored expression as he droned on.

Rory arrived with the drinks, threw his coat over the back of the shabby draylon banquette and flung himself down beside her. He took a long swig of his pint, wiped his mouth with the back of his hand and exhaled loudly. 'Christ, that's better. I needed that.'

'Hungover as usual, Rory, I've no doubt. You look a bit rough, I must say.'

'Spot on as ever, m'dear. My outward appearance is a pretty accurate reflection of my inner state.'

'Where were you last night?'

'In bad company.'

'Whose?'

'Oh – I was on the skite with my good pal and drinking buddy, Jonathan Hughes. Fins and Lawless joined in.'

'*David* Lawless?'

'Yeah,' said Rory, looking mildly surprised at her incredulous tone.

'*You* went out and got rat-faced with David *Lawless*?'

'Jesus, Deirdre, do you have a problem with that? Even an über-dude like David is allowed to behave badly from time to time. I would have thought that you'd be more surprised by the fact that Finbar was part of the equation.'

Deirdre was doubly curious. 'Yeah, that's weird too, actually – why him?' She knew that Rory rarely socialized with Finbar de Rossa if he could help it.

'He has entrée to a late-night drinking den that I was curious to investigate.'

'Oh? Where?'

'Some small hotel in Ballsbridge. It was a pretty sad gaff, as it turned out, but we stayed the course and got gently scuttered.'

'I can't imagine David Lawless getting drunk.'

'He makes a great drunk. Like a lord. Unlike Fins. Fins gets malicious.' Rory reached into the pocket of his coat and produced two packets of peanuts. He skidded one across the table at her. 'Here. Get fat. You could do with putting on a few pounds, you know, Deirdre. Marian reliably informs me that these are packed with calories. No super-model worth her heroin-chic would look at one.'

Deirdre wanted to hear more about David Lawless. 'How long did you stay drinking?' she asked.

'Dunno.' Rory threw a handful of peanuts into his mouth. 'Late. We were finally driven out by Finser's third rendition of his Liam Neeson story.'

'Which one?'

He smiled at her. 'Yeah – I thought you'd have heard most of them by now. The one that starts: "When Liam and I were working on *Excalibur* we frequented a terrific pub call Sheehan's . . . blah-de-blah-blah . . ."' Rory started snoring.

'Actually, I don't think I've heard that one yet,' said Deirdre, smiling back.

'Well, sweetie, you simply haven't lived! Look – there he is over there. Shall I call him over for you?' And rising to his feet, he waved at Finbar across the room while Deirdre clung to his sleeve trying to pull him back into his seat and begging him to shut up.

Finbar waved back, obviously delighted to have been spotted with his gorgeous companion. 'Hi there, Rory. How's your hangover?' he shouted over the din.

'Worse than yours, I expect, but not as bad as Lawless's. He looked *very* seedy indeed earlier on this evening. We ended up in MacNamara's after we left you.'

'Silly fellow,' smiled Finbar, returning to his Eastern princess.

'Where's MacNamara's?' asked Deirdre.

Rory wasn't listening. 'Very tasty,' he muttered, half to himself as he eyed Finbar's sultry friend. 'How does he do it? Maybe if I encourage him to tell her all his film-star friend stories she'll get real and come home with me.'

Deirdre was dogged. 'Where's MacNamara's?' she repeated.

'You mean you don't know?' he said, with some incredulity. 'Oh, I forgot. You're Deirdre O'Dare.'

Stung by the implication that she had no social savvy, Deirdre hit back. 'I'm not devoid of urban after-hours experience, Rory. I know you think I'm from the sticks, but that doesn't mean I'm more into step-dancing than clubbing. I was in Renard's last Friday, and Lillie's the weekend before, and the POD for Jessica's birthday. And I'll probably join some friends in The Kitchen later on this evening.'

Actually, she had no intention of heading off to The Kitchen now. She wasn't really in the mood any more.

Rory threw back his head and laughed. 'No, I don't imagine you're *totally* devoid of after-hours experience, Deirdre, although the clubbing aspect's of secondary importance. It would be wishful thinking, for instance, to imagine you're intacta.' Deirdre looked blank, and he adopted an exaggerated expression of hope. 'You're *not*, are you?'

'Sorry?'

'Intacta. As in virgo. I thought they were as scarce as unicorns these days. If you answer the question correctly then this could be your lucky night, Deirdre O'Dare.'

'Actually, I'm a Capricorn.'

Rory crowed again. 'Jesus, Deirdre, are you for real? Even Suki Hayes would have picked up on that one and she hasn't been intacta for years.'

'What do you mean by intacta?'

'Educating you is such fun, Deirdre. The word "intacta" refers to the unbroken hymen of a virgin.'

She had walked into it. Her cheeks were on fire. 'You are intolerable, Rory,' she said, looking away from him.

'I know,' he said complacently as he downed his pint and signalled to Meagre Meagher for another. 'Want another glass of horse's urine, sweetheart?'

Deirdre actually wanted to tell him where to put it and walk out, but she was still intrigued by his drunken spree with David Lawless. 'OK,' she said without much good grace. 'I'll get it.' After she'd paid for the drinks and brought them back to the table she reinstigated the conversation.

'So you ended up in a place called MacNamara's last night. I suppose that's some kind of shebeen?'

'You are right, Ms O'Dare. It *is* a shebeen – a real lowlife drinking den. And we ended up there this morning, not last night.' Rory sent her an indolent smile and stretched himself with unselfconscious relish, folding his arms behind his head. Deirdre noticed that the hairs on his forearms were the colour of white gold against his tanned skin. She could make out ridges of muscle under the taut cotton of his short-sleeved black T-shirt, and she suddenly felt an impulse to reach out and run a hand over his belly. Jesus, wise up, Deirdre, she thought, surprised at herself. Rory was surveying her through half-closed eyes, and she felt uncomfortable and cross when she realized that he was focusing on the tomato-juice stain on her T-shirt.

'I take it you were there till the very *early* hours of this morning.' To her dismay the words came out sounding unintentionally prudish.

'If you can call around ten o'clock the early hours. Actually, I think we were there till nearly eleven because we didn't hit Johnny Eagle's until around half-past. My recollection of events is, you may appreciate, a little hazy.'

'So you and David Lawless were drinking until eleven o'clock this morning!' Deirdre's jaw had dropped appreciably.

'Well, no – not continuously. The three of us took

time out for a fry in the Meridian Grill before we hit MacNamara's. Then Hughes fell by the wayside – literally, I seem to remember – and we put him in a taxi.'

Deirdre knew the Meridian Grill. It was an all-night greasy spoon frequented by insomniac alcoholics and ladies of the night on their tea-breaks. She somehow found the idea of David Lawless eating there profoundly shocking. And where on earth was Johnny Eagle's?

'This Johnny Eagle's – it's not *another* pub, is it?'

Rory smiled and shook his head. 'Johnny Eagle is a tattoo artist. The best. And it might surprise you to know that it was Lawless's idea. He kept rambling on about how he'd always been meaning to have a tattoo done, and that he regretted not doing it years ago. It was like some kind of Shamanistic thing. He insisted that I get one too. It was bloody sore, actually, despite the anaesthetic effect of the alcohol.'

A tattoo artist. Things suddenly connected in Deirdre's brain.

'So *that's* what happened!'

'Take me with you, darlin'.'

'David Lawless got drunk and decided to get a tattoo!'

'You could be a detective, Deirdre.'

She gave him a scathing look. 'No, it's just that when I saw it earlier on this evening I wondered about it, you know? I mean, it's a strange thing for a man like him to do, isn't it? It's OK for you, Rory – you're just a bloke. But I never thought that–'

Registering the look on Rory's face, she stopped dead, and when he gave her his incendiary laugh she realized what she'd just said.

'Oh. Oh – I don't mean – I mean, you mustn't think that – oh shit!' Deirdre knew her cheeks had gone crimson, and she covered them with her hands as Rory shot her a sceptical smile.

'Relax, Deirdre. Your private life is your own concern.'

'But there's nothing–'

'Don't *worry*, Deirdre. Your secret is safe with me.'

'Mind if we join you? This is Jasmine.'

Oh – not bloody Finbar de Rossa again. He seemed to have the knack of descending on her at critical moments. She might have known that he wouldn't be able to resist the temptation to show off his Asian beauty. Deirdre sank back in her seat, resigned and hopeless. She'd never be able to convince Rory that she wasn't doing something extramarital with David Lawless. She just hoped that he wouldn't say anything to anyone. She thought with horror of the repercussions *that* would have. But she knew from Maeve that Rory wasn't really that kind of a guy. She was reasonably certain it would go no further than him.

As she feigned interest in Finbar's interminable anecdote about his experiences on some movie set with Harrison Ford, she noticed that the beauty's sloe eyes kept sliding towards Rory McDonagh. Although Finbar seemed oblivious, it was pretty obvious to Deirdre that Rory was aware of her too by the brazen way he was playing up to her. As he gave her a particularly lazy smile, Deirdre felt a sudden stab of annoyance. Insufferable git, she thought. Any minute now he'd be offering to show her his tattoo. Why hadn't he *listened* to her when she'd tried to explain to him about David Lawless's tattoo instead of jumping to the wrong conclusion like that?

The image came back to her of her director as he had looked in Eva Lavery's dressing-room, dripping with water and smiling at her – and she was flooded with confusion again. She wished she'd never thought of delivering the bloody eggs. The whole sorry incident would never have happened if he'd bothered to lock the door. She felt like Alice in Wonderland. Things just kept getting curiouser and curiouser.

Chapter Eight

On Monday morning, Deirdre climbed the steps up to the front door of an elegant Georgian building on Baggot Street. Checking her watch, she decided against pressing the bell labelled 'Sally Ruane Management' just yet. Anxious to be as organized and punctual as possible she'd actually got there ten minutes too early. She laid the blue cardboard folder that contained two hand-picked ten-by-eights and her CV down on the top step and sat down on top of it, glad that she had something to come between her and the stone slab. She didn't want to run the risk of getting her dress dirty. She had opted for a simple geometric print dress today. It was just right for her meeting with the agent, she decided. Not too trendy and not too formal.

At precisely ten o'clock she stood up and went to ring the doorbell. As she reached out a hand the door opened without warning and a burly motor-cycle courier wearing leathers and a black-visored helmet barged out on to the steps straight into her. The force of the collision sent Deirdre reeling and her folder went flying down into the basement area of a restaurant below. It fell open, and CV photographs scattered. 'Sorry, love,' muttered the courier as he took the flight of steps in one bound and leapt on to his bike like an actor in a bad western.

'You might have stopped to help me,' shouted Deirdre at the eagle transfer on the back of his jacket as he gunned the engine ostentatiously and roared off down Baggot Street at breakneck speed, obviously a man with a mission.

She peered over the area railings and saw that her photographs had landed right next to a small mountain of black rubbish bags, one of which was oozing some kind of oily, evil-looking liquid. She couldn't believe it. She'd so wanted to create a good impression and contrive to look at least halfway efficient for Sally Ruane, and now she'd blown it.

She tried the gate at the top of the area steps. It was locked. The restaurant wasn't open yet. She gazed down at her photographs in despair, realizing that the only solution was to climb over the railings. There were a lot of people passing and she was going to look like a complete eejit, but she couldn't go in to see Sally Ruane without her CV and her ten-by-eights. She braced a foot against the bolt of the gate and slung a leg over the cold wrought-iron, feeling the cotton of her dress ride up her thighs as she did so. A passing business man ogled her bare legs, and she made a face at him. She slung her other leg over the gate with difficulty, cursing the clumsy courier.

At the bottom of the steps she knelt down and retrieved her photographs. One had landed face-down on top of the spillage and was too far gone to be of any use to her now. She'd have to trash it. The folder, too. The second photograph was salvageable – just. She carefully wiped away the worst of the oily stuff with a tissue. It would leave a stain on the white border, but at least it hadn't gone all over her face. Unlike the egg she'd be wearing when she walked into Sally Ruane's office looking as if she hadn't bothered to make an effort.

Her watch read four minutes past ten when she rang the bell. An efficient-sounding voice came over the intercom. 'Who is it, please?'

'It's Deirdre O'Dare to see Sally Ruane.'

'Come on in. We're on the first floor.'

The buzzer on the front door sounded, and Deirdre pushed it open to find herself in a beautifully proportioned lobby with a stone floor, decorated in restrained grey tones. She quickly climbed the stairs to the first floor and knocked on the door which had a plaque screwed on to it. 'Sally Ruane Management' was etched on the shiny brass surface.

'Come in,' repeated the voice.

A plump woman with a kind face and small wire-rimmed glasses was sitting at a big teak desk with a computer on it. There was a neat pile of mail to one side of her and a stack of what looked like screenplays on the other. Light flooded through the tall window behind her, giving the room an airy feel. There were two giant couches on either side of a long coffee table with a selection of magazines and newspapers fanned out symmetrically along its highly polished glass top. Framed theatre posters lined the eau-de-Nil walls, and iridescent fish shimmered in a tank in the corner. Three doors led off the reception room, two to the left and one to the right, and Deirdre hoped fervently that one of them led to the loo. She badly needed to wash her hands after her encounter with the oil-slick in the basement.

The woman looked at Deirdre over her glasses. 'Deirdre?'

Deirdre nodded. 'That's right.'

'Nice to meet you.' She stood up and extended a beautifully manicured hand for Deirdre to shake. Deirdre took it gingerly, half expecting the woman to recoil at the state of her own grimy hands, but her grasp was firm and somehow reassuring. 'I'm Mary Sheridan, Sally's secretary.' The woman had a friendly face. 'I'm afraid Sally's been detained by a call. I expect she'll be on the phone for some time. Make yourself comfortable and have a browse through the papers while you're waiting. Can I get you some coffee or tea?'

'Um, no, thank you.' Deirdre felt the first tremulous stirrings of nerves. 'Could you tell me where the loo is, please?'

'Through there.' She indicated one of the doors on her left and gave Deirdre an amicable smile before returning her attention to her computer.

In the loo Deirdre turned on the taps, helped herself liberally to liquid soap and scrubbed her hands as though she was rehearsing Lady Macbeth's sleepwalking scene. Examining her reflection in the mirror, she saw the muck on her hands had somehow transferred itself to her face. There was a dirt track running down her right cheek. Using loo-roll to clean herself up she thought with horror that she could have sat through her interview with Sally Ruane completely oblivious to the fact that she looked like a mechanic.

She returned to the reception area unobtrusively, and sat perched on the edge of one of the oversized couches, thinking that if she sat back into it she might never be able to get up again unaided. Unfolding a pristine copy of today's *Irish Times* she sat there pretending to read it, swallowing hard from time to time. She was sneaking a glance at her watch when the door to the hall opened suddenly, and an elegant, Nordic-looking woman swept in. It was Ann Fitzroy. Deirdre gulped like a cartoon character, but thankfully it went unnoticed. Ann Fitzroy sailed straight past her.

'Oh, Ann – what perfect timing,' said Mary Sheridan. 'I was just about to courier that script to you.'

'I've saved you the trouble then, haven't I? I was passing by on my way to the studio and I thought I might as well pick it up myself. Is Sally in?'

'Yes, but I'm afraid she's up to her eyes. Jerome's gone AWOL and nobody seems to know where to find him. He reminds me of one of Bo Peep's sheep at this stage.'

Ann Fitzroy didn't smile at Mary's little joke. 'Dear God – not again. The last time he did that they finally located him in New Orleans. I can't understand why people continue to employ that man. Even if he does decide to honour his contract he'll waste everyone's time and patience by pickling himself in alcohol.'

The sound of a ringing mobile came from Ann Fitzroy's expensive-looking suede bag. She extracted the phone and deftly extended the aerial. 'Hello? Ann Fitzroy.' The pitch of her voice was suddenly husky and warm – in sharp contrast to the glacial tones Deirdre remembered from the one time she'd spoken to the soap opera star on the phone.

'Hello, Eddie.' She moved gracefully to the couch opposite Deirdre and sat down, crossing long, golden, meticulously waxed legs. 'Yes, I think I have a window at four. Let me check my book.' She produced a pigskin Filofax which immediately fell open for her at the right page. 'Eddie? Could you make that half past? You're an angel. How many scripts? Television or radio? Oh – just a pitch, is it?' Her inflection on the word 'pitch' had a slightly steely quality to it. Deirdre noticed. 'Never mind. Yes, yes – I'll see you there at half past.'

Ann Fitzroy leant back on the massive couch, and, with a little sigh, depressed a button on her mobile. She was as svelte as ever this morning in a toffee-coloured suede tunic and soft suede mules which matched exactly the colour of her bag. A simple gold slave bangle encircled one of her lightly tanned arms, and Deirdre saw that she had the lean, sculptured physique of the compulsive exerciser. She certainly wore her age well. Better than Eva Lavery, who had an unashamedly lived-in look about her. But there was a telltale dearth of laughter-lines around those ice-blue eyes.

'Darling. Hi.' Ann Fitzroy swept a curtain of shiny, silver-blond hair back from her forehead. 'I'm not going to make it home at all today.'

Deirdre's heart lurched. She must be talking to David! She turned the page of the *Irish Times* and studied it intently with unseeing eyes, trying hard to look as if she wasn't listening.

'I've a session at half-past-four. You've a rehearsal around then anyway, right? Honestly, you're such a perfectionist, David. The show's up and running now – do you really have to do so much fine-tuning?' With her free hand Ann Fitzroy produced a powder compact from her bag and studied her face in its mirror. 'I thought you might need reminding that we're meeting the Johnstons tonight. Yes. Cooke's at eight o'clock.' There was a frigid pause. 'Well, you're going to have to cancel it. I arranged this dinner last week and we can't let them down now. It's *important*, David. Very well. Let me know as soon as possible please. Leave a message if the mobile's powered off. Bye, darling.'

Deirdre winced inwardly. The endearment had been totally unconvincing. From her tone, Ann Fitzroy might as well have said, 'Bye you bastard from hell.' She noticed that Mary Sheridan's attention was firmly fixed on her computer screen.

Ann Fitzroy smoothed an eyebrow and then snapped shut the lid of her compact and stowed it in her bag along with her mobile. She sighed again. 'Why does life have to be so stressful?' she said irritably to no one in particular. Throughout her telephone conversations she had given no sign that she was aware of Deirdre's presence. Now she fixed her with a gimlet eye, and her appraisal felt as sharp as a diamond.

Mary Sheridan came to the rescue. 'Do you two know each other? Ann Fitzroy, Deirdre O'Dare.'

Deirdre rose awkwardly to her feet, conscious that her palms were sweaty. She rubbed her right hand surreptitiously on her dress before holding it out. 'Hello, Ann. Nice to meet you.'

Ann Fitzroy did not shift from her relaxed position on the couch, but reciprocated the handshake in a languid fashion, surveying the younger woman coolly. Her eyes were the colour of the Bombay Sapphire gin bottle. There was no warmth in them, even though the actress contrived to curve her subtly lipsticked mouth into an approximation of a polite smile.

'Deirdre O'Dare?' She seemed bereft of interest. 'Oh, yes. You play Hermia in my husband's production of *A Midsummer Night's Dream,* don't you? Was that *you* I spoke to on the phone the other day?' Her tone had become increasingly vague.

'That's right.' Deirdre's heart was hammering. Why oh why did she have to meet this woman just before her interview? Her nerves were lacerated already.

'So unfortunate, wasn't it, that he got the casting wrong.' She looked at Deirdre in a calculating way and then put an elegant hand to her mouth and said: 'Oh! The *first* time round I mean, of course, with Suki Hayes.' She emitted a little icicle of laughter. 'You must have had to work very hard to keep up.'

'Yes, I did.' Deirdre could think of nothing else to say. She felt like a mumbly adolescent in her simple geometric print shift.

'I believe you're playing Ophelia as well? What a shame Maeve wasn't available. Still, I'm sure you'll be perfectly adequate.' She gave Deirdre a disingenuous smile and glanced at her discreet gold watch. 'I'd better fly.'

'Don't forget your script, Ann.' Mary Sheridan passed a chunky jiffy bag across the desk to her. 'Thank you, Mary. Send my love to Sally, won't you? Oh – and tell her I'm really not interested in endorsing that moisturizer unless they hike up the fee. The television scripts are execrable.' And Ann Fitzroy glided out of the room.

Deirdre felt as if she'd been incinerated.

Mary Sheridan gave her a sympathetic look. 'Don't pay any heed, my love. She doesn't mean half of what she says. It's just her manner.'

Deirdre was unconvinced. Maeve had been right, after all, she thought, hotly. Ann Fitzroy *was* a prize bitch. How dare she say such vile things! Deirdre shouldn't have allowed her to get away with it. She should have stood up for herself. If she ever came across Ann Fitzroy again she'd be ready for her. She wouldn't be such a walkover next time! As she stared blindly at the *Irish Times* her anger gradually subsided, to be replaced by a sense of humiliation so strong that she wanted to cry. She felt utterly defeated.

The intercom on the reception desk buzzed. 'Mary? I've finished at last, thank God. They located the bastard in Rio. Has Deirdre O'Dare arrived yet?'

'Yes, she's here.'

'OK – you can send her in now.'

'Sally – can I have a quick word first?' asked Mary Sheridan with a sideways glance at Deirdre.

'Sure – come on in.'

Mary disappeared through the door on the right, and Deirdre was glad to be left alone for a while. It meant that she could take deep breaths and try to recover a shred or two of her slashed confidence.

Moments later Mary returned. 'Deirdre? You can go in now.'

Deirdre stood up and gathered her things together. She was aware that Mary Sheridan had clocked the fact that her photograph and CV were lacking an envelope.

'It might be an idea to slip those in here,' she said, handing her a manilla envelope and giving her a smile of encouragement.

'Oh – thanks. I had a bit of an accident. I dropped my folder in a kind of oil-slick, I'm afraid.'

'That won't worry Sally. She's very down-to-earth, you know. You'll like her.'

Deirdre gave what she hoped sounded like a confident knock on the door and passed through into Sally's office. It was bigger than the reception area, but not as elegant. This was very definitely a work place. There were papers on just about every available surface, and a virtual Manhattan skyline of towering piles of ring-bound scripts, books and video tapes ranged the walls. A couple of year-planners hung behind Sally's desk, so dense with kaleidoscopic high-lighter that they looked more like colour-charts for Berger. A notice-board was crowded with newspaper cuttings, Post-It notes, Gary Larson cartoons and numerous photographs. Deirdre recognized nearly all the faces.

'Nice to meet you, Deirdre. Sit down,' Sally Ruane was sitting behind the desk, partially obscured by small hills of paperwork. She rose to her feet to shake hands. 'Excuse the mess. And please don't mention the rain forest. I hate being made to feel guilty.'

'Nice to meet you too, Sally. Thanks for sparing me the time.' Deirdre noticed that her voice was wobbly. She still felt a bit floored by her encounter with Ann Fitzroy.

Sally carefully shifted a rather precarious pile of documents to one side so that she could get a better view of her prospective client and sat back down. 'All this is superficial, you know – a kind of organized chaos. *I* know where everything is, though people find it hard to believe. Mary keeps trying to tidy things up, but I never let her.' Sally drew one leg up onto her chair and wrapped her arms around it. She was wearing black jeans and a floppy black Viyella shirt. Her black hair was cut into a sharp Louise Brooks bob, and she had the longest legs Deirdre had ever seen. She sent Deirdre a smile so warm that the actress felt herself beginning to relax at last.

'You come highly recommended. It's very unusual for David to personally recommend anyone. You should be extremely chuffed.'

'Oh – I am. I'm really grateful to him.'

'I was in at the show on opening night. You're good, Deirdre.'

'Thanks very much, Ms Ruane. That's a real compliment.' She meant it.

'It's a fact. I don't do flattery, Deirdre. And please call me Sally.' She rested her chin on her cocked knee. 'You can be sure that I'll always be perfectly candid with you. This isn't a business for wimps, and you'd better expect to get bruised black and blue if you're going to survive out there.' Sally's gaze was frank and uncompromising. 'This may sound like B-movie speak, but I have to give it to you hard and I have to give it to you straight up. You *have* to understand from the outset that if you go into this profession dreaming about fame, fortune and Hollywood, you might as well get out now. I won't have anyone on my books starting out with any illusions.'

Deirdre nodded solemnly. What Sally was saying had already been drummed into her at college.

'You've been incredibly lucky to have come so far in such a short time, Deirdre. To set foot through my door is no mean achievement – and I'm not saying that out of arrogance. In the past eighteen months I've only taken on one newcomer. She made an impressive debut, but then she decided to take London by storm. She hasn't worked for nearly a year, and she's an extremely accomplished girl. It can be very frightening to realize how quickly and how unpredictably a promising actor can plunge into obscurity.' Sally took a cigarette from a pack on the table and lit up. Deirdre dreaded to think what would happen if there was ever a fire in the office. 'The bubble that you're riding on now has got to burst some time, Deirdre – and you've got to be prepared for it when it happens. Once your contract's up with Lawless Productions you'll be back in the real world of unemployment. I'll give you all the help I can, but you're going to have to help yourself, too. You know that, don't you?'

'Yeah.' Deirdre nodded. 'I'm going to try my hardest, Sally. I was warned at college that it's a dog-eat-dog world out there.'

'It can be a bitch-eat-bitch world, too. There's a strange dearth of sisterly feeling in the acting profession. You may already know a little bit about that? I believe Ms Fitzroy was less than charitable to you out there earlier.' Sally raised an eyebrow in inquiry, and her smile was knowing.

So that's why Mary Sheridan had asked to see Sally before Deirdre went in! It had been to advise the agent that Deirdre had just been emotionally mauled. She was beginning to like this woman and her secretary more and more.

Sally suddenly swung her leg down from the chair, leaned her elbows on the desk and looked at Deirdre with intense scrutiny. 'Hell. It's a pity I didn't know about you last week. Juliet Rathbone–Lyon was over, casting the Grace

O'Malley film. I'd love her to have seen you for the young Grace.'

Deirdre had heard about the Grace O'Malley film from Maeve. The film was a big-budget American production based on the life of Grace O'Malley, the legendary Irish Pirate Queen, and Jessica Lange had been cast in the role of the older Grace. Now they were searching for someone to match up with her as the young Grace.

'I don't suppose,' Sally's expression was dubious, 'I don't suppose you'd be able to fly to London next week to see her? We'd have to clear it with the theatre, of course, but if you were to fly over next Sunday there's a possibility that I could arrange for you to meet Juliet first thing on Monday morning. You'd be back in time for the show on Monday night. Have you somewhere you could stay overnight in London?' Deirdre immediately thought of her cousin Nuala. She hadn't seen her for years, but she was sure she wouldn't mind putting her up for one night. 'Yes,' she told Sally without hesitation. She neglected to mention that she had no idea where the money for the air fare would come from.

'Good. Remind me. When does *Macbeth* go into rehearsal?'

'Tuesday week. It was meant to be Monday, but Finbar de Rossa had post-synching to do on some film, so David decided to postpone rehearsals for one day.'

'Perfect. I'll see what I can do.' Sally got up from her chair to see Deirdre to the door. Deirdre was of average height, but she felt positively dwarfish beside Sally.

'Well, Deirdre,' she said as she turned the door handle. 'It was good to meet you. I'm sure we'll get along famously just as long as you don't expect to *get* famous, OK?'

Deirdre returned the agent's warm smile, and then suddenly remembered something. 'Oh – my CV and stuff. They're in an envelope on your desk.' Deirdre hesitated, looking over at the desk and wondering if Sally Ruane would ever be able to locate the envelope amid the clutter.

Sally interpreted her anxious expression correctly. 'I'll *find* them, Deirdre, don't worry! Talk to you soon. Bye.'

'By the way, Sally. My photograph's a bit – um –'

But the phone on Sally's desk was ringing. 'Bye, Deirdre,' she said, gently pushing the actress through the door. She gave a little wave of dismissal, and was gone.

Deirdre went straight to the nearest telephone box to let her mum know she'd landed herself an agent.

'That's wonderful news! You must be over the moon, Deirdre.'

'I am. I was dead scared to begin with, but she's actually really nice – not intimidating at all.'

'We'll toast you over dinner tonight. You've worked hard for this.'

'Mum? There's only one snag.'

'What's that?'

'She wants me to fly to London on Sunday to meet a casting director. They're looking for someone to play the young Grace O'Malley in a blockbuster film, and she thinks I might be right for it.'

'More wonderful news!' said Rosaleen exuberantly. 'Where's the snag?'

'I've no money, Mum, and the flight'll cost a fortune. I hate to ask, but could you lend me some? I promise I'll pay it back as soon as I can – I'll do it in instalments out of my pay every week.'

There was a pause before Rosaleen said: 'Deirdre? Have you checked your account since I told you I'd lodged a surprise for you?'

'No, I haven't had a chance to get to the bank.'

'Well, I suggest that you take a look.'

'Oh, Mum!' Deirdre felt a sudden thrilling sense of apprehension. 'How much did you lodge?'

'I got a lot of money for those paintings, Deirdre. More than I can usually command. You got a present of three hundred pounds.'

Deirdre was weak with relief. 'Mum! I love you! Oh, I'm so happy – I can't tell you how much! Oh thank you, Mum, thank you–' Her burblings of gratitude were cut off as the beeps sounded and the line went dead.

* * *

Later that afternoon she arrived at the theatre and made her way to the green room. David Lawless wasn't happy with the blocking in the final scene and he had called the cast for a rehearsal at four o'clock. Deirdre remembered how Ann Fitzroy had called him a perfectionist on the phone earlier that day and the bitter tone she'd adopted, and once again her heart went out to him. How hellish to be married to that woman!

People were late, as usual, so there was a delay before they could start work. She sat down beside Maeve, who was having her daily fix of *Hello!* She was dying to tell her all about her meeting with Sally Ruane and the trip to London, even though she still knew nothing definite. She'd hung around her flat all afternoon waiting for the phone to ring, and had taken her courage in both hands just before she'd left and dialled Sally's number. She had a suspicion that she'd never be any good at playing waiting games. She didn't want to pester the agent and look like she was going to be a perpetual nuisance, but she was desperate for feedback. As it transpired, there wasn't any. She'd spoken to Mary Sheridan who told her that yes, Sally had put through a call to Juliet Rathbone-Lyon that afternoon, but the casting director had been out of the office. She'd just have to be patient and hold on until tomorrow.

She sat down beside Maeve on the leatherette couch and peered at the magazine over her shoulder. 'Who's in it this week? Anyone I know?' she asked facetiously.

'Tara Palmer-Tomkinson, as usual. And actually, there's someone *I* know.'

'Oh?' Deirdre was intrigued. 'Who?'

'Gabriel Byrne.'

'You *know* Gabriel *Byrne*? I don't believe you, Maeve!'

'It's true. I even got to snog him in a film once, years ago. I was just starting out then, and I'd only a tiny part, but he was an absolute sweetheart and looked after me like a daddy.'

Deirdre realized that Maeve must be older than she'd thought. She was surrounded by grown-ups, even though most of them didn't behave in a particularly adult fashion.

'Oh, shit, Maeve – what a waste!'

Maeve looked at her curiously. 'What d'you mean?'

'Well, you know – getting an opportunity to snog Gabriel Byrne and not being able to enjoy it because you're gay.'

Maeve gave her friend a thoughtful smile and remarked: 'Actually, I *did* rather enjoy it . . .' before resuming her perusal of *Hello!*.

Deirdre saw Rory arriving and she looked at her watch. He was ten minutes late. A thought occurred to her. 'Maeve? Do you know what an oenophile is?'

'Mm. An oenophile is a connoisseur of fine wines. Why?'

'Oh – no reason.'

Eva Lavery wandered past, wafting Eau d'Issey in her wake. She was wearing faux snakeskin trousers and a tight black T-shirt. 'Jesus, Eva,' Deirdre heard Rory exclaim in a raw voice. 'What can I say? You look – well, ravishing is one word for it.'

Eva made a little moue. 'What's the point of *looking* ravishing? I'd really much rather *be* ravished, sweetheart, to be perfectly frank.'

'Can I be the perpetrator?' he asked.

Eva leaned over and gave him a kiss on the mouth which was, Deirdre noticed, a fraction longer than was proper. 'Mm. Maybe,' she said, and her smile was foxy.

'Hi, Eva,' said Maeve as the actress joined them in ritual scrutiny of *Hello!*. 'How did you spend your weekend?'

'Oh, not bloody Tara Palmer-Tomkinson again. My weekend? Oh, quietly – at home. In bed with my lovers, drinking too much champagne. Dancing round the house by myself with no clothes on. You know – the usual sort of stuff.'

The actress looked up from the magazine. David Lawless was standing only feet away from them, studying his notes. Their eyes met, and something tacit and unfathomable passed between them. Then David turned and walked out of the room. Eva watched him go, and then she gave a little start as Jessica Young approached and laid a deferential hand on her arm.

'Eva? Would you mind checking the prop garland? I understand you've been having a few problems with it, but it should be fine now. I left it to dry on the prop table.'

'Of course, Jessica.' Eva linked arms with the

ASM. 'You know, I wish Jenny hadn't insisted on all that lobelia in the garland,' she said, as they headed towards the door.

'Why's that?'

'It's frightfully unlucky. It means mischief and malevolence. She should have used lily of the valley instead. Or potatoes. They mean benevolence.'

'What does lily of the valley stand for?' asked Jessica.

'Return of happiness.' And Eva and Jessica disappeared into the wings.

'Maeve? Do you think Eva meant all that about the champagne and the lovers?' Deirdre inquired in a surreptitious tone.

'Sure.' Maeve stretched herself and yawned. 'The brilliant thing about Eva is that she's incredibly candid. If someone like Sophie came out with that it would just sound like pretentious guff, and we'd all know she was trying it on. Eva just states the truth pure – or maybe that should be impure – and simple.'

'Really?'

'Oh, yes. Who'd let on that they'd been dancing round a house with no clothes on? *Some* people may do it, and most people probably *want* to do it, but I don't know many people who'd be artless enough to admit it. It has to be true.'

Nick McCarthy called them for rehearsal. Deirdre rummaged in her backpack for her script, wondering how long the rejigging of the blocking was going to take. She hadn't eaten since breakfast, and she was starving. When she left the green room she came across Eva with the garland on her head, swinging her legs and playing a little tune on a hunting horn. 'This hunting horn is brilliant,' she said. 'If you half cover it with your hands it sounds like a constipated cat. Have a go.'

She handed the horn to Deirdre, who blew experimentally into the mouthpiece, half covering the other end as Eva had told her. Both actresses burst out laughing at the sound that emerged.

When they'd sobered a bit, Deirdre set the horn carefully back on its allocated place on the prop table.

'Eva?' she queried.

'Mm-hm?'

'I've got hold of some old photographs that might interest you. I'll drop them down to your dressing-room later, if you like.'

'Thank you, darling. What are they of?' Eva hopped off the table and strolled on to the stage with Deirdre.

Deirdre suddenly wondered if presenting Eva with the photographs was such a good idea. She might just succeed in opening old wounds, for all she knew. But it was too late to unsay it.

'Oh – you know – just some old production shots.'

'I'm intrigued.'

The company straggled to the edge of the stage, waiting for David to take charge. Lounging in the front row of the stalls, he had his long legs stretched out in front of him and his thumbs hooked into his belt-loops. He was immersed in his notes, and was repeatedly and abstractedly running the middle finger of his right hand over the black denim of his jeans on an area just below his hipbone.

'What on earth is David *doing*?' asked Eva in the manner of someone who doesn't expect a reply.

'Oh, it's probably the tattoo,' said Deirdre. 'I have a friend who got one done recently and she said it was really itchy for the first few days.' Deirdre suddenly realized to her horror that she'd just committed the exact same blunder as she had with Rory the other night. How on earth was she going to explain herself *this* time? She still hadn't enlightened Eva as to the reason behind her presence in the dressing-room that evening, and the longer she left it the more difficult it was going to be. She certainly didn't want to confess that she'd seen David Lawless stark naked.

'What tattoo?' Eva was staring at her.

'Well, um – Rory McDonagh told me this, so of course I don't know whether to believe it or not, but apparently he and David both got tattoos done last week. He said it was David's idea.' Deirdre was delighted that she'd had the bright idea of dragging Rory in to it. At least now she wouldn't have to admit to Eva that she'd seen the tattoo with her own eyes.

But Eva hardly seemed to be taking in what she was saying. She had turned her face away and was looking at David as he brushed back his hair and lifted his head from his notebook, surveying the assembled company with eyes that looked uncharacteristically lifeless. In comparison to David, Eva suddenly looked utterly incandescent. Her eyes shone as she gazed at him. 'It's a Siamese Fighting Fish, isn't it?' she breathed.

Deirdre said nothing.

Chapter Nine

The following Monday morning, despite all her best plans, Deirdre found herself running late for her appointment with Juliet Rathbone-Lyon. Sally had warned her on the phone that her interview with the casting director would not be plain sailing. 'Juliet's a tough lady, Deirdre, and doesn't suffer fools gladly.'

Deirdre was slightly taken aback, hoping that the agent wasn't making specific reference to her, but Sally continued. 'Don't take that personally, by the way. She thinks just about everybody else in the world is a fool bar her. She's spiky and not easy to like, but she's held in great respect by the industry. Just try not to say anything to rile her, and don't let her faze you. Keep it in mind that it's in her interest to meet you just as much as it's in your interest to meet her. And don't try too hard to make an impression – just be yourself.'

Oh God. She hated it when people said that.

Deirdre had arrived in Gatwick the afternoon before, and stayed with her cousin Nuala in Clapham. But instead of having a sound night's sleep and an early start, she'd had a horrendous time babysitting Nuala's wailing infant son, and had overslept her alarm. She'd woken in a panic, raced through the bathroom and screamed into the phone for a cab while the Tellytubbies mooned around on Nuala's television screen, looking a million times more Zen than she could hope to be on this nightmare morning.

Although Nuala's flat wasn't far from the station, it took an age to get there in the morning traffic. If Deirdre had been more sure of the way she'd have got out of the cab and ran. It was a blisteringly hot day and the gridlocked drivers were already seething with road rage.

As soon as she spotted the familiar logo of the underground she paid off the driver and sprinted to the station. She'd consulted the underground map in her diary while in the cab and was relieved to see that the Northern line which served Clapham Common would take her straight to Leicester Square. Her A-Z had told her that it was a short walk from there to Juliet Rathbone-Lyon's office in Soho. She bought a ticket and ran down to the platform to discover that a train had just pulled in. She was in luck for once – it would all be plain sailing from now on.

There were just seven stations between Clapham Common and Leicester Square, and she marked her progress on the map above the window, ticking the stops off mentally as the train went along. Clapham North, Stockwell, Oval, Kennington, Elephant and Castle. Elephant and Castle! She should be in Waterloo according to the map – how had she ended up in Elephant and Castle? Deirdre broke into a sweat and pushed her way through the crowd of passengers so that she could examine the map at closer quarters. The people around her sent her curious glances, but right now she didn't care how uncool she looked. She saw where she'd gone wrong immediately. She'd been so relieved to have found the right train waiting at the platform in Clapham Common that she hadn't thought to check out where it was heading. She would have to change.

As soon as the doors opened she hit the platform running, and made her way through the labyrinthine corridors in the direction of the southbound platforms. She could have been in hell. Maybe she was. Maybe this was her punishment for thinking murderous thoughts about people like Sophie Burke and Ann Fitzroy. The tunnels were crowded with commuters, all intent on getting to their destinations as fast as possible, irrespective of who was in their way. People were barging their way through the maze of corridors and thronging the escalators.

It was as hot as hell, too. Deirdre could feel sweat trickling down her sides, and her hair was sticking to her forehead. The air was dry and dusty, and her throat felt raw as she laboured for breath. There was a booming noise of machinery somewhere in the distance which was making her feel dizzy and even more confused. She doggedly followed the signs that would take her to the southbound train until she heard an announcement over the tannoy: 'Due to signal failure at Morden, southbound trains are not running at the present time. We apologize for any inconvenience.'

Deirdre sank on to her hunkers and buried her face in her arms. She didn't care who saw her at this stage, but the passersby were oblivious anyway. She was in a state of pure despair. She'd just have to forget about the interview. She was so overwrought anyway that she knew she'd make a total mess of it. She would give up. She hauled herself to her feet and leant against the wall of the Tube station feeling so drained that she couldn't muster tears even though she had never felt more like crying in her life. How could she have blown it so spectacularly? This was an archetypical Deirdre O'Dare scenario. She could have written it herself.

The dirt and dust in the Tube had lodged uncomfortably in her nose and she fished around in her bag for a packet of tissues, extracting one and blowing into it hard. It didn't seem to help. Where to go now? She was in no mood to take advantage of the couple of hours remaining to her in London trailing round the shops looking at things she couldn't afford, or visiting a gallery. She'd just make her way out to Gatwick and wait for her flight.

She thought miserably of what she was going to say to her colleagues in the theatre this evening. She was going to look like a complete and utter imbecile. She cringed at the thought of David Lawless finding out about this shambolic incident and she could not even entertain the notion of filling Rory in on what had happened. He'd use it as ammunition to make her life unbearable for the rest of the season. Then she thought of Sophie. That was the worst thought of all. She pictured the sham look of concern, the smug expression, the whispering behind her back. She couldn't allow it to happen. She picked up her bag and walked purposefully towards the up escalator. She would get to Soho somehow.

Something came back to her – something she'd overheard David Lawless say one day in the rehearsal room when Jessica Young had gone to him with a problem concerning an uncooperative crew member. He had listened to her carefully and then advised her how to handle the situation. His final words had been: '*You* have control of your life, Jessica, and you don't have to let other people keep you down.' No matter how aggressive Juliet Rathbone-Lyon might be she couldn't be such an ogre that she wouldn't be able to understand how easy it was to make the kind of mistake that Deirdre had just made. How could she be expected to know that there'd be signal failure on an obscure stretch of the southbound line?

There was no point in getting back on the Tube. Time was precious to her now and she was prepared to pay for it. She'd take a taxi. She got to the surface, hailed a cab and settled back for the journey. Now that the rush hour was over there'd be less risk of being stuck in traffic. With a bit of luck she'd be there in twenty minutes.

She took out her make-up bag and checked her appearance. She looked like someone's mad Irish cousin. Come to think of it, she supposed she *was*. She certainly couldn't walk into a major casting director's office looking the way she did. She wiped the smuts from her face with spit and a tissue, brushed her bird's nest hair and put on a touch of lipstick. Then she closed her eyes and concentrated on staying calm, taking deep breaths in through her nose and letting them out through her mouth.

The cab finally pulled up outside a tall building in Lexington Street. It was now nearly eleven o'clock and she was a whole hour late – not just the half-hour she'd anticipated.

'That'll be a tenner, love,' said the taxi-driver indifferently. A tenner! She was certainly paying through the nose for the pleasure of being seen by Juliet Rathbone-Lyon.

There was a force ten gale brewing inside her as she rang the bell, but she kept her shoulders straight and held her head high. She was admitted after a brief hiatus, and instructed over the intercom to take the lift to the top floor. The inside of the building was smart – gleaming with glass and chrome – and the lift floated up the shaft in scary silence.

She emerged at the top floor into an intimidating reception area. Like the lobby below there was a lot of highly polished metal around, and some very angular chairs which looked as if they might strut around when there was nobody there and boss each other about. Deirdre felt her resolve evaporating. A very pretty receptionist was sitting behind a glass-topped desk at the other end of the room. She looked up at Deirdre with a slightly fearful expression on her face. She didn't look much older than Deirdre herself.

'Deirdre O'Dare?' she asked.

'Yes – I'm afraid I'm terribly late.'

'We got a phone call from someone called Nuala to say you'd be here at ten thirty. It's eleven o'clock now.'

Deirdre was relieved – and rather surprised – by the total lack of accusation in the girl's voice.

'Yes, I know. I'm really sorry. I got completely lost on the Tube and ended up having to take a taxi.' She bit her lip. 'Will Ms Rathbone-Lyon still see me, do you think?'

'I don't really know. She's with someone at the moment – I'd better wait till she's finished before I let her know you're here.' The little receptionist stood up. She had spiky bleached blond hair and she was wearing a bright red suit with a neat, tailored jacket and a straight ankle-length skirt. She had a gold belt around her waist and was sporting some rather ostentatious costume jewellery. The look was kooky, but Deirdre could tell it was also expensive. 'Would you like some tea or coffee?' she asked politely.

'I'd love some water.'

'Sparkling or plain?'

'Plain, please.'

'With or without ice?'

'With, please.' Deirdre wondered how many times a day the unfortunate girl had to run through this litany.

'Sit down and make yourself comfortable and I'll bring it straight out to you.'

No-one could contrive to make themselves comfortable on such furniture. A chaise longue tightly upholstered in belisha-beacon orange looked challengingly at her. She tested it with her bum. She was right – it was perfectly unyielding.

The receptionist reappeared with her water. Deirdre thanked her and continued sitting ramrod straight on the chaise, studying the prints on the wall. They were all posters for films cast by Juliet Rathbone-Lyon and they covered a period of nearly two decades. Deirdre had seen most of the films and was impressed by the famous names which appeared above the titles. She was in very illustrious company indeed.

Her nose was at her again, and she had run out of clean tissues. 'Excuse me?' she asked the receptionist. 'Would you happen to have a spare tissue?'

'Certainly.' She produced a tiny tomato-red bag and took a packet of tissues out of it. 'You can keep the whole pack, if you like. I've another one in my desk.'

'Oh, may I? That's really kind of you. I've a feeling I'm going to need them.'

The receptionist looked startled. 'You're not on a crying jag, are you?' she asked in a concerned tone.

'Oh, no – I just think I may be getting some sort of summer cold.'

'I seem to have a permanent cold these days. I'm sure it's from all the travelling I do on the underground. The air down there's disgusting.

How did you manage to get lost, by the way?'

Deirdre explained as economically as she could.

'Hang about.' The girl produced a map of the underground from a drawer in her desk. 'Look – if you'd only carried on to Bank you could have taken the central line to Tottenham Court Road and walked from there. That's how I got here today.'

Of course that's what she should have done! It was staring her in the face now that the receptionist had pointed it out to her, but she'd been so fixated on getting to Leicester Square that she hadn't considered any other option. She could have saved herself a tenner and a lot of grief.

'Oh! I shouldn't have said that, should I?' said the receptionist, suddenly looking stricken. 'You probably spent a fortune on that taxi, and the last thing you needed to know was that you could have got here on your tube fare, anyway. I'm always doing things like that – thinking I'm being dead helpful and then realizing that I've actually made things worse. Sorry.'

'It's alright. I do it all the time too.' Deirdre decided that she liked this girl. She looked around at the framed posters again. 'It must be great working here and getting to meet loads of famous people,' she said.

'Actually I haven't met anyone famous yet, though there's a real babe in there at the moment. I'm a temp. It's my first day. I wish it were my last,' she added gloomily.

'Hard work?'

'It shouldn't be, but because of *her*' – the receptionist nodded her elegant little head towards the door behind her '– it is.'

'Juliet Rathbone-Lyon?'

'Mm hm. I've never met anyone quite so rude. I'm genuinely thinking of ringing the agency and complaining about her. If she gives out to me one more time I will. She said the most frightful thing to me this morning – I won't repeat it to you. She's the most foul-tempered–'

The appalled look on Deirdre's face stopped her in her tracks and the little blonde clapped her hands over her mouth. 'Oh my God – I've done it again. I forgot you haven't even met her yet. I hope I haven't spooked you too much. I'd hate to think that I'd made you even more nervous than you probably are already. I'm truly sorry.'

'It's OK.' Deirdre was actually feeling very unsettled. 'My agent warned me about her already.'

'We'll talk about something else, OK?' She cocked her head at an angle. 'Do you know something? You're the second person I've met today with that accent. Isn't that strange? Where are you from?'

'Dublin.' Deirdre didn't feel much like chatting any more. She was thinking about the dragon behind the closed door and was seriously dreading the thought of meeting her. She wished she could fast-forward her life until she got to the good bit.

'Oh – that means the girl who was in here earlier must be from Dublin too, then,' said the little blonde happily.

Deirdre's curiosity was suddenly aroused. 'What was her name?'

'Um – let me see – it's here in the appointment book. Oh yes – here we are. Sophie Burke. She had an appointment with the witch at half-past nine.'

Deirdre almost – but not quite – laughed. Hollowly. Trust bloody Sophie to set up her own interview with Juliet Rathbone-Lyon!

Suddenly the door behind the reception desk opened and the most beautiful young man Deirdre had ever seen in her life came through. She barely had a chance to register how drop-dead gorgeous he was before he turned back to say something to someone in the room behind him. From where she was sitting Deirdre couldn't see who it was but when she heard a female voice talking in a painful Home Counties accent she guessed that it must be Juliet Rathbone-Lyon.

'Don't take too long to think it over, darling. I'm a notoriously fickle individual and I don't like to be kept waiting. I'm a glutton for instant gratification, as you may have guessed.' Deirdre couldn't hear the low response, but it was met with a strident laugh. 'Darling, you are delicious and I'm voracious. I could eat you for breakfast. Talk to you soon.'

The door shut, and the young man advanced into the room. Deirdre didn't dare look up. She knew that if she let her gaze be drawn to him she would never be able to tear her eyes away, and she was damn sure he wasn't going to catch her staring. She was aware that he had taken a thick script out of a jiffy bag and was leafing through it.

She heard the receptionist talk into the phone

in tones which sounded rather strained. 'Deirdre O'Dare is here to see you, Ms Rathbone-Lyon.'

There was a beat for the response. Then the little blond girl made a face at the phone and put it down with a bang. 'She says would you mind waiting. Although she didn't put it as politely as that,' she added in a muttered undertone.

Deirdre stiffened and then tried to look cool, but without success. Her nose had started to run again. She slid a tissue out of the packet she was clutching and blew into it with as much discretion as she could manage, but it only succeeded in sounding like a surreptitious snuffling of some small hedgerow animal. She looked up to find the beautiful young man looking at her.

'Hello,' she said. 'It's a lovely day, isn't it?' She winced at herself.

'Hello,' he said back. 'Yes, it is.'

He didn't look as if would bite her, she thought. She half wished he might. He was all the things a handsome stranger should be. Tall and dark, with a smile that made her insides melt. He was even the right age for her – early to mid twenties, Deirdre reckoned. He narrowed eyes the colour of syrup and studied her for a moment.

'You going in to see Juliet?'

'Yes. If she still has time. I'm running late.'

'What are you up for? The Grace O'Malley film?'

'That's right.'

'I suspected as much from the accent. What part of Ireland are you from?'

'Dublin. I'm flying back this afternoon. I've got

to get back for a show this evening.' Deirdre was delighted to get a chance to let drop the fact that she was working. Being a working actor counted for a lot amongst the acting fraternity simply because most actors are terminally unemployed.

'What's the show?'

'*A Midsummer Night's Dream.* I'm playing Hermia,' she said, pleased to be able to show off a bit again.

'Is that David Lawless's *Dream* by any chance?' His voice was carefully neutral, but there was no concealing the interest in his eyes. Deirdre thought she'd seen him somewhere before – possibly in a film or on the telly.

'Yes.' She leant back on the chaise, trying to look relaxed. 'You're very well informed about what's going on in Irish theatre.'

'Well, it got amazing reviews in the British press. Eva Lavery's playing Titania, isn't she?'

'That's right. She's incredible in it.'

'Yeah?' said the beautiful actor.

'Yeah. She's also one of the nicest people I know.'

'She's not a diva, then?'

'Not at all.'

The phone sounded. 'Certainly, Ms Rathbone-Lyon,' said the receptionist with exaggerated courtesy. She looked up at Deirdre with sympathy in her eyes. 'You've to go in now.'

Deirdre was suddenly filled with intense alarm. Some instinct told her she should get out of there now, but at this stage escape was impossible. She turned to the stranger uncertainly, as if he might be able to help her somehow, but he was no longer looking at her. He was frowning at the carpet. The friendly little receptionist was looking apprehensive. 'Good luck,' she said, as Deirdre approached the door to Juliet Rathbone-Lyon's office.

'Yes. Good luck.' She turned around to find her stranger smiling at her.

'Thanks,' she said. 'I've a feeling I'm going to need it.' She walked into Juliet Rathbone-Lyon's office resisting the impulse to bleat, like a lamb on the way to the slaughter.

As she closed the door behind her a phone shrilled. Ignoring Deirdre, the casting director picked it up. 'Yeah? Oh, Daniel, hi. No, it's cool – I'm not busy at the moment.' She got up from behind her desk and wandered over to the window, leaning against the frame and looking down into the street. She had tucked the cordless phone expertly into the hollow of her collarbone and was idly pleating a sheet of typewritten paper.

Deirdre hovered by the door, not sure what to do. She didn't want to sit down without being invited. She'd just have to wait until Juliet Rathbone-Lyon had finished on the phone. The woman's back was still firmly turned to her, but the glimpse that Deirdre had got of her before she'd moved to the window had been enough for her to establish that she was actually extremely good-looking. For some reason Deirdre found this surprising. From all that she'd heard about Juliet Rathbone-Lyon and from the sound of her strangulated posh accent, she'd put together a mental image of someone who looked very different. She'd pictured someone a bit like Cruella de Vil in *One Hundred and One Dalmatians.* In reality she had very long, lustrous black hair caught up in a comb on the nape of her neck, navy-blue eyes and a fabulous figure, which was displayed to advantage in a midnight blue silk body. She wore hipsters to match, with high slim-heeled sandals.

Contractual details and legal niceties were the subjects under business-like discussion on the phone. The conversation went on and on while Deirdre stewed with nerves.

It was with a mixture of relief and anxiety that she heard Juliet Rathbone-Lyon say: 'Four o'clock Friday? I should be back by then. OK, Daniel. And just let me warn you – I'm not loving this. Yeah. Bye.'

She clicked off the phone, turned from the window and fixed her eyes on Deirdre with one brow raised. The mouth's a giveaway, thought Deirdre. Juliet Rathbone-Lyon's mouth was a thin line in her face. It looked as though it was set in a perpetual sneer.

'Deirdre O'Dare?' She walked slowly back to her desk, looking Deirdre up and down as she did so. Her expression would not have been out of place if she'd just seen something crawl out from under a stone.

Deirdre's heart sank. If there'd been a stone around she would have been glad to crawl under it. She was going to have to crawl anyway. 'I'm terribly sorry to be so late, Ms Rathbone-Lyon.

There were no southbound trains running because of signal failure and I–'

'Sit down.'

Deirdre was quite relieved to be interrupted. Her Tube story was so convoluted that she'd never be able to make it sound convincing. She was reluctant to sit down, but she thought it might be wise to do as she was told.

'My *temp*' – the casting director spat the word, – 'informed me that she'd received a call to say you were running late because you'd slept in.'

Thanks, Nuala, thought Deirdre.

'Well, that's true too, I'm afraid – but I wouldn't have been anywhere near as late if it hadn't been for the–'

'Let me tell you something, Deirdre.' Juliet Rathbone-Lyon leant back and crossed her slender legs, swivelling her chair slowly from side to side. 'A colleague of yours from Dublin who was under the exact same time constraints as you was able to get here at half-past nine this morning. She had done all her homework on the film, had read every available biography on Grace O'Malley–' (That's not fair! thought Deirdre with feeling. She had been preparing herself all last week for this interview, too, but she hadn't had the opportunity to prove it yet.) 'She looked fresh and behaved charmingly. In other words, she was consummately professional, despite the fact that she, like you, is just out of college. Indeed, I see that you were in the same year.'

She looked at the sheet of paper she'd been

pleating while she'd been talking on the phone and smoothed it out. It was Deirdre's CV. 'Shall I tell you something, Deirdre? I would advise you to take a leaf out of your friend Sophie Burke's book. By arriving here more than an hour late this morning all you have succeeded in doing is inconveniencing me and making me feel hostile, and I've no room in my life for negativity. I'm a take-no-prisoners kind of person, you understand, and I've an inkling that you badly need to get your act together. I'm going to suggest that you start by leaving my office and digesting the lesson I hope you've learned here today.' She screwed Deirdre's CV into a tight ball and tossed it into a wastepaper basket. Her mouth was like a hyphen, but her eyes were glittering with a kind of perverse satisfaction. She was waiting for Deirdre to grovel. Juliet Rathbone-Lyon was actually *enjoying* seeing her squirm.

She looked at the older woman with total incomprehension. Imagine getting off on treating people like shit! For the second time that morning David Lawless's words came back to her. You have control of your life, and you don't have to let other people keep you down. Then Deirdre unaccountably found her mouth starting to curve in a smile.

'What are you smirking at?' Ms Rathbone-Lyon asked tersely. 'I wouldn't have thought there was anything remotely amusing about this situation.'

'I was just thinking,' Deirdre raised her eyes from her hands which, she realized with mild surprise, were lying in an attitude of calm indifference in her lap. 'I was just thinking that I'm really glad I'm not you.'

She saw Juliet Rathbone-Lyon's self possession suddenly slip as she rose to her feet, turned on her heel and walked out the door.

'Did it go well?' the receptionist asked in a dubious tone.

Deirdre laughed from nervous release. 'Well, as far as I'm concerned it did. It's the best thing I've ever done in my life. I walked out.'

'What? You didn't!' The little blonde's reaction was simultaneously incredulous and gleeful.

'I did.' Deirdre laughed again, nodding her head. She herself could hardly believe what she'd just done.

'What a gutsy thing to do.' Deirdre looked round. Her stranger was looking at her with admiration.

'Oh!' Deirdre was taken aback. 'Are you still here? I thought you'd have been gone ages ago.'

'I was chatting up this lovely creature.' He sent the receptionist a smile which she reciprocated unhesitatingly from under thickly mascaraed lashes.

'Come with me.' He took her hand and started to stride out of the office. 'I'd say you deserve a double espresso after what Rathbone-Lyon must have put you through. Let me buy it for you.'

Deirdre flustered a bit as she trailed across the reception area after him. At the door he stopped and turned back to the elfin blonde. 'Nice talking to you.'

'Likewise.' She waved her fingers at Deirdre.

'Nice to meet you, brave girl,' she said. A little smile crept on to her mouth as she gave an expressive glance at the actor who was dragging her off for coffee. 'You're a lucky girl, too – aren't you just?'

Just then there came the noise of something smashing in the office beyond. '*Fucking* hell,' screamed Juliet Rathbone-Lyon, and as the interconnecting door between the two rooms was flung open the little blonde in the red suit lurched for the phone. 'That's it. I'm phoning the agency now!' she exclaimed.

Deirdre and her companion slid like eels through the door before the casting director could register that there'd ever been anybody there.

* * *

As they walked through the streets together he asked her exactly what had happened in Juliet Rathbone-Lyon's office, and she obligingly filled him in.

He took her to a small café in Soho which, he informed her, did excellent coffee. He ordered an espresso, and she ordered a cappuccino and a sandwich, suddenly realizing that she was ravenously hungry.

She was also beginning to come down from the adrenalin rush generated by stalking out of the interview with Juliet Rathbone-Lyon. How the hell was she going to explain her behaviour to her colleagues – and more importantly – to her brand new agent? She knew there was an element of thrilling bravado about what she had just done, but there was no denying that her behaviour had been irresponsible and reckless. Juliet Rathbone-Lyon was probably on the phone to Sally this very minute.

'What's your name?' Her new friend was studying her across the table.

Deirdre resolved to forget about the whole ghastly mess for the time being. The thing had been done and she couldn't undo it. 'Deirdre O'Dare.' She realized she didn't know his either. She almost didn't want to know it. Then he wouldn't be a handsome stranger anymore.

'I'm Sebastian Hardy.' Hell's bells. He even had a sexy name.

They shook hands across the table, laughing at the slight absurdity of the formal gesture. Deirdre felt shy, suddenly. She had never been able to feel at ease when talking to ludicrously handsome men. She brushed her hair back from her face, trying to think of something to say, but was relieved of the compulsion to talk small by the arrival of the waiter with their order.

'Thanks for helping me to escape,' she managed after the waiter had gone again.

'My pleasure.' He stirred a teaspoon of sugar into his coffee. 'You're having second thoughts, aren't you?'

'What about?'

'About whether you did the right thing back there.'

'Yeah. It was actually a pretty stupid thing to do.'

'Don't get too upset about it. Juliet isn't the only casting director in the world, and *Grace* isn't the only film. Talent will out. If you're any good, people will cast you. It's as simple as that.' He paused to drink some of his coffee, making a face and putting it down when he realized it was scalding.

'Won't she badmouth me all over the place?'

'Probably not. You'd be surprised. She won't do you any favours, that's for sure, but she won't want word getting out that she was trounced by some unknown from Dublin. No offence.'

'None taken.' She smiled back at him, grateful for his reassurance.

'Anyway, she's had it coming for ages. It's about time she took a couple of knocks. There aren't many people like you who'd have the nerve to deliver them, that's all.'

Deirdre couldn't help feeling flattered. She looked down at her sandwich. It was one of those enormous ones made from the kind of ciabatta so crusty it hurts your palate and it was crammed with frilly lettuce, tomatoes and chunks of char-grilled chicken in some kind of gloopy dressing. She knew it was going to be a nightmare trying to eat this with any degree of dignity, but she was so hungry she'd have to. She tried an experimental bite and managed to gnaw through the ciabatta with difficulty. A slice of tomato slithered to the plate, but Sebastian didn't seem to notice.

'Tell me about yourself,' he said. All her life Deirdre had cherished fantasies about a beautiful stranger asking her this very question. She nearly choked on her chicken.

'Are you sure you want to know?'

'Why else would I ask?' he replied, blowing on his coffee. His mouth was curved and sensual, and Deirdre caught herself looking at it. She quickly looked away again. 'Are you enjoying working with Lawless Productions, Deirdre?'

'Oh yes! I'm loving every minute of it.' Well, *nul points* for cool, Deirdre, she thought.

'I believe Lawless is a pretty inspirational guy.'

'Oh, he really is, Sebastian. He's a real actor's director – not one of those awful puppeteers. He has no time for mind games. D'you know what I mean?'

Sebastian smiled and nodded. 'Yeah, I've worked with some fuckwits in my time. Tell me more.'

'Well, David's theory is that an insecure actor will deliver an insecure performance – he has this incredibly positive approach to his work, you know?' Deirdre waxed lyrical, and Sebastian listened with unfeigned interest. She liked him. She hadn't met that many men who could converse with enthusiasm on a topic of conversation other than themselves.

'What's Eva Lavery like to work with?' he asked when she'd run out of steam on the topic of David Lawless. Deirdre obliged him by singing Eva's praises. She knew that she was talking too much, but she was still a bit uncomfortable with his beauty, and Sebastian Hardy genuinely didn't seem to mind. His expression of intense interest didn't flag and he actively encouraged her to elaborate on the smallest details.

Deirdre eventually had to admit defeat. 'Please tell me to shut up,' she said. 'You must be bored witless listening to me rabbiting away.'

'Not at all,' he said. His eyes bored into hers. 'You've been positively bewitching.'

Deirdre coloured and laughed. She took another bite of her sandwich and chewed earnestly for a while before swallowing hard and saying: 'What about you Sebastian? It's your turn to tell me about yourself.'

His face took on a slightly guarded look. 'Not a lot to say. I graduated from RADA a few years ago and somehow I've been kept working ever since.'

'Theatre or television?'

'A bit of both. I had a season with the Citz in Glasgow. I did a couple of shows in Manchester last year at the Royal Exchange and I was at the National till recently. I've been lucky enough to fit in a couple of films and a BBC series as well.'

Lucky or very talented, thought Deirdre. This actor came with credentials. 'What was the series?'

'*Hurting People.*'

Suddenly she remembered where she knew him from. *Hurting People* was a Northern drama which had been televised at the beginning of the year. It had been massively successful. '*Now* I know who you are! You were the heroin addict in that, weren't you? What was the name of the character again?'

'Soup.'

'That's right! Oh, you were so *good* in that! I'm surprised I didn't recognize you earlier.'

'Not many people do. I looked pretty ropy in it.' He leaned across the table and removed a shred of lollarossa from her chin. 'Excuse me. That's been annoying me.'

Deirdre felt herself colour up again. 'Yeah. You did look a bit wasted. The difference is amazing. I mean, you really are much more good-looking in real life.' The colour intensified. 'Whoever dreamt of casting *you* as a drug addict must have been inspired! I mean, it just seems so against type.'

'It was Juliet Rathbone-Lyon, actually.'

Deirdre spluttered and a shower of ciabatta crumbs shot out of her mouth. Thankfully Sebastian laughed instead of looking appalled.

'Sorry to bring up your *bête noire* again so soon.'

'That's OK.' Deirdre smiled. 'Ha! She'll regret treating me the way she did when word gets back to her about how good I am as Ophelia,' she said with mock-heroism. She pushed away her plate with the half-eaten sandwich still on it. She wasn't going to risk suffering any further indignities.

'Ophelia? I didn't know that *Hamlet* was part of Lawless's season.'

'Well, it wasn't originally.' Deirdre proceeded to fill Sebastian in on the reasons behind the change to the programme. When she had finished she noticed that he had gone very still.

'So Eva Lavery is playing Gertrude,' he said, and there was a careful look about his eyes. 'Who's playing Hamlet?'

'It's on offer to Mark Llewellyn.'

'Yeah? He's a friend of mine.' Deirdre was impressed. 'I haven't seen him in a while. I must look him up.' He gave a slow smile and looked at his watch. 'It's time I went.'

Deirdre realized that if she was going to make Gatwick in time she'd have to start running again. She reached for her bag, but Sebastian Hardy put a hand on her arm. 'Let me get this.'

'Oh. That's very kind of you. Thank you, Sebastian.'

As he opened his wallet to pay the waiter, a cutting from a magazine fluttered to the ground. Deirdre stooped to pick it up, but Sebastian was there first. He retrieved it and put it back, but not before Deirdre had been able to catch a glimpse of the photograph that had been on it. She herself had seen it in her mother's *Vanity Fair* only last month. It was from a profile of luminaries of the British theatre photographed by Snowdon, and it was of Eva Lavery. Someone else with a crush, thought Deirdre ruefully. She knew exactly how he felt.

'What were you doing in Juliet's office, Sebastian?' she asked as he waited for his change.

'I've been offered a part in a movie in Australia.'

'Australia! Wow. I've always wanted to go there. What is it and when do you start?'

Sebastian looked down at the table top. 'Look, Deirdre – I don't mean to be rude, but I'd rather not talk about it until it's in the bag. I still haven't talked money, you see.'

He had been perfectly polite, but Deirdre was

embarrassed by her lack of sensitivity. 'Oh – I'm sorry, Sebastian. I should mind my own business.'

'It's OK,' he lifted his head and looked at her. His eyes were those of a dark angel. 'I just don't want to hex myself, you know?'

They left the café and prepared to go their separate ways. Sebastian took her hand. 'It's been a revelation to meet you.' He looked at her levelly but his expression was unreadable. 'It's unusual to meet someone and to like them straight away, isn't it? I like you very much, Deirdre O'Dare.'

'Thank you, Sebastian. I like you too.' What a nice change to be able to be so absolutely frank with someone, she thought. 'I hope we meet again some time.'

'I've a suspicion we will,' he said. He leant forward and brushed her lips briefly with his. Then he smiled and, turning away from her, strode in the opposite direction.

Deirdre nearly forgot to breathe.

Chapter Ten

The journey home was, to Deirdre's relief, quite uneventful. After the Tube incident she'd half-expected another catastrophe. Back in Dublin she took the airport bus into the city centre and walked to the theatre, picking up a McDonald's as she went. She was miles too early for the show, but there was a major chore that she was determined to get out of the way. She had to phone Sally Ruane.

She ate her Big Mac in the green room and then took a deep breath and picked up the phone. Mary Sheridan answered in her usual unflappable style.

'You're on a pay phone, Deirdre, by the sound of it,' she said in response to Deirdre's jittery preamble. 'Put it down and I'll get Sally to ring you straight back.'

The phone rang back almost instantly, and for the second time that day Deirdre braced herself to crawl. David Lawless had been right. She seemed to spend her entire life apologizing these days.

Sally's voice came over the line. 'Well, Deirdre. It didn't take long for you to put us in a highly compromising situation, did it? What the hell happened this morning? I spent nearly half an hour on the phone to Juliet Rathbone-Lyon trying to smooth her exceedingly ruffled fur, and it wasn't a pleasant task, as I'm sure you can imagine. What did you *say* to her?'

Deirdre filled Sally in, feeling ashamed and contrite.

'Dear Jesus, Deirdre. You really fouled up. You've wasted a lot of people's time and your own money, as well as blowing your chance of landing a very sweet role – and that chance had been looking good up until this morning, I might add.'

Deirdre flinched, waiting for the final blow.

'If you're going to stay in this business you've got to learn that you don't get anywhere by offending influential people. A little guile is essential, and don't be ashamed to use it. You'd better start practising how to eat crow.' As far as Deirdre was concerned, she'd been eating more crow than Pop Tarts recently. She hated the way it tasted. 'You could begin by writing Juliet Rathbone-Lyon an excruciatingly humble letter of apology. She's not going to acknowledge it, of course, but it might let me off the hook with her. I'm damn sure Sally Ruane Management isn't going to take the rap for your bad behaviour.'

'Sorry, Sally.' More crow. Deirdre was nearly crying.

'Having said all that,' continued Sally, 'I have to admit that I can't really blame you for doing what you did. Juliet's become insufferably arrogant recently – everybody's commenting on it, and a lot of people would love to pluck up the courage to tell her where to put it. And that includes me. Now, go away and write that letter, Deirdre. Oh – I've got

RTE interested in you, by the way. There's a new character coming in to *Ardmore Grove.* When you get your rehearsal schedule for *Macbeth* let me know how you're fixed and I'll set up an appointment for you.'

'What?' Deirdre was incredulous. 'You mean you're not going to scratch me off your books, Sally?'

'Deirdre, I didn't put you on my client list for your people skills, believe it or not. As far as I'm concerned you've got something else going for you – which is just as well. It's your skill as a performer that I'm interested in, OK? Just do me a favour and work a little harder on your sense of tact before I send you out to Montrose. See you soon.' And Sally put down the phone.

Deirdre was dizzy with relief. She *loved* her agent. What an understanding, tolerant, totally *fab* person she was. She'd have to buy her a present to say thank you.

In the meantime there was the letter to Juliet Rathbone-Lyon to get out of the way. What on earth was she going to say to her? She hated writing business-type letters. In fact, the only letters she wrote these days were to Sarah and her Granny in Westport. She'd leave it till later and ask Maeve to help her concoct something. It would be the biggest work of fiction since Grimm's fairy tales.

She was reading her horoscope in a back issue of *Cosmopolitan*, trying to work out if it had come true, when Sophie came in looking slinky in dévoré velvet. Deirdre noticed that she had the good grace to be wearing a slightly guilty expression.

'Hi, Deirdre,' she fluted. '*Love* your get-up. Is that what you wore to your interview this morning?'

Deirdre was still wearing her useful little geometric print dress. 'Yup,' she said, with a distinct lack of graciousness. 'Don't tell me you wore *that*?'

Sophie looked pink. 'Oh – so you heard I was lucky enough to get a chance to see Juliet as well? No, no – I didn't wear this. Of course not. This is for going out later on. I'm having dinner with Ben in Frères Jacques. It's my birthday.' Deirdre managed to refrain from wishing Sophie a happy birthday. 'I wore my Louise Kennedy to *my* interview,' she continued. 'How did you get on, by the way? She's nice, isn't she?'

Deirdre made a noncommittal noise. She was damn sure she wasn't going to give Sophie Burke the pleasure of knowing how spectacularly she'd blown it. Someone else could do that later. She would also have to take great care that Sophie didn't get to hear about the part going in *Ardmore Grove.* She'd be pretty sure to find out about it through her expert networking tactics, Deirdre knew, but she certainly wasn't going to get any useful information out of *her.*

Sophie looked arch. 'I thought I did rather well, actually. I seemed to have a really good rapport with her.'

If there'd been a Luger handy Deirdre would have had no hesitation in using it. She was spared the necessity to make any kind of response by the arrival of Maeve.

'Hi Deirdre. How did the interview go?'

'Come with me.' Deirdre took Maeve by the hand and dragged her off to the privacy of the dressing-room where she revealed all.

Maeve sat down at her dressing table and listened with interest to Deirdre's story. When she had finished she sent her a look of great approval. 'Brave girl, Deirdre. Nobody should be expected to put up with that sort of shit. Actors have been cannon fodder for the power trips of egomaniacs for too long.' She picked some dead blossoms from the posy of flowers that Deirdre had given her on the opening night and rolled them between fingers which would have been wonderfully elegant if it weren't for the bitten nails.

'You know something, Deirdre? The world is full of despotic little men who use people like pawns. For them, bullying is a way of life. It's sad to have to acknowledge that there are some despotic women out there too.'

'Thanks for the reassurance, Maeve.' Deirdre gave Maeve a kiss on the cheek. 'What on earth'll I say in the letter?'

'Make it very brief and formal. Apologize for being late and apologize for wasting her time, but don't apologize for what you said. After all, you didn't hurl insults at her or anything like that. By saying "I'm really glad I'm not you" you were simply stating an opinion.'

Deirdre looked at Maeve admiringly. 'How did you get to be so wise, Maeve?' she asked, fiddling with the little plastic sheep and sheepdog that Rory had given them on opening night. 'I wish I could think of stuff like that by myself.'

'I've lived longer than you have, Deirdre. Don't worry – you're learning all the time.'

* * *

By the time Deirdre hit Meagher's later on that evening she discovered that word of her attempt at committing professional suicide in Juliet Rathbone-Lyon's office had got round the cast and that she had become something of a heroine. She had repeated the story so many times at this stage that she was beginning to feel like the Ancient Mariner, and in spite of the fact that she'd had the most nerve-shattering day of her life, she was in flying form. She was regaling Eva with the most recent, improved version of her saga when Rory strolled over. He was singing the song about the little lamb that gets lost in the woods, but he substituted the word 'Tube' for 'woods'.

'I hear congratulations are in order, Deirdre,' he said, setting a glass of white wine down in front of her. '*Slainte.* Here's to the little lamb who bearded the Lyon in her den.' He sat down beside them. 'I've been having awfully impure thoughts about you, Lavery. You're looking particularly luscious these days. Who's the lucky man?'

'Impure thoughts. How nice! Call me later, why don't you, and relay them to me down the phone. That might be a way to get them off your chest. You could try an Italian accent.'

‘My French one’s better.’

‘OK. That’ll do. Now pay attention to Deirdre, darling. She met a particularly riveting young man this morning.’

‘I suppose he was a looker, was he, Deirdre?’

‘Yes, Rory, he was, actually.’

‘How astonishing.’ Rory yawned.

‘Dark or fair?’ asked Eva.

‘Very dark, with the most amazing sexy eyes.’

‘Mm. Sounds like my type,’ said Eva, smiling at David Lawless, who had just come into the pub with Nick McCarthy.

‘You really enjoy being a girl, don’t you, Lavery?’ asked Rory, looking at her with interested, sleepy eyes.

‘To the hilt, darling,’ she said happily. ‘I simply adore men. I suspect I’d have made a terrific courtesan.’

‘Anyway,’ said Deirdre, annoyed with Rory for interrupting. ‘His name’s Sebastian Hardy. He was in that BBC series earlier this year – did you see it? *Hurting People.* He was the drug addict in it – he was brilliant. And he’s really much more gorgeous-looking in the flesh.’

‘The flesh?’ Rory’s smile was provocative. ‘That’s a rather carnal expression for you, Deirdre. Did you manage to get *at* any of this dude’s flesh?’

‘Oh shut up, Rory. You’re beginning to sound like Finbar de Rossa.’

‘Never. *He’s* lecherous. I’m just plain horny.’

‘Anyway,’ Deirdre continued, ignoring Rory and turning to Eva who was at least looking interested.

'He was really nice – not big-headed at all. He bought me a cup of coffee and a chicken sandwich after–'

'Generous, too,' murmured Rory laconically. He was really starting to get on her nerves.

'Have you got a problem, Rory?' she said, spiking. 'I think you're just jealous.'

'Yes. I am jealous. With your usual uncanny perspicacity you have guessed right, sweetheart. It has been the height of my burning ambition for some time now to buy a chicken sandwich for Deirdre O'Dare. Please let me do it some time, Deirdre. Let me die a happy man.'

Eva intervened. 'Sebastian Hardy? I think I know him. I mean, I've never met him, but I'm sure I saw him in a production of *Streetcar* at the Royal Exchange. It must have been a year or so ago – I was working for Granada at the time.'

'That's right!' said Deirdre excitedly. 'That would be him! He said he'd spent some time working in Manchester.'

Eva looked thoughtful. 'He was very good,' she said. 'I think someone said he'd been the gold medal winner at RADA. I wanted to be introduced, but somebody had cocked up a restaurant reservation and we didn't have time to go backstage. Yes.' The actress nodded to herself. 'You're right, Deirdre. He's an extraordinarily intense actor.'

'Dull in here tonight, isn't it?' said Rory. He yawned again and rose to his feet, stretching ostentatiously.

'Don't do that, Rory. You know it only makes me

want to undress you at once and have you for supper.'

'Let me tell you something, Eva.' He leant down so that he could talk into the actress's ear, but didn't bother to whisper. 'It won't surprise you to know that I'm a lot more satisfying than a chicken sandwich.'

Eva sent him an amused look. 'Oh look – there's Marian,' she said.

'Ah. Got to run, I'm afraid,' said Rory, straightening up. 'She's on the midnight flight to Brussels and I'm her chauffeur. A bientôt, Eva. Mon dieu! Que tu es ravissante! Je voudrais te déshabiller et–'

'Oh, Lord – do stop, Rory. You were absolutely right about that accent. I'm already on the verge of swooning.'

The two actors exchanged another smile before Rory sauntered over to where Marian was ignoring Finbar de Rossa who was trying to chat her up.

'He can be a real pain in the arse sometimes,' said Deirdre, cross with Rory for showing her up in front of her heroine.

'But he's gorgeous, Deirdre. That means he can get away with murder.'

* * *

Macbeth rehearsals started the next day. The company assembled for the first read-through and this time Deirdre was pleased to find that she didn't feel nervous at all. She thought back to the day of the first rehearsal of *A Midsummer Night's Dream* and how terrified she had been then. It seemed as if the Deirdre O'Dare who'd stumbled through the First Fairy speech was a completely different person to the Deirdre O'Dare who was chatting animatedly to Maeve Kirwan as they waited for Jenny Cummings to display her model box and costume designs. Maeve was cast as Lady Macduff, Rory was Macduff, Adrian Pierce was Malcolm and Jonathan Hughes, Banquo. Sophie and Jessica were playing the other two witches and Finbar de Rossa was, of course, playing Macbeth. Eva was his Lady.

Nick McCarthy and David had devised and printed out a rehearsal schedule which Jessica was now handing round the cast. The constraints of overtime meant that the schedule was a lot tighter than that of *Dream*. Because the actors were now working evenings, most of the cast was called for either morning or afternoon sessions only. Three sessions a day would cripple the company financially, as well as being exhausting for them. Deirdre noticed that she had all day Friday and Saturday off as well as most afternoons this week. She'd ring Sally and let her know so that the agent could arrange an appointment for her with RTE.

After the read-through David Lawless asked them all to take an early lunch break. Maeve and Deirdre took sandwiches to the park. There was a lot of bare flesh on display – some of it rather unattractive. Deirdre undid as many buttons on her crop-top as decency allowed, and hiked her skirt up so that the sun could get at her legs.

Across the way Rory was lying on the grass

talking to Jonathan Hughes and chewing the stem of a daisy. His gaze had slid in Deirdre's direction and he was eyeing her legs with blatant enjoyment. Deirdre clocked the expression on his face. 'Bloody Rory – wouldn't you know it,' she said in indignation, pulling at the hem of her skirt. His brigand's eyes met hers and he laughed at her. 'He seems to really enjoy riling me, Maeve. When I first met him I thought he was OK, but his latest hobby seems to be Deirdre O'Dare baiting. He spends all his time sending me up rotten. He's a savage.'

'Your first impression was right, you know, Deirdre – he *is* nice. I've known him for years – we both started in the business at the same time on a film about highwaymen. God – what was it called? It was so awful that I've forgotten. Oh, yes – *Horse Power.* Can you believe that title?' Maeve turned over on to her stomach so that the backs of her legs could get some sun. 'But he *is* incorrigible. Finbar's furious with him, you know. Rory went off with that Asian girl he'd been working so hard at getting into bed last week.'

'What? He took her home?'

'No – *she* took *him* home. I think even Rory would draw the line at suggesting a *ménage à trois* to Marian.'

'How do you know all this, Maeve?'

'Unfortunately, while Rory is the soul of discretion he's also quite well known. A friend of mine spotted him coming out of the girl's flat in the small hours of the following morning. She lives in the same apartment block.'

Rory had got up and was getting into the T-shirt he'd discarded so that he could work on his tan. He strolled past them. 'Farewell, comrades,' he said. 'I'm off to shoot some pool.'

'Have you the afternoon off, Rory?' asked Maeve. 'I have too. Maybe I'll join you.'

'Be my guest. What a shame you're called back for rehearsal, Deirdre. You could have spent the afternoon showing off your lissom legs in the park.'

'Marian's an intelligent woman isn't she Rory?' said Deirdre, getting up and brushing the grass from her clothes.

'Correction, Deirdre. She's an *extremely* intelligent woman.'

'Then what on earth makes her stay with someone like you?'

'For the fucking astonishing sex, of course, airhead.'

* * *

Early on Friday Deirdre had her camera test out in RTE. She had found out as much as she could about her screen character from Sally Ruane, and Sally had faxed her a few pages of script so that she could learn her dialogue. It was the first time anyone had sent her a fax on Sarah's uncle's machine, and it made her feel nicely grown-up to be able to fax Sally back a thank you note.

Because the newcomer to *Ardmore Grove* was meant to be provocative, Deirdre decided she ought to dress for the part. She didn't want to look tarty – that wouldn't be right for the character, who seemed to be quite a classy piece of work – but it would do no harm to project a little sex appeal. The Marc O'Neill frock she'd bought to impress David Lawless on the opening night of *Dream* would be perfect. She gave a shudder at the memory of her pathetic attempt at seducing him. It still had the power to make her cringe.

* * *

The camera test went smoothly enough, although she'd come off her heel at one point and dried stone dead. But the director went for another take to give her a chance to get it right, and second time round was an improvement. She'd had a good rapport with the actor working opposite her, and she'd been careful to be polite, enthusiastic and attentive. At least this time Sally Ruane wouldn't have any complaints to make about her professional attitude.

When they finished, Deirdre apologized again for blowing the first take. 'Not to worry,' said the director amiably. 'You did fine. Thanks for your time. We'll be on to your agent when we know anything. It may take a while,' he warned her, 'so don't hold your breath. And remember. If you're not successful this time it's got absolutely nothing to do with your ability. Your talent isn't in dispute here. It simply means you didn't match up physically.'

Deirdre wondered who she was meant to match. Maybe the character was somehow related to Ann

Fitzroy? If that was the case, she knew she didn't stand a chance. They were chalk and cheese.

Still, she'd done a good test. She was feeling quietly confident until she snuck a look at the list of names on the call-sheet on her way out of the studio. There were at least another dozen actresses to be tested, and directly under her name on the list was printed '10.30 – SUKI HAYES.'

Deirdre was no longer quietly confident. She spent the entire journey back into town feeling despondent and wondering if she was in the wrong business. She couldn't cope with the way her hopes seemed to be raised one week and dashed the next. In spite of everything Sally had said to her that day in her office she still secretly harboured dreams of fame and fortune.

At Stephen's Green she got off the bus and thought for the first time about how she would spend the rest of her day. She badly wanted to talk to someone and she could do with a cup of coffee. Who lived nearby that she could drop into unannounced? She could go down to Trinity and meet up with her friends from third year, but they wouldn't be free until lunchtime. Eva was only ten minutes walk away but Deirdre felt shy at the thought of ringing the actress's bell. What if she had one of her lovers with her?

What about Rory? He lived just round the corner from Eva; she had pointed his house out to Deirdre the afternoon they'd driven home from rehearsal together. If she dropped in on him she could get that book from him at last. He'd mentioned that someone had given him a copy of *Playing Shakespeare* by John Barton, and it was a book she was dying to read. Rory had said he'd let her have his copy because he had no intention of ever reading it himself. But every night when they met in the green room and she asked him about it he told her he'd forgotten it again.

That's what she'd do. She'd pick up the book and spend the afternoon on the roof of her apartment building reading. Deirdre O'Dare set off in the direction of Rory and Marian's house as purposefully as her high heels would allow her.

Chapter Eleven

She rang Rory's doorbell and waited for quite a long time. Perhaps she'd got the wrong house? She debated whether or not to ring again, and decided against it. If he *was* in it would be uncool to have to ring twice – it would only make her look as if she were dead keen to see him, and she wasn't really. Maybe she should walk past Eva's house and see if her car was outside. If it was she might just pluck up the courage to drop in on her.

She was just starting to trail down the street when she heard a door behind her open. She turned round. Rory was leaning against the door jamb watching her. His dark blond hair was pulled back in a loose ponytail and he was wearing a big towelling bath robe. He was rather rumpled-looking, and wore his usual louche air. 'Well, dainty duck – if it isn't Deirdre O'Dare,' he said. 'How's it going, Deirdre?'

'Oh, hi Rory.' She immediately felt uncomfortable in her little black dress and wished she hadn't called. She'd obviously got him out of bed. 'I'm sorry to disturb you. I was in the neighbourhood and I thought I might as well drop by and pick up that book you promised me.'

'Well, come in, sweetheart, and stop skulking

about on the pavement outside my house looking like the Wicked Witch of the West. I don't want the neighbours clocking you and reporting back to Marian that I was entertaining young ladies while she was away in Brussels.' Still leaning against the door jamb, Rory beckoned with a finger and gestured for her to enter.

Deirdre hesitated and then moved towards the door. She didn't really want to go in, but it would look a bit strange now if she didn't. As she slid through the door, being very careful not to brush against him, she noticed that he smelled of soap.

The hallway of Rory and Marian's house was painted white and was lined with bookshelves. Deirdre saw that there were lots of well-thumbed travel books amongst some rather serious-looking political stuff.

'This way.' Rory passed by her and headed down the hall to the kitchen. It was an airy room filled with light from big windows and a skylight, and it bore a look of rather Spartan efficiency. There were two big white porcelain sinks and the walls were lined with white units behind which all the appliances had to be concealed, because there was no sign of them anywhere else.

The minimalist style of the room was compromised, however, by the pile of washing-up left undone in the sink, a chrome bin overflowing with empty food cartons and several empty wine bottles on the floor by the back door. Last Sunday's newspapers were strewn on top of the kitchen table along with an empty bottle of Saint Emilion, two elegant wine glasses with lees in them, cigarette papers, an intricately carved sandalwood box, a couple of travel books on Peru and an unplunged cafetière.

'You arrived bang on time for coffee. What a prescient little witch you are.' Rory produced two white mugs from a cupboard and then looked her up and down with an appreciative expression. 'Well, well, Deirdre O'Dare. You're looking *remarkably* wicked today. Sit down.'

The sound of loud barking came from just outside the back door. Rory crossed the room and opened it. 'Bugger off, Bastard,' he said.

Deirdre came over and joined him, looking round his shoulder at a mongrel which was standing there with an expectant look on its intelligent face. She could see that there was border collie in there somewhere. It made her feel suddenly full of nostalgia for her own dog at home. She hadn't seen Miró for ages. 'Don't be so horrible, Rory,' she scolded. 'How can you call such a beautiful dog a bastard?'

Rory looked at her with amusement. 'That's his name, witch. He found me when I was playing the Bastard in *King Lear*, so that particular moniker seemed appropriate at the time. Anyway, he's in the doghouse, is Bastard. He made off with one of Marian's new shoes last night. Look what he did.' He retrieved a mangled mule from the bin and held it out to her. She could just make out the Manolo Blahnik label on the inside of what looked like one of those chewy dried-beef toys she gave Miró at Christmas.

'You're not allowed in for at least another hour, mate,' he added, shutting the door firmly in the dog's face. 'Sit down, Deirdre,' he said again.

She sat down stiffly on one of the kitchen chairs, pushing aside the carved box so that she could rest her elbows on the tabletop.

Rory resumed his scrutiny of her appearance. 'Lipstick too, I see?' He deposited the mugs on the table and depressed the plunger on the cafetière. 'What lucky man has you looking so good so early in the day, Deirdre O'Dare? I'm almost afraid that you might have come here to seduce me, knowing that my doxy's away. Or have you got a hot date with Lawless later?'

She gave him a withering look. 'Don't be ridiculous, Rory. I had an interview out in RTE first thing this morning. And I wouldn't call *this* early in the day. It's after eleven o'clock, you know, and you're hardly even out of bed.'

'Oh, so you're still Ms Goody Two Shoes, not a wicked witch after all,' said Rory sadly. 'How disappointing. I was beginning to think I might be in luck. And for your information I have been up for some time.' He poured coffee into the mugs, sat down in a chair opposite her and lifted a hand to release his hair from the band that held it in its ponytail. As he shook his hair free Deirdre could smell the soapy smell again. 'It may even surprise you to know that I've actually been very busy this morning. How did the interview go?' he asked, leaning back and looking directly at her with lazy, interested eyes.

Deirdre realized with a sense of discomfort that *her* eyes had wandered to a gap at the neckline of Rory's robe which had left an area of his chest exposed. She looked away immediately and picked up her mug of coffee. 'Oh, OK. I thought I'd done quite well and then I saw Suki Hayes's name on the call-sheet and realized that I'd probably wasted my time. She was going in to see them just after me.'

'I wouldn't be too worried about Suki. Not everybody succumbs to her charms, you know. I certainly didn't.'

For some reason Deirdre was surprised by this information. 'Didn't you, Rory? I was under the impression that most of the male members of Equity would jump at the chance of – um – shagging Suki Hayes.' Oh God. Should she have said 'going to bed with' or 'making love to' or 'having sex with' or 'screwing' or 'fucking' or 'riding'? She was way out of her depth.

Rory laughed. 'You've a quaint turn of phrase, Deirdre. As it happens, I'm not a total debauchee. Nor am I officially a member of Equity – I haven't paid my sub this year. And I only sleep with women I find amusing.'

'Yeah? You seem to find *most* women amusing though, don't you, Rory?' His lopsided smile was beginning to disturb her.

Just then the phone on the wall behind her shrilled, and she jumped. 'Oh – I'd better go.'

'Stay where you are. I still have to locate that book you've been nagging me about so boringly for the past week, remember?' As he got to his feet to answer the phone Deirdre noticed that his robe had slipped open even wider. She found herself speculating whether or not he was wearing anything underneath. She somehow suspected that he wasn't.

'Yeah?' Rory picked up the phone. He had to insinuate himself around the back of her chair to get at it and she found herself flinching as his thigh brushed her shoulder. She tried surreptitiously to edge her chair forward a little and gave up when she only succeeded in making a squeaking noise against the tiled floor.

Rory leaned against the wall. 'Jake. What's the story? No – we ended up going for the music option. They were pretty cool, yeah. There's a good buzz there.'

Deirdre was feeling distinctly awkward. Her feet were killing her and she was uncomfortably aware of Rory's physical presence behind her. She furtively slid her feet out of her sandals and stretched them out under the table, wriggling her toes with relief.

'*Very* late. Yeah, good time.' There was something feral about his laugh. 'No comment. Oh, yeah – thanks, Jake – just let me write that down.'

Rory leant over her, stretching for a pen on the other side of the table. His rough towelling sleeve was grazing her cheek, and she could see the hard lines of the muscles on his stomach where the robe gaped open. Her cheeks were suddenly hot and she was extremely conscious of her breathing. He scrawled a phone number in the margin of one of the newspapers and, instead of standing back up when he had finished, he leant his right elbow on the table. Deirdre tensed. He had draped his left hand on her shoulder and his fingers were toying abstractedly with a strand of her hair. The contact seared her nerve-endings and she was appalled to realize that she had experienced such a sensation only once before. It had been when David Lawless had touched her bare shoulder on the evening of the dress rehearsal.

All the time Rory continued his conversation on the telephone. 'No, tomorrow night's out – Marian's due back from Brussels some time in the evening. I know.' Another laugh. His fingers were resting against the skin of her neck now, and Deirdre resisted an absurd impulse to rub her cheekbone against his sleeve like a cat. She was feeling as if something was slowly unfurling inside her.

Rory moved to stand up, and as he did so he let his right hand brush casually against hers where it lay on the table. Deirdre found herself turning her wrist so that her palm was exposed, and she watched as Rory's middle finger traced its curve and then continued to meander up her wrist and along the inside of her forearm, lingering on the inner crook of her elbow. He straightened up slowly, letting his hand trail against the side of her right breast. She felt her nipples harden, and suddenly she wanted him to touch her all over.

'Next week, some time. Yeah.' Deirdre barely registered what Rory was saying into the phone. 'I thought it was *you* she liked. Well, my mistake, man. You know me – I don't dish dirt. Nah – she was cool about that. A couple more months. Peru. Yeah.' A pause, then the laugh again. Deirdre was feeling sticky. Rory's right hand was undoing the buttons on the front of her dress very, very slowly. She would have to make him stop. She would in a minute. He slid his hand inside the front of her frock and ran it lightly over her bare breast, flicking a finger against her nipple.

She could hear her own intake of breath. She remembered that something like this had happened to her some time ago, but that had been in a dream. Then she was arching her shoulders, blatantly encouraging Rory to cup her breast in his hand and feeling vaguely surprised by her shamelessness. The pressure from his hand increased to comply with her mounting libido, and when he took her nipple between his thumb and forefinger and rubbed it gently her breathing grew too ragged to control. She was even finding it difficult to suppress a moan.

'Sorry, Jake – I've got to go,' she heard him say. 'I've just realized that I've something rather urgent to attend to.'

He hung up the phone and then let the receiver hang off the hook. Now he had both hands free, and he used them. Deirdre responded by reaching up and pulling his head down to hers. This was unlike any stage kiss they had ever exchanged – they allowed each other to use their tongues with abandon now. She had never dreamt that kisses could be like this. She felt that she was being kissed for the first time and in fact she may as well have been, because it was the first time she had ever been kissed by an expert.

Rory slid to his knees beside her and then pulled her on to the floor on top of him, rucking her dress up above her hips. His fingers performed as expertly as his mouth. His robe had dropped open and Deirdre's earlier suspicion that he was naked was confirmed. She ran her hands under the rough towelling and down his smooth back. It felt as if she were rubbing some sleek beast. Then she clung to him with arms and legs too as he rolled her over on to her back.

Rory knelt up and she felt helpless with desire. Reaching into the pocket of the robe which now hung loosely around him, he produced a condom and pulled open the sachet. Until now, Deirdre had never believed that putting on a condom could look sexy. He pulled her up into a sitting position and adeptly removed her dress before shrugging the robe from his shoulders and laying her back down on the floor. The tiles were cool and hard against her back as she shucked off her pants and raised her hips to him, inviting his tongue into her mouth again as he entered her.

She felt that she had never known anything so sweet as the sensation of Rory inside her. She wanted him never to stop. His voice was in her ear now, low and rough, and the sensation of it only increased her pleasure. 'Dear God – you're glorious in there, sweetheart. Like a ripe fig. You are quite,

quite succulent.' He was right – she *did* feel succulent inside. *He* had made her feel succulent. He glided a hand from where he supported the small of her back round to her belly and down, and Deirdre cried out as his practised fingers found her clitoris in the most exciting way. She was feeling even more syrupy inside as his other hand sought to spreadeagle her further. She stretched her limbs as widely as she could to accommodate him, opening like a flower, and then she wrapped herself round him tightly as she felt a core of pressure rising inside her. Every muscle in her body was suddenly bowstring tight with tension – she could even feel it in her toes. Her release was cataclysmic. Deirdre O'Dare was having the first orgasm of her life.

When she was spent, Rory allowed himself to follow suit and she watched in awe as he worked to a crescendo, looking down at her with an intense expression in his slanty eyes and a half smile curving his mouth. There was something pagan about his climax and Deirdre felt a kind of absurd ecstasy that she had been able to give it to him.

They lay side by side for quite a long time afterwards. Rory was the first to speak. 'Well, well. Welcome. The real Deirdre O'Dare has finally arrived. Thank *you* ma'am,' he said, raising himself on one elbow and studying her with amusement in his jade-green eyes. 'That was something of a revelation. I've heard about the wolf in sheep's clothing, but this is ridiculous. Who'd have thought that little lambkin was really a ravening wolverine under that prim exterior?'

Deirdre felt self-conscious suddenly. She reached out for Rory's discarded robe to cover herself, but he saw her intention at once, and took it from her. 'Nothing doing, sweetheart,' he said, chucking it across the room. 'Now I have you naked in the flesh instead of in my mind's eye I want to look at you.' He spread her legs again and she felt the last vestiges of shame drift away as he breathed out in manifest admiration. 'Wow – you're *so* kissable there.' He leaned down to turn words into action and she blossomed at the touch of his mouth. 'Beautiful. Like a Georgia O'Keefe painting.' Deirdre smiled at him as he straightened, and he smiled back, looking down at her. 'Look how svelte you are,' he said, tracing the geography of her body with a lazy hand and running his fingers lightly over her flank again and again until the muscles underneath shuddered involuntarily. She felt the stirrings of renewed arousal.

'Stop it, Rory,' she said, regretting the words the minute they were out of her mouth.

'Why? Jesus, you're symmetrical, Deirdre.'

Then she took his hand and guided it to where she wanted him to touch her again, no longer bothered by her own wantonness.

'Oh God – your hands are so – you're making me – oh!' She could not refrain from arching her back and reaching out for him where he knelt between her legs. He evaded her, sitting back slowly and unleashing a lethal smile. She rose into a kneeling position and took his face between her hands, kissing him languorously and stroking the back of his neck. 'Shit, Rory McDonagh. How did you get to have such a sure touch? Your hands seem to have a kind of – of *intuition.* D'you know what I mean?'

Rory laughed. 'Intuition is probably bang on. You need gentle hands to be a horseman. I was a wrangler before I became an actor.'

'Oh?'

'It's how I got into the business. I was handling horses on some totally crappy film – God, it was so bad I can't even remember its name.'

'*Horse Power*?' said Deirdre, rubbing her face against his collarbone and breathing in his clean, soapy smell.

'Yeah – that's right.' He sounded surprised. 'How did you know that?'

'Maeve told me,' she said, feeling a bit silly. She hoped he wouldn't think she'd been probing Maeve for information about him. Closing her eyes, she lay her head on his shoulder and slid her legs around his waist. Rory ran a hand down her right leg and stroked her instep. Her foot arched automatically.

'Wow, Deirdre,' he said. 'You even have sexy feet.'

'They're too big. Eva Lavery has sexy feet.' She smiled and wound her legs tighter around him.

'Anyway,' continued Rory, turning his attention to the concave area just below her ankle. 'They needed actors who could ride. And since all actors tell lies about their riding abilities they ended up with most of the cast shambling around on horseback incapable of hitting their marks. That's when they roped me in.' His lips brushed her collarbone. 'Jesus! That was some cowboy outfit.'

'Who directed it?'

'An amateur with lots of money and no talent. He was crazy about horses, and thought he was making the definitive equestrian movie. He called all the shots. Producer, director, screenwriter, dickhead.' Rory curled the tip of his tongue behind her right earlobe and trailed it slowly down the side of her throat, making her crane to the left. The syrupy feeling started its slow surge inside her again and she could not suppress the low moan that escaped her. 'That little fireworks display', he said into her neck, 'was just for starters.' His horseman's hand trailed the length of her spine, producing a domino effect in Deirdre's reflex muscles. 'I think I'll have you again, but this time not on the kitchen floor.'

He gathered her in his arms and stood up. 'Perhaps we should continue your education upstairs, O'Dare. I'd like to see you stretched out on a white sheet.' He climbed the stairs with Deirdre clinging to him, tensing her tummy muscles in an attempt to make herself look more sylph-like. The bedroom was white all over too, with white muslin curtains at the window and plain white linen on the bed.

'The sheets are pristine, in case you're wondering. I had to change them this morning after an accident with a mug of coffee. Marian will go ballistic if it's left a stain – they're her favourite Egyptian cotton. I don't suppose you're any good at ironing are you, Deirdre?'

He stopped her mouth with a kiss before she

could come out with an indignant response, and she melted all over again. Rory laid her on the bed and did everything he'd done to her on the kitchen floor and much, much more – only this time he took things much, much slower. And their lovemaking lasted much, much longer. As a finale, he took her to the stratosphere.

They lay back exhausted. Deirdre's hair was stuck to her face with sweat and she felt completely gorged with sex.

'Wow,' said Rory eventually. 'I think I may have accidently located your G-spot, Deirdre. Ironic, that. I've been searching for Marian's without success for years.'

Deirdre was in a complete daze, looking at Rory with a kind of awed bewilderment. She still wasn't quite sure what had hit her. Suddenly her face crumpled like a paper bag and she clung to him, curling herself into a ball. Great gloopy tears were sploshing on to his chest. Rory put an arm around her shoulders and pushed the hair back from her face.

'There, there, sweetheart,' he said gently. 'It's all right.' He let her weep on for a while, all the time stroking her hair and murmuring reassurance, the way a parent would to a small child. When her sobs had finally subsided he wiped away her tears with a corner of the sheet.

'A little post-coital tristesse is perfectly normal, you know. Though I imagine in the sort of books *you* read, Deirdre O'Dare, the afterglow is rosy – am I right? No tinge of blues there.' Slowly, she managed to return his smile. She was feeling extremely dopey and kitten-weak.

Rory got up from the bed and went to the wardrobe. He came back with a big white T-shirt. 'Here. Put this on and I'll go and get us some water. We could do with some re-hydration.'

But Deirdre's limbs had gone completely slack, and she was unable to get the T-shirt over her head. At her second futile attempt she simply gave up and keeled over on to the mattress.

'All fingers and thumbs?' said Rory, amused. He helped her up and dressed her himself as though she were a rag doll. Then he deposited her back on the mattress, stroking her face in an oddly tender gesture before disappearing downstairs.

It was a while before he returned. He was wearing his towelling robe and had a big bottle of water in one hand and a roll-up in the other.

'I didn't know you smoked, Rory,' said Deirdre as he sat down on the bed beside her and lit up.

'I don't. Only hash. Hash and sex make great bed-fellows.'

Deirdre remembered the cigarette papers and the carved box she'd seen on the kitchen table. And the two wine glasses. He'd taken coffee back to bed this morning, he'd said, and there were two mugs on the bedside table. And Marian was in Brussels. Deirdre methodically fitted the pieces of the puzzle together, and she didn't much like what she came up with. Part of her felt absurdly disappointed – piqued, even. But she wasn't going to say anything. She supposed Rory could do as he wanted without censure from her. She wished she could rid herself of the aggravating thoughts. She took a long swig from the bottle of water and averted her face so that he couldn't see her expression.

'Want some?' he questioned, offering her the joint.

She shook her head. 'It'd mess me up for the show.'

He leaned back against the pillows and looked at her sleepily. 'Come here,' he said, holding out his right arm so that she could tuck herself into its crook. She did as he suggested, laying her head against his chest and stretching herself against him, luxuriating in the feel of his flank against her belly. She was incredibly weary now, and very confused and she could hardly remember how the whole thing had started. Her brain was beginning to shut down and her eyes felt as if someone had rubbed sand into them. She yawned and cuddled herself up tighter in the curve of Rory's arm, and then she slid slowly into sleep.

* * *

Some time later Deirdre awoke. There were white sheets tumbled tempestuously all over the place, and sunlight was filtering through filmy white curtains. Her hair was spread out all over the pillow and she felt satiated with sex. Their limbs were intertwined. She had a peculiar sense of *déjà vu*. Where had this scenario originated? Then she remembered. It was one of her favourite David Lawless fantasies. Except it wasn't David Lawless lying next to her in the bed. It was Rory McDonagh. She'd fantasized once about tracing the outline of David's tattoo with a finger. Instead it had been Rory's tattoo she'd run her nails across – the one between his shoulder blades. A tattoo of a yellow rose with a snake coiled around its stem. One of her lines from the play came unbidden into her head: *Methought a serpent eat my heart away.*

She lay there and tried to make sense of the morning's chain of events – although it wasn't morning any more, she could tell by the clock on the bedside table next to her. It was now nearly three o'clock in the afternoon. How could she have let Rory seduce her like that? It was an appalling deviation in her scheme of things – that much was clear. What was unclear was exactly what course of action she should take now.

Inch by inch she edged herself out from underneath Rory's left arm which he'd slung across her, effectively pinioning her to the bed, and sat up, careful not to make any sudden movements that might disturb him. Maybe she should just sneak downstairs, get dressed and leave the house without saying anything, the way people did in films. Except she'd have to face him again this evening, and – she could barely bring herself to think of it – she'd have to kiss him on stage in front of an auditorium full of people! How on earth was she going to handle that? After the frenzied way she'd kissed him earlier she wasn't sure that she could even look him in the face, never mind kiss him on the lips.

She looked down at him where he lay and her eyes gravitated towards his mouth. Its usual slightly ironic cast had relaxed and it seemed even more sensual in repose – indeed all his features had taken on a softer aspect. Something started to furl or unfurl somewhere inside her, and she wasn't certain whether it was apprehension or desire. Whichever it was, she had to deny it. She stood up and made towards the door.

'Where are you going?'

She turned round to meet Rory's green eyes.

'Oh – hi.' Deirdre was suddenly unnerved. 'I thought you were asleep. I didn't want to wake you.'

'I haven't been sleeping. Just lying here with my eyes closed thinking of all the unspeakable things I'd like to do to you.' He stretched himself like a big cat and yawned. 'Don't tell me you were going to disappear without saying good-bye? I am shocked, Deirdre. I'd always considered you to be such a well brought up girl.'

'No, I wasn't leaving – I was just going to use the bathroom,' she lied. She had no idea what sort of etiquette was demanded of the situation she found herself in.

'Why don't you run a bath while you're in there? We could both use a soak.'

'Together?'

'Well, unless you'd prefer a cold shower. Come to think of it, that might be more advisable.'

Deirdre dithered in the doorway. She actually

found the idea of sharing a bath with Rory rather appealing. He was lying back against a heap of pillows with his arms folded behind his head looking at her with very narrow eyes.

'Well. That was a very nice way to spend a morning, Deirdre O'Dare,' he drawled. 'What a good idea of yours to seduce me like that.'

She bridled. 'I did *not* seduce you, Rory!' she said with some vehemence. '*You* seduced *me*! You were the one who started feeling me up!'

'Excuse me, you little Jezebel. *You* were the one who called on me wearing lipstick and a demon dress, and you were the one who instigated courtship behaviour by displaying your erogenous zones so flagrantly.'

'What erogenous zones?' Deirdre queried indignantly. 'I did nothing of the sort.'

'The little telltale proffering of a palm to be stroked? Your body language isn't the most subtle thing about you, Deirdre.'

'I didn't *ask* you to do it.'

'No – you're right,' he conceded. 'You *commanded* me to do it. You were positively quivering with lust. I have an unerring instinct for these things.'

Deirdre wanted to retaliate, but she knew that she was playing a losing game. 'Oh, shut up, Rory,' was her final quip before she flounced off to find the bathroom.

When she had finished she went down to the kitchen. Rory had got there before her and was cracking eggs into a bowl.

'Hungry, lambkin? I'm ravenous. All that activity

has given me one hell of an appetite. I decided the bath can wait, so if you started to run it, nip back up and turn the taps off, will you?'

'I didn't run it, actually,' said Deirdre with some *hauteur*, feeling smug that she had resisted the temptation to do so. Then she looked over to where he stood with his robe hanging loosely around him and suddenly had second thoughts. 'Yet,' she added as a precaution.

'Make some coffee, will you? The kettle's over there – the beans are in the fridge behind that cupboard door on your right. You'll have to rinse out the cafetière.'

Deirdre found herself doing as he asked. She padded across the kitchen in her bare feet and filled the kettle. Performing the mundane tasks seemed to diffuse the awkwardness of the situation and she was starting to feel more relaxed.

'I'm starving too, Rory. I'm glad you thought about food.' She slooshed the old coffee grains down the sink and turned to look at him. He was leaning against the kitchen table beating the eggs with a whisk. 'I'd never have thought that you could cook, though.'

'I can't. The only culinary task of which I'm capable is scrambling eggs. But I do them perfectly. I was taught by an expert.'

'Oh? Who?'

'An ex-girlfriend of mine was a cordon bleu chef.'

Deirdre wished she hadn't asked. She opened the fridge door and found the coffee beans.

'Root around and see if there's any cream. There

should be some smoked salmon, too.' Rory threw butter into a pan. 'And you could slice some bread for toast.'

Deirdre ground the beans in an electric grinder and cut thick slices of brown bread. Soon the smell of cooking eggs and smoked salmon filled the kitchen, and Deirdre thought that she'd never felt so hungry in her life. She also wished that Rory had told her that he was a demon at scrambling eggs before now. If she'd known that a week or so ago she could have off-loaded her free-range ones on to him and she might have avoided that embarrassing encounter with David Lawless in Eva's dressing-room altogether.

After they'd eaten they remained sitting at the kitchen table, talking. Deirdre was curious about Rory's career as a wrangler and she barraged him with questions about that and about his childhood in Galway. He had family in Mayo, too, she discovered, and he used to holiday in a place on Clew Bay called Carrowcross which wasn't far from where her granny lived, and where Deirdre had often gone swimming as a child. She found it amazing that she and Rory could easily have bumped into each other on summer holidays years ago when they'd visited the same remote beach. He told her about how he'd been bitten by the acting bug when he'd got the part in the awful highwayman movie by default, and about how his career had taken an upward turn since the first time he'd been cast in a show by David Lawless five years previously.

In turn she confided in him all her ambitions and

aspirations, told him how excited and scared she was at the prospect of playing Ophelia, and how it was her most cherished dream to one day be an actress of the calibre of Eva Lavery.

'Don't dream it. Be it,' he responded, draining his mug of coffee.

'That's Shakespeare, isn't it? *The Tempest.*'

Rory laughed.

'*A Winter's Tale*, then?'

'Nope, sweetheart, you're way off the mark. It's *The Rocky Horror Show.*'

They talked again and then they talked some more, and suddenly Deirdre realized that it was nearly five o'clock. She didn't want to go into work in her interview frock – she'd have to go home and change first, and she liked to be in the theatre no later than half past six. If she was going to be on time she'd have to make a move.

Instead she went upstairs and ran a bath.

* * *

Rory and Deirdre arrived at the theatre at twenty-three minutes past seven, only just making their half-hour call. Maeve gave her a curious look when she tore into the dressing-room undoing the buttons on her dress as she went.

'Hi, Deirdre. What happened? It's not like you to be so late.'

'Oh – I just got tied up, that's all.' Deirdre sent Maeve a radiant smile, slid into her dressing-gown and proceeded to quickly scribble make-up on to her face.

Maeve raised an eyebrow. 'What's with the sexy dress, O'Dare? Where are you going later? Or, come to that, pussy-cat pussy-cat, where have you *been* already today?'

'I had an interview out in RTE, remember?'

'*That* doesn't account for the Cheshire grin. You're the absolute personification of the cat who got the cream. How did the interview go?'

Deirdre shrugged. 'Hard to say. Suki Hayes was in after me.'

'Don't let that faze you. Not everyone falls for that trick.'

'That's what Rory said.'

'Rory!' Maeve shot her an eloquent look. '*Rory?*'

Deirdre bit her lip and averted her eyes, but not before she saw Maeve give a knowing smile.

When Act One beginners were called she danced down to the wings with her heart in her mouth. She felt that if she opened it her heart would fall out on to the floor and she'd either have to pick it up and stuff it back in again or put it on a plate and hand it to Rory McDonagh. After their bath that afternoon he had wrapped her in a big fluffy towel and dried every intimate inch of her, and as he rubbed the inside of her thigh dry, he had made a suggestion.

'You know that Marian's away tonight, Deirdre?'

Her reply was so faint that she had to repeat it. 'Yes? I mean, yes – yes I do.'

'How would you like to come back here with me after the show and share a bottle of wine?'

She'd remembered the empty bottle of Saint Emilion she'd seen in Rory's kitchen that morning and the pair of coffee mugs on the bedside table. She wouldn't give him the satisfaction of adding her name to the list of overnight guests he'd probably had since Marian had been away. He had stopped rubbing her with the towel and was rubbing her with gentle, insistent fingers instead. 'All right, Rory,' she'd said in a very small voice.

He was in the wings already, waiting for her along with Adrian Pierce. 'Hi, Deirdre,' he said when he saw her. 'How was your day?'

'Fine thanks,' she replied, trying to ignore Maeve's sudden repressed snort of laughter. 'How was yours?'

'Oh – I just spent most of it in bed.'

'You're a lazy bastard, McDonagh,' said Adrian, before heading towards the darkest corner of the wings where he did his pre-show preparation.

'On the contrary,' replied Rory, sliding Deirdre a very oblique look. 'By the way, sweetheart, your lipstick's a bit crooked-looking.' He reached out a hand and wiped the corner of her mouth with his thumb.

Once on stage, Deirdre found herself giving the most disciplined performance of her life. She knew she couldn't let her concentration slip for an instant, and when it came to the plotted embrace between Lysander and Hermia she found herself tensing unbearably. Rory's look was as guarded as hers.

When his mouth met hers the temptation to get lost in the kiss was almost irresistible, but she could feel the tension in his body language too, and it warned her to pull back. If anything, their stage kiss that night was more chaste than it had ever been.

At the interval most of the cast headed to the green room as usual for coffee. Deirdre ignored Rory with difficulty, and deliberately chose to sit at the opposite end of the room to him, between Maeve and Jessica Young. She tried hard to engage in the *Cosmopolitan* quiz they were sending up. Suddenly Jessica gave a little start.

'Oh – I nearly forgot,' she exclaimed, jumping to her feet. She called to Rory across the room. 'Rory? I've a message for you from Marian. She rang earlier from the airport in Brussels to say that she finished her assignment sooner than she thought, and she's flying back tonight. You're to pick her up from the airport straight after the show. I've got all the flight details written down – I'll get them for you now.'

Deirdre's eyes met Rory's and the blood drained from her face. His eyes narrowed and she saw him tense up. The signal he sent her was so subtle that nobody in the company could have discerned it, with the possible exception of Maeve, who was watching him closely. He shrugged his shoulders and spread his palms in an ambiguous gesture. The message he sent was clear to Deirdre. It read: 'C'est la vie, sweetheart.' She looked away at once, choking with emotion.

It meant that she failed to register the expression on Rory's face. It was one of defeated resignation, verging on despair. And there was something else there as well. There was genuine regret in his eyes.

Chapter Twelve

The next morning at rehearsal Deirdre didn't look at Rory. This wasn't difficult because they had no scenes together, but although she took great care not to come into contact with him, she was painfully aware of his presence. At the coffee break she was manoeuvring her way back to where she'd been sitting with Jessica and Kate, trying to carry three cups of coffee, when she narrowly avoided bumping into him. He put out a hand to steady her and she recoiled, sending coffee swilling over polystyrene rims on to his shoe. She managed a polite 'I beg your pardon,' without meeting his eye, and continued on her way.

The evening was even worse. There was none of the usual banter in the wings before the show went up. Instead the atmosphere was so stilted as to be almost formal. Maeve tried hard to pretend that everything was normal, but it was pretty obvious that things between Rory and Deirdre were strained. When Rory went to kiss her during the first scene, Deirdre's instinct was to back off, even though she knew it was a most unprofessional thing to do. She could feel Rory tighten his grip on her arm, and when he succeeded in planting a clumsy kiss on her mouth all she could think of was that she wanted to push him away.

She spent the interval in the dressing-room by herself instead of in the green room as she usually did, curled up on the chaise longue, hugging her wretchedness and asking herself time and again why she had handed herself on a plate to someone as notorious as Rory McDonagh. She must have been out of her mind to let him do the things he'd done to her yesterday. And she'd even been gullible enough to acquiesce to his suggestion that she come back for more that night!

She hadn't gone to the pub after the show the night before, even though she would have loved to confide in Maeve. She felt too ashamed to confess what a total idiot she'd made of herself. Instead she'd gone home and wept angry tears under the duvet. She hated Rory McDonagh for making her feel this way, and thanked God that at least she'd have no dealings with him in *Macbeth*. Having to feign intimacy with him every night for the rest of the run of *Dream* was going to tax her acting abilities to the utmost.

She heard footsteps on the stone stairs outside and tensed, thinking that it might be Rory coming to apologize for having taken advantage of her. She got to her feet with a hammering heart and pretended to busy herself with something at her dressing table. It was Maeve who came into the room.

'Are you OK, Deirdre?'

'Yeah, fine thanks, Maeve.' She forced a brightness she was far from feeling.

'I'm not going to pry, Deirdre. You don't have to tell me anything you don't want to. I just want to let you know that if you need to talk, I'd be glad to listen to you.'

Deirdre stopped her unconvincing show of preoccupation, but kept her back turned to Maeve, toying with the edge of the towel on the back of her chair.

'It's pretty obvious you've had a rough time of it today, Deirdre. I'm concerned for you, you know.'

Deirdre's brow furrowed and she bit her lip hard in a huge effort to stop herself from crying. It was no good. Suddenly her shoulders were shaking and she was sobbing great racking sobs. She felt Maeve's hand on her arm, and she turned to her friend, burying her face in her shoulder. 'Oh, Maeve – I don't know what to do – I've made such a Godawful fool of myself.'

'There, there – poor wee thing,' murmured Maeve, stroking Deirdre's hair. 'That's right – cry all you like. Let it all out, sweetheart.'

Deirdre stood wrapped in her friend's comforting embrace and cried and cried. By the time beginners for the second half had been called she had calmed down slightly, although her breath was still coming in shuddering gasps and her eyes were red and smarting. Maeve cleaned up the runnels of mascara which had smeared her face, and urged her to take deep breaths. 'Come on now, Deirdre – we've got to get the second half of the show on the road. Don't worry – you can do it. There's nothing like having to go on stage to force unwelcome thoughts to the back of your head. If you want to talk later just let me know, OK?'

Deirdre blew her nose, did a hasty repair job on her make-up and made her way to the wings, following Maeve as a lamb would its mother.

The next scene was difficult for her. It was the scene in which Lysander violently forswears Hermia, despite her continued protestations of love for him. To her horror, Deirdre found it impossible to stand back emotionally, and the tears which had been plotted came faster and more furious than they ever had before. When Rory tried to rid himself of her embrace on the line *I will shake thee from me like a serpent*, she was barely able to articulate her response: *Why are you grown so rude? What change is this sweet love?* She saw a look of intense concern cross Maeve's face.

Deirdre was uncertain how she managed to get through the rest of the show. By the time the curtain came down she felt emotionally battered, and for the first time ever took no pleasure in the usual enthusiastic response from the audience at the curtain call. She caught up with Maeve on her way back up to the dressing-room. 'Maeve? I think I'll have that drink that you offered to buy me last night, if that's all right with you.'

'Sure,' said Maeve. 'You deserve a large one after getting through all that shit tonight.'

They decided to avoid Meagher's and went instead to O'Riordan's, the rival establishment. It was quieter and more civilized there, and there was no risk of running into Rory or Marian. She told

Maeve everything that had happened the previous day.

'Oh, poor Deirdre,' said Maeve when she'd finished. 'It must have been really tough on you to be let down after what was obviously a sensational day. I can imagine that McDonagh's an extremely – proficient lover.' Maeve chose the word with care. 'Probably even considerate, which is even rarer. No wonder you're feeling so grim.'

'It's got nothing to do with the fact that I didn't get to spend the night with him, you know, Maeve. I understand perfectly that Rory and Marian are an item, and of course I wouldn't expect him to suddenly dump her just because of me.' Maeve was looking at her carefully. 'I wouldn't *want* him to do that, for heaven's sake,' she added quickly. 'It's just that I was so kind of, well – I was *uninhibited* with him. I've never behaved that way with anyone ever, Maeve. I feel so humiliated now at the thought of it! He must think I do that kind of thing all the time! What if he tells someone and word gets around?'

'You mustn't worry about that, Deirdre. I *know* Rory, remember? And I can tell you he's not into all that macho bragging stuff. He would have reassured you of that himself if you'd given him a chance. You've just been too busy avoiding him.' A dude in black leather walked past them, eyeing them both blatantly. Deirdre averted her gaze rather snootily and was surprised when Maeve gave him a long, interested look and returned his slow smile.

'Maeve? I didn't think you were interested in men,' said Deirdre curiously.

'I'm not interested in going to bed with them, but that doesn't mean I can't flirt with them. Flirting is one of the more enjoyable things in life, Deirdre, and it's free. I hope I'll still be flirting well into my eighties if I'm lucky enough to live that long.'

'Oh,' said Deirdre dubiously. 'I'm not sure I'd like to be eighty. Although I suppose people have more respect for you when you're older. Maybe I'll be dignified by then.'

'Dignity, schmignity,' retorted Maeve. 'Could you imagine if you'd tried to be dignified with Rory yesterday? You'd have missed out on all that fun. Dignity and ballistic sex make poor bedfellows, Deirdre. Literally. And you're not to feel ashamed about it. All right? Nobody should be ashamed to have a good time as long as no-one else gets hurt. Just take care of yourself health-wise and contraception-wise. *And* emotionally, Deirdre. I wouldn't like to see you getting hurt.' And Maeve looked at Deirdre in an uncomfortably meaningful way.

'Oh, there's absolutely no chance of *that*!' said Deirdre with ostentatious carelessness, jumping to her feet. 'I owe you a drink, Maeve.'

* * *

Deirdre spent Sunday out in Kilmacanogue with her mum and dad, mostly out of guilt because she hadn't seen them for so long, but also because she felt that she badly needed some mollycoddling. Her mother seemed to have an intuition that she was feeling especially vulnerable because she did all the right mumsy kind of things that Deirdre craved. She gave her all the easy jobs to do in the preparation of their lunch and then sent her off to the garden to play with the dog until the meal was ready.

Deirdre was delighted to see Miró because he gave her an excuse to behave like a child again. They played around the garden until they were both exhausted and then flopped on the grass, Deirdre laughing as he covered her face with big slobbery kisses.

It was another beautiful summer's day, but the intense heat of the last week was made more bearable by a delicious whispering breeze. As she lay on the grass following the progress of a trail of little clouds so puffy that they looked as if they should be coming out of the funnel of a cartoon train, she felt very glad that she had escaped to the country for the day instead of sitting in her city-centre flat full of self-loathing.

The three of them had a late, very lazy lunch outside with a bottle of cold Chablis and big bowls of strawberries to finish, and Deirdre fell asleep in the sun while reading the Sunday papers. Later on, her mother loaded her with organic produce again – Deirdre had asked her not to put in so many eggs this time – and dropped her to the DART station in Bray.

'Come and visit again soon,' Rosaleen told her. 'I know you're all grown-up now and you've a life of your own to lead, but to me you're still my little girl and I can't help being anxious about you. If you have any problems, you will let me know, won't you, Deirdre? You're not so worldly-wise that you don't need help from time to time.' And she hugged her daughter and drove off, leaving Deirdre wondering if her mother realized quite how astute she was.

The day spent in Kilmacanogue had done her a lot of good. She knew she had made a terrible mistake with Rory McDonagh, but if he didn't broadcast it, as Maeve had assured her he wouldn't, there wasn't too much harm done. Maeve had been quite right. The only way to look at it was as a once-off, and as a valuable lesson learned. She would simply behave as if nothing had happened between them, and expect him to do the same. She would treat him with distant politeness so that their working relationship wouldn't be affected, and she would be consummately professional in all her dealings with him, but she would try to avoid him socially without making it too obvious to the rest of the company.

There was the physical intimacy of their stage relationship to contend with, of course, but there were only three more weeks of *Dream* to go, and she'd just have to look on it as yet another of the many pitfalls of her chosen profession. She supposed that every actor in the world was at some stage in their career obliged to embrace someone they found repellent in real life. She would have no stage involvement with him at all in *Macbeth*, and while they would have to work quite closely together in *Hamlet* because they were cast as brother and sister, at least there'd be nothing sexual about their relationship.

She got back to her flat at about nine o'clock that Sunday evening to find the light on the answering machine blinking dully, indicating that there was just one message on it. She hit playback and then sat down on the floor with a thump as Rory's voice came over the speaker.

'Deirdre, hi. I'm calling from a public phone – for obvious reasons I didn't want to use the phone at home – but I think this one may be banjaxed. Shit – hang on – let me stick another coin in. I hope you're getting this message. I just wanted to say that I'm sorry I didn't get a chance to talk to you yesterday. I could tell you were upset and – *shit*–' He was interrupted by an urgent bleeping noise. 'I knew this fucking thing wasn't working properly. Look – I've no more coins, Deirdre, so maybe you'd–' There was a prolonged bleep and then the line went dead and the machine turned itself off.

Deirdre continued to sit on the floor, feeling icy cold despite the warm evening. 'I could tell you were upset.' How dare he! How *dare* he presume that she had *any* feelings whatsoever towards him or the whole sorry affair! Did he think she was some lovesick schoolgirl mooning around after him, hoping that Marian might leave her some crumbs? Did he expect her to come running after him in case he might be able to fit her in along with all his other *rides* the next time Marian was away on an assignment? She was glad she'd already worked out exactly how to handle the situation.

Rory McDonagh was going to find out that Deirdre O'Dare wasn't as naïve as he'd so obviously believed, that she was growing up fast, and that she could handle a one-night – or one-afternoon – stand without getting emotionally involved. She could be as blasé as the best of them. She would just have to make it perfectly clear that it wasn't going to happen again, and she'd let him know that as soon as she possibly could.

* * *

There was something businesslike about her as she walked into the rehearsal hall the next day with an air of resolution and her head held high. A kind of homing instinct told her immediately where Rory was sitting and she veered in the opposite direction. He was talking to Eva, and she could hear his predatory laugh. She busied herself with minutiae, retrieving her script and pencil from her backpack and pulling on her jazz pumps.

David Lawless was standing close by immersed in conversation with Nick McCarthy. She took the opportunity to cast covert admiring glances in his direction, wondering how she could ever have contaminated herself with Rory McDonagh when her whole being craved this prince among men. He was laughing at something Nick had said, shaking his head, and Deirdre thought she had never seen him look so attractive. There was a real aura of contentment about him these days. His demeanour was less guarded, he seemed more readily inclined to laugh, and the gleam in his eye was amused rather than watchful. He must have felt her watching, because suddenly he turned his head to where she was sitting on the floor tying her laces. He cocked his head to one side and beckoned to her to come to him, stretching out his arm as she trotted over obediently and laying it around her shoulders.

'Deirdre. How are you?'

She was mildly surprised to find his touch less disturbing than usual.

'I'm fine, thanks, David.'

'Are you?' His eyes searched her face. 'I think I need a word with you – and another party. McDonagh!' he called across the rehearsal room floor. 'Come here for a minute, please.' Deirdre blanched and she could feel her shoulders stiffen under David Lawless's arm.

Rory looked up and a slightly wary expression crept over his face. He took leave of Eva with a smile and came over to them, steering his way around clusters of chattering actors.

David drew the pair aside. 'What's going on between you two?'

Deirdre felt colour flood her face and said nothing. Rory maintained his look of circumspection and merely gave his director a quizzical look. 'I'm not with you, David.'

'I noticed on Friday for the first time that there was something different about the way you two were playing your scenes. It was very subtle – in fact it only seemed to affect your first scene together that particular night – but on Saturday there was something more seriously wrong. Your love scenes had lost all their spontaneity, and the scene where Lysander rejects Hermia was way over the top. You seemed to have absolutely no rein on it, Deirdre. What's happened?'

Deirdre said nothing and cast down her eyes. She knew she looked like a sullen child, but she felt quite incapable of dealing with the situation. There was an embarrassed silence.

'Well?' prompted David.

'My fault, I'm afraid,' said Rory. 'I gave Deirdre a bum steer. She asked me on Friday before the show how I thought our scenes were going and I told her that I thought the love scene was too passionate and the rejection scene not passionate enough. She was just doing what I suggested.'

Deirdre looked up at Rory astonished. Then she looked at David. She had never seen such controlled anger. His eyes had darkened and the line of his mouth was hard. One eyebrow was raised sardonically.

'I wasn't aware that you had directorial aspirations, Rory. Personally, I suspect that you should stick to acting. Please don't volunteer your advice to any of my actors ever again.' He turned glittering eyes on Deirdre. 'If you need help with your interpretation in future, Ms O'Dare, I suggest that you come to me. In the meantime if I feel that either of your performances aren't up to scratch again this evening, you will be called to re-rehearse. I am a busy man and can ill-afford the time to fix what someone else has seen fit to tamper with quite unnecessarily, so I suggest you work your asses off tonight to get it right.' David Lawless turned on his heel and strode off.

Deirdre kept her eyes fixed on the ground. She felt that she should be grateful to Rory for taking the rap for her, but she couldn't articulate the words. She didn't want to be beholden to him for anything.

'Deirdre?' She slowly raised her eyes to his. There was a look of intense inquiry in them. It made them appear even greener than usual. 'I tried to call you from a banjaxed phone yesterday. Was there any message from me on your machine?'

She didn't want him to know she'd got his message. She didn't want to give him the chance to weaken her resolve. She'd surrendered to his persuasive tongue once too often. She'd make it perfectly clear that Deirdre O'Dare was no slapper.

She held his gaze for a second or two. 'No. No, I didn't,' she said, and then she looked down at her hands. The knuckles were white. She composed her face and looked at him again. 'Was it anything important?' she asked in a bored voice, trying to imitate the autocratic way Eva held her head.

Rory studied her for a long moment with calculating eyes. Then he assumed a parody of her pseudo-dignified stance and gave her the longest, slowest, most insouciant smile she'd ever received. Deirdre felt something stir uncomfortably inside her, and she tensed in an effort to control it. 'Sorry, Deirdre. I mistook you for a grown-up there for a minute,' he said. 'Don't worry. The message wasn't important at all.' Then he turned his back on her and strolled across the hall to rejoin Eva Lavery.

* * *

Deirdre went into the theatre that evening feeling very small and more than a little scared. She had been severely chastened by the knuckle-rapping she'd got from her director, and was determined that she was going to get her act together. She was a professional now, and she couldn't let her personal feelings get in the way of her work. Aside from anything else, David's threat to them that they would have to re-rehearse their scenes together if they didn't come up with the goods was a strong incentive to get it right. The last thing she wanted was to have to spend more time working on love scenes with Rory McDonagh.

She'd just gone through the stage door and was on her way up the stairs to the dressing-room when the door on the landing which led to the production office opened. Deirdre was on the verge of taking the stairs two at a time in case it was David Lawless, but she knew it was inevitable that she'd bump straight into him. She steeled herself and tried to look dignified.

'Thanks again, David. See you later,' said a vaguely familiar voice. The person emerging from the office shut the door behind him and started to come down the stairs towards her. Deirdre stopped dead. It was Sebastian Hardy.

'Sebastian!' she exclaimed. She could hardly

believe her eyes. 'What on earth are you doing here?'

'Deirdre – hi!' He ran down the rest of the steps and gave her a great bear-hug. 'I was hoping I might bump into you before the show. You're about the only person I know in this town.'

'But – what are you *doing* here?' Deirdre insisted, like a gobsmacked parrot. 'I'm so amazed to see you!'

Sebastian held her at arm's length and smiled. 'Have you got time before the show?' He glanced at his watch. 'It's a long story.'

'I'll make time,' said Deirdre firmly. She wasn't going to miss out on an opportunity of finding out what Sebastian was doing in Dublin. 'I'm always in too early anyway.'

'Excellent,' said Sebastian. 'But let's not hang about here – it's a beautiful evening. We'll talk outside, shall we?'

They walked as far as a nearby church where they sat down on the steps. Deirdre gazed at Sebastian, not bothering to hide her delight at seeing him again so unexpectedly. Suddenly all the nastiness of the past couple of days seemed to have evaporated and it felt like life could be fun again.

Sebastian stretched out his long legs and leaned back on the steps, resting on his elbows. 'You look good, Deirdre. God, is it really just a week since I saw you last?' He gave her a smile which made her feel weak. 'I'd better tell you what I'm doing here, hadn't I?'

'Oh yes, Sebastian – I'm *dying* to know.' Deirdre

hugged her legs with her arms and rested her chin on her knees, waiting for him to fill her in. He was even more devastatingly handsome than she remembered. She hoped that someone from the cast would walk by and see them together. Preferably Rory.

'Do you remember I told you after we met in Juliet's office last week that she was interested in me for that Australian film?'

'Yeah?'

'I turned it down.'

'But why Sebastian? That's a really prestigious production, isn't it?' Deirdre had read an article about the forthcoming film in one of the Sunday papers, and had felt chuffed to be able to tell her parents that she had actually met one of the actors who was to be involved in it.

'I was never really interested. It would have meant spending nearly five months in Australia, and I'd have been out of commission for work going at home. There's a film adaptation of *Nicholas Nickleby* happening later in the year, and Juliet told me there's a better than average chance of me being cast. So I weighed up the options with my agent and we reckoned it might be worth staying on in London and making myself available for that.'

Deirdre looked puzzled. 'That still doesn't explain what you're doing in Dublin.'

'Well, I hope I'm not hexing myself if I tell you. Can you keep a secret, Deirdre?'

'Of course I can!' Deirdre was aching with curiosity.

'You may remember me mentioning that Mark Llewellyn is a friend of mine?'

'Yes?'

'Well, when I turned down the film, Juliet needed a replacement pronto. I suggested Mark. He's actually much better casting than I would have been.'

'But he's playing Hamlet!'

'Not any more. It looks like I am.'

Deirdre couldn't believe her ears. '*What?* How?'

'I rang Mark last Monday to tell him about the film. I knew he'd be interested. He has family – a brother and a sister – out there, and he hasn't seen either of them for about five years. So in a few weeks time he'll be packing his bags for Australia and there's a reasonably good chance that I'll be packing mine for Dublin.' He smiled at her. 'Juliet was shrewd enough to wangle an audition for me with David. She didn't want to antagonize him by poaching Mark from Lawless Productions.'

Deirdre looked at him in admiration. 'So you and Mark swapped. What an inspired idea!' she said.

'I've always wanted to visit Dublin. After all, isn't it the grooviest city in Europe? Funny how things turn out, sometimes, isn't it?'

'So that's what you were doing in the production office just now!'

'Yeah. I don't want to sound arrogant, Deirdre, but I've a hunch that it's in the bag. I did a bloody good read, and David's seen my work at the National. I've a feeling they might let me know later on today.'

'Won't they wait till tomorrow to call you? You won't get back to London till all hours tonight.'

'I'm staying on here for a day or two. I wanted to catch *Dream* and there's a production on at the Abbey that I'd like to see tomorrow. An old girlfriend of mine is in it.'

'Oh.' Deirdre hoped the tone of her voice didn't sound too deflated at the mention of a girlfriend. At least he'd said "old". 'So you'll be in at the show tonight?' She made this sound much brighter.

'Sure. I'm looking forward to it. Eva suggested that I join you all in the local afterwards, so I'm interpreting that as another positive sign.'

'You met Eva, then?' Deirdre suddenly remembered the photograph which had fallen out of Sebastian's wallet in the café that day. 'Isn't she lovely?' She watched his reaction carefully. She thought that if he did harbour an infatuation for the actress she might see it in his face, but she could read nothing there but enthusiastic agreement.

'Yeah. She's pretty charismatic, all right. We read together after I'd gone through the soliloquies – you know the scene where Hamlet confronts Gertrude in her bedchamber?'

'Of course,' answered Deirdre. 'That's difficult stuff.'

Sebastian suddenly took a deep intake of breath and leant forward, shaking his head.

'Sebastian?' said Deirdre with concern, putting her hand on his shoulder. 'Are you all right?'

He straightened up and gave her a tired smile. He was suddenly composed again. 'Yeah, I'm fine, thanks. It's just been a hell of a rough week. And I hate auditions worse than death. I'm always wrecked afterwards.' He looked at his watch. 'Hey – isn't it about time you made a move?'

'Shit!' Deirdre jumped to her feet. 'You're right.'

'Sorry, Deirdre,' said Sebastian, standing up as well. 'It's my fault if you're late. I've been talking too much.'

'Oh, no, no – not at all, Sebastian.' She could see Sophie walking towards the theatre. She would have to pass by them on her way. Deirdre decided to linger on for a little while. 'So I'll see you in the pub after the show, then?' She raised the level of her voice slightly. 'Do you know which one to go to, Sebastian?'

'Eva mentioned a place called Meagher's? I might go and grab a sandwich there now.'

'It's just across the road there, to your left.' Deirdre pointed ostentatiously, using her peripheral vision to keep tabs on Sophie. She had drawn level with them, and Deirdre could just make out the gobsmacked expression on her face. 'Catch you later, Sebastian – enjoy the show! Oh – and it's lovely to see you again.' She took a huge risk. 'Darling,' she added.

'The pleasure's all mine, Deirdre. Didn't I tell you the first time I met you that we were fated to meet again? See you later.' And Sebastian headed across the road in the direction of the pub.

Deirdre strolled towards the theatre with a deliberately unhurried tread and a singing heart. She could see the other actress turning the corner into the laneway which led to the stage door. She knew that Sophie was lagging intentionally so that Deirdre could catch up with her. When she rounded the corner she saw that Sophie must have dropped her bag on the ground, because she was stooping down and was laboriously putting back the bunch of keys and the make-up pouch which had fallen out of it. Sophie looked around at the ground as if to make sure she hadn't dropped anything else as Deirdre drew abreast of her.

'Oh – hi, Deirdre!' said Sophie, as if Deirdre was the last person she expected to find going into the theatre at ten past seven on a Monday evening. She zipped up her bag with a satisfied air now that she'd made sure its contents were intact.

'Hi, Sophie,' said Deirdre in a careless voice. 'How's it going?'

'Oh, the usual, you know.'

'Good.' Deirdre threw her a smile and carried on down the lane.

'Was that you I passed sitting on the church steps?'

'Um – yeah.' Deirdre sounded as if she wasn't quite sure, and then started to hum a little tune.

Sophie couldn't bear it any more. 'Who was the guy?' she asked with contorted casualness.

'The guy?' Deirdre contrived to sound a little puzzled. 'Oh – you mean Sebastian? That was Sebastian Hardy. You may have heard that I met him in London last week.'

'Oh – did you?' said Sophie vaguely.

Deirdre knew damn well that Sophie had heard

about her meeting with Sebastian. 'Yeah. He took me out for lunch and we got on really well. He's really simpatico.' She preceded Sophie through the stage door.

'What's he doing over here?' Sophie's voice was practically strangulated with the effort to sound uninterested.

Deirdre paused with her back to Sophie for a beat or two and then turned with a mysterious smile. 'Oh, let's just say he wanted to see the show,' she said lightly. And as she turned her head away, she tried not to laugh at the expression on her rival's face.

Chapter Thirteen

She kissed Rory that night with a passion so intense that it took even him by surprise. 'Jesus Christ, Deirdre – take it easy,' he muttered in her ear as their embrace was interrupted by the arrival on stage of Maeve. But Deirdre was firing on all cylinders. Her performance felt as fresh to her as it had done on the opening night, and nothing was going to cramp her style. She was determined that she would shine tonight, not just for David Lawless, but for Sebastian Hardy too.

Rory gave her a curious look as they headed towards the green room after the first scene. 'David should give you notes more often, sweetheart. That was dynamite.'

She was in too good a mood to be snotty with Rory. After all, she had promised herself to maintain as smooth a professional relationship with him as possible. She decided to be gracious instead of just ignoring him. 'Thanks, Rory,' she said. 'I can't say I'm too unhappy with my performance so far this evening.'

'I wasn't referring to your performance, O'Dare. I was referring to the sensational snog. Oh – sorry, Deirdre,' he said in response to her look of contempt. 'Was that a bit *jejune* for you?' And he disappeared in the direction of the notice-board where there was at least a week's accumulation of letters waiting for him. Death threats, probably.

At the interval she bumped into Jessica, who was looking flustered.

'What's the problem, Jessica? Someone giving you a hard time?' Deirdre knew that Finbar de Rossa had been in hot pursuit of Jessica since she had inadvertently let slip that she wore stay-ups in preference to tights.

'Not really – hang on a sec – just let me finish writing this down. "Jeremy phoned. Please phone back later",' she intoned to herself as she scribbled a message on a scrap of paper. 'Jesus, Deirdre – sometimes I wish our leading lady wasn't quite so popular. I seem to spend half my life running up and down those stairs with messages for her. And there's some problem with the ass's head that I have to deal with before the second half. Sophie got that bloody wreath stuck round one of the ears and just made it worse when she tried to untangle it.'

'Can I do something to help?' asked Deirdre. 'If that's a message for Eva I'll take it up to her if you like.'

'Oh, that *would* be a help Deirdre – thanks a lot.' And Jessica thrust the message into Deirdre's hand and raced towards the wings.

Deirdre was glad to have an opportunity to visit Eva's dressing-room. She hoped that the actress would be forthcoming about Sebastian Hardy. As she raised her hand to knock, she remembered what had happened on the last occasion she'd called to Eva's door, and this time she made sure her knock would be heard even in the shower room.

'There's no need to break the door down. Come in,' called Eva peremptorily.

Deirdre slid through the door with an apologetic expression.

'Oh, it's you, honey. Hi,' said Eva. She was sitting back in her chair with her feet up on the counter, looking at a book. She threw it on to the counter top, stretched herself and yawned. 'Funny, isn't it? I remember studying the poem I've just been reading in Latin class at school and thinking it was boring and stupid. How one changes – there's so little in life that's constant, isn't there?

Suns when they sink can rise again
But we, when our brief light has shone,
Must sleep the long night on and on

Eva shook her head and laughed. 'It's not like me to be philosophical! That must be the first meaningful thought I've had in years. Yet another sign of creeping middle age, I suppose.'

Deirdre smiled. 'You'll never be middle-aged, Eva.'

'I'm rather looking forward to it, actually. They say one's sex drive goes into orbit. But thank you anyway, darling, for the lovely compliment – and for the wonderful photographs. I'm sorry – I've been so distracted recently that I completely forgot to thank you.' Eva was gazing at the opposite wall with a supremely happy expression on her face. Deirdre turned to see that the three photographs her mother had given her had been framed and were hanging on the wall above Eva's couch. 'Now.' Eva returned her attention to Deirdre. 'What can I do for you?'

'Oh – I was just bringing you a phone message.' Deirdre handed over the scrap of paper and hovered, wondering how she might bring up the subject of Sebastian.

'Bloody Jeremy again,' said Eva, perusing the message. 'What a tiresome boy he's becoming. Oh, by the way – I had occasion to meet *your* beau today, the one you bumped into in London. What's his name again?'

'Sebastian Hardy?'

'Yes. You were absolutely right, sweetheart – he is drop-dead delicious. And very talented indeed.' Eva peered at her reflection in the dressing table mirror and took up a lipstick. 'Shall I be incredibly indiscreet and let you into a secret?'

'Oh, yes please, Eva!'

'He's going to be our Hamlet.'

Deirdre whooped inwardly but feigned surprise. 'Oh how wonderful! But what about Mark Llewellyn?'

'Oh, he's buggered off to do some movie in Australia. You *are* a lucky girl, aren't you. I must have a word in David's ear and persuade him to put in lots of snogging scenes for you.' Eva leant towards the mirror and coloured her lips carmine. 'Come to think of it, that bedchamber scene between Hamlet and Gertrude can be played pretty raunchily even though they're mother and son. Oh, goodie – that's something to look forward to. It'll be a welcome relief from bloody Iggy, anyway.' It took Deirdre a second or two to work out that Eva was referring to Finbar de Rossa. 'I think David plots all those snogging scenes I have with him deliberately to annoy me. He put another one in this morning, and I had to drop big hints to Iggy that the Macbeths were probably pretty clued in when it came to oral hygiene.'

Second half beginners was announced over the tannoy.

'You're on soon, darling, aren't you? Better make tracks. McCarthy's in stinking form tonight – he bawled Rory out for being late for the half hour. Oh – and make sure you're in the pub after the show, Deirdre. Sebastian's going to be there.'

The recasting of Hamlet wasn't a secret for long. News travels fast backstage in a theatre. Because she had actually met the famous Sebastian Hardy, Deirdre found that she was very popular all of a sudden. Everybody was offering to buy her a drink after the show – even Sophie.

When the show came down Deirdre changed and scrubbed her face clean of make-up quicker than she'd ever done. She regretted that she wasn't wearing something sexier than jeans and a T-shirt, but then she supposed it wouldn't do to look as if she was trying *too* hard. She couldn't wait to see the look on Rory's face when he came into the pub and saw her sitting with Sebastian. She passed him on the stairs on the way out.

'You're in a tearing hurry this evening, Deirdre, aren't you?' he said as she ignored him. 'By the way, sweetheart,' he called over his shoulder. 'I note with pleasure that you're starting to put on a bit of weight at last. It suits you.'

* * *

Deirdre was among the first of the cast to arrive at the pub. To her disappointment there was no sign of Sebastian. She hazarded a guess as to what he would drink. Guinness, she reckoned, since visitors to Ireland always wanted to try genuine Irish stout. She ordered a pint for him and a glass of white wine for herself. There was a large party of people just vacating a table, and she immediately commandeered it, pushing the empty glasses and overflowing ashtray to one side.

She didn't have long to wait. Within minutes the door to the pub opened and Sebastian came through, deep in discussion with David Lawless. She sat up very straight in her chair in an attempt to attract his attention, and when he failed to notice her, gave a little wave. That didn't work either, so she went over to the bar and hovered, feeling rather foolish. She wished she hadn't bought the pint of Guinness now after all, because David Lawless had just put in an order for two Budweiser. Deirdre cleared her throat. 'Hi, Sebastian,' she said tentatively. 'Hi, David.'

'Deirdre – hi.' Sebastian gave her a gratifyingly

brilliant smile. 'Hey – you were terrific tonight,' he said, kissing her on the cheek. 'I can't tell you how glad I am that David's decided to cast me – I'm really looking forward to working with you.' He made the standard phrase sound absolutely genuine. 'I just hope I'll be able to keep up with you!'

'Oh – so you *are* going to be playing Hamlet! That's wonderful news, Sebastian!'

'I can't quite understand why you sound so surprised, Deirdre,' said David, looking amused. 'Eva must have told at least half the cast before the interval tonight.'

Deirdre gave a rather sheepish laugh.

'You two obviously know each other already,' he continued. 'So there's no need for me to introduce you.' He gave them both an appraising look. 'You'll work well together, I hope. You certainly look good together. A pretty inspired bit of casting, if I say so myself. And I'm glad you've got our leading lady's imprimatur, Sebastian. She's very choosy about whom she works with. Sorry, Deirdre – how rude of me. Can I get you a drink?'

'Oh – no thank you, David. I have one already – over there. I actually managed to get a decent table tonight.' She indicated where she'd left her glass of wine and the now redundant pint of Guinness, and after David had paid for his drinks they all made their way over.

'Is Eva likely to join us tonight?' asked Sebastian as they sat down.

'Yeah, later,' said David, looking at his watch.

'The lady takes her time. She needs space to herself after a show – likes to let the adrenalin subside a little before being sociable. Whose is the pint of Guinness?'

'Oh, I bought that,' said Deirdre. 'It's for – for Rory.' He was the first person she could think of off the top of her head who drank Guinness, and as soon as the words were out of her mouth she regretted them. She didn't owe Rory McDonagh any favours – not even a pint.

'I was glad to see that you two had managed to resurrect your scenes together after the fiasco of Saturday night,' said David Lawless. 'I was beginning to wonder if there was some personal agenda there which was colouring your performance, Deirdre.'

Deirdre stayed schtum.

The pub was starting to fill up now. Most of the cast had arrived and Sophie and the other fairies had congregated in a little knot over by the bar, and were casting covert glances towards where Deirdre sat with David and Sebastian. She couldn't help preening a little, knowing how privileged she was to be in such illustrious company. Nor could she help looking towards the door from time to time to see if Rory would come through. It was unlike him not to be among the first into the pub after the show, and Deirdre was irked by the thought that he might not show. She wanted him to see how familiar her behaviour with Sebastian Hardy was. She wanted him to witness her laughing and being perfectly at ease with the most beautiful man in the room.

Just then the door opened and Rory walked in at last, heading straight for the bar. Deirdre allowed herself a little smile and then wiped it from her face immediately. He was followed by Marian who was talking earnestly to a bearded man whom Deirdre recognized as a presenter of a heavyweight political programme on RTE. Deirdre immediately swivelled in her seat so that she was unlikely to make eye contact with any of the party who had just come in, and tried to concentrate her attention on what David Lawless was saying instead. She wasn't really listening. She heard Rory's wicked laugh ring out suddenly and saw David's gaze shift in his direction.

'McDonagh!' he called. 'There's a pint waiting for you here.'

Deirdre decided to study her nails. Then she heard Rory's voice behind her.

'Thanks, David,' he said.

'Don't thank me – thank Deirdre,' replied David Lawless.

'Well, Deirdre – what an unexpected surprise.' To her horror Rory slid into the seat opposite her and raised an eyebrow at her. 'Could this be in return for services rendered?'

Deirdre felt her face flare up, and she hated Rory McDonagh more than ever.

'Rory – meet Sebastian Hardy,' said David Lawless. Deirdre was relieved that the focus had been taken off her. 'He'll be joining us to play Hamlet later on in the season.'

Rory looked across the table to where Sebastian

was sitting beside Deirdre. He reached over and shook hands.

'Nice to meet you, Rory,' said Sebastian. 'That was a terrific show tonight.'

'Nice to meet you too, Sebastian,' Rory said carefully. Then: 'Where have I heard your name before? It was some time recently, I'm sure.'

Deirdre felt herself going cold.

'Oh yes – I remember now. Didn't you meet Sebastian when you were in London last week, Deirdre?' Rory fixed his dangerous green eyes on her and smiled. Then he reverted to Sebastian. 'I think you bought her – a sandwich?'

'That's right.' Sebastian gave Deirdre a warm look.

'Nice for you to bump into each other again so soon,' said Rory. 'The long arm of coincidence stretches across the Irish Sea. Can I get you a drink, Sebastian? David?'

'No thanks. Not right now,' returned Sebastian with a smile.

'Maybe later,' said Rory, rising to his feet. 'What about you, Deirdre? Your usual horse's – I mean your usual white wine?'

'No thank you, Rory,' she said in a tone which could have been interpreted as 'Fuck off, Rory.'

'Well – cheers.' He looked at her again, raising his glass to her, and then included Sebastian and David Lawless in his smile. 'Excuse me. I'll catch you later,' he said, and moved off. On his way to rejoin Marian at the bar he ran into Eva, who had just come in and was strolling towards their table.

She was wearing her snakeskin trousers and had something of a just-got-out-of-bed look about her. Rory looked wolfishly at her and said something in her ear, whereupon the actress threw back her head and laughed her wonderful, throaty laugh. Rory bowed, and, taking her hand, held the palm to his lips. Deirdre remembered how he had done the same to her just before they had gone to their separate dressing-rooms on Friday evening before the show and something inside her went taut. She was aware that beside her Sebastian too had gone rigid, and she shot a glance in his direction. He was looking at Rory and Eva and there was an intensity about his expression which Deirdre found a little unsettling. For some strange reason she felt she'd seen it somewhere before.

As Eva came towards them, Deirdre saw the muscles in Sebastian's face relax into a smile. He stood up and, taking the actress's hands, kissed her on both cheeks. 'I'm so star-struck that I'm practically inarticulate, Eva. That was the most stunning piece of theatre I've seen in years, and I just don't have the words to tell you how good you were. Please let me get you a drink?'

'Well, thank you Sebastian.' Eva's smile was radiant. 'And yes – I'd love a drink. Noilly Prat, please. You'll have to let the barman know that it's for me – he keeps a bottle behind the bar specially. I'm the only person who ever seems to drink it.'

'I don't think he'd heard of it before you started ordering it, Eva,' said Deirdre. 'This isn't the hippest gin-joint in all of the world, as you may have noticed, Sebastian. Rory McDonagh discovered it.'

'I'll be right back.' Sebastian returned Eva's smile and relinquished her hands.

'What a stunning looking boy he is,' Eva said, as he disappeared in the direction of the bar. She sat down beside David in the chair recently vacated by Rory, following Sebastian's progress with thoughtful grey eyes.

'Hands off, Lavery.' David was looking at her with a kind of indulgent amusement.

Eva laughed. 'Don't worry, darling. I'm rather tired of the old cradle-snatching lark. Boys tend to get *involved* and then they become so biddable it's boring. I've decided I'm going to stick to men my own age from now on.'

'Men?' asked David. He reached out a hand for his pint, and Deirdre noticed that it grazed Eva's snakeskin-clad thigh as he did so.

'Well, maybe even one man. I dare say there's *some* novelty to be had from exclusivity.' She smiled and yawned, stretching herself like a cat. 'God, I'm sleepy. I'm not sure that love in the afternoon is such a good idea when there's a show to do in the evening.' Deirdre wondered why David Lawless was suddenly studiously avoiding Eva's eyes and smiling.

'You're happy with our new Hamlet, Deirdre?' he asked, leaning forward. For some reason she didn't find his sudden display of interest in her opinion wholly convincing.

'Oh, yes!' she said with enthusiasm. 'I was saying

to Eva only the other evening what a brilliant actor Sebastian is.' Deirdre started to rave about his performance as the drug addict in *Hurting People*, and about how coincidental it was that she should have met him for the first time just last week.

'I told Deirdre that I'd try to persuade you to put lots of sexy bits into her scenes with Sebastian,' said Eva. 'You're a very lucky girl, you know, Deirdre – first Rory McDonagh and now Sebastian Hardy. A vicarious sex life is one of the perks of the job – as long as the other party is amusing, of course. Goodness – it must be absolutely earth-shattering for you, darling, having two such edible actors all to yourself.'

Deirdre felt herself blushing again. Sebastian was on his way back with a tray of drinks, and she hoped he hadn't overheard anything Eva had said. As the actress had a habit of never bothering to lower her voice it was highly probable he had.

'Noilly Prat, Eva. And a glass of white wine for you, Deirdre.'

She sent him a radiant smile.

* * *

As the evening wore on she hoped that Rory could see how much fun she was having. Eva was outrageous as ever, David Lawless was trenchantly witty, and Sebastian was charming and easy to like. Rather to her dismay, Deirdre's suspicion that he had a crush on Eva seemed to be well-founded. Actors often fell in love with their leading ladies in much the same way as she had fallen in love with her director. She couldn't help feeling a small tug of jealousy. She had hoped that Sebastian might take a shine to *her.* It would have been so cool to have a relationship off-stage as well as on, especially since they were playing such romantic parts. Hamlet and Ophelia. Sebastian and Deirdre.

She took a sideways look at him. He was listening with rapt attention to Eva, who was being incredibly indiscreet about a leading British actress. Deirdre didn't want to look at him too closely, but there was something about his expression which she found curious. It was as if he was trying too hard to appear relaxed and in control, and there was something quite unfathomable behind his eyes.

Deirdre volunteered to buy the next round of drinks, and was glad when Sebastian asked her for another Bud. David and Eva both declined, saying that they'd be leaving soon. She was standing at the bar trying to attract the attention of a barman when she heard a rather sexy female voice behind her ordering three pints of Guinness. Deirdre was annoyed. It was *her* turn to be served. She turned round with the intention of sending a dirty look to whoever had pre-empted her and found herself face to face with Marian.

'Oh hi! How are *you*?' she said, effusively.

Marian looked slightly taken aback. Although they had been briefly introduced weeks ago they had never yet had a conversation.

'How was Brussels?' Deirdre blundered on. 'The weather must have been fabulous. Oh, thanks,

Michael – I'll have a glass of white wine and a pint of Bud, please.'

'Actually, it was too hot in Brussels,' Marian replied politely.

'Oh – that must be why you decided to come home early?' asked Deirdre, trying as hard as she could to sound conversational.

'That was one of the reasons, yes.'

Deirdre inferred from the slightly cool tone that Marian's early return was absolutely none of her business, but she knew that she was going to have to continue this parody of dialogue for as long as it took the barman to fetch their drinks. She flailed around mentally for something else to say. Travel was obviously a good topic. 'You must be really well-travelled. Peru next, is it?'

'What? No.' Marian looked rather at a loss, as if she wished Deirdre would go away. When it became obvious that she was stuck with her she had the good grace to break the rather embarrassing silence that was accumulating. 'Actually, I hate travelling. I only do it when I have to cover stories.'

'Oh?' said Deirdre with an expression of intense interest on her face.

'Yes,' said Marian. There was a beat and then she continued with an obvious effort. 'Rory's the one who suffers from wanderlust.'

'I take it your reference to wanderlust is in its strictly geographical sense, my love?' Rory's voice came from over Deirdre's shoulder. She was extremely glad that her drink hadn't arrived yet. She would have choked on it.

'Of course, my dear beau. Everyone knows your reputation for constancy,' returned Marian.

'You two do know each other, do you?' Deirdre was aware of a barely perceptible guardedness in Rory's question.

'Yes.' Marian sounded rather resigned. 'I'll take this pint back to Barnaby. Will you pay for the drinks, Rory?' And, to Deirdre's unutterable relief, she helped herself to two pints from the counter and was gone.

Deirdre wanted to bang her head off the bar. How could she have made the mistake of assuming that the travel books in the Marian/Rory McDonagh household were Marian's and not Rory's?

'Sorry to interrupt your nice girly chat,' said Rory. 'But something made me think that Deirdre O'Dare might find social intercourse with my partner rather laborious. Evidently it was the case vice versa as well,' he added as he watched Marian set down a pint in front of the political presenter. 'Marian's not that into playing with Barbies.'

Deirdre shot him a look laced with venom.

He pitched his voice slightly lower. 'I trust you didn't drop too many gaffes, sweetheart? What was your opening gambit, for instance? Something along the lines of "Rory's a really phenomenal ride, isn't he, Marian?" Delivered no doubt with your usual tact and circumspection.'

Deirdre's cheeks were flaming. 'Fuck off, Rory,' she said.

'Well parried, as ever, sweetheart. I've always

found that particular riposte never fails to floor me. Don't hang about to pay for your drink. I'll get it – and your boyfriend's as well.'

Deirdre didn't hang about. Even though the last thing she wanted was to be beholden to Rory McDonagh for her drink, she couldn't bear to be in his presence for an instant longer.

She pushed her way through the crowd back to the table, spilling some of Sebastian's pint as she did so, and feeling full of loathing for Rory. How had she ever let him seduce her? She must have been out of her mind. She wished more than anything that she could undo the events of last Friday. She knew that for the rest of his life Rory McDonagh would have something over her. She would never be able to let down her guard in company as long as he was around.

As she stomped across the room she bumped into Eva, who was leaving on the arm of David Lawless. 'Deirdre? What's happened to you? You look awfully upset.'

'Oh – I had a hard time trying to get a drink, that's all. They're short-staffed in here again this evening.'

'Poor child. Maybe we should start going to O'Riordan's instead,' she said vaguely.

'I think that's a brilliant idea, Eva!' Deirdre pounced on the opportunity which presented itself. If anyone could start a trend towards drinking in another venue Eva Lavery could. Then Deirdre wouldn't ever have to associate with Rory McDonagh again. He'd never abandon his beloved Meagher's. 'Are you leaving now?'

'Mm-hm. I want to get an early night. I've a costume fitting for the film first thing in the morning.'

David Lawless bent his head and said something *sotto voce*, and she looked at him with meaning. 'Don't even think about it, darling,' she said, in a voice that dripped warning. David raised an eyebrow, giving her the kind of smile he gave to Deirdre in her fantasies, and Eva suddenly said: 'Oh, all right then.' She stood on tiptoe and kissed his mouth. 'By the way, darling,' she added to Deirdre. 'You might want to start sharpening your claws.' She directed a look back to the table where Sebastian was sitting. Sophie Burke had just slid into the seat which Deirdre had vacated, and Jessica and Kate had gravitated closer to the table.

Eva smiled and blew Deirdre a kiss. 'See you tomorrow, darling.' And as she turned to leave, Deirdre noticed that David's hand was resting low down on the actress's hip. He slid it up to the small of her back and steered her through the crowd in what Deirdre thought was a rather proprietorial fashion. One might almost take them for a couple of newlyweds.

Then she turned around to see that Sebastian was watching them as well. There was something predatory about his expression. When they had disappeared into the crowd he turned towards Sophie and smiled at her. Deirdre had never seen the actress dimple so abjectly. She walked back to the table full of purpose. Poor Sebastian. There was nothing she could do about his infatuation with

Eva Lavery, but she was damn sure that she'd protect him from Sophie's cringe-worthy attempts to impress him. Sophie had Beautiful Ben, and good luck to her. But she bloody well wasn't going to get her dinky little claws into Sebastian Hardy too.

She placed the two glasses on the table with emphasis. 'Hi, Sophie,' she said lightly. 'I see you've introduced yourself to Sebastian at last.'

'Oh, hi, Deirdre,' Sophie's tone was equally casual. 'Pardon me – have I taken your seat?' she said, without making any move to get up.

'Yes, but it doesn't matter. I'm quite happy here.' She sat in the chair immediately opposite Sebastian and gave him a dazzling smile.

'I may be drawing the wrong conclusion here, but are those two an item by any chance?' he asked casually, nodding his head in the direction of the door through which Eva and David had just departed. 'I was under the impression that David Lawless was married to some Irish soap opera star.'

Deirdre leaned back in her chair with a little smile. She'd let Sophie jump at the chance of filling Sebastian in on the Lavery/Lawless/Fitzroy saga. She didn't want to look like some indiscreet showbiz gossip type in front of him. She'd let Sophie have that accolade. With a bit of luck, Sophie wouldn't be able to resist the temptation to bitch about their leading lady, and Deirdre suspected that she wouldn't be doing herself any favours. Sebastian wouldn't enjoy listening to Sophie badmouth Eva Lavery.

As she'd anticipated, Sophie picked up her cue immediately.

'Yes, Sebastian – they are an item, actually,' she said.

'What?' Deirdre turned to Sophie with undisguised curiosity.

'Oh, hadn't you heard, Deirdre? Of course, I forgot that you're always about six weeks behind everyone else. Too busy thinking about yourself, as usual. Not,' she added hastily as she saw the expression which crossed Deirdre's face. 'Actually, you weren't in the pub on Saturday night, were you?' Deirdre cast her mind back. Saturday had been the night she and Maeve had gone to O'Riordan's to avoid Rory. 'That's when it all broke. Of course, I'd been in the know for a while, Sebastian, because my grandfather is a great friend of Ann Fitzroy's father you know.'

'Who's Ann Fitzroy?' Sebastian had crossed one long denim-clad leg over the other. His relaxed posture was belied by a fierce concentration behind his almond shaped eyes.

'Ann Fitzroy is married to David Lawless – she's the soap opera actress you mentioned.' Sophie looked around and then leaned forward in the manner of the habitual gossip. 'Well, maybe I should say they *used* to be married. He left her a couple of weeks ago and divorce is in the air. Apparently he just upped and left and moved in with' – Sophie paused for effect before delivering her trump card – 'your leading lady, Sebastian.

David Lawless dumped his wife of over twenty years for Eva Lavery.'

Even the horribly self-satisfied expression on Sophie's face could not put Deirdre off tapping the actress for more information. 'They've been perfectly open about it, Sophie, have they?' she asked.

'Well, Deirdre, even you must have noticed that they haven't been able to keep their hands off each other for the past while. But it wasn't until Saturday that it became official.'

'Official? Did they make some kind of announcement or something?' Deirdre was itching with curiosity and wondered vaguely why she wasn't more upset by the revelation that David Lawless was now lost to her forever.

'No. Ann did that. She actually organized a party on Saturday to announce to all her friends that they were splitting up – a bit like an engagement party, only in reverse. And David wasn't invited, of course. He was here in the pub with Eva after the show that night, and they just let the fact that they're now living together drop quite casually. It was all over the place within half an hour.'

Deirdre's mind was spinning. 'This party that Ann Fitzroy had – was it to *celebrate*?'

'I'm not sure. Why don't you ask Maeve? Her girlfriend' – Sophie's voice went a bit stiff on the word 'girlfriend' – 'Jacqueline did the catering. Anyway, as I said, *I* knew it was on the cards. And it's not really surprising when you take their past history into account.'

Deirdre could hardly believe that Maeve could have withheld this nugget of information from her. She would have to seek her out immediately.

Opposite her Sebastian was watching Sophie carefully. 'What do you mean by their past history, Sophie?' he asked.

Sophie looked unbearably pleased with herself. 'Well . . .' she began.

Fascinating though the story of the Lawless/Lavery relationship was, Deirdre didn't think she could sit through Sophie's one-woman show a second time. 'Excuse me for a minute will you, Sebastian? I'll be back shortly.'

Deirdre stood up and her eyes ranged the room. She spotted Maeve and Jacqueline sitting at a crowded table on the opposite side of the pub, and negotiated her way towards them. It was just as she joined them that she noticed that Rory was part of their company. She hovered indecisively for a moment or two, trying to catch Maeve's eye without attracting his attention. She noticed that Marian and the political presenter were nowhere to be seen, and that Rory was nursing what looked like a very large whiskey. He looked up suddenly, caught her gaze and held it. His mouth smiled at her, and all Deirdre could see was contempt in its curve. She broke contact with his eyes before his smile had a chance to register there and signalled to Maeve.

'Oh, hi, Deirdre – come and join us.'

'No thanks, Maeve. Um, can I have a word?' Her eyes slid in Rory's direction and Maeve copped on to her discomfort immediately.

'Sure.' She rose to her feet and followed Deirdre to the corner of the bar. 'You're not going to be able to avoid him for ever, you know, Deirdre. Although I wouldn't blame you for wanting to avoid him in the mood he's in right now. He's a devil this evening, and obviously out to get totally rat-faced. What's up with you?'

'Is it true that David has hooked up with Eva Lavery?'

'Seems so.'

'Why didn't you tell me?' she asked. 'I found out – from Sophie Burke of all people – that Jacqueline did the catering for Ann Fitzroy's party on Saturday night.'

'You may recall that you were somewhat distraught on Saturday night, Deirdre. I didn't think the fact that Jacqueline was catering for some party of Ann Fitzroy's would have been of much interest to you in the state you were in. Anyway, I didn't know myself that it was such a bizarre soirée until Jacqueline came home in the early hours of Sunday morning and told me all about it.'

'What do you mean, bizarre?'

'Well. Remember I told you before that I thought Ann Fitzroy was cracked?'

'Yeah?'

'Her party on Saturday night proved it beyond all reasonable doubt.'

'Why? What happened?'

'Keep this to yourself, Deirdre, will you? It won't do Jacqueline's reputation as a society caterer much good if word gets out that she can't be trusted to keep schtum about what goes on at private parties. Discretion goes with the job, you know.'

'Don't worry. I'll only tell Sophie,' said Deirdre. 'Joke,' she added apologetically.

Maeve leaned back against the bar counter. 'When Jacqueline arrived to start work on Saturday night Ann was already half-pissed. Jacqueline said she opened the door with a glass in one hand and a half-empty bottle of burgundy in the other, screaming at her housekeeper for not answering the doorbell. Then she swanned off up the stairs and closeted herself in her bedroom until it was time for the guests to arrive.' Maeve suddenly glanced over Deirdre's shoulder. 'No, I really think the Gossard one is your best bet. The lace-trimmed ones are really pretty and the underwiring gives you a terrific cleavage.'

'What?' Deirdre looked at Maeve in astonishment, and then comprehension dawned as Sophie hoved into view.

'I never thought you were one for girly talk, Maeve,' she said. 'Actually, La Perla is top of the range, if you can afford it. That's what I have on now.' And Sophie thrust out her chest in the manner of a preening pigeon.

'Really?' said Maeve. 'You must show me some time, Sophie. Maybe we should organize a lingerie party one evening after the show.' Maeve sent Sophie a suggestive smile, and the actress immediately sidled off down the bar looking horrified.

Deirdre laughed with delight. 'Wow, Maeve –

that was excellent! I've never seen her look so scared!'

Maeve gave a satisfied smile. 'Anyway, where was I?'

'Ann Fitzroy had gone up to her bedroom.'

'Oh, yeah. Well, just as Jacqueline and her team were starting work, a delivery van arrived and off-loaded all these toy animals – you know, the really expensive stuffed velour ones.'

'For their daughter? But I thought she was well into her teens. Why would Ann Fitzroy be buying her furry toys at her age?'

'They weren't for the daughter,' said Maeve. 'She wasn't even there. Apparently she's spending the summer in France before she starts university. She's off to Cambridge in the autumn.'

Deirdre looked puzzled. 'Who *were* they for, then?'

'For the guests.'

'What?'

'Yep. Every single guest was presented with a cuddly toy when they arrived and told that if they took care of it for the duration of the party, they'd be allowed to take it home.'

'But that's so *weird*!'

'That wasn't the only weird thing she did. She took Jacqueline's team down to a kind of pantry in the basement which had been converted into a wine cellar. Jacqueline said it was amazing – full of racks of the most extraordinary wine. Apparently David Lawless is something of a connoisseur–'

'An oenophile, you mean?' said Deirdre.

Maeve smiled. 'An oenophile, yeah. Anyway, she made them take every single bottle of wine upstairs to the reception room and uncork them. All told, Jacqueline reckoned there were around five hundred bottles. There was even some Château d'Yquem.'

'Shit. How many people arrived?'

'Not that many, funnily enough. Jacqueline had been told to cater for fifty, but only around thirty showed in the end.'

'Wow. Five hundred bottles of wine for only thirty people! Did the cast of *Ardmore Grove* show up?'

'No – most of the guests were socialites. Only two or three of the cast arrived in the end.'

'And you weren't invited?'

Maeve laughed. 'God, no. Ann Fitzroy wouldn't let *me* near her nobby do.'

'They must all have been pissed as newts by the end of the evening.'

'Apparently the evening wasn't that long. People made their excuses and left pretty early. Jacqueline said that everyone just looked really embarrassed, sitting around clutching these fluffy toys and trying to pretend that it was another normal event in the social calendar. By eleven o'clock there was just Ann Fitzroy and some die-hard boozers left.'

'Was she off her face?'

'No, surprisingly enough. She should have been, according to Jacqueline, but she said Ann was wired to the moon, not falling down drunk.'

Just then Sophie swanned past carrying a bottle of Sol and a pint of Budweiser.

'For Sebastian,' she said to Deirdre, indicating the pint with a complacent little smile.

Deirdre turned her back on her and raised her eyes to heaven.

'You must introduce me to this Sebastian dude,' said Maeve. 'I'd love to find out if he's as fascinating and charming as you've made him out to be.'

'Oh – he is, Maeve!' replied Deirdre. 'I'll introduce you now, if you like.'

Maeve nodded in the direction of Jacqueline, who was waving at her and pointing at her watch. 'I don't have time right now – I'd better make tracks. We're going to see some new stand-up at the Da Club.' Maeve smiled and made a move to go.

'Hang on a sec, Maeve. There's one more thing I want to know. Why did Ann Fitzroy open so many bottles of expensive wine? She can't have thought it would all be drunk.'

'It's pretty obvious, isn't it? Revenge on David. At the end of the evening she insisted that what hadn't been drunk was to be poured down the sink. Gallons of the stuff went down the plughole.'

'I don't believe you!' Deirdre was aghast.

''Fraid so. It nearly broke Jacqueline's heart. She managed to sneak an unopened Margaux, though – a Grand Cru Classé. We're saving it for a special occasion.'

'What a doolally thing to do!'

'That's not the end of it. She insisted that all the bottles be put in black rubbish sacks and then booked taxis for her drunken friends, gave them Eva's address and told them to dump the bags outside her door.'

'Oh my God – David must have been fuming!'

'Did he look like an unhappy man to you this evening?' asked Maeve. 'I've a feeling that Eva's more precious to him than a whole Château full of Margaux.'

Jacqueline arrived at Maeve's elbow. 'Lover, if we don't go now we're going to miss the beginning. Hi, Deirdre, how's it going?'

'Fine thanks, Jacqueline. Maeve was filling me in on Ann Fitzroy's bash the other night.'

'You witness some pretty peculiar goings-on in my job. Don't repeat it, Deirdre.'

'Don't worry.' She saw Jacqueline glance at her watch. 'Look – I won't delay you. Enjoy the show. See you in the morning, Maeve – you're called, aren't you?'

'Yup. Night, Deirdre.'

'Night.'

Deirdre made her way back to where Sebastian and Sophie were sitting. They had now been joined by Kate and Jessica, who were laughing loudly at something Sebastian had said. Her mind was reeling. She had never suspected that grown-ups – and until recently she'd considered Ann Fitzroy to be as grown-up as you could get – could be capable of behaving like particularly spoilt six-year-olds. She sat down next to Sophie who, she realized to her dismay, was just about to opine on the current production at the Gate.

Sebastian looked up and gave Deirdre his beautiful smile. 'It's about time I went,' he said, looking at his watch. 'No offence to the present company, but I'm really exhausted. I was up at the crack of dawn to catch my flight this morning.'

'Where are you staying, Sebastian?' asked Sophie.

'The Clarence. Do you know it?'

'Of course I do – everyone knows the Clarence. It's U2's hotel.' Sophie looked urbane. 'In fact I had lunch in the Tea Room just last week.'

'Isn't it a bit pricey to stay there, Sebastian?' asked Deirdre.

Sebastian looked a bit embarrassed. 'Well, actually, I'm staying there gratis. Bono's a bit of a mate of mine.'

Four jaws dropped, and Sophie actually said 'What?' instead of 'Pardon me?'

'Yeah,' Sebastian smiled apologetically. 'I met him during the filming of *Twitchers*. I only had a small part, but Bono hung out with the cast while we were on location in Scotland – the band was touring at the time. He's a really sound bloke, Bono, and when I knew I was coming to Dublin I gave him a bell. He invited me to stay at his hotel and told me not to worry about the tab.'

Deirdre was dying to see *Twitchers*. It was a cult new wave British film which had just been released, and U2 had composed the soundtrack. She was impressed. Imagine knowing Bono and not feeling the need to boast about it! The more she found out about Sebastian Hardy, the more interesting he became. 'Are you going to see him while you're here?' she asked. Maybe, just maybe, she'd get an introduction.

''Fraid not. The band's still on the road.' Sebastian stood up. 'Temple Bar isn't that far a walk, is it?'

'No, but it can be quite easy to get lost,' said Deirdre. She was having an inspired idea. 'Actually, it's not far from where I live, Sebastian. I could show you the way, if you like?'

Opposite her Sophie went all stiff.

'I've got a better idea,' smiled Sebastian. 'Let's get a cab and I'll drop you off. That is, if you don't mind leaving now?'

Deirdre's heart started to flitter like a humming-bird. 'I'd love to,' she said, trying not to beam too radiantly.

'Fine,' said Sebastian. Deirdre hoped that Sophie saw the smile he gave her as he slung his jacket over his shoulder. 'Let's go, then. Goodnight, Sophie. Goodnight, Jessica, Kate. I look forward to seeing you all again next month.'

'Goodnight, Sebastian,' they called in unison as he and Deirdre headed towards the door. She snuck a look towards where Rory had been sitting, but he was no longer there. Dammit, she thought. She'd hoped that she'd be able to score a point by letting him see her leave the pub escorted by Sebastian Hardy.

As they passed by the bar, she spotted him. He was leaning on the counter with another large whiskey in front of him, talking to a Demi Moore clone. Sebastian paused to have a word with Nick McCarthy, and Deirdre felt rather uncomfortably as if she was treading water. Rory was laying on his stupid sexy laugh, and the gorgeous girl was obviously falling for it. Deirdre felt like giving her a warning. Suddenly his eyes met hers, and for the second time that evening Deirdre found it difficult to look away. He studied her for a moment or two through narrowed lids and then let his glance slide to where Sebastian stood next to her. He grinned. Then he turned to his companion, excused himself, and steered himself in her direction. Deirdre noticed that his gait was very slightly unsteady.

'Where's your friend staying tonight, Deirdre?'

Deirdre didn't like the look in Rory's eyes. Maeve had been right. He was dangerous tonight. She wanted to ignore him, but something made her think it wouldn't be a wise thing to do, so instead she shifted her gaze away from him and looked intently into the middle distance. 'The Clarence,' she said with careful carelessness.

'Not The Seraglio? I'm surprised.' Rory's gaze travelled down her body and back up again, and finally came to rest on her breasts. To her horror, she felt her nipples harden under her thin cotton T-shirt.

Rory looked at her closely and smiled. 'You look flushed, sweetheart. Better get some air. It's never a good idea to get too hot too soon. But of course, you already know that. Have fun,' and he returned to the bar where Demi Moore was waiting for him.

Thankfully Sebastian was just coming to the end of his conversation with Nick McCarthy.

'Can we go now, Sebastian? It's got awfully stuffy in here,' she asked.

'Sure,' he answered. 'Bye, Nick – and thanks for everything.'

The air outside, though sultry, still felt welcomingly refreshing, and Deirdre breathed it in deeply as they strolled to the taxi rank. Being Monday, getting a cab wasn't a problem, and they were soon on their way to Sebastian's hotel.

'I'll get out at the Clarence, Sebastian. I'm literally only about five minutes' walk away.'

'Nonsense. I'll leave you at your door, Deirdre. I'm not going to allow a beautiful woman to walk two steps down the street on her own at this hour of the evening.' His arm was draped along the back of the seat, and Deirdre wished that Sophie could see her now.

'It's going to be a nice crowd to work with,' he said. 'I'm glad I didn't sign a contract for that Australian movie.'

'Will you be around tomorrow, Sebastian?' Deirdre asked hopefully. 'I could show you around Temple Bar, if you like? I'm free in the afternoon.'

'I don't think I'll have time tomorrow. I'll have to see about organizing somewhere to live. Nick told me there are a couple of flats in town which are let exclusively to visiting theatre and film people, and I might try to recce them.'

'What about tomorrow evening? Do you think you might come to the pub again?' Deirdre realized that she was starting to sound slightly desperate, and gave herself a mental warning to back off a bit.

'I arranged to meet my friend in the Abbey bar after the show. We might move on to your local afterwards, though, if there's time.'

Deirdre wished she hadn't said anything. She didn't want Sebastian turning up in Meagher's with some looker on his arm.

'It would be nice to see you again before I go,' he continued. 'And I'd love to get another opportunity to talk to David and Eva.' There was a pause, then: 'That's some story, isn't it – about the two of them finally getting together after all these years? It would make a wonderful film.'

'Yes – with Gabriel Byrne as David Lawless,' said Deirdre enthusiastically. 'He'd have to wear coloured contacts, though. His eyes are too blue. And who would be Eva?'

'I'm not sure there's an actress alive who could play Eva Lavery,' said Sebastian slowly.

Deirdre smiled. 'I think you're right,' she said.

'I know I am,' said Sebastian. But there was no answering smile in his voice. His arm on the seat behind her shoulders was no longer relaxed, and he had turned his face away from her and was staring out the window into darkness. Deirdre could have kicked herself for bringing up the subject of Eva.

'Oh – can you drop me right here!' she called to the taxi driver. He obligingly pulled up alongside the kerb just outside her apartment block.

Sebastian turned back to her and smiled into her eyes. 'Goodnight, Ophelia,' he said. 'If I don't see you tomorrow evening I'll see you on the first day of rehearsal. You know something? David was absolutely right. We'll work well together, you and I.' Then Sebastian leaned down and kissed her on the mouth. It wasn't a passionate kiss but it was quite clearly the kind of kiss you reserve for someone who is more than just a friend. It was, Deirdre decided, an exploratory kiss, as if he was trying to ascertain whether or not she would respond. She did.

After a minute he lifted his lips from hers. 'You'd better go in,' he said gently.

Deirdre did as she was told.

Chapter Fourteen

Costume fittings had been arranged for the following day, and Deirdre was called first, along with Kate and Sophie. Jessica hadn't been cast in *Macbeth* because there was no part for her, so she'd glumly scratched the 'Acting' from her title and resumed her duties as an ordinary ASM. However, when she'd seen some of the costume designs that Jenny Cummings had shown them on the first day of rehearsal, she'd almost breathed a sigh of relief that she wasn't in it. Jenny's design concept was drawn from the era of the Thirties and was inspired by the Depression. The witches were to represent vagrants in cast-off clothing that was meant to look as if it had been scavenged from second-hand shops.

Deirdre arrived at Jenny's studio to find the designer sitting at her desk sketching. Deirdre noticed that the designs she was working on were for *Hamlet*, and she hoped that maybe she'd get a sneak preview of her Ophelia costume. Jenny's assistant Roxanne showed her to the rail where her costume was hanging. Deirdre's heart sank like a stone. It comprised a knitted jumper, a man's jacket, a mid-calf tweed golfing skirt, thick woollen socks and a pair of battered, mannish boots. The crowning glory was a knitted bobble hat.

The outfit she was to wear as Lady Macbeth's lady-in-waiting was a bit better, she was glad to see, although it wouldn't do too much to flatter her either. It was a fitted wool suit in the rather strict, masculine style favoured by Wallis Simpson and was a particularly drab shade of grey. Deirdre didn't care if grey was the happening fashion colour – she knew it did absolutely nothing for *her*. She also knew that all that wool meant that she was going to be hot as hell on stage under the lamps.

It was some consolation, she supposed, that the costume hanging next to hers on the rail which bore Kate's name was nearly as bad as hers – although at least Kate had trousers and an old top hat to wear which Deirdre would have much preferred to her spinsterish skirt and trainspotter's hat. She thought with longing of her gossamer-light *Dream* dress as she struggled into the shapeless jumper and tied the laces on her heavy boots. There was something inside the left one, so she took it off again so that she could inspect it. She gingerly poked around inside the boot with her fingers until she made contact with the unidentified object and extracted it. It was a used corn plaster. She dropped it as though it had burnt her.

'Oh – *gross*, Jenny – there's an old corn plaster in my boot! Oh – yeuch, yeuch! Oh – *yeuch*!'

'Sorry about that, Deirdre. Roxanne picked a load of shoes up in the thrift shop down the road. I've actually known worse things to come out of that shop. I'll spare you the details.'

Bloody Roxanne might have checked the boots out before letting her try them on, Deirdre thought crossly. She slid her foot back into the boot as if expecting it to bite her.

'Perfect!' exclaimed Jenny with pleasure as Deirdre shuffled out of the changing cubicle. She stood back and looked at her critically and then circled her, pulling at the fabric of the jacket from time to time and pointing out details that needed changing to the wardrobe mistress. Deirdre looked at her reflection in the cheval glass and wanted to die. Sebastian had mentioned that he'd come over in time for the opening night. What on earth would he think when he saw her like this?

Just then the door opened and Sophie waltzed in, squawking on her mobile. She stopped dead when she saw Deirdre and then let out a shriek of laughter. 'Wow – the Bag-lady from the Bog! Sorry, Daddy – I'd better go. I'm speechless, suddenly. Yeah – thanks again, Dad.' She switched off her phone and gave Deirdre the once-over. 'Wow, Deirdre, you look amazing. The absolute cutting edge of grunge. And that hat really sets off the look. You should have a makeover more often.' And as she started to laugh again Deirdre unleashed a filthy look and Jenny looked nettled.

'Just get into your costume, will you, Sophie?' she said tersely. 'It's on the rail with your name tag on it.'

As Sophie rummaged among the items on the rail Deirdre thought dark thoughts. She hadn't thought to look at the design for Sophie's costume on the first day of rehearsal because she'd been too devastated when she'd seen her own to think about anyone else's, but she fully expected it to be as grim as hers. Worse, she hoped. She couldn't wait till Sophie came out of the cubicle and had to face herself in the mirror. She'd take care not to laugh, though. That would be a bit juvenile. The most she'd allow herself would be a covert smirk.

'The Thirties was such a bleak period, wasn't it, Jenny?' she said, trying to avoid looking at her reflection.

'Yeah. It was David who came up with the idea of setting it in the inter-war era. It's a real contrast to *Dream*, isn't it?'

'Mm,' responded Deirdre, trying not to sound too glum. 'What's Lady Macbeth wearing?'

'Oh, I've got some stunning stuff for Eva.' Jenny had finished issuing instructions to the wardrobe mistress and was jotting down details in a big notebook. 'For the banquet scene she's wearing white satin, based on a gown by Vionnet – you know, those gorgeous bias-cut dresses that flow out when you move? Lady Macbeth would have been at the forefront of fashion, we reckoned, and would have worn nothing but designer stuff. That's when I got the idea for Sophie's costume.'

Roxanne floated past with a pair of exquisite silk pyjamas on a hanger.

'For Lady M. in the sleepwalking scene,' said Jenny, indicating the pyjamas. 'Anyway, where was I? Oh, yes – well, you know the way we want to convey the idea that the three witches are supposed to have scavenged for their clothes in second-hand shops? Well, Sophie's the witch that got lucky. She visited the second-hand shop on the day that Lady Macbeth's maid was off-loading last season's stuff.'

Deirdre wasn't really listening. She wasn't interested in Sophie's costume. She wanted to steer the conversation round to the subject of the next production so that she could find out what she'd be wearing as Ophelia. 'Oh yeah?' she said. She was just about to ask her what period *Hamlet* was going to be set in when the curtain to the changing cubicle was pulled back, and Sophie drifted out.

'Oh – look at my beautiful replica Chanel!' cried Jenny.

Sophie was wearing a stunning gold lamé evening dress with a matching pleated jacket and a radiant smile. The outfit had been distressed to look second-hand, with a great rip in the skirt, one arm missing from the jacket and dirt plastered around the hem to look as though it had been trailed through mud, but there was no denying that the dress retained much of its original glamour, and that Sophie wore it extremely well. The single bare shoulder looked incredibly sexy, and the tightly belted waist showed off her slender figure to perfection.

Deirdre thought she might throw up. 'Shall I get into the Gentlewoman's outfit now, Jenny?' she asked with forced carelessness. She needed an excuse to get away from Sophie.

'Yes, do, please, Deirdre. I think there may be a problem with that. I've a hunch it may be a tad too elegant.' She turned her attention back to Sophie. 'I'll have to break this dress down a little bit more, I think. You look so fab in it, Sophie, that we'd run the risk of you upstaging the other witches.'

'Not hard to do!' laughed Sophie.

Deirdre slouched back into the cubicle feeling venomous and thinking that really things couldn't get very much worse. She'd have to devise some subtle way of letting Sophie know that Sebastian had kissed her in the taxi last night – she might feel a bit better if the other actress knew about that.

* * *

They were now into their third week of rehearsals for *Macbeth* and Deirdre found that she wasn't enjoying herself as much as she'd done during *Dream*. Rehearsals weren't as demanding, and she spent a lot of time hanging around doing nothing. In spite of her history with Rory, she kind of missed working with him. He'd always been able to make her laugh.

She also knew that she wasn't concentrating hard enough on her work. Instead of observing David from the sidelines as she had done when he'd directed *Dream* and learning from his example, she tended to obsess about Ophelia. She had even taken to reading *Hamlet* in the evenings when she went back to the flat in preference to doing her homework on *Macbeth*, trying to justify her behaviour by reminding herself that Ophelia was a much tougher role than either First Witch or Lady

Macbeth's lady-in-waiting. Then she would remember what David Lawless had said to her that night on the terrace of Meagher's – that there *are* no small parts, only small actors – and she'd feel guilty.

She also felt guilty because she wasted a lot of time in the rehearsal room thinking about Sebastian, and fantasizing about what it would be like to work with him, in much the same way that she'd fantasized about David Lawless during previous rehearsal sessions. It was funny, she thought, that the demise of her obsession with David Lawless had seemed to happen just around the same time as his reunion with Eva Lavery. David had been a kind of father figure for her, she decided. It was probably a better idea to stick to someone closer to her own age – especially someone as gorgeous as Sebastian.

He hadn't shown up with his old girlfriend in Meagher's on his last evening in Dublin and she had to admit that, although she would have loved to have seen him again, she wouldn't have been able to tolerate the look on Rory's face if he'd seen Sebastian with a different woman the very evening after Deirdre had left the pub with him.

She also thought a lot about the kiss Sebastian had given her, and wondered what it signified in terms of their relationship. She was a bit confused by it. Was he intending to take her to bed in due course, or had he simply felt that it was *de rigueur* to kiss a young woman in the back of a taxi? She'd kissed loads of men – well, a few, anyway – in the backs of taxis and never bothered to take things any further. Maybe it was just a kiss between friends. Although it had been intimate, it had had none of the awful carnality of the abandoned kisses she'd exchanged with Rory.

She shuddered now when she thought of those kisses. Thank God she seldom saw him these days. She took care to avoid him in rehearsal and in the pub after the show. Her hopes that Eva might persuade some of the cast to switch allegiance to O'Riordans had never materialized – in fact, neither David nor Eva showed up much in Meagher's any more. They were probably too busy making up for lost time.

Although she rarely socialized with the actress after the show, she often gravitated towards her in the green room, and occasionally visited her in the dressing-room for a chat. It was unusual, she knew, for an ingénue like her to have such a familiar relationship with an actress of the stature of Eva Lavery, but since the day when Eva had invited Deirdre into her home, they'd become quite friendly. Deirdre had even found out from something Nick McCarthy had let slip that it had been Eva who had originally suggested to David that Deirdre take over as Hermia in *Dream.* In a way she felt that she had become a kind of protégée in Eva's eyes. It was as if an honour had been conferred upon her. She sometimes toyed with the idea of visiting the actress in her home again, but now she knew that David Lawless was living there too, she found the prospect too embarrassing.

She still watched Eva when she wasn't too busy fantasizing about Hamlet and Ophelia. Eva's Lady Macbeth was a totally passionate creation, and Deirdre was so mesmerized by her performance that, on a couple of occasions during the sleep-walking scene, she had completely forgotten to come in with one of her lines as the attendant Gentlewoman.

The scene in Act One where Lady Macbeth urges her husband to murder Duncan was white-hot with adrenalin and energy – Eva and Finbar sparked off each other as they did in the evenings when they became Titania and Oberon – and as she watched them Deirdre would sometimes realize that she was holding her breath. There was one speech in particular that fascinated her. It wasn't just the shocking imagery of the language that made it memorable – it was the ferocity with which Eva delivered it. Deirdre knew it by heart, and she would recite it inwardly along with Eva as the actress rehearsed:

I have given suck, and know
How tender 'tis to love the babe that
milks me:
I would, while it was smiling in my face,
Have pluck'd my nipple from his
boneless gums
And dash'd the brains out, had I so
sworn
As you have done to this.

Eva invested the speech with such extraordinary fervour that one afternoon as she was rehearsing the scene she broke down and wept. The company went silent as David put his arms around her and held her for a while until she calmed. Then he told the company to take fifteen, and he left the room with Eva leaning her head on his shoulder.

It was strange, Deirdre thought, that the actress should find it so problematic to keep her emotions in check during this particular speech. The way she played it reminded Deirdre of the way she played the speech in *Midsummer Night's Dream* where Titania makes reference to her 'changeling child' – the speech David Lawless had warned her about during the notes session just before the show had opened. She'd had difficulty reining herself in back then, too.

As she meandered into the coffee room she overheard Finbar talking to Nick McCarthy. 'It's the old biological clock, of course. Lavery's wondering if she's left it too late to have babies – especially now that she and David are back together. She's probably a bit broody at the moment.'

Deirdre reckoned that Finbar was probably right – even though he wasn't renowned for his insight into the female psyche. Poor Eva. Maybe she was really desperate to have a baby before time ran out for her, and all the references to babies in the parts she was playing were upsetting her.

* * *

Late on the Sunday morning before production week, Deirdre went down to her local Spar shop to get some tins. She had hoped to be able to go out to her mum and dad in Kilmacanogue and get something decent to eat, but they'd gone off to the West of Ireland to visit her grandmother. She had no other social inclinations. She was a bit hungover from celebrating the last night of *Dream* the night before and she knew it wasn't wise to be too sociable the day before the tech and dress rehearsals, so she decided she'd spend all day in the flat with *Macbeth* and the Sunday papers and chill.

As she rounded the corner of the road she saw a dirty white Karmann Ghia parked on a double yellow outside the shop. She immediately suspected that it was Eva's, and a glance at the untidy interior confirmed that this was the case. Inside the shop Eva, wearing chandeliers in her ears and nothing on her feet, was buying papers and croissants and looking out of place. Somehow it had never occurred to Deirdre that her leading lady was capable of doing mundane things like Sunday morning shopping.

'Hi, honey!' she said as Deirdre approached her. 'Goodie gumdrops – what a stroke of luck to have run into you! Come home with me and have breakfast. You can keep me company for an hour or two. David left for London at the crack of dawn and I'm feeling unbearably lonely.'

'I'd love to, Eva,' said Deirdre happily. 'Why are you wearing the crown jewels to the local supermarket, by the way?'

'The crown jewels?'

Deirdre indicated the glitzy earrings. 'Oh – these! They're rather gorgeous, aren't they? I must have forgotten to take them off before I went to bed last night. They weren't high on my list of priorities when I was undressing.' She delved around in her bag for money. 'Hah! If you come back with me it means I'll have an excuse to put off loading the dishwasher. We had people round for supper after the show last night and the place is a complete mess. Two more croissants, please,' she said to the star-struck shop assistant.

Deirdre followed Eva to the car and prepared to suffer a degree of trauma as Eva drove back to her house in her habitually erratic fashion. Being Sunday morning, the streets were mercifully empty.

Eva had been quite right. The house was a mess. The long refectory table was littered with crumpled napkins, half-empty wine glasses, side plates with the remains of cheese and biscuits on them, and coffee cups. There were lots of flowers in vases all over the room, and a small platoon of wine bottles stood by the back door, looking as if they were ready to march out by themselves. Deirdre spotted a note on the table in David Lawless's bold black handwriting, held down by the kind of little boxes you get from jeweller's shops.

She found herself wondering who Eva and David's dinner guests might have been, and what kind of conversation had flowed along with the wine around that table the previous night. A host of celebrities had been in to catch the show before it closed, and she pictured Eva and David sitting at opposite ends of the table chatting and laughing with Jim Sheridan and Frank McGuinness and Brenda Fricker and all the other luminaries of the Irish film world she'd seen leaving the pub with Eva last night. As she passed through to the garden she noticed a framed costume design by Monica Frawley of the leading lady in some period drama, with a message scrawled in the corner. 'Thanks for the grub, Lavery,' she read.

'Ignore everything, darling. Just go through into the garden and I'll bring the coffee out in two shakes. Dammit, I'll have to rinse out the cafetière, won't I?'

'I'll do it, Eva,' volunteered Deirdre.

'It's all right. I'm going to ask you to help me load the dishwasher later, though. I *hate* doing that.'

'I thought you hated cooking as well. How did you manage to feed all those people last night?'

Eva looked at her blankly. 'David did it, of course, darling,' she said.

Deirdre went through the glass doors which led out on to a patio where a blue slatted wooden table and four matching chairs stood. Deirdre had seen them in the window of Habitat as she'd passed by the week before.

Eva's garden was rather wild, but very beautiful. There were three wide steps flanked by two enormous Japanese urns leading down from the patio onto a long strip of grass which was bordered by densely planted flower beds. At the far end of the garden was a pergola over which clambered a mass of small pink roses. Deirdre strolled down the lawn along a slate pathway, marvelling that such a perfectly lovely, secluded place could exist only a few minutes' walk from the city centre. The high, ivy covered walls meant that Eva's garden could not be overlooked by neighbours. There were two deck-chairs under the beams of the pergola. Yesterday's *Irish Times*, yellowish from lying out in the sun, and a biography of Sam Beckett lay beside them on the paved area. There was a raised pond in a recess, virtually overgrown with pink water blossoms and choked with weed. Deirdre peered in and saw a dead fish floating on the top.

'Eva? There's a dead fish in your pond,' Deirdre called to the actress as she emerged onto the patio carrying a big wooden tray.

'Shit. Another koi bites the dust. Or should I say bites the scum? I completely forgot to ask David to clean out the pond. I'll be in trouble with Barbara again.'

'Who's Barbara?' asked Deirdre as she walked back up the path to where Eva was transferring cups and plates from the tray onto the table.

'She does the garden for me. She's a wizard. She looks at a plant and it thrives. I look at the same plant and it keels over. That's why I always wear sunglasses in the garden even in the winter so that the plants won't see me looking at them – or else I sneak through apologetically with downcast eyes.' Eva plunged the coffee and poured it into cups. 'Sit down, darling. Help yourself to croissants.'

'What's David doing in London?' Deirdre asked.

'Meeting actors for his next RSC gig.'

'On a Sunday?'

'It's the only day he has free. When he gets back this evening he'll be heading straight into the theatre. I probably won't see him till the morning.'

'Will he be seeing Sebastian while he's in London?' Deirdre realized that her attempt at nonchalance was really pretty pathetic.

'No.' Eva looked at Deirdre shrewdly. 'Do you fancy Sebastian, darling?' she asked.

Deirdre was fazed by the actress's directness. 'Oh – well, I mean, I'm not really sure,' she said, suddenly uncertain. 'I suppose I must do. He's a really nice guy. And he's seriously good-looking.'

'That's not a reason to fancy anyone, Deirdre. I fancy David rotten, but he's no Adonis.'

'Oh, but David's so *sexy*.' It came out before Deirdre could stop herself.

Eva laughed. 'Oh, Deirdre, you blush divinely! You're absolutely right. He's the sexiest man I know, and I'm very lucky to have him. God knows, I waited long enough,' she added with a thoughtful look. She took a sip of coffee. 'Do you know something, darling? We might never have got together if it hadn't been for you.'

'What do you mean, Eva?' Deirdre asked curiously.

'Well, do you remember the time you told me that David had had a tattoo done?'

'Yes?'

'It was a sign to me that he'd reached a turning

point in his life, and that it was time for me to rescue him by taking him back into my bed at last.'

Deirdre was slightly taken aback by Eva's revelation, but she was dying to find out exactly what the actress meant. 'What do you mean, Eva?'

'I presume you're aware that we had a relationship once? A rather passionate one as a matter of fact.' She looked down at her plate with a private little smile on her face.

'Well, yes I do, actually,' Deirdre confessed.

Eva's smile broadened. 'I'd be more surprised if you didn't know. This town has little respect for secrets. Anyway,' she tore off a bit of croissant and applied butter liberally. 'Once upon a time David and I were so besotted with each other that we decided we needed permanent symbols of our undying devotion. We made a plan to go together one afternoon to a tattoo parlour to have identical tattoos done.'

'Johnny Eagle's?'

'The very place. How did you guess?'

'Rory had his done there too.' Deirdre wished she hadn't mentioned Rory's tattoo. It brought back an image of her on a white sheet, dragging her nails down his back.

'How interesting,' said Eva with a smile, and then continued. 'Well, David didn't show and I got very cross. So instead of getting a romantic, hearts-and-flowersy type of tattoo I opted for something a little more aggressive. I could have had a tiger or a dragon, but I thought that might be a bit butch. I wanted something beautiful that would still suggest ferocity and so I asked Johnny to do–'

'A Siamese Fighting Fish,' said Deirdre.

'You're on the ball today darling. How did you know that?'

'I saw it on the nape of your neck that day you asked me for a massage.'

'Observant creature!' Eva smiled at her over the rim of her big coffee cup.

'Where had David got to, Eva?' Deirdre prompted tentatively.

There was a pause, and then Eva said: 'I only found that out the next day. David had been summoned to Ann Fitzroy's father's house. There he was made to feel that he had no alternative but to do the honourable thing and agree to marry Mr Fitzroy's daughter because she was pregnant by him.'

Deirdre didn't say anything. Eva was looking off down the garden. They both sat in silence for a while. Then: 'She miscarried, so they say,' she said. She gave a little shake of her aristocratic head. 'Poor David,' she continued. 'If *I* went through hell then so did he. He was stuck in that marriage for over two decades.'

'Why did he *stay* with her?' The thought of David spending two decades in hell filled her with indignation. She hadn't survived five minutes in Ann Fitzroy's company.

'David has the most integrity of any person I know.' Eva leant forward with her elbows on the table and her elegant hands wrapped around her coffee cup. 'He struggled for a few years to try and make the marriage work. He even asked me to consider continuing our relationship clandestinely, but I knew I could never hack that. It had to be all or nothing.' She took a sip of her coffee. 'Once his daughter Aoife was born David vowed that he would continue with a parody of wedded bliss until she was old enough to leave home. And she's just left – she's going to university in England soon. Cambridge, in fact. She's a very bright girl. David's devoted to her.'

He'd named his daughter Aoife, the Irish for Eva. Deirdre remembered with some embarrassment that she'd actually once entertained a fantasy about one day becoming Aoife Lawless's stepmother.

Just then the cordless phone on the table between them started to ring. Eva picked it up and pressed the talk button. 'Hello?' she said. 'Oh, hi, darling.' The actress leaned back in her chair and an expression of near-beatification crossed her face. 'No, I haven't been up for very long. Oh, just sitting in the garden having breakfast. Not yet – I promise I'll do all my homework later. Yes. I found it. It's absolutely beautiful, thank you, darling.' Eva stretched out her left hand and gazed at it. Deirdre followed the actress's eyes and saw that she was wearing a circle of small diamonds on the third finger which she had never seen before. It flashed brilliantly in the sunlight.

It really was dead romantic, she thought – the two of them getting together after all those years spent apart, yearning for each other. She felt a kind of delighted pride that she had actually been instrumental in their reunion. She picked the last crumbs of croissant from her plate.

'No, not too lonely, thanks,' said Eva on the phone. 'I ran into Deirdre O'Dare at the supermarket when I was buying the papers and brought her home to keep me company. Yeah – she's here right now.'

Deirdre picked up the tray and quickly stacked cups and plates onto it from the table. Then she disappeared off in the direction of the kitchen, stopping on the way to add some of the empty wine glasses from the previous evening's dinner. As she started to load the dishwasher she couldn't stop thinking about Eva and David and the misery they'd both gone through.

What, she wondered, had those two lost decades cost them?

Chapter Fifteen

The first day of production week dawned, and Deirdre fetched her frumpy witch's costume from the rail with a heavy heart. She sprayed her feet furiously with Doctor Scholl's Refreshing Foot Mist before putting on her second-hand boots. Sophie kept making excuses to leave the dressing-room so that she could swish past in her golden dress, humming little tunes.

The costume Jenny had designed for Maeve was based on a suit by Schiaparelli with a sequinned jacket over shocking pink palazzo pants. Not everybody could get away with such a dramatic look, but Maeve had the height to carry it and she looked stunning. Deirdre wished that the First Witch had visited the second-hand shop on the day that Lady Macduff had done *her* bit for charity, but knowing her luck she'd have ended up with one of Schiaparelli's famous fashion follies – a cast-off 'chest of drawers' suit or a witty 'shoe' hat.

She trundled down to the stage in her clumpy boots feeling miserably self-conscious, but contrary to her expectations nobody sniggered or looked askance at her – not even Rory. She thought she'd have been a sitting target for his fatuous remarks. It began to dawn on her that vanity in an actor was as undesirable and counterproductive as squeamishness in a nurse or fear in a stunt man.

But she still steered well clear of the green room mirror. The Wicked Witch of the West had style when compared to this particular First Witch of the Blasted Heath. She remembered how Rory had compared her to a wicked witch that day when she'd made the mistake of calling to his house, except he'd said it in a way that had made her feel that she was sexy, whether she liked it or not. Even Finbar de Rossa wouldn't find anything about her sexy now.

At least now she didn't have to kiss Rory every night. During the last week of *Dream* she'd counted down how many more times she'd have to embrace him, and she went through the final performance congratulating herself on what a consummate actress she was that she could kiss someone she hated so much with such easily feigned ardour.

Sebastian's good luck card to the company for the opening night of *Macbeth* had arrived a day early. It had been pinned along with all the other early arrivals to the green room notice-board, which was looking festive once more. In a few days the cards would be replaced by the usual Equity notices, repeated futile requests from Stage Management to restrict smoking to the green room, and rehearsal schedules. And this time Sebastian's name would feature on the call sheets! Deirdre couldn't wait until she read that the Mousetrap scene was scheduled for rehearsal – that was the scene where Hamlet lays his head in

Ophelia's lap. She prinked at the prospect.

Sebastian had sent her a card too – a reproduction of Klimt's 'The Kiss' with a message inside which simply read: 'Good luck tonight – see you after the show. Love, Sebastian.' The only other member of the company to have received a card from him was Eva. Deirdre got revenge on Sophie for the frock by announcing 'From Sebastian – how nice,' and reading the message out loud, pausing for effect before the word 'Love'.

Deirdre visited Eva in her dressing-room well before the half-hour call this time. It bore its usual opening-night resemblance to the hothouse in the Botanical Gardens. Eva was sitting in her white gown idly opening cards and then throwing them aside after a perfunctory perusal of their contents. They were strewn like bright petals across her dressing-table.

This time Deirdre had felt brave enough to present the actors with individual sketches she'd made of them as their opening night presents. She'd had more time on her hands in rehearsal to execute them, and was actually quite proud of them. She hadn't wanted to give Rory or Sophie anything, but she thought that by leaving them out it might look as if she actually had any kind of opinion of either of them, so she deliberately gave them unflattering portraits. She was particularly pleased with Rory's. He'd been sending lecherous looks to Eva at the time, and he looked all squinty in the drawing.

'This is beautiful, darling!' exclaimed Eva. 'Why, you have a real talent, don't you? I'm going to frame this and hang it on my dressing-room wall, along with the photographs.' Eva smiled at her and then cocked her head to one side and adopted a meditative expression. 'Actually, maybe I've a better idea. I'll put it in one of those travelling photograph frames and make David take it with him every time he goes away. It might remind him that I have an extremely jealous nature. Thank you, darling. I'm extremely touched.'

Feeling pleased, Deirdre started towards the door, but a strange little gasp from Eva made her turn back to the actress.

'Oh – how horrid!' She had just opened an envelope and taken out a sheet of note paper. She dropped it as if it was white hot.

'What is it, Eva?'

The actress didn't reply. She had gone very white and was holding her hands up to her face. She sat utterly still for a long moment, looking as if she had been carved from marble.

Deirdre was terribly concerned. She wanted to know what had upset her friend. Without thinking what she was doing she retrieved the sheet of paper from where it lay on the floor and looked at it. There was one typewritten sentence on it and no signature. It read: 'Bring forth men-children only!' Deirdre made the connection immediately. The sentence was a quote from the play that was to open that very evening. It was a line spoken by Macbeth to his Lady at the end of Act One.

'What does it mean?' Deirdre was puzzled. She also felt suddenly very disturbed.

Eva slowly let her hands sink to her lap. She took a long, rather ragged breath and said: 'It's nothing. It's not important.' She was still ashen and obviously very shaken. Then she turned to Deirdre. 'Listen to me, Deirdre. *This* is important. You mustn't tell anybody about this – not a single soul. Do you give me your solemn promise that you won't?'

Deirdre was uncertain. 'But what about David, Eva? Don't you think you should tell him? He might be able to help – to suggest a reason behind it, even?'

'Absolutely not. Please promise me that you won't breathe a word to David about this. I can handle it myself – honestly I can,' and the actress attempted a rather crooked smile of reassurance.

'All right, Eva. I promise.' Deirdre was actually extremely doubtful. She wasn't at all convinced that Eva was doing the right thing, but she'd made a promise, and Deirdre O'Dare kept her promises. 'Is there anything *I* can do to help?'

'No. Yes. Pick up that envelope and see if there's a postmark on it. I can't bring myself to touch it.'

Deirdre did as she was told. The front of the envelope read simply 'For Eva Lavery' in type-written letters. It hadn't been addressed and there was no stamp. 'It was hand-delivered, Eva,' Deirdre said in a small voice.

'OK.' The actress took another deep breath. 'Now, Deirdre, listen to me again. This is what I want you to do. Will you take both the envelope and the note and rip them into very small pieces?

Then dispose of them please. I don't care how you do it as long as you make sure they're destroyed.'

Deirdre hovered with the envelope and the paper in her hand. She was reluctant to leave the actress on her own when she was still so obviously upset.

'Please, Deirdre. I'm fine, really I am.'

'Are you absolutely sure?'

Eva nodded.

'All right.' Deirdre stuffed the note into the pocket of her dressing-gown, kissed Eva on the cheek and then backed towards the door. 'Good luck tonight, Eva,' she whispered.

'Thanks, Deirdre. Good luck to you, too.' The actress's smile was strained. Deirdre realized that she'd never seen Eva force a smile before.

When Deirdre returned to her dressing-room there was a little round cactus with tiny pink flowers waiting for her on her dressing table. It was from Rory McDonagh. The attached card bore the legend: 'Ha! Deirdre O'Dare doesn't have the monopoly on childishness! Good luck tonight, wicked witch. From Rory. PS: I'll miss the snog.'

Deirdre sighed and raised her eyes to heaven. She was just about to screw the card up and fling it in the bin when she saw in her mirror the reflection of Sophie Burke's dressing-table. There were so many cards pinned up around her mirror that it looked like an elaborate collage by Jeff Koons. Deirdre's place, in comparison, looked a bit empty. Comparing her place to Kate's and Maeve's reassured her a bit. The two other actresses had around the same number of cards as she had.

She debated the merits of taking the high moral ground and trashing Rory's card – as it deserved – against the temptation to add it to the ones already hanging round her mirror. It wasn't a particularly nice card, she thought, as she turned it over. It had a picture of a sheep on the front. Or was it a goat? The animal was so clumsily depicted that it was difficult to tell. Rory had no taste whatsoever. Still, it would augment her collection. She stuck it up with some sellotape, hoping that nobody would be so low as to snoop around her cards reading the messages inside. The animal's face looked down at her. It had a rather intelligent expression. She decided that it was a goat, not a sheep. He must have remembered that she was a Capricorn, she thought, as she tried to partially conceal it with something rather more classy.

Deirdre's concern for Eva put the lid on her own rising nerves that night. She listened with more than usual attention to the show over the tannoy – especially to the end of Act One – but nothing in Eva's voice betrayed anything untoward. In fact, her performance seemed to be as flawless as it had been on the two previews.

During the interval Eva sent word to Deirdre to come to her dressing-room. 'Did you get rid of it?' she asked.

Deirdre nodded. 'Yes. I tore it up and put it in the sanitary disposal unit in the ladies' loo.'

Eva managed a smile. 'Clever girl. Thanks, darling, I owe you.'

'How are you feeling now, Eva?' Deirdre

thought the actress was still looking a bit pale.

'Better, thanks. It takes more than an anonymous note to faze me, Deirdre. I'm certainly not going to let it upset my performance. Although I might be a bit of a party-pooper after the show tonight.' Eva was sitting with her elbows on the countertop in front of her, her face between her hands. She looked very vulnerable all of a sudden, and Deirdre's heart went out to her. She moved forward and gave the actress an impulsive hug.

'I think you're wonderful, Eva,' she said.

'Thank you, darling. I think you're wonderful, too. Enjoy the rest of the show.'

* * *

The curtain came down to the rapturous applause they now expected. As she took her bow, Deirdre wondered what it would be like to be in a show that bombed. She knew she was spoilt rotten working for Lawless Productions. She let her gaze wander round the auditorium, hoping to see Sebastian's among the other smiling faces. It was extremely unlikely, she knew. She didn't even have the first idea of where he was sitting. Suddenly, and totally unexpectedly, she saw him. He was sitting in the fifth row of the stalls in an aisle seat. The bright light from the stage had spilled over into the auditorium and she could read the expression on his face quite clearly. He was clapping hard, but he wasn't looking at her. He was gazing at Eva Lavery. Another one smitten, thought Deirdre O'Dare.

* * *

Because her mum and dad were still away on holiday, she'd given her two complimentary tickets to two old college friends, whom she'd arranged to meet afterwards in the pub. Meagre Meagher's was even more crowded than it had been on the opening night of *Dream*, and finding Sebastian wasn't going to be easy. The cigarette smoke was stinging Deirdre's eyes and constricting her throat and she knew that her clothes and hair were going to stink tomorrow. She was wearing her short little black number as she usually did for special occasions, this time for Sebastian's benefit. Pretty soon she ran into Jessica, who had changed her mind about the costumes and was now lamenting that she'd missed out on being cast. 'Those costumes are inspired. You've no idea how evil the three witches look in that first scene – especially Sophie, unsurprisingly enough. Oh, by the way, Deirdre. I bumped into Sebastian on the way out of the theatre and asked him if he was coming over. He said he wanted to take a walk – the show had knocked him for six and he needed some head space, so I suggested he meet up with us all in the Troc later.'

'Oh. OK.' Deirdre had thought it a bit strange that Sebastian hadn't come backstage after the show. He was one of the company, after all. She felt slightly disappointed, and decided she wouldn't stay long in the pub.

A number of tables had been booked in the

Trocadero, the restaurant in the centre of town favoured by show-biz types, and the cast were to meet up there later on to eat. It wasn't far to walk, so after a quick drink Deirdre hit the street with Maeve and Jacqueline. They hadn't got far when a gold-coloured '65 reg Jaguar pulled up beside them, and one of the windows was wound down. Eva was sitting in the passenger seat beside David Lawless.

'Going to the Troc?' she inquired.

'That's right,' said Maeve.

'Get in then – we'll take you there.'

Deirdre climbed into the back of the car after Maeve and Jacqueline feeling relieved. She hadn't been able to get a seat in the pub and even the short distance to the Trocadero would have been difficult for her in her heels. There was a price to be paid for vanity.

She had never been inside such a luxurious car. The interior smelt of leather, and the seats were rock-a-bye-baby comfortable. There was something soothing and classical playing. She sat back and enjoyed the ride, noticing that Eva wasn't as voluble as usual and admiring the way David Lawless handled the wheel as he drove. He had the air of a man who was totally in control, yet he contrived to look relaxed at the same time. Any time they stopped at lights he let his left hand rest lightly on Eva's thigh beside him. The actress was wearing something long and fluid in silk, and delicate silver earrings hung from her ears.

The car pulled up outside the restaurant and

David told them to go on in while he found somewhere to park. Deirdre had only been in the Trocadero once before, and she felt a flurry of excitement as she walked in and saw Eva being greeted with warm hugs from the maitre d' and all the waiters.

It was an unashamedly theatrical restaurant, with dramatic red decor and metres upon metres of swathed fabric everywhere. Framed and signed photographs of actors and actresses lined the walls. Deirdre wondered if her photograph would ever hang here too. She could see Eva's in a conspicuous place. It was a wonderfully spontaneous shot of the actress laughing with her head thrown back and her hair flying, looking directly into the camera with a wicked expression. It hung directly opposite Ann Fitzroy's dignified portrait on the far wall. Ann Fitzroy looked stunning, as usual, but there was something contrived and artificial about her pose, and her eyes looked dead.

Deirdre cast her eyes around to see if Sebastian had arrived yet, but there was no sign of him.

A waiter took their coats and led them down to the back of the restaurant where a number of tables were reserved for them. Not many people from the cast had arrived yet, most of them opting to stay on in Meagher's until closing time. There were just two people sitting at a round table laid with eight place-settings. They were Marian and Rory.

Oh, God, no! Deirdre wailed inwardly as Eva drifted in their direction. Why wasn't Rory in the pub with his drinking cronies as usual, swigging back copious pints? Marian must have arranged to meet him in the restaurant directly after the show. She was probably fed up with hanging out in the awful Meagher's, and Deirdre couldn't really blame her. She watched with horror as Eva settled herself at the table and Maeve and Jacqueline followed suit. She had no alternative. When Sebastian arrived he'd make straight for Eva Lavery – there was no question about it. If she wanted to keep company with Sebastian Hardy tonight she'd have to sit down and break bread with Rory McDonagh.

He was talking to Eva now, with his back to her and wasn't aware of her presence until she rounded the table and came into his view. At least he had the good grace to look slightly horrified as she slid into the seat beside him. She'd done some rapid mental calculations as she'd approached the table and seen the seating arrangements shaping up. Maeve and Jacqueline had sat down together and Eva had earmarked a space for David, which meant that there were only two remaining seats free between Eva and Rory. If Deirdre sat on Eva's left it would mean that the only place for Sebastian would be between herself and Rory, and somehow she didn't much like the idea of Rory and Sebastian sitting together, especially when quantities of wine were likely to be consumed. Rory was unpredictable enough when he was sober. She didn't want him telling lies about her to Sebastian. Why did life have to be so complicated, she thought. All these machinations were making her feel like someone in a PD James novel. She decided she'd brazen it out.

'Hello, Rory,' she said pleasantly. 'Hello, Marian.'

She couldn't help noticing the expression of fortitude that came over Marian's face when she saw Deirdre, as if she was about to take some kind of endurance test. 'Oh, hello, Deirdre. How are you?' she said, immediately turning to the person on her left who happened to be Maeve. Deirdre wasn't surprised. The only time they'd ever exchanged words had been during those excruciating minutes at the bar in Meagher's, before Rory had intervened, and *that* particular encounter could only have led Marian to believe that Deirdre was a complete social dunce.

'Thank you so much for your sketch, Deirdre.' Rory gave her a polite smile. 'Do you know, it gave me a terrific idea for a career departure for you. If you don't make a success of this acting lark, you could always earn a crust by doing pencil sketches of passersby on O'Connell Street. You know those artists' – Deirdre noticed that his voice put quotation marks around the word 'artists' – 'who display samples of their genius sellotaped up on sheets of plastic-covered cardboard and who volunteer to dash off an uncanny likeness of you in two minutes? You could do that, Deirdre. It would be the perfect outlet for all your creativity.'

Deirdre helped herself to a bread roll and some butter, wishing she hadn't sat down next to Rory after all. 'Eva liked hers,' she said, rather testily.

'Oh? Well, maybe Eva's didn't squint as much as mine.'

It was going to be a long evening, Deirdre

thought. The waiter came to take their orders. Rory asked for blue fillet steak and then turned to Deirdre and said: 'Fillet of a fenny snake for you, Deirdre?' Everyone at the table laughed at Rory's allusion to her witch's speech, so Deirdre felt she had to smile too, but the smile felt rather rictus. Rory's witticisms were becoming increasingly irksome.

She spent the next half hour wishing that Sebastian would arrive. Marian had fixed Maeve and Jacqueline with her undivided attention and Eva was less than her usual scintillating self. Anyway she and David were too absorbed in each other to be much fun.

Rory drank too much claret and continued to needle her incessantly. At one point he threw back his head to crow at one of her more erudite remarks. She caught a trace of his sweet, clean smell and felt more uncomfortable than ever.

The restaurant was filling up now, with cast members arriving in flying form every few minutes. Rory looked over his shoulder to respond to some banter from Jonathan Hughes. He turned back to her and she noticed that the habitually sardonic smile that he wore when talking to her these days had been replaced by something more intelligent. He looked directly in her eyes. 'Your boyfriend's here,' he said.

Deirdre's head turned so fast that she was in danger of whiplash. Her gaze flew to where Sebastian stood talking to Sophie, who'd obviously grabbed him on his way past her table. He was smiling at something she'd said, and pushing his hair back from his forehead with an easy hand. Then he turned and his eyes met Deirdre's. She rose to her feet instantly. 'Hi, Sebastian – come and join us,' she called, ignoring Rory's heavy sigh beside her. Eva looked up when she heard Deirdre's greeting and gave Sebastian a shattering smile, which Deirdre tried to copy. Despite her best efforts, she knew she was miles wide of the mark.

Sebastian headed straight for Eva.

'You're sensational. Pure and simple.' He leant down and kissed her on the cheek. Deirdre noticed that his hand lingered on the actress's shoulder as he straightened up. 'And David, you're – well, you're just incredible.' His gesture indicated that he could say no more, and he gave a laugh at his own inarticulateness. Sebastian sat down between Eva and Deirdre in the only available chair, and Deirdre was pleased that her seating plan had worked. 'Hi, angel,' he said, kissing her cheek. 'Rory. Nice to see you again.' The two actors nodded at each other and then Sebastian returned his attention to her. She could feel Rory watching. 'I'm sorry to say I was running late, Deirdre, so I missed the first couple of witches' scenes. My flight from Heathrow was delayed, and then there was a problem getting a taxi, so I didn't get to the theatre until around a quarter past eight. Is it all right if I help myself to wine?' he asked politely.

'Oh, yes, Sebastian, please do,' said Deirdre happily. 'Now, let me introduce you. This is Maeve; Jacqueline; Marian.'

Sebastian shook hands all round, and Deirdre sat back with a big smile on her face. The fun was about to begin.

* * *

In fact, the evening wasn't much fun. Not long after Sebastian arrived Eva and David left – Eva pleading a headache. She looked tired, Deirdre thought, and she smiled at her with sympathy as she kissed her good night. Eva returned the smile with a little pressure on Deirdre's hand, as if to acknowledge the secret they shared. Then, around twenty minutes later, Maeve and Jacqueline got up to go. Jacqueline had an especially heavy day in the morning, with a lunch and a dinner party to cater for.

Deirdre, Sebastian, Rory and Marian were left looking at each other.

'Well, this is nice,' said Rory, signalling to the waiter for another bottle of claret. 'Tell me, Deirdre – any word from RTE about the soap?'

Deirdre had heard from her agent the previous day. Suki Hayes had got the part. Sally had told her not to be too disappointed because there was something further down the pipeline for which the director felt she'd be better suited. 'Well – yes, actually,' she said, trying to sound unconcerned. 'They cast Suki Hayes.'

'Oops,' said Rory, flashing Deirdre an enormous smile.

'Who's Suki Hayes?' asked Sebastian.

'Oh, she's a famous MAW.'

'Model, Actress, Whatever?'

'That's right. She has other talents as well. Or so I'm told,' he added as Marian shot him a frosty look. He smiled lazily back at her.

'It's probably just as well that you didn't get it, Deirdre.' Sebastian's tone was both sympathetic and reassuring. 'Once you're cast in a soap it can be difficult to get work elsewhere. Your availability's stymied for starters, and there's a kind of snob thing attached to it. A lot of directors steer clear of casting soap opera actors. There's an arrogant fuckwit of a director in London who's been quoted as saying that soap opera actors are vulgar, conceited and as witless as sheep.'

Rory opened his eyes wide. 'Well, Deirdre. I'm surprised you didn't get the part.' A sudden image flashed across her mind's eye. Rory McDonagh was on his knees begging her for mercy and she had a pistol in her hand.

'That soap is rubbish, anyway,' said Marian.

'How do you know, Marian? You never watch it.' Rory helped himself to more wine. 'Or so you say. Maybe you do, secretly, when I'm at work. Maeve tells me that when members of the viewing public approach her in the street practically the first thing they say is: 'I never watch it myself, of course.'

Marian sighed. 'Don't have any more wine, Rory.'

'Why not? It's extremely good wine. And I'm not driving.' He drank down some more. 'What do you think of the wine, Deirdre? I'd be terribly interested in your opinion.' His smile was demonic.

Marian rose to her feet. 'I'm going,' she said. 'You can come with me or not, Rory, as you like.'

'I think I'll stay, if you don't mind, beloved. I'm having great fun.'

Marian turned on her heel and stalked out of the restaurant.

As Rory fixed her with his devilish grin again, Deirdre panicked.

'I must go to the loo,' she said. 'Excuse me, Sebastian.'

Down in the loo, Deirdre dithered. She desperately wanted to get out of there, but she didn't want to leave without Sebastian. Bloody Rory was fouling everything up. Maybe she could pretend that she wasn't feeling well, and ask Sebastian to call a cab for her. But it didn't necessarily follow that Sebastian would want to share it as he'd done the last time. She didn't even know where he was staying.

She peered at her face in the mirror and decided that she needed more lipstick. Then she wiped it off again, remembering that she'd read somewhere that men didn't like kissing women who wore too much lipstick. She couldn't hang around in the loo much longer. She didn't know what evil Rory could be poisoning Sebastian's mind with while she was absent from the table. She'd just have to face up to the intolerable situation and hope that some excuse to lure Sebastian away would soon come to her.

To her dismay, when she returned to the table Sebastian and Rory were roaring with laughter.

They'd been joined by Jonathan Hughes, who had obviously drunk the best part of the bottle of Chianti he was brandishing.

As Deirdre approached the table she overheard Rory saying something like: 'If fellatio ever became an Olympic sport she could represent Ireland,' and she thought for one hellish moment that he was talking about her. She sat down in agony, but Rory didn't pay her any attention, thank goodness, and then she saw that they were looking at Jonathan Hughes's *Irish Times*. 'At least that's what Finbar claimed when he bored us all to death with tales of his amorous exploits that night we ended up in that poxy hotel of his.'

Suki Hayes's photograph had made the television page already, Deirdre saw. The caption underneath read: 'Suki Hayes: Newcomer to *Ardmore Grove*.'

Sebastian turned to her as she sat down beside him. 'I was thinking of ordering a cab,' he said. 'Do you fancy sharing it with me?' She thought she could detect something meaningful about the smile he sent her.

Deirdre's heart immediately started a tap-dance. 'Oh, yes please, Sebastian,' she said.

The taxi didn't take long to arrive, and Deirdre got to her feet beside Sebastian, hoping that people were noticing her. Unfortunately Sophie had already gone.

Rory looked up at them with a vaguely quizzical expression on his face. 'No bags, Sebastian?' he asked.

Sebastian was putting on his jacket. He brushed at a bit of fluff on his sleeve with a casual hand. 'I left them at the theatre.'

'Not even a toothbrush?' persisted Rory. Deirdre wished he would shut up. What business was it of his where Sebastian's stuff was?

Sebastian patted his pocket. 'It's in here.'

'I'm impressed,' said Rory. 'You travel even lighter than I do.'

Sebastian smiled. 'Goodnight, Rory – Jonathan,' he said. 'See you at rehearsal on Monday.'

'See you, Sebastian. Good night, Deirdre.' To her horror, Rory stood up to kiss her goodbye. She felt his lips brush her cheek, and then his tongue briefly grazed her left ear like an electric eel. She knew he heard the gasp she gave. She quickly picked up her bag as Rory nonchalantly sat back down beside Jonathan and poured wine into their glasses. Then she followed Sebastian out of the restaurant.

In the cab she asked Sebastian where he was staying.

'I've taken a flat off the South Circular Road. It's not far from you,' he said.

It wouldn't be far from Eva Lavery, either, she thought darkly. But at least now David was safely ensconced there with her.

'What's it like?' she asked.

'It's perfect,' he said. 'It's in the basement of a solicitor's house. She's literally only just finished doing the place up and this is its first let, so its pristine. I must have you round some time. There's a wonderful garden to sunbathe in.' Sebastian stretched himself and smiled. 'The only snag is that it still smells of paint.'

Deirdre was a bit puzzled. 'When did you see it?' she asked.

He took rather a long time to answer. Then: 'Well, the last time I was over I told you that I was going to view some apartments the next day, remember?' Deirdre thought he sounded rather cautious. 'That's when I saw it.'

'Oh,' said Deirdre. 'I thought you said it still smelled of–'

Suddenly Sebastian was kissing her. It took her quite by surprise, but she soon got used to it. She kissed him back, her heart and mind cheering. What a coup for Deirdre O'Dare! She could hardly allow herself to believe that this was happening after the fiasco that had been the earlier part of the evening. She felt as if she'd just been awarded a trophy.

Sebastian carried on kissing her until the taxi stopped. Deirdre broke the kiss reluctantly and looked up. They were parked outside her apartment block. 'Do you want to come in?' she asked.

Sebastian looked at her with an unreadable expression. Then: 'Not right now, Deirdre,' he said.

She resisted the temptation to say: 'When, then?' and said 'Sure,' instead, thinking that she sounded very grown-up.

'Let's make it some other time,' he said, and smiled as he caressed her cheek. 'We'll make it some time soon, OK?'

'OK. See you at rehearsal on Monday, then?' She

half-hoped he might suggest that they meet up at some stage over the weekend, but he just smiled and said 'Yeah.'

Deirdre smiled back and got out of the cab. She gave a careless little wave as it started up and then let herself into the lobby of her apartment block. As the door closed behind her Deirdre O'Dare jumped for joy.

Chapter Sixteen

Deirdre spent most of the weekend worrying about what to wear to the first read-through of *Hamlet* on Monday morning. She wanted to avoid looking as if she'd made any kind of special effort, so it had to be simple. A couple of months ago *Marie Claire* magazine had run a feature on 'Timeless Classics', and one of the suggested combinations was a big white cotton shirt and a pair of black Levis. That wouldn't be too difficult to get right, Deirdre thought, and she'd made sure to pay a visit to the laundrette on Saturday so that her white shirt would be pristine.

She turned up early for rehearsal. Sophie was already there, doing a warm-up in state-of-the-art practice gear. She'd almost forgotten that Sophie had been cast as the Player Queen, even though she'd been droning on about it in the dressing-room ever since she'd found out. It was her biggest part so far this season, and Deirdre realized with a sinking heart that there'd just be the two of them sharing the dressing-room once the show was up and running. She wondered if she wouldn't be better off in the extras' dressing-room next door. As soon as Sebastian came through the door Sophie struck a particularly sexy pose and Deirdre felt like throwing up. To her delight, Sebastian was wearing jeans and a plain white shirt, too. Deirdre rolled her sleeves up to show off her tan and sidled over to him. 'Snap!' she said, touching him lightly on the arm.

Sebastian looked puzzled until Deirdre pointed at their identical shirts. Then he gave a gratifying laugh. 'You wear it better than I do, gorgeous. You look great today,' and when he smiled at her she felt all warm inside.

A couple of hours later after a pacy read-through of the play the cast put down their scripts and looked at David Lawless, waiting for his verdict. 'Well. That was as close to a perfect reading of *Hamlet* that it has ever been my privilege to listen to,' he said. 'Thank you all very much. You can take fifteen.'

Deirdre had watched Sebastian covertly from time to time as he had read, taking great care to ensure that Rory wasn't watching her watching him. She didn't want to leave herself open to any further pathetic jibes from that quarter about 'her boyfriend'. Sebastian had given an exceptionally disciplined, intelligent reading of the role and it was obvious that he'd done his homework. Not only was his reading informed and razor-sharp, but Deirdre could tell by the *way* he read that he was already dead-letter-perfect.

Sophie had changed from her warm-up gear into a skin tight pair of electric orange vinyl trousers and a tiny T-shirt. It was at least two sizes too small, with obvious intention. After the read-through she'd made a beeline for Sebastian, and

Deirdre was fuming. Rehearsals weren't going to be as much fun as she'd hoped if bloody Sophie was going to monopolize Sebastian. She hung around on her own for a while pretending to be absorbed in her script, but he didn't seem to notice her much. After he'd managed to escape from Sophie he went off to make himself coffee and then started talking to David Lawless. At this stage Deirdre had given up her pretence of studying her script and was looking out of the window of the rehearsal hall with what she hoped was a dreamy, enigmatic expression on her face. She cast a sidelong glance at Sebastian to see if he was looking at her, but he was still listening intently to David. Maybe she should stop playing so hard to get and just think up another excuse to talk to him. The shirt stunt had been a bit feeble, she had to admit.

'You're looking very pensive, Deirdre,' came Rory's dreaded tones as he ambled past. 'You know, I've a suspicion that there's very little woolly thinking going on inside your shapely cranium these days. I might even go so far as to say there's a cunning streak in you, O'Dare.'

Deirdre didn't even bother telling him to shut up. She just carried on trying to think up ways of attracting Sebastian's attention.

* * *

He didn't pay her very much attention at all for the first week of rehearsal. He was obviously an incredibly thorough, dedicated actor and he wasted no time fooling around the way Rory sometimes did. He even spent his tea and lunch breaks either in conference with David Lawless or with his head in his script, analysing the text and fine-combing it for nuance. His perseverance was paying off, because his performance was changing and growing every day like a living thing. Deirdre found him fascinating to watch, and felt guilty that she was wasting so much of her own time devising opening gambits and stratagems to get him to notice her.

Because Hamlet spends so much time on stage she didn't get much of a chance to socialize with him in the coffee room, which was where the actors went to be sociable when they weren't involved in the scenes being worked on. She hadn't even had a chance to do any scenes with him yet because Hamlet and Ophelia didn't meet until Act Three, and they weren't going to be starting work on that until the following week. She didn't see him after rehearsal because she had to get herself something to eat before the evening's performance of *Macbeth*. And he hadn't once set foot in Meagher's to meet up with the cast after the show. He was just totally focused on delivering the goods.

Deirdre remembered what Sebastian had said in the taxi that night about having her round to his place one day, and she gradually faced up to the miserable realization that he must have forgotten all about it. He couldn't have forgotten about the kiss as well, surely? She wondered equally miserably if she'd ever kiss him again.

At the end of the week she had a brainwave. If

he wasn't going to ask her over to his place, maybe she should think about asking *him* over to hers! How to do it, though, was the problem. She didn't feel confident enough to just invite him over for coffee or a glass of wine, and dinner was out of the question. That was just *too* intimate – she might as well just ask him right out to go to bed with her. Which she'd practically done in the taxi that night she'd asked him in, she remembered with some embarrassment. But things had changed since then, and she no longer felt as relaxed with him as she once had.

What if she were to invite someone else around as well? Then it wouldn't look as if she was trying too hard to seduce him, and there was a chance that he might hang about a bit after the other guests had gone. Who could she invite? She thought of Maeve and Jacqueline and then rejected the idea. She'd be far too embarrassed to put any of her cooking on a plate in front of a gourmet like Jacqueline.

For some strange reason the word gourmet reminded her of the excellent scrambled eggs that Rory had cooked for her in the kitchen that day he'd inveigled her into bed. He'd told her that he'd been taught how to scramble eggs by a gourmet – an ex-girlfriend. She'd never dreamed that scrambled eggs could taste so good. Imagine if she were to invite *him*! She almost laughed out loud at the total absurdity of the idea.

She tried to banish the memory of sitting with Rory at his kitchen table – and of what he'd done to her on his kitchen floor – by thinking harder about who she could invite to dinner. Some of her old friends from Trinity? No. That might be rather an awkward situation. Sebastian didn't know them, and she wanted him to be in the company of people with whom he could feel really relaxed.

Her second brainwave nearly sent her reeling. Would it be too totally audacious to invite David and Eva? If Sebastian heard that Eva Lavery was coming she knew he simply wouldn't be able to turn her down. She didn't know if she had the nerve, though. She looked at the couple where they stood talking together across the room surrounded by an aura of contentment so intense they practically glowed. She couldn't interrupt them now. But when would she get another chance? It was Friday already, and Sunday was the only night she'd have free. She was running out of time. If she was going to do it she'd have to do it now.

She took a deep breath and strode across the room, suddenly uncomfortably aware that Rory McDonagh wasn't a million miles away. She'd have to be careful he didn't overhear anything.

'Excuse me, please, Eva –' she said, keeping her voice very small indeed '– but I was thinking of having a dinner party at my flat on Sunday evening. Would you and David be interested in coming?'

'Oh! What a lovely idea, Deirdre!' said Eva. 'We'd be delighted to come, wouldn't we, David? How sweet of you to think of asking us! Who else is coming and what time do you want us?'

'Oh – eight for eight-thirty, please.' That was what her mother always said. 'And Sebastian's the only other person except I haven't asked him yet.'

Actually, Deirdre had known that there was no point in asking him until she'd made sure that Eva would be there.

'Jolly good!' said the actress with enthusiasm. 'We'll look forward to it with pleasure.'

Deirdre turned away with a smile to recce the room for Sebastian. There was no stopping her now. As soon as she spied her quarry she advanced towards him, determination in her step. 'Hi, Sebastian,' she said.

'Deirdre! Hi! How are things?'

'Oh – fine. I wanted to ask you something.' She could see Sophie watching her, so she lowered her voice again. She'd let Sophie know all about it later, but she wasn't going to run the risk of her overhearing Sebastian turn her down. 'Would you like to come to dinner at my flat on Sunday evening?'

'Oh God – I'm not sure I can, Deirdre,' he said doubtfully. 'I was hoping to get some work done on the soliloquies on Sunday.'

Deirdre was in like lightning. 'Eva and David will be there,' she added brightly.

There was a fractional pause. Then: 'Oh – to hell with the soliloquies,' he said. 'I could do with a break. I'd love to come. Thank you, Deirdre. What time?'

'Oh – say eight for eight-thirty?'

'Terrific. I'll look forward to it.' He gave her an urbane smile and inclined his head.

Just then Nick McCarthy strolled up. 'Sebastian? Jenny would like a word when you've a minute.'

'Sure, Nick. I'm on my way. I'll see you on Sunday then, Deirdre. Oh – what number's your flat?' he called over his shoulder as he moved off. His pitch was gratifyingly audible.

'Thirteen,' she called back. 'And I'll let you have my phone number before we finish just in case you need to contact me before then.'

'Thanks, Deirdre – see you later.' He raised his hand and smiled his glorious smile before turning away. He could make a fortune doing toothpaste commercials thought Deirdre, looking after him with a thrill of anticipation. Sunday evening couldn't come quick enough.

As she strolled casually in Sophie's direction she had to pass Rory, who was lounging against the doorway into the coffee room, looking like a gunslinger.

'You ought to start a coven, Deirdre. What plots are you hatching now? There's something very fishy cooking in your cauldron today.'

She was almost glad she'd walked by him. What on earth *was* she going to cook? She didn't possess a single recipe book. She'd just have to cheat.

* * *

When she pulled up the blind on her bedroom window on Sunday morning bright sunshine leapt through. Another blue sky day in the life of Deirdre O'Dare, she thought, hugging herself with excited anticipation. Sadly, she'd have to start her day by doing a bit of housework. She hoovered and dusted and plumped cushions. Then she looked at her pile of magazines. There was a *Hello!* that she'd had to buy because there was a big feature on Johnny Depp in it, and someone had nicked the green room copy. The covers of her *Cosmopolitans* had loads of sex-related features listed, and she blenched at the sensationalism of her trashier magazines. She'd hide them and just keep the *Vanity Fairs* her mother had passed on to her – they had class, even though they were a bit out-of-date. She'd get the new one when she went down to the Spar shop for the papers. Maybe she should splash out and get a *Vogue* as well. *Newsweek* too, perhaps? That would give just the right intellectual impression. She trashed the idea almost immediately. She had enough cop-on to know that *Newsweek* would be stretching credibility a bit.

Singing along to her Cardigans album she carried the more embarrassing of the magazines into her bedroom and threw them under the bed where they joined her dust-covered yoga book. What about her bedroom? What if Sebastian did decide to stay on after Eva and David had gone? She hardly dared hope. Her humming grew more intense as she surveyed the room. Yes – it might be a good precaution to tidy up a bit. It was well overdue, anyway. She hung up all the clothes that were lying around, and stuffed her underwear back into its overflowing drawer, taking care to set aside her prettiest knickers and the dangly earrings she'd purloined from Sarah's room. For the first time she was glad that she had the flat to herself. Getting

Sebastian into bed would be a bit more problematic if her flatmate was around. The walls were very thin and she'd have felt awfully self-conscious.

As she was leaving the room she saw her ancient one-earred teddy-bear lolling on the bed. She picked him up and threw him under the bed too. Then she reconsidered. She took him out, made a little nest of the woollies in her jumper drawer and laid him gently on it, trying to avoid looking at the expression on his face as she slid the drawer shut.

* * *

At eight fifteen the doorbell went and she picked up the intercom. It was Sebastian. She pressed the entry button, leaned against the wall and took a very deep breath. Then she saw that the upmarket Sunday papers she'd bought were still pristinely folded. She ran back, shook them out and opened the review section of one of them at random so that it would look as if she'd been reading it when the doorbell rang. It fell open at an article entitled 'Seduction in the Nineties. A Woman's Prerogative?' Yelping inwardly, she scrabbled quickly through the pages to find something less pertinent. She was thankful when she found an item about Damien Hirst, and she folded the paper open at that page and left it casually strewn on the couch.

Sebastian kissed her on both cheeks when he came through the door. He was carrying a bunch of flowers wrapped in cellophane and a bottle of wine. 'I'm afraid the flowers aren't very special,' he said as he handed them over. 'The shop only had yesterday's mixed bouquets.'

Deirdre didn't mind. She'd never had a present of flowers from a man before. 'They're lovely, Sebastian. Thank you. Oh – Château Raspail!' she exclaimed as she slid the wine bottle out of its wrapping. 'How delicious!' Making any comment on the wine was a bit of a risk. She hoped Sebastian wouldn't expect her to elaborate. She dived into the kitchen to get a corkscrew and a vase for the flowers before they got into a big discussion about the comparative merits of wine. She had heard somebody once describe a wine as 'amusing, if a bit presumptuous', but she didn't want to say that about Château Raspail in case it was neither of these things. For all she knew, Château Raspail might take itself very seriously indeed. 'Will you do this?' she said, handing him bottle and corkscrew.

'Sure. Eva and David not here yet?' he asked as he sat down on the couch in the sitting room. She loved the expert way he pulled the cork.

'Not yet.' Deirdre was arranging the flowers as artistically as she could. They'd make a nice centrepiece for her dining table. She had put candles on the table, too, that she'd bought from the local Spar earlier in the day when she'd gone to buy her glossy magazines. Unfortunately they were very ordinary candles – the white kind you buy in case of a power cut. Spar didn't have any trendier ones. She lit them now, and then wished she hadn't. It felt a bit silly to be lighting candles when the sun was still splitting the trees outside.

'You're looking gorgeous.' Sebastian was lounging back in the couch with his long legs splayed out in front of him. She felt her heart accelerate a little.

'Thanks.' She was wearing her little black Marc O'Neill number again. She didn't care that Sebastian had seen it before. It was simply the sexiest thing she owned. 'So are you.' Yikes! She hung over the vase of flowers, tweaking them this way and that. They weren't being terribly co-operative, but she carried on tweaking them anyway because she wanted something to do. She didn't want to go over and sit beside Sebastian on the couch in case it looked like a come-on, and she couldn't think of anything to say.

'Christ – Brit Art's gone to hell,' said Sebastian, looking at the photograph of Hirst's latest formaldehyde masterpiece.

'Oh – I'm so glad you think so, Sebastian!' she exclaimed. 'I mean – I'm not *totally* anti all those Bright Young Brit Art types, but some of them *really* get up my nose.' Deirdre was delighted that Sebastian had hit on a subject about which she wasn't completely ignorant. She was just about to launch into a tirade against the new wave of conceptual art when the phone rang. It was Eva.

'Deirdre? Can you hear me?' Eva's voice was a bit fuzzy. She was obviously on a mobile in some crowded place.

'Hi! Yes, I can hear you. Just about.'

'Listen to me. This is a nightmare scenario. I'm sitting here in the casualty department of St James's

Hospital waiting to see a doctor. It looks like I'm going to be here for hours, darling – there are people on crutches and with their arms in slings milling around all over the place.'

'Oh Eva – what's happened?'

'I've banjaxed my ankle. We were on our way over to you when I slipped on the rug in the hall. We were running a bit late – I'd fallen asleep in the bath, I'm afraid – and as we were dashing out the door I executed such an amazing pratfall that I would have laughed if it hadn't hurt so hard.'

'Oh, Eva – I'm so sorry!'

'Yes. So am I. It's a total pain in the arse, darling. Literally. Mrs O'Toole polished the floor with more than her usual gusto on Friday and I've been skating about on it all weekend. I felt I should be wearing one of those dinky little tutu things that ice-dancers wear. I'm surprised I came off as lightly as I did.'

'How bad is it?'

'Just a sprain, I think, but I gave it quite a nasty twist. There's going to be an amazing bruise – it's going all purple already.'

'I don't suppose you can make it this evening, then?' Deirdre couldn't keep the disappointment out of her voice.

'I'm sorry, darling. I wanted to pretend it wasn't that bad because I hated the idea of letting you down, but David insisted on taking me straight to hospital. I suppose he could carry on without me, couldn't he? I could take a taxi home after–'

Deirdre interrupted immediately. 'Oh no, Eva! He can't abandon you in out-patients!' The idea of her heroine sitting in the casualty department of St James's Hospital all on her own filled her with horror.

'You hadn't gone to too much trouble, had you Deirdre? I'd feel awful if I thought you'd been slaving over a hot stove all day on our account.'

'Oh no – please don't worry about that, Eva. I'll confess I cheated and bought everything from Marks and Spencers. I can't really cook, you see.'

'That's not called cheating, darling. It's called common sense. Is Sebastian there yet?'

'Yes.'

'Well, have a lovely time together, won't you? Give him a kiss from me.'

'I will. Good night, Eva. And I do hope your leg's not too serious. Will you be able for the show tomorrow?'

'Oh, yes – I'll manage somehow. Jolly old Doctor Theatre and all that. Come to think of it, I rather fancy the idea of Lady Macbeth carrying a wonderfully elegant cane. I'll get Jenny to look out for one with a silver top. And at least all those trailing evening dresses will disguise my horrible thick ankle. Good night, darling. And profound apologies once more for my confounded clumsiness.'

'Don't apologize, Eva. It wasn't your fault.'

Deirdre put the phone down and stood looking at it for a minute. She was dreading having to turn round and face Sebastian.

'Eva's not coming then?' he said lightly.

'No. She's sprained her ankle. She was calling

from out-patients. I'm sorry, Sebastian.' The evening was going wrong already.

'Not to worry. Is it badly sprained?' Sebastian folded the newspaper and put it down on the coffee table.

'She didn't seem to think so, but David wanted her to have it looked at.'

'I've never known an actress playing Lady M. to have got through a run of the Scottish play without some kind of upset. There's a lot of justification for that particular superstition, I think.' Suddenly Sebastian drained his wine glass and got to his feet. 'Let me top you up,' he said.

'Thanks.' She held out her glass and studied him as he poured. When he raised his eyes unexpectedly and smiled at her, Deirdre felt that she owed Eva Lavery the biggest debt of gratitude in the history of the planet. She hated the idea of the actress stuck in out-patients, but Fate had intervened and made her slip on the rug. Fate had intended that she, Deirdre O'Dare, could be alone tonight with Sebastian Hardy.

Sebastian poured wine into his own glass and took a sip before setting it down on the coffee table. 'Can I do anything to help in the kitchen?' he asked.

'Oh, no. I can cope.' Deirdre didn't want him to see the cartons of ready-made food, and then remembered that she'd blown it anyway by letting slip to Eva on the phone that Marks and Spencers were responsible for catering her dinner party. She gave him a bright smile and slipped into the kitchen.

The cross-section of the Chicken Kiev in the picture on the box looked gorgeous – crispy on the outside and succulent on the inside, with oodles of garlic butter flowing out of it like a river. 'Preheat the oven to 200C,' she read. She'd forgotten to do that and the stupid oven always took ages to heat up. If she hung around waiting for it to preheat there'd be too long a gap between the starter and the main course. She'd ignore the pre-heating bit and bung the stuff in anyway. She resumed her scrutiny of the instructions on the box. 'Remove carton and foil,' she read, as she reached out to switch on the cooker. The little red light came on, and then went out again almost immediately. Puzzled, Deirdre flicked the switch up and down a few times. Nothing happened. She was suddenly aware of an ominous silence emanating from the sitting room. The tasteful classical music she'd put on the CD player before Sebastian's arrival had stopped.

'Deirdre?' Sebastian's voice came from the sitting room. 'I think there's been a power cut.'

* * *

In the end they sent out for Indian food from the take-away Eva used. Sebastian insisted on paying, and Deirdre didn't protest too hard. She'd spent a small fortune on her Marks and Spencers dinner party. If she had to fork out for a rake of Indian dishes as well she'd be strapped for cash for the rest of the week.

She was glad she'd bought the box of candles from Spar. She lit all of them and stuck them into bottles and on saucers all over the room, and as the sky outside darkened and the level of wine in the second bottle got lower and lower, the atmosphere inside became more and more mellow.

'I'm sorry, Sebastian,' said Deirdre at around midnight. She was pouring the last of the wine into their glasses. 'This has been a total disaster.'

Sebastian was running a finger around the rim of his wine glass. 'I don't think it's been a disaster,' he said. He looked up at her. His eyes were even more like topaz in the candlelight, and she felt as if she were under some kind of spell which wouldn't allow her to stop gazing at him. He wasn't smiling when he eventually spoke again. 'Will I stay?' he asked.

'Yes please, Sebastian,' said Deirdre.

She had pulled it off.

* * *

In the bedroom he undressed her very slowly, kissing bits of her as they were exposed. She followed suit. They kissed for a long time. Sebastian's kisses were practised and sensuous and all that kisses should be, but for some reason Deirdre didn't feel aroused yet. They lay down on her bed and caressed each other until he was very hard. He was exploring her with a gentle finger.

'Come inside me now, Sebastian,' she said.

'You're not ready yet, angel.'

'Yes I am,' she said.

'Are you sure?'

'I'm very sure.'

There was a brief hiatus while he retrieved his jeans and produced a condom packet from his hip pocket. He tore open the packet, slid on the rubber and then he entered her. She gave a little gasp and Sebastian stopped moving at once.

'Am I hurting you, Deirdre?' he asked, looking down at her with concerned eyes.

'No,' she lied.

'You must tell me if I do. Promise?'

'I promise,' said Deirdre, and Sebastian proceeded to make love to her with considerate thoroughness.

There must be something wrong with her, she thought as she writhed obligingly. Here she was, in bed with the most beautiful man in the world and she wasn't feeling anything. What on earth could she do? She returned Sebastian's kisses with a feeling close to despair as he moved inside her. She could feel his urgency mounting, and suddenly she just wanted this sham to be over.

She started to make little moaning sounds of excitement, and realized that she sounded exactly like Meg Ryan in that film where she'd faked the orgasm in a restaurant. What on earth was the name of that film? she wondered. It annoyed her that she couldn't remember. How had her orgasm happened that time with Rory? She cast her mind back to that fateful Friday, trying to remember exactly how she'd behaved when she'd climaxed, and wondering if she'd be able to replicate it. It wasn't easy to do without feeling like a total fraud. And after all, she hadn't had that many orgasms in her life to judge by. Only three, in fact. She started to wonder how good an actress she really was.

Sebastian was breathing hard now, and she raided her memory bank in desperation. She'd tensed unbearably just beforehand, she remembered, so she strained against him, still making the moaning noises. Then an image of Rory as he had looked when he had come inside her flashed across her mind and she felt something start to happen. The image persisted, and Deirdre realized rather uncomfortably that she was feeling the first stirrings of arousal. She tried to push Rory to the back of her mind as Sebastian celebrated his orgasm.

Afterwards he lay back and turned his head on the pillow so that he could study her. She hoped he wouldn't register her rather guilty expression.

'You didn't come,' he said.

'Yes, I did.' Deirdre told a lie for the second time in thirty minutes.

Sebastian shot her a sceptical look. 'Come here,' he said. 'Let's try something different.' And as his tongue travelled down her body and she stroked his head with her hands Deirdre tried hard not to think of Rory McDonagh.

* * *

Later she lay beside a sleeping Sebastian with her eyes open. She had done it. She had got Sebastian

Hardy into her bed. How would she let Sophie know? But strangely, the notion of scoring points off Sophie didn't thrill her as much as it usually did. She turned over and tried to force herself into unconsciousness.

Beside her Sebastian moved in his sleep. 'Miching malicho,' he said, quite clearly. Deirdre's eyes shot open. The words weren't quite as nonsensical as they sounded. The room seemed to be buzzing with silence, and her mind felt crystal-clear. She'd heard him speak those words before at the first read-through of the play. They were from a line that Hamlet delivers to Ophelia in the Mousetrap scene.

Marry, this is miching malicho; it means mischief . . .

It was a reference to his own deviousness.

The notes on the text had told her that 'miching' meant 'secret' and that 'malicho' meant 'mischief – or the cherishing of vindictive feelings'. She felt a bit uneasy. Then Sebastian spoke as Hamlet once again, and Deirdre was more than uneasy – she was suddenly quite scared. 'Mother, mother, mother,' he said, and his voice was suffused with heart-rending sorrow. 'Go not to my uncle's bed. Refrain tonight.'

Dear God, thought Deirdre. His identification with the role must be phenomenal if he was even *dreaming* as Hamlet. She lay there feeling tense, wondering if she should wake him. She hated the thought of him sleeping in a state of such obvious anguish. She *would* wake him if he spoke again. But Sebastian slept on silently, and Deirdre finally fell asleep beside him wondering how they would conduct their relationship in public from now on.

* * *

The following morning Sebastian was as tender and considerate as ever when he woke her to make love. Afterwards, Deirdre lay in his arms watching the progression of the numbers on the digital bedside clock and hearing for the first time the almost inaudible click each time they changed. Sebastian was due in rehearsal in less than an hour's time. He was toying with a strand of her hair. 'Deirdre?' he said.

'Mm hm?'

'I'm not sure that this was such a good idea.'

She stiffened. 'What do you mean?' she asked.

'I'm not sure that we should have gone to bed together.'

She sat up and looked down at him with blank eyes, brushing her hair back over her shoulders. 'Why not, Sebastian?'

'I know it's a cliché, but it's one that usually makes sense. And I'm afraid I'm speaking from experience. It really doesn't do to mix business with pleasure, Deirdre.'

She'd heard someone say virtually the same thing once, and it wasn't in the too far-distant past.

David Lawless had said as much that night she'd flung herself at him on the pub terrace.

'It's my fault it happened,' he continued. 'It was terribly irresponsible of me. I'm sorry. We'd had such a lovely evening and drunk too much wine and you were looking so fab in your sexy dress that I couldn't resist the temptation. Can you find it in your heart to forgive me?'

There was a pause, and then Deirdre nodded. Numbly, she gathered the duvet up and pulled it over her breasts. Why did she make so many bloody awful mistakes when it came to men? She felt choked inside and knew she wouldn't be able to say very much for a while.

'It's just that I'm going to be working my ass off and I'm not going to be able to give you any time. It wouldn't be fair on you, Deirdre.'

She remembered the searingly sad tone in his voice when he'd called out in his sleep. 'Mother, mother, mother.' He was yearning for Gertrude. He was yearning for Eva Lavery. If Deirdre hadn't been so fond of Eva she might almost have felt resentful of her. She'd already bewitched one gorgeous man. It didn't seem fair that she should have the power to bewitch two. Ha! Sebastian needn't bother worrying about being unfair to her, she thought grimly. *Life* wasn't bloody fair to her. She sat there looking at her folded hands, hoping she wouldn't cry. On the street below an ambulance went by, siren blaring.

'Maybe when the show is up and running we could try again, Deirdre. But it would be impossible right now. I'm just too totally focused on the play.'

'I know.' Deirdre finally spoke but she was still looking at her hands. 'You were saying things in your sleep.'

'What things?' Sebastian was suddenly alert.

'Lines from the play.'

'Can you remember which ones?'

'Yes.' She quoted the lines back at him, and then she finally allowed herself to look at him. 'Hamlet has bad dreams, too,' she said. 'He says so in the play.' They held each other's gaze for a long time.

Then: 'I'm so sorry,' repeated Sebastian.

Deirdre nodded again. 'So am I,' she said.

'Let's not allow what happened last night to sour our friendship, Deirdre, please? I'd really hate myself if that happened. And it would make it incredibly difficult for us to work together. I like you too much, you know.'

'It's OK, Sebastian. I'm a rock-solid pro at this stage – I've been dealt a lot of punches. I'm not going to behave like some emotional adolescent.' Ever again, she could have added.

Sebastian leant forward and kissed her gently on the lips. Then he stood up and Deirdre took one last look at her handsome prince in all his glorious nakedness. 'I'll take a quick shower. Then I'd better haul ass if I'm not going to be late for rehearsal.'

When he had gone Deirdre trailed into the kitchen to start on last night's dishes. Maybe she should have a long talk with Maeve. Maeve's shoulder was the most comfortable one to cry on when her mum's wasn't around.

But as Deirdre scraped plates and dumped empty cartons into the pedal-bin she realized with some surprise that she hadn't cried yet.

Chapter Seventeen

In rehearsal on Tuesday Sebastian and Deirdre took the floor to block the first scene of Act Three. She had known that the scene was going to be tough on her. It was nearly as bad as that awful time when Rory as Lysander had had to spurn her on stage the day after she'd gone to bed with him. Now Sebastian was rejecting her as Ophelia and denying that he ever loved her. Deirdre found it difficult to look him in the face, and her line 'I was the more deceived' came out in little more than a whisper.

She made a heroic effort to face up to him for his answering speech, but she found that his expression quite unnerved her. His eyes burnt with a passionate intensity as he delivered the lines:

> *It were better my mother had not borne me. I am very proud, revengeful, ambitious; with more offences at my beck than I have thoughts to put them in, imagination to give them shape, or time to act them in.*

Because Sebastian had till now portrayed Hamlet as something of a control freak, the ferocity he invested in the words was all the more shocking.

When they had finished, David Lawless drew the

pair aside. 'Put a curb on the intensity, Sebastian. Play up the sardonic aspect as we agreed. I know the natural inclination is to play a lot of the speeches with emotion, but try to take it easy, especially in these early days when we're really only messing around with the blocking. OK? Now. Let's try it once more before we break for coffee.' He started to move back to the chair at the top of the room from which vantage point he observed rehearsals, and then he turned back to Deirdre. 'The whisper worked beautifully. Keep it in, Deirdre,' he said.

The more they worked together, the easier it became for Deirdre to distance herself from the events of Sunday night. Sebastian had been right. It was of paramount importance that they remain friends while they were working in such close proximity. She was glad that there was no antagonism between them, the way there still was between herself and Rory. She continued to steer clear of *him.* He seemed to derive perverse pleasure from goading her every time he encountered her.

The only scene they had together was in the first act of the play, when Rory as Laertes advises his sister to be wary of Prince Hamlet's advances. The first time they'd rehearsed the scene Rory had looked at her with an amused air as he'd delivered the speech which warns her to steer clear of the prince. It seemed to her that he was deliberately relating the words to her real life situation, and she found herself not wanting to look at him. She had swung away, leaving him upstage of her as she faced front, and then she was suddenly uncomfortably aware that he had moved downstage again and was standing directly behind her. With a slow hand he lifted the dense mass of her hair from where it fell down her back and drew it up over her right shoulder, exposing the nape of her neck and her left ear. He snaked his right arm around her waist, holding her against him, and then he rested his head on her shoulder so that their faces touched and his mouth was practically against her ear. His delivery of the speech had been slow, measured and heavy with meaning:

Then weigh what loss your honour
may sustain,
If with too credent ear you list his
songs,
Or lose your heart, or your chaste
treasure open
To his unmastered importunity.
Fear it, Ophelia, fear it, my dear
sister . . .

He had pressed himself against her and she could feel his hot breath in her ear. Her own breath was coming faster, and she arched herself against him a little in an attempt to push him away and disengage herself. But his right arm had pinioned hers and he was holding her wrists together so that she couldn't use her hands. Her efforts to squirm out of his loathsome embrace were proving futile – he was too strong for her. Suddenly she felt the fingers of his other hand against the nape of her neck, and to her horror he trailed his left hand slowly down the front of her shoulder until it came to rest on her breast. Deirdre froze and her face went scarlet. She was glad there had been no-one else in the rehearsal room other than David Lawless, Nick McCarthy and the elderly actor playing Polonius, who was waiting to make his entrance and who had his nose stuck in his script.

She badly wanted to stop the scene and tell Rory in no uncertain terms to give over mauling her, but she knew it would be a really uncool thing to do – it would just make her look uptight. After all, Rory was only experimenting with the scene – playing about with it as David Lawless had instructed them to do before they had started to rehearse it. She made one last effort to free herself of his arms, then gave up and went limp against him. Rory was coming to the end of his speech. Suddenly he thrust her away from him as if he had suddenly discovered that he'd been embracing a slug. 'Be wary, then. Best safety lies in fear,' he said with meaning. Unprepared for the shove, Deirdre staggered and almost fell. She took a couple of breaths before she launched into her own speech, which she invested with a great deal more indignation than she had done at the read-through.

As Polonius strode onto the stage shouting 'Yet here, Laertes!', David Lawless spoke up. 'Can we stop there? Sorry to interrupt,' he added. 'OK, you two. Let's do that again.' He strolled up to join them on the rehearsal floor, rubbing his ear thoughtfully. 'I know we discussed the Freudian thing that exists between siblings, Rory, and there was some nice stuff beginning to emerge there, but the hand on the breast smacks too much of actual incest. You're broadcasting it rather than suggesting it.' He paused and then ran a hand over his jaw. 'The shove was presumably to indicate Laertes' disgust at himself rather than any real repugnance for his sister?'

'Yeah.' Rory nodded. 'Did it work?'

'It's not defined enough. Try moving downstage left after you push her away so that the audience can read your facial expression but Ophelia can't.' Then David Lawless turned to Deirdre. 'I loved the struggle and the capitulation. Keep it in, Deirdre. OK, let's take it up to the entrance of Polonius again.'

And as he returned to his chair and Deirdre braced herself to go through the hellish scene one more time, she sent Rory a basilisk look which was wasted because he wasn't looking at her. He was consulting his script with an expression of rapt concentration.

* * *

As the days wore on, Deirdre realized that her life had become more routine than it had ever been. She missed having Maeve around now that she was working on *Ardmore Grove*, and she didn't sit on the sidelines and watch rehearsals as much as she'd used to. Although she and Sebastian were on perfectly friendly terms outwardly, she didn't like the idea of being seen to observe him as he worked.

He might get the wrong idea if he caught her watching him.

Instead of hanging around doing nothing, Deirdre decided to pass the time more profitably by taking up knitting. She'd heard that loads of actresses did that or embroidery to fill in the long hours spent hanging around film sets.

She chose a very straightforward pattern for a man's jumper, thinking that if she kept at it, it would be ready for her dad for Christmas. She wasn't very good to start with and kept dropping stitches, but after a while she got the hang of it, although she didn't really know what all this tension stuff was about. The pattern had advised her to knit a sample square first and then measure it to find out whether her tension was right, but Deirdre thought that that was a total waste of time and didn't bother. She'd managed to get a really good bargain in knubbly cotton bouclé in Clery's. Cotton was tough to knit, but she'd bought all fourteen balls of the bloody stuff and she wasn't going to give up.

She was sitting in the coffee room by herself on the Friday morning of the second week of rehearsal when the door opened suddenly and someone came in. She looked up and realized that because she'd been concentrating so hard on her knitting, her tongue was sticking out and she was squinting a bit. It was Rory.

'Hey, Deirdre – you could enter a Bonny Baby contest. Don't move an eyelash – just stay like that and I'll fetch Amelia. She's just arrived. You could get her to do a whole new set of ten-by-eights.'

Amelia was a theatrical photographer who'd been commissioned to do rehearsal shots. Rory dropped a teabag into a cup and sloshed hot water over it.

Deirdre put down her knitting and sighed. 'Rory, you are becoming more vexatious by the day,' she said.

'Vexatious,' he repeated, helping himself to a Jammie Dodger. 'That's a good word, O'Dare. Vex-a-tious.'

He sat up on the windowsill, set his tea down and took a bite out of his biscuit.

'Those are Eva's biscuits.'

'She said I could have one. Who's the gansey for? Not the Prince of Denmark, by any chance?'

Deirdre didn't want to be having this conversation, but she was damn sure that she wasn't going to let Rory McDonagh drive her out of the coffee room. 'No, actually. It's for my father for Christmas.'

'Lucky fellow. D'you know something? You can sound awfully prim sometimes, Deirdre. It surprises me. I've reason to believe that Ms Goody Two-Shoes isn't entirely innocent of at least one of the seven deadly sins.'

Deirdre started knitting again.

Rory drank down some of his tea, looking at her over the edge of the cup. His eyes looked very narrow. 'You're looking very domesticated these days, Deirdre. I hear you've even started doing dinner parties. Pity Eva wasn't able to make it as far as your gaff the other night. Or maybe her fall was fortuitous? I'll confess that I'm quite surprised that your boyfriend's still alive. Something tells me that you'd be a practitioner of the Lucretia Borgia culinary school.'

Deirdre concentrated harder on her knitting, being careful to keep her tongue in. She wished Eva hadn't said anything about her party to Rory.

Rory started swinging his legs. 'The new improved Deirdre O'Dare sits well on you. You're looking very sexy these days, as well as domesticated. I even had a dream about you last night. You were–'

Just then Jessica Young put her head around the door and said: 'Deirdre? You're needed now – we're blocking the Mousetrap scene.' Deirdre got up with alacrity. She didn't want to hear anything about Rory's dream. The thought that she'd been roaming around inside his head last night made her feel very uncomfortable. As she got up to follow Jessica into the hall she had trouble controlling the almost irresistible impulse she felt to stab him through the heart with one of her knitting needles.

To Deirdre's relief, work on the Mousetrap scene – the scene where Hamlet lays his head in Ophelia's lap – had been postponed because of Eva's hectic work schedule. It would be pointless to continue blocking the play without her, so David had opted to cement what they'd already blocked. Deirdre had had to submit to Rory's pawing over and over again. She wished that she hadn't resisted him so vigorously the first time they'd rehearsed it, and that David hadn't decided it was a good idea to keep it in. Having to squirm against Rory like that was almost as bad as having to kiss him in *A Midsummer Night's Dream.*

Deirdre remembered how excited she'd once been by the idea of rehearsing the Mousetrap scene. It was ironic that she should look on it now with growing apprehension. After much discussion the cast straggled onto the floor to take up their allotted positions.

'Come hither, my dear Hamlet, sit by me,' called Eva to Sebastian.

'No, good mother; here's metal more attractive,' he replied, advancing towards Deirdre who was sitting downstage left. Sebastian knelt down beside her and nuzzled his face into her lap with the relish of a satyr, as David Lawless had suggested to him. As he continued, Deirdre could feel her face becoming hot, and she had some difficulty in getting her lines out. She was having to hold her script at an awkward angle in order to allow Sebastian free access to her.

Looking up, she saw Rory McDonagh walk into the rehearsal room through the door of the coffee room. What was *he* still doing here? He was meant to be finished for the day. As the door swung shut behind him, he clocked what was happening on the floor. Raising an eyebrow, he settled himself in a chair by the door and settled back to enjoy the spectacle. The expression of polite interest he'd arranged his features into was belied by his mouth, which was curved in a barely perceptible smile.

* * *

When Deirdre went home late that afternoon there was a message on the answering machine from her agent, asking her to ring her.

Mary Sheridan put her straight through to Sally.

'Hi, Deirdre. What's your schedule like next week? I want to set up an interview for you.'

'Things will be pretty busy towards the end of the week because we'll be doing runs, but I'll be reasonably flexible for the first half.' Deirdre could hardly believe that she was hearing herself having a telephone conversation like this. It was the kind of stuff she'd fantasized about saying for the past five years. 'If they stick to schedule, that is,' she added. 'It keeps being changed to accommodate Eva.'

'OK, let me make a note of that.' There was a brief pause. Deirdre imagined Sally at the other end of the phone sifting through pyramids of paper. 'Now. Let me fill you in on this one. There's a Texan company coming over to make a film – it's set at the time of the Famine, OK? The producer has put up all his own money and will be directing his own screenplay. He's a millionaire ex-pat and it seems this has been a pet project of his for years.'

Deirdre started to feel excited, even though she knew she shouldn't. She remembered what Sally had said to her before about grandiose dreams.

'Having said that, I don't want to get your expectations up. The guy is a dilettante – a complete amateur with a lot more money than sense. He came over some years ago to make a truly abysmal feature which as far as I know didn't even make it to video. What was the name of the bloody thing?

It had something to do with horses. It was so awful I can't even remember–'

'*Horse Power?*'

Sally sounded surprised. 'How did you know that?'

'Maeve Kirwan was in it. And Rory McDonagh.'

'Well at least you can check this geezer out with them. I imagine they'll have horror stories to tell about him.'

'Sally – d'you mind me asking? If it's such rubbish, why are you putting me up for it?'

'Because there's very little happening at the moment and I want you to take every opportunity you can to work on your interview technique, Deirdre. You badly need experience in that field. I'd send you up for an interview for the Civil Service if I thought it would be of some use after that débâcle with Juliet Rathbone-Lyon.'

'So even if I was offered the part you'd advise me not to take it?'

'Yes. Although a lot would depend on how much they'd be prepared to pay you and how much you needed the money.'

Pretty badly, thought Deirdre. She'd had to bring tuna sandwiches into rehearsal all week. At least she'd been able to cash her cheque this afternoon. She'd celebrate the end to the penury her dinner party had forced her into by going clubbing tonight.

'When are they shooting, Sally?'

'Not for a while, but they're casting now because they're over recceing locations at the moment. They'll probably be starting some time in October.

You could be finished on *Hamlet* by then, and if you're not you'll still be available to them during the day.'

'But I thought you didn't want me to do it? Wouldn't you prefer it if I *wasn't* available?'

'They want assurances that you'll be available before you get in to see them. There's no point in interviewing an actor who's going to be tied up with other projects.' From her demeanour over the phone, Deirdre could tell that Sally was sifting papers again. 'I'll try and set up something for you early next week. I'll talk to you on Monday, Deirdre, OK? Enjoy your weekend.'

'Thanks, Sally. Same to you.'

'Oh, by the way, Deirdre – this is important. Can you ride?'

'Yes,' came the prompt reply.

'Are you sure? Actors are notorious liars when they're asked that question.'

'Sally, I've lived in Wicklow all my life, remember? That county is teeming with equestrian centres.'

'I believe you. Bye, Deirdre.'

'See you soon, Sally. Thanks.'

Deirdre put down the phone and bit her lip. She'd only been on a horse twice before, and that had been when she was about ten. Not to worry. Sally had told her she should turn down the part anyway, even if she was offered it on a plate. And if she *did* decide to do it she could always take a crash course in riding lessons. Then nobody would know she'd been bluffing. She could ask her dad to lend her the money for tuition, and she'd be able to pay it back when the film money came through.

Riding would be a useful skill to have, she thought, even though she wasn't mad about horses. Perhaps she should invest in a course anyway. Then the next time she was asked that question she could put her hand on her heart and say yes, she could ride. She remembered what it had been like on the two occasions she'd been pony-trekking. Her horse had attracted loads of flies. She'd spent the afternoon brushing them off with flailing arms, and her legs had been in agony for days afterwards. Maybe she'd put off having lessons for a while.

That evening in Meagher's, Sophie joined Deirdre and Maeve who were sitting tittering over the *Irish Times* crossword, writing in incorrect solutions like 'Bum' and 'Scrotum' with juvenile glee. Maeve was in giddy form because she'd found out that day that she would have no scenes at all with Ann Fitzroy for the rest of the season on *Ardmore Grove.* Sophie was wearing a pair of snakeskin trousers almost identical to Eva's, but knowing her they were probably real, and probably from an endangered species of snake.

'Heard about the new movie that's coming to town?' she asked breezily.

'Yeah,' said Deirdre casually. 'I'm going up for it next week.'

'So am I,' said Sophie smugly. Shit, thought Deirdre.

'What movie?' asked Maeve.

'Something set during the Irish Famine. They

need actors who can ride and I'm an excellent horsewoman,' pronounced Sophie. Double shit, thought Deirdre. 'Apparently the director's absolutely crazy about horses, so at least we'll have something in common.'

'Horse crazy?' said Maeve. 'That sounds ominous. It's not the same eejit who was on that totally embarrassing film I did years ago – what was it called? It was so desperate that I can't even re–'

'*Horse Power*.'

'That's right. You mean you actually *remember* it, Deirdre? I wouldn't have thought it would ever even have–'

'Made it to video? It didn't, apparently.'

'I'm not surprised. How come you're so well-informed?' asked Maeve.

'You told me about it while we were doing *Dream*, and I was talking to Sally about it today on the phone.'

'Well at least you're forewarned – you'll know to steer clear of it,' said Maeve.

Deirdre looked down at her nails and shrugged. 'It depends on how much money they're offering.' Now that she knew Sophie Burke was up for what was presumably the same part she suddenly wanted to get it rather badly.

'Just be careful, Deirdre. That *Horse Power* film was the worst thing I've done in my entire career. I cringe when I think of it.'

'Oh, well,' Deirdre wanted to change the subject. 'Suki Hayes will probably get it anyway – if she's up for it.'

'She's not up for it,' Sophie said knowledgeably. 'She's not available. She's doing *Ardmore Grove*, remember? The part you tested for?' She gave Deirdre a bright smile which made her want to accidentally knock her pint over Sophie's snake-skin trousers. She'd stopped drinking Meagre Meagher's wine since she'd had a taste of Sebastian's scrummy Château Raspail and had taken to drinking Guinness instead.

Just then Rory McDonagh rolled up. Oh, God – not him *and* Sophie, thought Deirdre as he slid into the seat beside Maeve. She was beginning to think she'd have been better off not coming to the pub after all, especially when the door opened and Boring Beautiful Ben came through, casting his eyes around for Sophie.

'I've got some news that will amuse you, Maeve,' said Rory.

'I bet I can guess it,' she answered. 'The *Horse Power* people are in town again.'

'Spot on,' said Rory. 'How did you know?'

'Deirdre and Sophie are going up for it next week.'

Rory opened his eyes wide. 'Well. I wish you luck, girls,' he said.

'I'm surprised they haven't cast you in it, Rory, since they know what a formidable wrangler you are. Why don't you contact them?' Maeve's inquiry was plainly facetious.

'They've already contacted me, sweetheart.'

'No!' Maeve burst out laughing. 'What did you tell them?'

'I told them to go eat horse shit, of course,' said Rory. And as Maeve and Rory continued to laugh, Deirdre stole a look at Sophie who was stealing a look at her at the same time.

Miching malicho, thought Deirdre O'Dare. It means mischief.

* * *

'Howdy!' The following Wednesday morning TP O'Reilly, the director, producer and screenplay writer of the Famine film leaned across the boardroom table of a soulless hotel function room to shake Deirdre's hand. He was a florid, avuncular-looking man in his early fifties.

'Hi!' Deirdre gave him a big smile. 'Nice to meet you! I'm Deirdre O'Dare!' She had sensed immediately that exclamation marks might be a good idea.

'Big TP O'Reilly, Deirdre!' he said in a drawly Texan accent, pumping her hand vigorously. 'The name's officially Thomas Patrick, but everybody just calls me Big TP. I'm big in stature' – he patted his large paunch with both hands and grinned at her – 'and big in heart. And I've a larger than life personality!' He gave her a big wink. 'Take a seat, Deirdre.'

She sat down opposite him with her smile still in place. Behind the smile she was thinking that Big TP probably had an ego to match everything else that was big about him. In a far corner of the function room a rather flushed-looking PA was sitting working on a laptop. A mobile rang and the woman picked it up crossly. She muttered into it briefly and then returned her attention to her computer screen.

'Well, Deirdre,' said TP O'Reilly in a jocular tone. 'Let's see if we can find you among all these other lovely young things.' He indicated a stack of photographs on the table and picked up Suki Hayes's from the top. 'A real pussycat.' He did a bad imitation of a growl, looking at her with his teeth bared and his eyebrows raised. Deirdre refused to betray her discomfort. She wasn't going to blow this interview. Maybe she could contrive to let him know that Suki Hayes wasn't available. Big TP set Suki's photograph carefully to one side and started leafing through the others, making appreciative noises as he did so. Her smile faded as she watched him. 'You've a great smile,' he said, when he finally located her photograph.

'Thank you, Mr O'Reilly,' she said, switching it on again. Her facial muscles were starting to feel stiff.

'No, no, no – Big TP.'

'Of course. Big TP.' Deirdre felt extremely foolish calling a man she'd only known for two minutes Big TP. It sounded as if she were addressing an Indian Chief.

'D'you know something, Deirdre?' He put her photograph on the top of the pile and extracted a large cigar from the breast pocket of his checked jacket. 'It's great to be back in the country of my forebears. It truly is. It's like coming home.' He shook his head sadly. 'Can you credit it, Deirdre?

My ancestors were forced to flee their native land without a penny, and a century later here am I returning a millionaire. A *multi*-millionaire.' He repeated the mournful head-shake and then flicked on a lighter and held the flame to the cigar, sucking hard on the end. 'There's a word for that, isn't there, Deirdre?' he said between sucks. 'I'm not very good with words. I prefer to express myself through pictures. That's why I make films. What's the word I'm looking for?'

'Ironic?' suggested Deirdre.

'Yes, yes, yes! Ironic! That's the word.'

'Ironic, to be sure,' added Deirdre, thinking it was probably a good thing to sound a bit more Irish.

Across the table from her TP had gone very quiet and nostalgic-looking, obviously lost in some reverie of the Emerald Isle. The silence went on and on, and Deirdre decided she'd better kick-start the interview again. She cleared her throat. 'You know, I've a feeling you're a man after me own heart, Big TP. Someone told me that you have a passion for horses.'

The effect the word 'horses' produced on TP O'Reilly was metamorphic. He lifted his head at once and beamed at her. 'A passion? That's some understatement, Deirdre! If I'd lived in the time of the Greek myths I'd have been a centaur for sure! Ha ha ha!'

'They are magnificent beasts, horses,' replied Deirdre, with a faraway look on her face. 'I sometimes feel that I was born to ride.' She suddenly realized what she'd said and stopped short, giving

TP a quick glance to see if he'd registered her gaffe, but he was rummaging in a wallet he'd produced from his inside pocket.

'Here. Take a look at these,' he said, throwing a handful of snapshots onto the table between them. 'My wife often jokes that I never travel with a picture of her or the kids in my wallet – I only ever travel with pictures of my horses!'

Deirdre picked up the photographs with a foreboding heart and a fascinated expression. What on earth was she going to say about them? One horse was indistinguishable from the next as far as she was concerned. 'Oh my God – what magnificent animals!' she exclaimed. She thought Big TP's horses looked like – well, like horses.

'Ain't that the truth,' Big TP concurred, leaning back in his chair and stretching his arms above his head. 'They're almost dearer to me than my own children.'

Deirdre didn't doubt it. 'I just – I'll just have to admit it, Big TP. They have rendered me absolutely speechless. I have never seen such magnificent creatures. I am gobsma . . . – absolutely dumbfounded by their sheer – their incredible – you know . . . ?'

'Yeah. I know just what you mean.' TP smiled and nodded at her slowly. 'They're magnificent, aren't they?'

There was a photograph of a goldy-coloured horse amongst the bunch. Suddenly something came back to her in a flash. She remembered a story that had been serialized in *Bunty* years ago, when she'd been about ten years old. It had been about an orphan girl who'd escaped from the circus run by her wicked foster mother. She hadn't wanted to leave her favourite circus pony, so she'd stolen him and taken him with her on her travels through the lonely Scottish highlands in an endeavour to trace her real parents. It hadn't been Deirdre's favourite series because it had had a horse in it, but it was better than the one about the girl steeplejack. It had been called 'Paloma's Palomino'.

'The palomino is particularly magnificent,' she hazarded, sneaking a look at Big TP to make sure she hadn't got it wrong. She also thought that she might be over-using the word 'magnificent'. 'I've always thought that the palomino is a truly – um – majestic breed. They have real –' Deirdre searched around for another good word '– charisma. And mystery,' she threw in for good measure.

'I can tell you know your horses, Deirdre. I handed over a lot of bucks for that little lady.'

He blew a couple of smoke signals out of his mouth and Deirdre suppressed a cough. 'I can well believe it,' she said in a knowledgeable way. The cigar was probably top-of-the-range but it still stank.

To her relief he stretched his hand out across the table and reappropriated the snapshots. He gazed at them lovingly for a minute or two before replacing them in his wallet. 'Well, that's enough about our mutual passion,' he said jovially. 'For now, anyway,' he added. 'I've a feeling we might be spending more time together in the future, Deirdre.' He gave her another wink and Deirdre brightened.

That seemed like a good omen, she thought, as she tried to dimple. She'd begun to realize that she wasn't particularly good at dimpling. Sophie had the monopoly on that. She wondered if Sophie had been in to see Big TP yet.

'There was another actress in here today who knew about horses, Deirdre. She prattled on for a long time before I realized that, although she knew a lot about them *here* –' Big TP pointed to his head '– she knew nothing about them *here.*' He pointed to his heart. 'I can tell a horse lover at a thousand paces, Deirdre, and you have horses in your soul. I'm right, aren't I?'

'That you are, Big TP.' Deirdre nodded solemnly, but her heart was starting to hum a tiny little tune. It was *Home, Home on the Range.*

'Anyway, she was a blonde, and I don't want a blonde in the part. Gentlemen may prefer blondes, but gentlemen marry brunettes, ha ha ha, as the famous Dorothy Parker once said.' Deirdre knew for a fact that it was Anita Loos who'd said it, but she wasn't going to enlighten him.

Big TP leaned his elbows on the table. 'Let's talk some business, Miss Deirdre. I'd better start by telling you about the part I have you in mind for.' He sent her another wink and she dimpled quite well this time. 'It's the part of the daughter of the local wealthy landlord' – (Uh-oh, thought Deirdre. She'd better start phasing out the brogue.) – 'who takes pity on the local starving peasants, and visits them with food and drugs.' (Drugs? thought Deirdre in astonishment. Why would she offer them drugs if she'd taken pity on them?) 'You know, those herbal remedies and – uh, what d'you call them? – tissons and stuff like that that they used back then.' (Tissons? Oh – *tisanes.*) 'Then her father finds out and tries to stop her from doing it because he's a really evil British officer as well as being a landlord so he has shit-loads of power. But his daughter Tracey' – Deirdre was starting to hear warning bells – 'defies him because she's fallen in love with one of the local peasants, so they escape his wrath on horseback. Then Bob gets killed by evil British GIs–'

'Excuse me, Big TP,' said Deirdre politely. 'Sorry to interrupt you, but who's Bob?'

'Bob's the peasant. I decided to name the heroine of the film Tracey after my daughter and the hero Bob after my son.'

'Oh – I see. What a nice idea.' Deirdre nodded brightly.

'Anyway Bob's dead, right? So Tracey decides to seek revenge on her father and becomes an outlaw. From being the fabulously wealthy and beautiful daughter of the local landlord she goes to nothing. Just like that. Nothing!' Big TP thumped his fist on the table and Deirdre jumped. 'All she has left in the world are her wits and her trusty horse.' (Uh-oh, she thought.) 'So she roams the country on The Lady Tara, helping the poor and setting up traps for the Brits and then one day her father stumbles across one of the traps and gets blown into a thousand smithereens!' Big TP sat back in his chair with a challenging expression on his face. There was a long pause.

Then: 'Is that the end?' Deirdre enquired tentatively.

'No! We find out that Bob didn't really get killed – he's been an outlaw all this time too, setting traps for the Brits just like Tracey. They meet up by accident one day when they're both setting a trap in the same place – this is the bit I'd like you to read for me – and realize that they're still crazy about each other despite all they've been through, so they get married. Then the Famine's over and they both go back and live in the big house.'

For a while the only sound was the tip-tapping of the PA's fingers on her laptop. 'It sounds fascinating, Big TP,' said Deirdre finally.

'I knew you'd think so! OK – let's read it together. Here's the scene I told you about where Tracey and Bob meet up. It's only a couple of pages, but that's all I need to tell whether an actress has got what it takes or not. I'm a very perceptive man when it comes to recognizing genuine talent, and I've a feeling you've got *just* what it takes, little lady!'

He pushed a couple of printed pages across the table to her and Deirdre looked at them cautiously. She was starting to feel slightly panicky. Tracey was landed gentry. She'd have to remember to do a sort of posh voice. She took a deep breath. 'Bob!' she exclaimed. 'It's you! But it can't be you. Bob's dead.'

Big TP's Texan drawl had been replaced by an

execrable Irish accent. 'No, Tracey – don't go! I'm Bob. I am Bob. Believe me I am Bob.'

'How can I believe you when I saw your dead body with my own eyes. This is some trick of the Brits. I'm getting out of here.'

'No! (He seizes her by the arm).' Oh God, thought Deirdre. He's going to read all the stage directions as well. 'You mustn't go now that I've found you again after all these years. Look! (He rolls up his sleeve to show her his birthmark.) Here is the proof!'

'I must believe you. There could be no other Bob.' Deirdre decided that since Big TP was reading the stage directions aloud, she'd better do so too. '(She falls into his arms. They kiss passionately.)' Oh God, she thought. Who was going to be playing Bob? At least she knew it wouldn't be Rory McDonagh. '(They draw apart. She strokes his face tenderly.) But Bob, how could this be? How come you're still alive after all this time?'

'I feigned death to fool the Brits. But it's a long, long story, Tracey. We don't have time right now. The Brits will be here soon.'

'You're right, Bob, we must go. Have you still got Old Madge your horse?'

'No, Tracey. Sadly Old Madge lay down and died that time I had to feign death to fool the Brits. (He looks away from her, obviously moved.) Old Madge died of a broken heart, Tracey, but it was really the Brits that did it. I'll never forgive them for what they did to her.'

'I'm so sorry, Bob. I'll never forgive the Brits

either. I'll never forgive them for what they've done to you. I'll never forgive them for what they've done to me. And I'll never forgive them for what they've done to my country.'

'Your country? But you are the daughter of a noble Englishman, Tracey.'

'Correction, Bob. *Was* the daughter.'

'(He gives her a quizzical look),' interjected Big TP.

Deirdre resumed. 'Yes, Bob. I blew my father to bits. I am as Irish as you now. The blood that flows through my veins is no longer the blue blood of a noble English Earl. It is the green blood of Ireland. (She produces an Irish passport from her handbag and brandishes it.)' Deirdre wondered if she ought to mention that Irish passports didn't exist until the 1920s and then decided against it.

'Tracey I love you.'

'Bob I love you too. (They kiss again.) But we had better hurry. It is getting late.'

'You're right, Tracey. Ah – I see your horse The Lady Tara in the next field. Make haste and flee this place.'

'I'm not going anywhere without you, Bob. Not ever again. The Lady Tara is strong enough to carry us both. (They cross quickly into the next field, mount The Lady Tara and gallop off over the horizon.)'

'Wow, Deirdre!' TP blew out more smoke. 'You read that like a dream. That's just the way I've always imagined those words would sound some day.'

Deirdre didn't bother with the dimple this time. She wasn't sure that she shouldn't have blown this interview after all. 'Thanks, Big TP.'

Big TP got to his feet and stretched out his hand. 'Well, little lady, it's been a pleasure meeting you. And I can say with every confidence that I'm sure we'll meet again.' He gave her another enormous wink, which she found herself automatically returning. 'Ha ha ha!' roared Big TP. 'You surely are my kind of gal, Miss Deirdre O'Dare!'

And as he showed her to the door he rested an avuncular hand just fractionally too low on the small of her back.

Chapter Eighteen

They were well into their fifth week of rehearsal when Deirdre got a message on her answering machine from Sally to tell her that she'd been offered the part of Tracey. She didn't know what to feel. She certainly didn't feel the thrill she would have felt if she'd heard she'd landed a part – however tiny – in the Neil Jordan movie, for instance. And somehow victory over Sophie didn't seem that important any more.

Her instinct told her that she should turn the film down. She knew it wouldn't do anything to advance her career and that it would only result in real humiliation and plummeting self-esteem. Then she thought of the financial implications. She had just over six weeks of employment left to run with Lawless Productions. There had been a rumour that the run of *Hamlet* might be extended because of the phenomenal public interest, but that had been quickly scotched because too many cast members had already committed themselves to other projects. They were the lucky ones. There was absolutely no sign of any other work coming up with the exception of the Grace O'Malley film, and Deirdre knew that that was blown into another galaxy as far as she was concerned. She rang Sally to ask for her advice.

'Well done on getting an interview right, Deirdre. You must have worked hard on that one. Something of a Pyrrhic victory, though, all the same.'

'You really don't think I should take it then, Sally?'

'No. Sorry, Deirdre. You'd be doing yourself no favours professionally. Are you very disappointed?'

'Not really. I wasn't mad about TP O'Reilly. And his script was just embarrassing.'

'Good. I'm glad. I'll phone the production company today and quote them a totally unrealistic figure. They'll back off immediately if they realize they won't be able to afford you.'

'The problem is I've only six more weeks of work, Sally. What'll I do when *Hamlet* closes?'

'Are you telling me you're having second thoughts?'

'Well, no – I really don't want to do the film. It's just that I'm going to be stony broke.'

'That goes with the business, Deirdre. It's the actor's perennial problem. You've been extremely lucky to date, you know. Either you sign on the dole – you should have enough stamps by now – or you find some kind of part-time work.'

'What about *Ardmore Grove*?' Deirdre knew that a note of desperation was starting to creep into her voice. 'Are they still interested?'

'I haven't been in touch with them for a while. I'll bring it up next time I need to contact them. But even if they are interested, Deirdre, remember that you're talking months ahead. The episodes involving the character they have you in mind for aren't happening until after Christmas.'

'You will let me know, Sally, if anything else comes up?'

'Of course I will. In the meantime, just enjoy *Hamlet*.'

Deirdre put the phone down feeling frightened. Maybe she should start putting out feelers about getting work as a waitress or as a chambermaid in one of the new city centre hotels that were springing up all over the place.

She'd had a letter from Sarah a couple of days ago to say that her uncle had cut short his sabbatical. He'd be returning to Dublin in a couple of months and wanting his apartment back, and then she'd have to go home to Kilmacanogue. She wouldn't be able to afford to get a flat in town – rents were punishingly expensive for anything within walking distance of the city centre – and the thought of possibly having to share a bed-sit in Rathmines after the comparative luxury of the flat she'd been caretaking filled her with gloom. Then she gave herself a mental rap over the knuckles. Sally was right. She had been extremely lucky to date, and she should really be concentrating on her current work instead of worrying about what was down the line.

Hamlet rehearsals were becoming slightly fraught. Nearly ten weeks of working on two shows simultaneously was beginning to tell on the actors, and now that they had hit production week they were working three sessions a day. Everyone was feeling tired and irritable, and tension was inevitably building. Even Eva's sanguine disposition was being tested to the limit. Of all of them, she was the most under pressure. Juggling two shows and a film was taking its toll, and she had displayed temperament on one or two occasions, invariably apologizing all round afterwards.

The weather had changed at last, and the company was starting to dress in rather drab autumnal colours instead of their bright summer garb. Finbar de Rossa had come down with a virus and was having awful problems with his voice as a result of having to play the demanding role of Macbeth every night as well as rehearsing Claudius during the day. He was under strict doctor's orders not to use his voice unless he absolutely had to, which at least put a stop to his interminable movie set anecdotes.

Sebastian was the only member of the company who wasn't revealing signs of strain, but then he was the only member of the company who wasn't working nights as well. Still, it had to be taken into consideration that Hamlet was the most demanding of Shakespeare's roles, and Sebastian was busting a gut in terms of the work he was putting in. His interpretation was intelligent, witty and sophisticated, but one could sense that, beneath the urbane exterior, his Hamlet was plagued by demons. Sebastian positively shimmered with surface tension.

He must have extraordinary reserves of energy, thought Deirdre, as she watched him rehearse the duel with Rory. It was the afternoon of the day Deirdre had turned down Big TP's film. Rory's hair was clinging to his face, and there were damp patches of sweat on his T-shirt, but Sebastian was scarcely out of breath.

When they finished, Rory staggered over to where she was sitting knitting and sank gasping onto the chair beside her. 'Let me have some of your water, Deirdre,' he said, indicating the big bottle of Tipperary water at her feet. She found herself breathing in the smell of his sweat with something she was surprised to identify as pleasure. She'd noticed before that there was nothing offensive about the way he smelt, as there was with some of the other actors. The shower in one of the men's dressing-rooms was out of order and some of the male members of the cast were pretty rank every night after the fight scene in *Macbeth.* Sitting anywhere near them in the pub after the show had become something of a trial. In the green room one night Eva had provocatively offered Rory the use of her own shower until his was fixed. Catching sight of the expression of David Lawless's face, Rory had politely declined her generous offer.

'Thanks,' he said now, as Deirdre handed him the water bottle. He put it to his mouth and took a couple of swigs. Then he lowered it, wiping his mouth with the back of his hand before handing it back to Deirdre. She took it from him and carefully ran her sleeve round the rim of the neck before screwing the top back on.

'Oh – good idea, Deirdre. I'd forgotten how unhygienic it was to exchange bodily fluids,' he said. He gave her an ominous smile. 'How's the gansey coming along?' He took her knitting from her before she could stop him and held it up, looking at it admiringly. 'It's looking good, Deirdre. That dishcloth stitch must be dead complicated. Lainey Keogh'd better watch her ass.'

'Don't you think it's about time you started working out or something, Rory? You're obviously terribly unfit.' Deirdre snatched the knitting back from him.

'Work out? Me? What's your address, O'Dare? Doolally Lane, Cloud Cuckoo Land?'

'Well you could at least try jogging. That's how Sebastian keeps fit. He jogs before rehearsal every morning.'

'The only jogging I am interested in, Deirdre, as I know you're aware from personal experience, is of a horizontal nature.' Deirdre had walked into it yet again. 'And I'm reasonably certain that your boyfriend, that hip, hot, happening dude, Sebastian, has a penchant for that kind of jogging, too. But I'm sure you know that already? May I?' he asked politely, taking the bottle of water from her again and drinking deeply.

'He's not my boyfriend,' Deirdre snapped, her face flaming.

Rory looked at her. There was something curiously speculative about his expression. Then he took another swig of water. 'Well, well.' He raised an eyebrow at her. 'I'm surprised to hear that, what with all the sheep's eyes acting you've been doing ever since he came on the scene. Do you mean to tell me that he doesn't reciprocate your warm feelings towards him?'

'Just get off my case, will you Rory?' She turned on him with blazing eyes.

'Wow – Deirdre O'Dare kicks ass. You should get lippy more often, Deirdre – it suits you. I've always liked that sassy streak in you.'

Deirdre turned away from him again. 'Go away, Rory,' she said in an excessively polite tone, articulating each syllable. 'You quite clearly have a jaundiced mind. You are odious and you are hateful.'

'And you are oxymoronic and tautological, sweetheart.' He handed back the bottle of water. 'Just let me say one thing before I go, witch. What does Hamlet say to Gertrude in the second scene of the play?'

Deirdre didn't answer. She wasn't about to play guessing games with Rory McDonagh. She went back to her knitting.

'He says: "Seems, madam! Nay, it *is*; I know not *seems*." Listen to me, Deirdre. You're not going to want to hear this, but Sebastian Hardy knows "seems" inside out. He's smiling and he's smiling, but there's some serious villainy going on there.'

'Don't be so stupid and melodramatic, Rory.'

'Let me tell you something, Deirdre. Do you

recall he said he'd missed the first fifteen minutes of *Macbeth* on the opening night?'

Something in his voice made her look at him. 'Yes? So what?' she replied dismissively.

'Well, it wasn't because his plane was delayed or because there were problems with taxis at the airport. I saw him unloading bags from a taxi into the basement of a house two streets away from me when I was on my way into work that evening. At around six o'clock.'

'Yeah?' Deirdre regarded him sceptically.

'And no mistake, sweetheart.'

Deirdre looked at him uncertainly. 'Well, maybe he missed his bus and that made him late. Or his taxi didn't show up on time,' she argued. 'There are loads of reasons why people can be late.'

'You're not listening, Deirdre. Why did he lie about his plane being delayed? And why did he say he'd left his bags at the theatre when I quite plainly saw them outside his door?' Rory stood up and looked down at her. '"Be wary, then; best safety lies in fear." Laertes' advice to Ophelia is good. I wouldn't like to see you getting your dainty fingers burnt, Little Bo-Peep.'

'I'm quite capable of looking after myself, you know, Rory,' she said snootily.

He shrugged. 'I have my doubts about that. Just remember this: There are more things in heaven and earth, Deirdre O'Dare, than are dreamt of in your philosophy.'

And as he strolled away, Deirdre's gaze returned to Sebastian.

* * *

That night in the pub, Deirdre told Maeve that she'd turned down the TP O'Reilly film. Maeve looked at her with admiration. 'Well done, Deirdre. That's a really gutsy thing to do – especially when there's no prospect of work in the pipeline. Ha! With a bit of luck Sophie'll get the part now. She'd never have the cop-on to turn it down. What did she say when you told her?'

'She doesn't know yet.'

'What?' Maeve looked mildly astonished. 'I'm amazed, Deirdre. It's not like you to miss an opportunity of crowing over Sophie. Actually, now I come to think of it it's strange that you didn't broadcast it all over the dressing-room this evening.'

'Well, I forgot.'

Maeve lifted her glass. 'How are rehearsals going?' she asked.

'Oh, all right, you know. I miss having you around. And everyone's really tired – especially Eva.'

'She's still working on the Jordan film?'

'Uh huh.'

'What's Sebastian going to be like?'

'Amazing. He's dead serious, though – tunnel-visioned. It means he's not really that much fun to work with. I know having fun isn't what it's all about, but it's nice to have a bit of a laugh from time to time.'

'Well. At least you've a scene with Rory. He doesn't take life too seriously. Or are you two still behaving like children?'

Deirdre shrugged. 'Yeah. I suppose so,' she said.

Maeve looked at Deirdre for a minute and then looked around the pub, which was heaving as usual. Since the spectacular success of David Lawless's season at the Phoenix, Meagher's had had to hire extra staff to cope with the punters who thronged in after the show every night. 'Look – there's Sophie over there. Will I wave to her to join us? Then you can subtly drop the news about the film into the conversation.'

'To tell you the truth, Maeve, I couldn't be bothered. Maybe she'll find out from someone else, maybe she won't. I really don't care either way.'

Maeve gave her a curious look. 'Why, Deirdre O'Dare – I do believe you're starting to grow up.'

Deirdre smiled wryly. 'Not much chance of that,' she said. 'I'll never understand real life.'

Just then Rory walked into the pub. He looked a bit wrecked.

Maeve looked thoughtful suddenly. 'I'm going up to the bar. Let me buy you a drink to celebrate your rite of passage, Deirdre.'

Maeve was gone some time. Deirdre normally felt self-conscious sitting in the pub by herself, but for some reason it didn't really faze her this evening, even when a rather gorgeous-looking poser started eyeing her with intent. Eventually he came over and smiled down at her. 'Hi. You were in the show tonight, weren't you?'

'Yes, I was,' said Deirdre.

'I was impressed.'

'Thanks a lot.' Deirdre returned his smile politely.

'D'you mind if I join you?'

Deirdre was dead tired. She didn't feel like making the effort to talk to anyone, especially not a poser, even if he was drop-dead gorgeous. She just wanted to take it easy with Maeve.

'I'd rather you didn't, if you don't mind. Sorry. I'm feeling a bit wasted.'

'Maybe you could do with an ego massage to perk you up? I'm good at that.' He sat down beside her and gave her a meaningful smile. He was sitting too close to her. 'The name's Gary, by the way. And you're . . . ?'

'Deirdre.'

'Well, Deirdre, it's nice to meet you. D'you know something? You're even sexier in real life than you are on the stage.'

Deirdre almost snorted. The last word to describe the way she looked in *Macbeth* was sexy.

'You're a very beautiful woman, Deirdre,' continued Gary. 'I love beautiful women. Especially beautiful women who are actresses. I know about them.' Deirdre really didn't like the way he was looking her over. 'I see you've finished your drink, angel. D'you fancy going on somewhere else? My friend's throwing a party in his flat in Rathmines later. It'll be kicking, Deirdre. You'll have a good time.'

Deirdre tensed. 'I don't want to be rude, Gary, but I'm with a friend.'

'Drop him. I bet he doesn't deserve you.'

This guy was persistent. Deirdre was starting to feel exasperated. She didn't want the hassle of a row but she'd have to think of some way to discourage him. 'Gary, I don't want to offend you, but let's just say I'm of a different sexual persuasion to you, OK?' This might put him off. 'Now, maybe you could leave me alone?'

'Hey – a lesbian! All right! That makes things even more interesting. Maybe I could watch. I've always found the idea of two beautiful women doing things to each other a real turn-on.' He stroked her cheek with a finger.

He was really invading her space now. Deirdre let him have it. 'Oh, just fuck off, will you? Haven't you got the message? I'm not interested, all right?'

He stood up slowly and shrugged, leering at her unpleasantly. 'Snotty little dyke,' he said. 'What use is your lesbian girlfriend to someone as uptight as you? You could do with a really good fuck, bitch.' And he made an obscene gesture at her before going back to his friends.

Deirdre was too tired to retaliate. She felt violated, somehow, even though she knew it was stupid to let the bastard get to her. What was the *point* of such nastiness? She had been quite right in what she'd said to Maeve earlier. She'd never understand real life.

Maeve returned with three pints. 'Was that geezer giving you a hard time? I saw him breathing all over you.'

'Yeah,' said Deirdre, feeling defeated. 'Why do some men take such pleasure in making women feel bad, Maeve?'

'What did he say to you?'

Deirdre told her. Maeve sighed and raised her eyes to heaven. 'Shit, Deirdre – the world is full of cretins like that – it's text-book. He wanted to get back at you because you weren't interested in him.' Maeve looked over to where Gary was sending out signals to Sophie Burke. Sophie was dimpling obligingly. 'Some men can't handle the fact that they're not God's gift to every woman on the face of the planet. You struck him a body blow and he didn't like it.'

'He gets off on making people feel bad? Well, it worked. It was like that time in Juliet Rathbone-Lyon's office when I could tell she was enjoying twisting the knife. The really stupid thing is that he actually *succeeded* in upsetting me, Maeve.'

'Try not to let it get to you. Wankers like him aren't worth wasting energy over.'

'I suppose.' Deirdre was half-heartedly tracing the rings that her pint of Guinness had left on the table. She gave a little sigh of resignation. 'You're always right, Maeve. D'you know, sometimes I wish I *was* a lesbian. I've had such bloody awful luck with men.'

Maeve laughed. 'Not a chance, Deirdre. You're a man's girl through and through. I can tell these things.'

Deirdre picked up her glass. 'Who's the other pint for?'

'Rory. I invited him to join us.'

'Oh, *no*, Maeve!' Deirdre suddenly stopped tracing patterns. 'Talk about morons. You *know* that Rory and I can't stand each other these days.'

She made a half-hearted move to get up, but Maeve laid a restraining hand on her arm. 'Give him a break, Deirdre. He's going through a really tough time at the moment. He and Marian are breaking up.'

'Oh.' Deirdre sat down again slowly. 'Are you serious, Maeve? But they've been living together for years, haven't they? I mean – they're practically married.'

Maeve nodded. 'Sad, isn't it?' There was something vigilant about the way she was looking at Deirdre. 'It seems that for the past while they've kind of drifted apart. Rory's never there for her and she's never there for him. I don't think the split's acrimonious, but it's always difficult when long-standing relationships come to an end.'

'How did you find all this out?'

'Rory told me in the Troc last night. We went for a meal after we left the pub.'

'Oh.' For some absurd reason Deirdre felt slightly jealous that Rory had confided all this in Maeve. She imagined the two of them sitting in the intimate ambience of the Trocadero, trading secrets over a bottle of wine. Then she shook herself mentally. After all, why shouldn't Rory use Maeve as a shoulder to cry on? They'd been close friends for a long time, ever since they started out in the business together. She made an effort to be conversational. 'The house belongs to Marian, doesn't it? Has he moved out yet?' Deirdre's mind flashed back to the pristine white bedroom and the white and chrome bathroom. She remembered how Rory had kissed her toes in the bath and then dried them carefully afterwards.

'He's looking for somewhere. He thought he might take Sebastian's flat after *Hamlet*'s finished.'

'What about in the meantime?' asked Deirdre.

'I said he could move in with us.'

'With you and Jacqueline?' Deirdre was surprised.

'Yeah. He can have the futon for a few weeks.'

'And you don't mind?' She didn't know how anyone could tolerate living with Rory McDonagh.

'Why should I mind? I love Rory to bits and Jacqueline's mad about him too. She claims nobody can lift her out of a fit of the blues the way he can. He's a natural born charmer.'

Maeve was right, Deirdre supposed glumly. After all, Rory McDonagh had charmed her into his bed. How gullible she'd been that day!

'Here he comes now,' said Maeve. 'And by the way, Deirdre – we didn't have this conversation. This is privileged information, OK?'

'OK.'

Deirdre watched Rory as he dropped down beside Maeve on the banquette. He gave her a tired smile and kissed her on the cheek. 'Thanks for the pint, Maeve,' he said. 'What a chum you are.' He picked up his pint and sank a good third of it.

'Guess what Deirdre did today, Rory,' said Maeve.

'That unfathomable creature sitting over there? I

couldn't hazard a guess, Maeve. Won the knitwear prize at the Irish Fashion Design Awards?'

Deirdre felt hot and inexplicably shy and wished Maeve hadn't said anything about her to Rory.

'Apart from that. She turned down her first film offer.'

'Not Big TP's venture? Well, Deirdre, I am impressed. You're starting to show signs of intelligent life at last.'

Deirdre was too tired for this. She got up. 'I'm going to the loo, Maeve,' she announced, and headed in the direction of the ladies. As she walked past a table she noticed two geezers lounging ostentatiously. One of them was the guy called Gary who'd been horrible to her. He leaned over and said something to his friend in a low voice which prompted a snort of raucous laughter. Then he stepped out in front of her and thrust a fist between her legs.

Before Deirdre had a chance to react, Rory was there. He grabbed Gary by his shirt collar and the expression on his face was dangerous. He was white with rage. 'Back off, friend,' he said in a very calm, very scary voice. 'If you ever touch that woman again I will rip your head off, do you understand? I will do it if that's what it takes to teach you respect. Now. Tell me this. What are you going to learn from me?'

Gary's eyes were bulging. He was sweating and his face had gone bright red. He spluttered something incoherent.

'I'm sorry – I can't hear you.' Rory's tone was perfectly level. 'What are you trying to say, man? Respect? Yeah?'

'Yeah,' Gary finally managed to get out. 'Respect.' Around him the punters had gone very quiet. Nobody tried to intervene.

'Good.' Rory let go of his collar. 'Now. Apologize to the lady.'

Deirdre's face was as white as Rory's. Gary looked at her like a sullen child and said: 'Sorry, babe.'

He immediately put his hands up in an attitude of surrender. Rory was at his throat again.

'She's not a babe.' His voice was oily with menace. 'She's a lady. What do you say to a lady? You call her madam, don't you? Do it.'

'Sorry, madam.' Gary was craven now.

'That's better,' said Rory. 'You're learning manners now.' He released him and Gary went stumbling backwards. 'Get out of here,' said Rory, sounding ominously pleasant. He indicated Gary's friend with a nod of his head. 'You too. Get out of here now.'

It had all happened very fast. The pair of posers turned and ambled through the crowded pub trying to look casual. Then Gary turned and spread out his hands. 'Cool it, man,' he said rather feebly as he followed his friend through the door with an unconvincing strut.

Deirdre looked at Rory numbly. 'Thanks, Rory,' was all she could say.

'Yeah,' said Rory. He gave her a smile that didn't quite reach his eyes. 'You can buy me a pint now, Deirdre, if you like.'

* * *

By the time *Hamlet* was due to open the entire company was exhausted. There had been problems with the set and the crew had been working round the clock. Jenny had decided to set the play in Regency times with Elsinore being inspired by the Brighton pavilion, and the necessary opulence and Jenny's insistence on period detail had sent the budget soaring and the crew stark staring mad from working overtime. In the end it was worth it. Everyone agreed that Jenny had excelled herself.

The costumes were beautiful, too. Deirdre would have been happy to wear a bin bag after her experience in *Macbeth*, but she had practically swooned when she'd first tried on the dress which Jenny had created for Ophelia. It was Empire line, made from layers and layers of fine sprigged muslin, fitted around the bust and gathered so that it fell in soft folds to the ground. It had tiny puffed sleeves, was very low-cut and it virtually floated with her as she moved.

Jenny insisted that all the actresses wear what she called 'bananas' to push their breasts up as was the fashion in Regency times. These were curved calico wodges stuffed with kapok which were pinned into the actresses' costumes and which worked on the same principal as a balcony bra. Deirdre had nearly died of self-consciousness the first time she'd tried her frock on. She felt as if her breasts were sitting on a tray, and she kept trying to pull the flimsy fabric of her frock up over them, but Jenny was adamant. 'No, no, *no*, Deirdre. Wear it the way Eva does, so that your nipples are practically exposed. They weren't ashamed to show their bosoms during the Regency – a bit like the way we're not ashamed to show thigh today. I mean – just look at the tiny skirt that Sophie's wearing. In fact,' Jenny went on, musingly, 'it might be rather nice if your nipples actually *are* exposed and maybe highlighted with rouge when you're carried on drowned. I might run that by David and see what he thinks.'

Deirdre was horrified. A kind of dumb-show had been plotted into the action of the play where Laertes was to carry the dead body of his sister across the stage in silence, the only sound being the tolling of a funeral bell in the distance. For this brief appearance, Deirdre was to look as if she'd just been lifted from the river. Jenny had had a second, broken-down version of Ophelia's gown made up and had instructed Deirdre that she was to change into it after the mad scene and get into the shower. She needed to be dripping wet with water. The thought of being manhandled across the stage by Rory McDonagh with her breasts on display made Deirdre want to die. Maybe Jenny would get distracted and forget about the idea. But her hopes were dashed when Jenny produced her notebook and started scribbling in it with characteristic enthusiasm. She wished that the designer wasn't quite so imaginative.

In fact, when they came to the dress rehearsal, it was a *fait accompli.* The way Rory carried her, with his left arm under her spine and his right arm under her knees meant that her head fell back so far that her breasts spilled out of the top of her dress anyway. Because the scene was conducted in virtual darkness, it meant that the audience wouldn't clearly discern her nakedness, but she knew that Rory was well aware of it, even though for once he made no ribald remarks.

Deirdre might as well have been carried onto the stage stark naked. The soaking wet muslin moulded itself to the contours of her body like a second skin, accentuating the curve of her belly, the line of her thigh and the jut of her hip. Although the water was warm when she took her shower, by the time she got out onstage, she was freezing and it was obvious. Her nipples were hard and prominent. She suffered agonies of embarrassment as Rory lifted her and gathered her against his chest just prior to the slow walk across the stage and she could tell that he wasn't entirely comfortable with the situation either. She was completely oblivious to the fact that she had never looked more desirable.

* * *

In spite of the fact that the opening night of *Hamlet* was the most successful one of the season, the celebrations afterwards were more subdued than any to date. There was the usual champagne backstage and then a party in the function room of Meagher's, but everyone seemed tired and dispirited, and the jollity was rather forced. Only the liggers seemed to be having any real fun.

Eva looked exhausted and didn't bother to show up at the party because she was due on location at some unearthly hour the next morning, and David only put in a brief appearance before disappearing with two of the financial backers. Rory and Jonathan Hughes got quietly and morosely drunk in a corner and then shambled off somewhere together – probably to that shebeen he'd told her about, Deirdre supposed. Some of the other cast members gave up on the party after an hour or so as well, and disappeared off to Lillie's or the River Club.

Maeve had been in to see the show by herself because Jacqueline was catering for a function, and Deirdre joined her afterwards. She was rather dreading the rest of the run, especially since Sophie was now the only other person sharing the dressing-room. She'd have nobody to swop secrets with now that Maeve was gone. There was really only Sebastian left. The two of them still got on well, but there was an awkwardness between them which Deirdre didn't quite know how to handle.

Sebastian puzzled her enormously. Sometimes he seemed to actively seek her out, and was almost protective towards her. He'd engage her in long conversations and listen to her intently, and on a couple of occasions it had seemed as if he was about to kiss her, but he always backed off. She noticed that he'd automatically gravitate towards her if she was in Eva's company. The actress's effect on him was still magnetic even though her chronic fatigue had drained her of most of her vibrancy, and she wasn't particularly sociable these days. On other occasions, he would retreat into himself and cut himself off from everyone except David Lawless. She didn't think she'd ever get to really know Sebastian Hardy. There was something closed and rather mysterious about him, as if he'd erected defences around himself which no-one could ever penetrate.

At the party, he had insisted on buying Maeve and Deirdre drinks before joining his agent who'd flown over from London for the opening night.

'Curious type, Sebastian, isn't he?' observed Maeve as he had politely taken leave of them.

Deirdre shrugged. 'I suppose he is. Enigmatic's the word I'd choose.'

'Or secretive. Did Rory tell you that weird story? The one about the time he saw Sebastian unloading his bags from a taxi even though he claimed later that he'd left them at the theatre?'

'Yeah. I'm not sure what to make of all that.' Deirdre suddenly thought of something else she'd found confusing. 'There's another weird thing, Maeve. We shared a taxi home from the Troc on the opening night of *Macbeth* –'

'That was the night he arrived, right?'

'Yeah. Remember he told us he'd missed the first

fifteen minutes of the play because his plane had got in late?'

Maeve nodded.

'Well, on the way home in the taxi he said that his flat still smelled of paint.'

'I don't follow.'

'How did he know it smelled of paint if he hadn't had time to even drop his bags off before the show?'

'I see what you mean.'

'So Rory must have been telling the truth when he said he'd seen Sebastian moving in that same afternoon.'

'I've never known Rory to tell a lie, Deirdre.'

Deirdre was silent for a while, casting her mind about in an effort to make sense of things. 'What does it all mean, Maeve?'

'That there's more to Sebastian than meets the eye, I suppose.' There was a pause and then Maeve sent her a shrewd look. 'You've been to bed with him, haven't you Deirdre?'

Deirdre's sudden high colour betrayed her. 'How did you guess?'

'I told you before – I have an instinct for these things. I may not be heterosexual, Deirdre, but that doesn't mean I can't see what goes on between men and women.'

'It only happened once.' Deirdre coiled a strand of her hair around her index finger. 'Afterwards he told me he didn't think it was a good idea to mix business with pleasure.'

'What a shit.' Maeve's tone was scornful.

'He's not a shit, Maeve – honestly he's not. I like

him a lot, and I know he likes me, but maybe he just doesn't fancy me that much. That's not his fault – he didn't force me to go to bed with him.' Deirdre looked over to where Sebastian was standing talking to his agent at the bar. 'He's just so beautiful.'

'That's not a good reason to go to bed with anyone, Deirdre.'

'I know.' Deirdre looked chastened. 'That's what Eva said, except she said it *before* I went to bed with him, and I still didn't bother to take her advice. I was going to tell you about it, Maeve, and ask what you thought, but somehow the whole thing just seemed like a lost cause, and the longer I left telling you the less it seemed to matter.' Deirdre gave a big sigh. 'As a matter of fact, Maeve, I think Sebastian's cracked over Eva Lavery.'

'That wouldn't surprise me,' said Maeve dryly. 'You could almost see it on stage tonight.'

Deirdre was curious. 'What do you mean?' she asked.

'In the bedchamber scene between Hamlet and Gertrude. It was practically incestuous.'

'Well, that's the effect David wanted to produce. He *wants* the audience to feel a bit uncomfortable with it.'

'It seemed to me that Eva was a bit uncomfortable with it, as well. I got the distinct impression that there was a lot of unplotted stuff going on.'

'Like what, Maeve?'

Maeve tugged gently at a nail with her teeth. 'It's hard to pinpoint. It was as if Sebastian somehow lost the run of himself during that particular scene. And it was all the more noticeable because he'd been so tightly reined in up till then. There was something dangerous about him. I dunno,' she shook her head. 'I just got an odd feeling about it, that's all.'

'That *is* odd,' Deirdre agreed. 'The night he stayed over at my place he was quoting from that scene in his sleep.'

Maeve looked meditatively at Sebastian where he was handing over money at the bar. 'He's an impressive talent.' She drained the last of her pint and turned back to Deirdre. 'Talking of talent, Rory was on form tonight, wasn't he? Those scenes between the two of you were beautifully tuned. And the duel with Sebastian was electric.'

'Mm,' said Deirdre noncommittally. 'Has he moved in with you yet?'

'He hasn't had time. He'll probably get round to it some time next week. Look, Deirdre – there's Sally Ruane waving at you.'

Deirdre looked up and saw Sally on the other side of the room. The agent beckoned to her.

'Sorry, Maeve – I'd better go and see what she wants.'

'That's OK. I'm going to head off now, anyway. I'm in studio first thing in the morning. Give me a ring some time soon, won't you?'

'Sure. D'you think you'll come in and see the show again?'

'Definitely. I might leave it till the last night, though. It'll be interesting to see how much has changed by then.' Maeve wrapped herself in her coat, and then wrapped her arms around Deirdre. 'Bye, you. Take care of yourself.'

'Bye, Maeve,' Deirdre hugged her back. 'And thanks for everything.' She watched for a minute as the actress moved towards the door, saying goodbye to her ex-colleagues as she did so, and stopping for the occasional embrace.

'I'm glad I caught you,' said Sally when Deirdre joined her. 'I tried to contact you this afternoon but you'd obviously already left for the theatre, so I just left a message on your machine. Oh – by the way – that was excellent stuff this evening, Deirdre. Well done. You have terrific stage presence for someone with so little experience.'

'Thanks, Sally.' Deirdre went pink. She wondered if tomorrow's reviews would reflect Sally's opinion. She'd love to get some real praise from the press for once. Eva's name had dominated all their reviews so far.

'I need to run something by you.' Sally's voice took on a businesslike timbre. 'Remember I told you that I'd get back on to Big TP Productions and ask for an impossibly high fee for you so that we could get them off your back?'

'Yes?' Deirdre nodded, feeling curious. 'How much did you ask them for in the end, Sally?'

'I made it as unrealistic a figure as I possibly could, Deirdre. I asked them for seven hundred and fifty pounds a day. That's *way* over the rate an actress of your experience can command. With a shooting schedule that would involve you for around eighteen days plus overtime and expenses you're talking in the region of more than fifteen thousand pounds.'

Deirdre laughed out loud. It was an insane amount of money to ask for someone who was just starting out in the business. No-one in their right mind would even consider it.

'I wouldn't laugh too hard, Deirdre. I've a suspicion you might decide to have second thoughts about this movie. Big TP apparently didn't bat an eyelid. He agreed the fee. The part's still yours if you want it.'

Deirdre didn't say anything simply because there was nothing *to* say. She'd have to book a crash course in riding lessons.

Chapter Nineteen

The next day Deirdre looked in Yellow Pages under H for horses. There were very few stables listed, and they were all very far away – most of them in Wicklow. It would take forever to get out to them – she might as well go back and live with her mum and dad in Kilmacanogue. But how on earth would she get all the way out there after the show every night? She could hardly expect her mum to drive into Bray and pick her up from the DART.

She tried under E for Equestrian, but there was absolutely nothing listed there. Then she had an idea. Rory McDonagh would be bound to know. She hated the thought of asking him for advice, but she really didn't have much choice. She got through to Maeve at the studio and asked her for Rory's phone number.

'What do you want Rory for?' asked Maeve. 'I thought you and he still weren't getting on?'

Deirdre told Maeve about the TP O'Reilly film.

'Shit, Deirdre – I don't believe you. That's incredible money! I can't say I blame you for changing your mind.'

'You reckon I'm doing the right thing, then?'

'For that sort of money? For sure. Anyway,

knowing TP O'Reilly the film won't even make it to video and there'll have been no harm done.'

'That's what Sally said. She said that with a bit of luck it'll never see the light of day and nobody will ever be any the wiser.'

'TP must want you really badly. You take care of yourself, OK?'

'What do you mean, Maeve?'

'He's a bit of a lech. I remember on that awful *Horse Power* thing he had a habit of feeling up some of the younger actresses – including me until he realized I was more streetwise than the others and didn't have a problem about telling him where to get off. Make sure he keeps his hands to himself, and don't get yourself into a situation where you're alone with him.'

'Oh, God, Maeve. I'm really dreading this.'

'Just take the money and run, Deirdre. The most important thing for you right now is to get on with those riding lessons. Here's Rory's number.'

Deirdre wrote it in her book, and then put the phone down to Maeve and picked it straight up again. There was no point in delay, and no time for it either. She punched in the number.

To her relief, he picked up. She really didn't want to have to talk to Marian.

'O heavy day – not Deirdre O'Dare. What a surprise to hear your voice, Deirdre. You're not thinking of calling round here again, are you, wanting to make the beast with two backs? I'm too knackered and hungover to be of any service to you today, I'm afraid.'

Deirdre wanted to tell him to shut up, but she was too badly in need of a favour to run the risk of antagonizing him. She filled him in on why she was ringing.

Rory whistled when she mentioned the sum of money involved. 'Wow. Old TP must have taken a real shine to you. I'd watch out if I were you.'

'I know. That's what Maeve said. Does nobody realize I'm a grown-up? I *can* take care of myself, Rory, you know, and I'll cope with that problem when I come to it.'

'Sweetheart – the savviest person of my acquaintance you are not.' She made a face at him down the phone. 'Why didn't you just look up the Yellow Pages for a riding school, by the way?' he asked. 'It must stick in your craw to come to *me* for advice.'

'I did. There weren't any listed.'

'No riding schools listed?' Rory sounded incredulous. 'What did you look under?'

'H for horses, of course. And I even tried E for equestrian.'

Rory's laugh was so robust that Deirdre had to hold the phone away from her ear. 'Jesus Christ, Deirdre – did you never think of looking under R for riding?'

'Oh shut up laughing, Rory. I'm up to ninety already about this riding lark – I could do without you taking the piss.'

'You really land yourself in it, don't you, O'Dare?'

'You've got to help me, Rory,' she insisted, adding 'Please' for diplomacy's sake.

He sighed down the phone. 'OK. Let me make a phone call to a friend. He has a riding school in Wicklow and he owes me a favour.'

Deirdre bit her lip. 'Wicklow's awfully far out, Rory. I'm not sure I could manage all the travelling.'

'I'll drive you. I'll be the one who's teaching you.'

'But when you said a friend–'

'He doesn't owe me *that* big a favour, Deirdre. He'll let me use his horses, but I don't expect him to teach somebody as dizzy as you how to ride as well.'

'But that means *I'll* owe *you* a favour, Rory!' she wailed, before she could stop herself. This was too much to bear.

He laughed. 'Can't hack that, can you, Deirdre?'

'Well, no – I mean, it's just–'

'It's OK, sweetheart. I rather fancy the prospect of riding out in Wicklow in the autumn. It'll be a good way to pass the time before I start rehearsals again.'

'Oh?' Deirdre hadn't known that Rory was doing anything after *Hamlet*. She'd assumed he was going to Peru – he'd mentioned it on a couple of occasions. 'What you are doing?'

'I've been offered *Les Liaisons Dangereuses* at the Abbey.'

'Which part?' She knew she hardly needed to ask.

'Valmont.'

Deirdre remembered the two film versions she'd seen – one with John Malkovich, the other with

Colin Firth. It was the sexiest role in the world.

'You should get your agent to put you up for Cécile, Deirdre. You'd be perfect for it. I'd almost say typecast.'

Cécile was the innocent who was seduced by Valmont in the play. It would mean she'd have to kiss Rory on stage again.

'I'm not available,' she said quickly. 'It would clash with the film.'

'What's the name of this epic anyway?' asked Rory.

'Oh – well, it's only got a working title at the moment.'

'And what might that be? *The Crock of Horse Manure*?'

'Don't be facile, Rory.'

'You're stalling, sweetheart.'

She braced herself. '*The Revenge of Irish Bob*,' said Deirdre.

'Oh shit,' said Rory.

* * *

The first day they drove out to Wicklow, Deirdre felt rather shy sitting in the passenger seat of Rory's ancient Saab. She knew that, despite his protestations to the contrary, he was actually doing her a very big favour. She couldn't think of anything much to say to him, so she just kept quiet for most of the drive and listened to him as he filled her in on the type of stuff that would be expected of her when it came to filming.

'Once you've got a bit of experience in the saddle the most important thing for you to learn will be how to stop the horse. The job is about hitting marks, which, as you know, can be difficult enough on foot. On horseback it's a hell of a lot tougher.'

Deirdre had learned about hitting marks at college. She'd been told how important it was for an actor to walk into shot and stop at a point and at an angle previously agreed with the director and the cameraman. If you stopped wide or short of the mark the focus would be wrong, or you'd be half out of shot, or your physical relationship to the other actor or actors involved in the scene would be compromised. She couldn't imagine how she'd be able to keep all that stuff in her head when she was sitting on a horse! And what if there was dialogue on horseback as well? If the dialogue she'd had to read with Big TP that day was anything to go by, she was going to have serious problems. Bad dialogue was always more difficult to learn than well-written stuff.

'You're going to have to work on your physical strength, Deirdre,' said Rory as he moved up a gear. 'The riding itself will help you to build up muscle – and I may as well warn you that they'll be muscles you've never used before. Well, some of them, anyway.' He turned and glanced at her, and she could imagine the expression in his eyes behind the dark glasses. She looked away to study the view out of the passenger window. 'You'll need to put Radox on your shopping list, pet lamb. You'll be taking lots of hot baths to relieve those aching, symmetrical limbs of yours.'

They were hitting the motorway. He put his foot down. 'Timing is crucial as well. You'll need to be able to stop a horse like *that*–' he clicked his fingers. 'If you've got a good beast you can sometimes leave it to him. An intelligent horse will pick up on the smallest signal. And presumably if TP O'Reilly is forking out that kind of money for *you*, he'll be prepared to spend money on his horses as well.' Rory stretched his left arm back and dragged his leather coat from the rear seat into the front of the car. 'Take a look in the pockets, will you? You'll find a couple of apples. Don't throw away the cores.'

'Oh – take a right here, Rory, that's the road up to Mum and Dad's.'

Deirdre had told Rosaleen that she'd be dropping by to pick up a pair of wellington boots. Rory had told her that she'd need long boots to avoid chaffing her calves against the horse's flank and ones with a small heel so that her feet wouldn't get stuck in the stirrups. The only boots she could think of that came anywhere near that description were her old wellies, and he'd said they'd be fine. He'd also insisted that she wear jodhpurs. 'If you don't,' he'd said, 'you'll get "pinch".'

'What's "pinch"?' Deirdre had asked.

Rory had paused. Then he had raised an eyebrow and run the tip of his tongue slowly along his upper lip. 'Well, you know that appetizingly tender skin on the very inside of your thighs?'

Deirdre had started flicking at specks of dust on

her sleeve. 'Yes?' she'd replied in a careless voice.

'If you don't wear jodhpurs that skin gets rubbed raw, darling. It hurts like hell and you'll have big purple marks all down the inside of your thighs the next day. The only alternative is to wear the thickest leggings you own with at least two pairs of tights underneath. And I don't think I'd like that. The prospect of those racehorse legs and pert buttocks encased in three layers of synthetic fibre is pretty upsetting, to be perfectly frank.'

Deirdre had cleared her throat. 'OK. Are they terribly expensive?'

'You could pick up a cheap pair in a sports shop. Look on it as an insurance policy for your most intimate places, sweetheart. We're going to be doing a lot of riding.' Deirdre still hadn't been able to meet his eyes. 'I suppose you could ask Sophie Burke to lend you a pair. I've heard she's hot shit in the saddle.'

'I'd rather buy a pair,' Deirdre had said with finality.

They were rounding a bend in the road. 'Just here, Rory.' Deirdre indicated the house where she'd grown up.

'Pretty house,' he said, pulling up.

'Do you want to come in?' she asked.

Rory looked at his watch. 'Better not,' he said. 'I told Tommy we'd be there by eleven, and we're running late. Anyway,' he added as she slid out of the passenger seat, 'I'm sure you wouldn't want your parents to get a load of the reprobate you're hanging out with.'

Deirdre ran down the garden path feeling quite glad that Rory had turned down the invitation to come in. She'd have felt a bit silly introducing him to her family. They might have taken it up wrongly.

'Hi, Mum,' she called as she spotted Rosaleen doing something to a shrub by the front door.

'Hello, my love,' said Rosaleen, straightening up and pushing her hair back. 'Your boots are in the hall.' She looked over to the road where Rory was turning the car. 'Won't you stay for a cup of tea? I'd love to meet your friend.'

'I'm really sorry, Mum – we don't have time. Rory set up the session for me at eleven and it's five to already.' She gave her mum a peck on the cheek and picked up her boots from where they stood just inside the doorway. 'Thanks a lot for looking out the wellies.'

'Yeah – that took some doing. Your cupboards are a nightmare. By the way, I found this when I was rooting around for them. I thought you might find it amusing.' Rosaleen took one of the wellies from Deirdre and pulled out a couple of rolled-up pages covered with rather ostentatious, scrawly handwriting. Deirdre recognized the writing as her own, except she hadn't used that style for years. She took the pages from Rosaleen and cringed. The i's were all dotted with little round circles instead of dots. She remembered that she'd thought it was so cool to do that!

'What is it?' she asked curiously.

'It's an essay you did at school on *Hamlet*.'

'Oh God – I bet it's embarrassing.'

'It is a bit. But I think it's rather sweet.'

Rory rolled down the driver's window as they strolled up the path towards his car. 'Ms O'Dare senior? I beg your pardon,' he said, taking off his sunglasses after a moment's scrutiny. 'Perhaps I should make that not-so-very senior.' He flashed Rosaleen his highwayman's smile and Deirdre raised her eyes to heaven. He was the most compulsive flirt she had ever met.

Rosaleen smiled back at him. 'What a beautiful man,' she said in a low voice to Deirdre. 'You watch out for yourself, my love.'

'Don't worry, Mum. Rory wouldn't lay a finger on me.'

Rosaleen looked at her astutely. 'You'd like him to though, wouldn't you?'

'Don't be daft, Mum. We're just friends.' She supposed they *were* friends again, now that Rory was being more co-operative these days. She gave her mother another kiss and moved towards the gate.

Rory had his arm draped over the rolled down window and was still smiling at her mother, studying her. 'Your daughter looks just like you.'

Rosaleen raised an eyebrow and tilted her head to one side. 'I'll take that as a compliment,' she said. Dear Jesus, thought Deirdre. He even made her *mother* go all coquettish.

'That's how it was intended. She doesn't look much younger than you either. I mean that.' Rosaleen shook her head and laughed at him as he released the hand brake. 'Nice to meet you, Ms

O'Dare.' He sent her another smile and saluted her with a relaxed hand before putting the car into gear. The Saab slid away from the gate, and Rory maintained eye contact with Rosaleen until his view of the doorway was obstructed by the hedge.

Deirdre sighed and sat back in the passenger seat feeling indignant. How dare Rory McDonagh give her mother the once-over? It was lucky her gran hadn't been there as well. Then he'd have had three generations of women to be politically incorrect to.

Her indignation subsided as they swooped down through the Glen of the Downs. The autumn valley was breathtakingly beautiful. The forests on the hillsides which bordered the road were a mass of golds, yellows and russets. As the car sped along, Deirdre stared out at the view until it became a blur. It was like looking at a Turkish carpet through out-of-focus specs. In spite of her apprehension, she felt very happy. It was nice to be driving fast through some of the most beautiful countryside in Ireland on a sunny autumn day.

'What's that you've got?' Rory indicated the pages she was still holding with a nod of his head.

'Oh – it's an essay I did on *Hamlet* when I was at school. Mum found it when she was looking out my wellies.'

'Give us a go.'

'Oh, no, Rory. I'm sure it's awful.'

'I'm sure it is too. That's why I want to hear it. Go on, Deirdre – do something useful for once and entertain the driver.'

She smoothed out the paper on her lap. 'Oh God,' she said, and laughed.

'What?'

'"We are first introduced to Hamlet when he appears in the first court scene. He is in mourning for his dead father and he looks like a black blob,"' she read aloud.

'Well, it's pretty accurate so far,' remarked Rory. 'A bit – jejune, maybe.'

Deirdre smiled at him. He had his right hand on the steering wheel, his elbow resting on the rolled-down window of the Saab, and his left hand was lying completely relaxed between his thighs. He gave her a sideways look through his black glasses. 'Sexy, aren't I?' he said.

'Oh, stop it, Rory,' she said. Actually, she supposed, he *did* look sexy. She'd seen men driving around in cars with sunglasses on and their elbows hanging out of their rolled-down windows all summer, but they'd been posing. Rory couldn't pose if he tried.

'Go on with the thesis, Deirdre.'

She scanned the pages. 'Oh – here's a good bit. "Hamlet's mother, Gertrude, has married Hamlet's uncle, the dead king's younger brother, and Hamlet is furiously angry and raging with his mum."'

'Told you you were tautological. Where are the oxymorons? Hamlet is clearly jaundiced.'

She ignored him. 'Oh – I must just have discovered the word "vacillating". I've used it about ten times,' said Deirdre, turning the page. '"Hamlet is determined to get vengeance for his dead father even though he vacillates all over the place. He torments his mum in her bedroom and then–" Agh! Oh no, that's too embarrassing!'

'What? Tell me!' demanded Rory.

'Definitely not. It's too jejune, even for me.'

'Something to do with imagery, is it? "Shakespeare uses the image of the skull to illustrate . . ." blah, blah, blah.'

'Nah – it's worse than that. I hadn't got round to imagery then. This was pre-inter, you know. We were asked to read a book or a play during the summer holidays and write a synopsis of it. I remember wanting to read *Hamlet* because I'd seen a reproduction of that gorgeous Millais painting of Ophelia. You know the one I mean?'

'The one of her floating downstream with her hair trailing all over the place?'

'Yeah – that's the one.'

'I can't see you as a swot, somehow, Deirdre O'Dare.'

'I wasn't. All my school reports said I could do better. The teachers were always giving out to me about being lazy.'

'I got a lot of that as well.' He glanced down at the pages in her lap. 'Any more good bits?'

Deirdre had nearly finished reading the essay. Her lips moved silently as she ran her finger over the last few lines. '"Hamlet's girlfriend Ophelia goes mad. Then she disappears off to pick flowers and ends up dead as a dodo in the river,"' she read. She burst out laughing.

'Give me that essay at once!' Rory grabbed it

from her with his left hand, and Deirdre shrieked.

'No! Never! Give it back, Rory! You're a bastard!' She tore the sheets of paper from him, quickly rolled down the passenger window and flung them to the wind.

'You could be fined for that, Deirdre,' said Rory with equanimity. 'Littering the picturesque Irish countryside with your juvenilia. Here we are.' He hung a left, and then left again at a sign which read 'Glenview Equestrian Centre'.

'See?' said Deirdre, in a slightly piqued tone. 'They *are* called Equestrian Centres.' She picked a bit of apple-skin from her tooth with a nail.

Rory smiled and shook his head. 'You never opt for the simple route, do you, Deirdre? Not if there's a reasonable chance of complicating the plot.'

They went through a gateway into a tree-lined driveway which curved up to a low, timber-clad building. There were fields with horses grazing in them on either side of the driveway. Rory drove round to the back of the building and stopped the car at a brick archway. Through the archway was a courtyard lined with stables. Deirdre could see long, equine faces poking out above the half-doors, and her nervousness returned.

'Come and meet Tommy,' said Rory, getting out of the car. 'He owns the joint.'

Deirdre followed Rory through the archway into the yard and over to what she guessed was the tack room. There was a pungent smell of horses in the air. A couple of girl grooms stared at them curiously, looking away quickly and giggling when

Rory smiled at them. He reached the tack room door and looked in. 'Tommy. How's it going?' he asked.

A middle-aged man of stocky build with a tanned, weather-beaten face was sitting on a bench reading *The Irish Field* with a cigarette dangling from his lip. He rose to his feet and clapped Rory on the back. 'Rory! Nice to see you. It's been a while.'

Rory turned to Deirdre. 'Deirdre, this is Tommy Connors. He knows more about horses than anyone in the business. Tommy – Deirdre O'Dare – an actress who needs to learn to ride in a hurry.'

Tommy shook Deirdre's hand. His hand was surprisingly small, but he had a powerful grip. Deirdre noticed that his skin felt tough and rather horny. 'For a film, is it?' asked Tommy, squinting at her through piercing blue eyes.

'That's right.' Deirdre returned his smile.

'Big TP O'Reilly's back in town, Tommy,' said Rory. 'Remember him?'

Tommy looked at Rory with a slightly incredulous expression on his face. 'Not that Horse's Arse outfit?' he asked.

'The very same,' replied Rory.

'No shit,' said Tommy. 'You're not working on it, are you, Rory?'

'Unfortunately I'm otherwise engaged, Tommy,' said Rory with a smile. 'I'll be doing dandy acting in the Abbey.'

'Wise boy,' commented Tommy, folding up his newspaper and putting it in his pocket. 'Come here with me, Deirdre O'Dare. I'll saddle up Minerva for you, and then Rory can put you through your paces.' Tommy stubbed out his cigarette and swung a saddle and bridle from racks on the wall. He walked across the yard towards one of the boxes with Deirdre trotting obediently behind him. She noticed that he was slightly pigeon-toed and that his gait was rather slouched, and wondered that such a physically shambolic-looking man could be a master horseman, as Rory had claimed he was. A magpie was performing its clumsy sideways dance in the middle of the yard, and Deirdre muttered her usual spell to ward off evil and blew it a kiss.

Rory strolled over to the other side of the yard where a big brown horse was stalled. It shook its dark mane and whinnied when it saw him. Rory rubbed its nose and spoke to it in low, affectionate tones, and then produced his apple core from his pocket. He looked utterly contented.

'This is Minerva, Deirdre,' said Tommy.

Minerva was quite a pretty horse. She was a chestnut mare with a white star on her forehead. She had large, clear, kind-looking eyes and her ears were pricked forward, giving her an intelligent expression. Tommy opened the stable door and started to tack up. Deirdre noticed that Minerva had one white sock, which she thought was rather sweet.

'Go on.' Rory's voice came from behind her. 'Give her her present. You're going to want her to like you.' Deirdre took the apple core out of her pocket. 'Talk to her, Deirdre – get her used to the sound of your voice. And stroke her.'

She waved the apple core under Minerva's nose. 'Here, Minerva,' she said. It felt a bit stupid talking to a horse.

'Not that way. Set it on the palm of your hand otherwise she won't be able to take it without running the risk of biting you. Tell her you're glad to meet her.'

Deirdre did as Rory had instructed, and Minerva took the apple core obligingly. 'Hello, Minerva – it's nice to meet you,' said Deirdre, stroking the horse's nose. It felt pleasantly velvety under her hand. 'What a pretty girl you are! You're going to teach me to ride, you know.'

'She's the best teacher there is,' said Tommy Connors. 'She's just the right size for you and she has a lovely, easy-going temperament. She's the perfect horse for a novice.' He was doing something to a strap which ran under Minerva's belly.

'Tommy's tightening the girth,' Rory explained. 'Some animals hold their breath while this is being done, so that their sides expand. They don't like being constrained by the strap, you see. Then once it's been tightened they let out their breath and when you get up on them the saddle slips and you fall arse over tit.'

Deirdre looked alarmed.

'Don't worry – you won't have that problem with Minerva.' Rory smiled down at her. 'She knows her job is to help you. She's been trained for it.'

Tommy Connors gave Minerva a pat on her side. 'OK, Deirdre – she's all yours. Rory – you can take over now.'

Rory had brought a small selection of hard hats from the tack room. He handed one to Deirdre and instructed her to pull the strap fast under her chin. 'Let's have a look,' he said, lifting his hand and checking the strap to see how tight it was. She flinched involuntarily at the touch of his fingers against the vulnerable skin of her throat. He checked the crown of the hat for size against her skull. 'Too big. We'll have to try something smaller. I didn't think your brain was *that* minuscule, O'Dare.'

He repeated the procedure with the second hat, which fitted snugly. Then he stood back, ran his eyes down her legs and sucked in his breath. 'Look at those legs,' he said, half to himself. 'Uh huh – the boots are fine. OK, Deirdre. Let's get ready to rock and roll. I want you to walk Minerva out to the manege. Take hold of this – this is the bridle. Always lead from the left unless you're on the road, when you lead from the right. Put your right hand up under her chin groove near the headcollar, and hold the end of the bridle with your left hand. Now, stand by her shoulder and tell her to walk on.'

Deirdre followed Rory's instructions to the letter. To her surprise, Minerva moved forward with her. 'It's working!' she exclaimed, giving Rory a delighted smile.

'Jesus, Deirdre,' said Rory. 'You haven't even got up on her yet.'

They passed through the brick archway and out to what Rory had called the manege. This was a fenced-in outdoor area with a dark sand surface.

'Shall I get up on her now?' asked Deirdre, tentatively.

'Sure. Let's give it a go,' said Rory. 'I'll hold her for you. Put your left foot in the stirrup. Make sure it feels comfortable. Now, try and swing your right leg up and over her back.'

Deirdre gave up on the third attempt.

'I could give you a leg up, but I'm not going to. You've got to learn how to do it for yourself.' Deirdre felt quite relieved. She didn't like the idea of Rory shoving her up on to Minerva by her buttocks. 'You can help yourself by taking hold of her mane. It won't faze her at all – she's well used to it. Aren't you, beautiful?' Rory stroked the horse's nose with his free hand.

At the fourth try Deirdre managed to throw her leg over Minerva's back and landed with an undignified thump! in the saddle. Minerva didn't budge.

'You should see the expression on her face, Deirdre,' said Rory, laughing up at her. '"Patience on a monument."'

Once mounted, he showed her how to hold the reins, and how to use her heels against the horse's flank. 'Now try walking around on her to get the feel of her. Keep your hands relaxed – don't drag at the rein.'

Deirdre kicked Minerva lightly in the sides with her heels as Rory had instructed and the horse started to move. The sensation of the beast beneath her was very pleasant – relaxing, even – and for some reason she felt ever so slightly superior. She supposed it had something to do with being so high off the ground. 'Oh, Rory – this is going to be fun!' she said, looking down at him.

'For you, perhaps, witch,' he replied. But there was a smile in his eyes as he watched her.

* * *

Deirdre made progress quite fast. Every other day Rory would take her out through the Glen of the Downs to his friend Tommy's stables. She'd felt like a sack of potatoes on a pogo-stick when she had attempted to trot on the first day, but she had finally mastered the rising trot, sitting into the horse and being aware of Minerva's rhythm. She was soon able to manage a canter, which she found so exhilarating it left her breathless.

Rory had talked to her about how important it was to feel relaxed, confident and in control – though she found it almost impossible to remain in control when she happened to lose her stirrups while cantering one day. Rory reminded her that even great horsemen have difficulty keeping control if a horse decides it's having an off day and chooses to be stubborn. But Minerva never had off days. Deirdre felt very proud and privileged when she realized that the animal had actually started watching out for her, and displaying signs of pleasure when she approached her stall. She felt that she and Minerva shared a kind of sixth sense, and she loved it when the horse sometimes seemed to read her mind.

Rory rode with her now, on the beautiful bay gelding she had seen him talking to on the day of her first lesson. When they raced through the fields together she often found herself laughing out loud with delight. She felt that it was as close as a human being could ever come to flying.

He'd been right about her muscles. Her thighs and inside legs had ached like mad after the first few lessons, and she was exhausted after the show on the days when she'd gone out riding. Her appetite had sharpened too with all the fresh air and exercise she was getting, and she found herself wolfing down vast quantities of food. She suddenly became organized enough to make sure that her fridge was perpetually stocked with individual pre-cooked dinners, and on the days when she didn't go riding she found herself snacking out of sheer boredom.

Now that she didn't have rehearsals to attend during the day she had very little to occupy her. She'd finally given up on the gansey she'd been knitting. She wrote loads of letters to Sarah, who was so in love with her scenic artist that she hadn't bothered to come back to Dublin once since she'd started working at Stratford. How lucky she was, thought Deirdre, to be so in love and have that love reciprocated. Deirdre now knew that she'd never known what being in love was like. Beautiful Ben, David Lawless, Sebastian Hardy – they'd all been misguided infatuations. She wondered if she'd ever meet the right man.

They were leading their horses back into the

stable-yard after their ride one day when she noticed that Rory was looking her up and down approvingly. 'I'm glad to see you've put on weight, Deirdre. Your ass looks great in those jodhpurs. You were starting to look like something by Giacometti there for a while.'

Deirdre knew she'd turned red. She still didn't know how to handle remarks like that from Rory. Spending so much time in each other's company meant that they were relaxed around each other again, but the sexual nature of his banter had always made her feel uncomfortable, and she took pains to avoid any physical contact with him.

She led Minerva into her box and set about unsaddling her. To her surprise she realized Rory had followed her in. Startled, she turned around, losing her balance momentarily, and ending up with her back against the wall of the stable. Silhouetted against the light which streamed in through the open door Rory appeared even taller than usual, and the confined space suddenly seemed very claustrophobic. Deirdre's heart was palpitating, and she found herself wondering for some quite absurd reason if Rory was going to kiss her.

'You dropped your bracelet, sweetie-pie,' he said. 'Don't wear it next time, OK? Here – catch.' He tossed the bracelet in her direction and turned, whistling, on his heel. Deirdre put out her hand too late and the golden chain slid through her fingers on to the straw-strewn floor.

* * *

As the run of *Hamlet* drew to an end Deirdre became increasingly despondent. Even though she knew she was incredibly lucky to have landed such a lucrative film contract, she was dreading the actual shoot. The script had arrived, and Deirdre realized glumly that the scene she'd read with TP O'Reilly was actually one of the better-written ones. He had enclosed a note inviting her to have dinner with him, and she was relieved to be able to write back pleading the show in the evening as an excuse. She hoped he wouldn't suggest lunch instead.

She knew she was really going to miss the rest of the cast when the run finished. There was little prospect of maintaining much social contact with the friends she'd made while working with Lawless Productions. She knew that friendships in the acting world were quickly forged and quickly forgotten once people went their separate ways. Maeve was busy with *Ardmore Grove* and anyway, she had Jacqueline and Rory for company. He and his beloved mutt, Bastard, had moved in with them shortly after *Hamlet* had opened. Deirdre had volunteered to help him with the move so as to cut down on the expense of removal men. She thought it would be one way of returning the favour he'd done her by offering to teach her to ride, but Rory had laughed and said it would take him just one trip in his car. She'd bought him a big glossy book on South America as a present instead.

He had started rehearsals on *Les Liaisons* which meant that he had no time for riding lessons any more. She'd done OK, he said. She'd had twelve or thirteen sessions with him, and was now a reasonably proficient rider – although her attempts at jumping even the lowest bars Rory erected for her weren't terribly successful. She'd taken a couple of tumbles – nothing serious – but there just wasn't enough time to learn to jump along with everything else she needed to know.

David had already gone back to London to work on his next RSC project, although he travelled back to see Eva as often as he could. She would be joining him soon – immediately after she had finished work on the Neil Jordan film. Jessica Young was going to Galway to work with Druid, and Sebastian would be going back to London too. It felt like the end of an era.

Deirdre wondered if the actors on *The Revenge of Irish Bob* would be any fun. She hoped she'd know at least *one* other cast member. She remembered how ill-at-ease she'd been on the morning of the very first rehearsal of *A Midsummer Night's Dream* all those months ago, and realized to her dismay that she'd have to go through all that insecurity again soon. Her first day on the film was scheduled for early in the afternoon on the Sunday after *Hamlet* closed – she wouldn't have even a day's breathing space.

At least she wasn't having to work on two projects simultaneously, the way Eva was. The actress's punishing schedule had taken its toll, and she looked wrecked. There were great dark circles under her eyes, she had lost a lot of weight – which didn't suit her – and she was uncharacteristically spiky on occasion. Sometimes her grey eyes looked almost black with exhaustion. There was a haunted look about her too, as if she were being besieged by demons, and it was obvious that her work was being affected. Her concentration was poor, and on a couple of occasions she had had to wander down stage left to get help from the prompt corner.

Deirdre felt intensely sorry for her. Her golden aura seemed to be fading. She wondered if she could do anything which might bring a little colour to the actress's life. She hadn't been near her dressing-room for some time now, thinking that Eva probably needed space to herself.

She remembered how kind Eva had been to her from the very first time she'd come into contact with her, and she felt horribly guilty. *She* had spent the last few weeks having a ball careering round Wicklow on horseback and laughing at Rory McDonagh's stupid jokes, and all these weeks Eva had been slogging away, having no fun in her life at all. She never came to the pub any more, and Deirdre knew that she hardly ever saw David now that he was spending so much time away. She must be lonely, as well as everything else.

On the evening of the last performance of *Hamlet* Deirdre marched into a posh florists on her way into work and bought up every single sunflower in the shop. It didn't matter that she handed a small fortune to the rather surprised-looking woman behind the counter. After all, Deirdre O'Dare was a woman of substance now, thanks to Big TP O'Reilly.

She got to the theatre earlier than usual and went straight to Eva's dressing-room. 'Yes?' came the barely audible response when she knocked.

'It's Deirdre, Eva.'

'Come on in, darling.' Eva sounded very subdued.

When Deirdre entered the room the actress was lying on her couch with her eyes closed. She opened them with what seemed like an effort. 'Hi, Deirdre. Thank goodness it's only you. Heavens – you look like Byrnam Wood.' Eva managed a rather lacklustre smile.

'These are for you, Eva. To say thank you for' – Deirdre hesitated. Thank you for *what* exactly? 'For being my friend.'

To her horrified astonishment, Eva burst into tears. Deirdre wasn't quite sure what to do for a moment. Then she remembered how Maeve had behaved to her on the night she'd had that crying jag over Rory. She put the flowers down on the actress's dressing-table, went over to the couch and took Eva in her arms. 'There, there, Eva,' she murmured. 'Don't cry – everything's going to be all right.' She made little rocking movements and stroked the actress's blond head. She held her for what seemed like ages. Eva's tears were copious – 'Like Niobe, all tears'. One of Hamlet's lines drifted through Deirdre's mind as she continued to comfort her friend.

Gradually Eva's sobs subsided. Deirdre fetched tissues from the dressing-table and gently wiped her wet face. 'Tsk, tsk,' she said. 'Look at you, you naughty thing. You've made your beautiful eyes all red from crying.' Eva sniffed, and then accepted a tissue from Deirdre so that she could blow her nose. 'Oh Eva.' Deirdre sat back and looked at her with sympathy all over her face. 'You mustn't worry. You're over the worst of it now. After tonight you've only the film to worry about, and that's nearly finished too, isn't it?'

'Yes,' said Eva in a tiny voice. Then she started to cry again. 'Oh Deirdre – it's not the hard work that's killing me – I've never been afraid of hard work in my life.' She buried her face in her hands.

'*What* is it then, Eva?' Deirdre felt a bit frightened.

Eva slid her hands down her face so that only her mouth remained covered. Her eyes looked very scared. 'I think I'm going mad,' she whispered between her fingers.

Deirdre looked at her. For a while she didn't know what to say. Then she realized that if she was going to be of any help whatsoever she must encourage the actress to talk. 'Why, Eva?' she asked. 'What makes you think that?'

'Deirdre – you promise you won't tell anyone?'

Deirdre promised. 'And I keep my promises, Eva,' she added. 'I never told *anyone* about that anonymous note you got on the opening night of *Macbeth*.'

'That's when it started! That's the first thing that happened to frighten me. And it's been going on since *Hamlet* went into rehearsal – although it wasn't too bad in the early stages, and I just told myself I was imagining things.'

'What things, Eva?'

'It sounds really stupid, Deirdre, but I think Sebastian Hardy hates me. I think he was the one who sent that note.'

'Oh, Eva, no! I've always known that Sebastian's just *mad* about you. It even used to make me feel jealous!' Deirdre took Eva's hands in hers. 'I'll let you into a secret. When I first met him in London all that time ago, he actually had a picture of you in his wallet! He's a real fan, Eva!'

Eva's reaction shocked her. She tore her hands from Deirdre's and started to beat at her own head with her fists. '*No, no, no,*' she repeated over and over again, shaking her head as if trying to rid herself of horrible thoughts. Deirdre grabbed Eva's hands which fluttered around her halo of tangled golden hair.

'Stop it, Eva. You must stop it at once.' Deirdre knew that she must remain calm. She had never felt so much like a grown-up in all her life. She held Eva's hands prisoner between her own until the actress seemed to have steadied a little, then she went over to the dressing-table and poured some still Ballygowan into a glass. She returned to where Eva was sitting looking very white. Deirdre held the glass to her lips and persuaded her to sip a little. She couldn't manage it. The water dribbled down over her chin, and Deirdre found herself mopping Eva's face again. 'Where's David?' she asked. 'Can I contact him?'

Eva shook her head. 'He won't be here till after the interval – he rang me from Heathrow.'

'What's his mobile number, Eva?'

'Please don't try and contact him, Deirdre. You promised you wouldn't tell *anyone*, remember? Anyway, look – I'm calm now. Really I am.' She took a packet of Gitanes from the pocket of her robe, lit one, and inhaled the smoke deep into her lungs. She had calmed considerably, but she still looked utterly ravaged.

'Tell me about it, Eva,' said Deirdre, sitting down beside her again.

Eva let her head fall against the back of the couch. 'Sebastian's freaking me out, Deirdre, and he's doing it deliberately.' She took a deep breath and pushed her hair away from her face. 'I had a strange vibe from him quite early on in rehearsal, but it's been getting worse and I've been getting more and more paranoid. Since the show opened it's become unbearable.' She took hold of one of Deirdre's hands as if seeking reassurance. 'Do you remember we had a notes session the day after the opening night when David asked Sebastian to tone down his emotional level in the bedchamber scene?'

Deirdre cast her mind back. 'Yes,' she said. 'I remember. And Sebastian said he'd lost the run of himself because of first night nerves, and promised it wouldn't happen again?' Deirdre recollected how Maeve had remarked on Sebastian's lack of control in the pub after she'd seen the show on opening night.

Eva rubbed her left eye with a nicotine-stained

finger. Her eyes were raw from weeping. 'Well, he did hold back for another week or so, and then he started in again with a vengeance. Oh, Deirdre – I've started to dread hearing the line: "Mother, mother, mother," as he comes on stage every night. He plays the entire bedchamber scene as if he's possessed.'

Deirdre felt a little shiver run down her spine when Eva spoke the words: 'Mother, mother, mother'. She remembered again how anguished Sebastian had sounded when he'd talked in his sleep that night they'd gone to bed together. 'Why doesn't David tell him to stop it?' she asked, feeling horribly inadequate.

'He doesn't play the scene that way when he knows David's in the theatre.'

'But haven't you *said* anything to David about it?' Deirdre was puzzled.

'No.'

'Why not, Eva?' She was indignant now. 'How can you let Sebastian get away with that sort of behaviour? You should have made sure that David nipped it in the bud ages ago! Even though it's too late, you must tell him about it tonight!'

'I can't.'

It was only the second time Deirdre had ever heard Eva Lavery say those words. The two women looked at each other for a minute, and then Eva bowed her head. Deirdre knew that she mustn't ask Eva why she couldn't talk to David.

'Have you said anything to Sebastian?' she asked, in a gentler tone.

'No.' Eva raised her head and looked at her again. 'I'm too frightened of him. He's got something over me, Deirdre. I know he has.'

'Are you talking about some kind of blackmail, Eva?'

Eva gave a tired shrug. 'Emotional blackmail, yeah. He knows something about me he shouldn't.'

Deirdre was utterly shocked. She'd never dreamed that anything like this had been going on during the show. She had always noticed the intensity behind Sebastian's eyes when she had to confront him on stage, and he'd always been a bit unpredictable when it came to the very emotional scenes, but she was used to that by now. Eva's experience with him sounded grotesque. She tried to think back to what she'd been hearing over the tannoy for the last few weeks. Jonathan Hughes had remarked that the bedchamber scene had been sounding rather erratic, but Deirdre hadn't really bothered to listen to it. She was too busy avoiding Sophie or gossiping with Jessica or bantering with Rory in the green room to bother much about what was going on on stage.

'What exactly does he do to you, Eva?' she asked in a very quiet voice.

'He menaces me, Deirdre. Not just as Hamlet menacing Gertrude, but as Sebastian Hardy menacing Eva Lavery – I'm sure of it. He steps right out of character and becomes Sebastian Hardy on stage – and he's not the polite, charming Sebastian we know. He's a devil.' Eva drew her legs up onto the couch and wrapped her robe tighter round her.

She put out her cigarette in the overflowing ashtray and lit another one. 'It usually starts when he says that line –

You shall not budge; you go not till I set you up a glass/Where you may see the inmost part of you.'

'What's your reply to that?' For some reason Deirdre knew it was significant.

'I say:

What wilt thou do? Thou wilt not murder me?'

Deirdre tried not to let her alarm show.

'Then he gets more and more excited as the scene goes on. When he takes my head between his hands to show me the pictures of his father and his uncle I sometimes feel he's going to crack my skull open with his bare hands.'

'Eva, this is awful –'

'And when he comes to that line about "the rank sweat of an enseamed bed" – you know the one?'

Deirdre finished the quote for her:

'Stewed in corruption, honeying and making love over the nasty sty.'

'Yes, yes! It's vile, Deirdre. He says it right in my ear and looks at me as if he's not referring to Claudius, but to – to – Oh, God, Deirdre – I just know it, somehow! He means David.'

'David?' Deirdre was appalled.

Eva nodded and covered her face with her hands again. 'Please believe me,' she whispered. 'I know I sound as if I'm talking like a mad person, but it's true.'

Deirdre thought of Gertrude's response to Hamlet's taunts: 'These words, like daggers, enter in mine ears.' What agony it must be for Eva to deliver those lines! She made a decision. She would take control – or at least make it *look* as if she was in control. 'Eva, listen to me. This is the last night. You will never, ever have to do this again.' She took the actress's face between her hands and looked directly into her eyes. 'You are the bravest person I know. You can do this one last time, I know you can. And after the show you will never need to see Sebastian Hardy again.'

Eva looked at Deirdre searchingly. 'You don't think I'm being hysterical, do you?' she implored. 'Or that I'm just imagining things? You do believe me, don't you?'

'Of course I believe you, Eva.' She looked at her watch and then she stood up and helped Eva to her feet. 'It's time to get ready, sweetheart. I'll help you.' She knew it would make her late for the half-hour call if she helped the actress dress, but she didn't care. 'Don't worry – you're not going mad.'

'You're not just humouring me? You promise you believe me?' Eva's tone was still anxious.

'I promise I believe you, Eva.'

Deirdre meant every word she said. As she fetched Gertrude's costume from the rail she was remembering what Rory had said about Sebastian

Hardy, and she was filled with an awful dread. Sebastian hadn't been late for the opening night of *Macbeth*. His plane hadn't been delayed and he'd had no problems with taxis. He'd had plenty of time to check out his flat and leave his cases there before strolling into the theatre. In fact, he had even arrived early enough to deliver a note to the stage door before the show went up. A note which would never be traced back to him because he would claim that he hadn't arrived in the theatre until fifteen minutes after curtain-up. It had been the note Eva had got which had read: 'Bring forth men-children only'.

Deirdre O'Dare suddenly felt very cold.

Chapter Twenty

Half an hour later, on her way to her dressing-room, Rory raced ahead of her up the stairs. He was late, as usual. 'Fucking traffic,' he muttered, and then stopped and looked curiously at her. 'Are you all right, Deirdre? You look a bit spacey.'

'Do I?' she answered unheedingly. 'No, I'm fine.' More than anything else in the world at that moment she would have loved to have taken Rory into her confidence and tell him everything that had happened in Eva Lavery's dressing-room less than an hour previously. She almost wished she hadn't made her vow of silence to Eva. The grisly reality of her situation was that she had to handle this by herself.

As she continued on her way, Rory called after her before he disappeared through his dressing-room door: 'Oh, by the way – Maeve's in at the show again tonight. She said she'd see you in the pub afterwards.'

'OK,' said Deirdre without enthusiasm. The last thing on her mind was end-of-season partying. She had determined that she would be vigilant this evening. She would stay in her dressing-room instead of messing about in the green room during her time off stage, and listen to the progress of the show on the tannoy. She had also decided that she would watch the bedchamber scene from the wings during the second half, taking care not to be seen by either of the actors on stage. She would make sure that no harm would come to Eva Lavery tonight.

The first warning note came when she was slipping on her kid pumps towards the end of Act One. As she listened to the dialogue between Hamlet and the ghost of his dead father she was aware that Sebastian sounded unusually emotional. On the line 'O my prophetic soul! My uncle!' he peaked, howling the words like a wolf. Then he seemed to regain a measure of control and the playing of the scene settled back into its accustomed rhythm. It suddenly occurred to Deirdre that it was not Eva who was mad, but Sebastian.

The thought remained with her when he burst on to the stage before commencing their first scene together and launched like a demon into 'To be or not to be'. Deirdre was upstage of him, and, as she had her back turned to him, she could not see the expression on his face as he delivered the great speech. But there was an audible catch in his voice as he said:

To die – to sleep –
No more; and by a sleep to say we end
The heartache, and the thousand
natural shocks
That flesh is heir to; 'tis a
consummation
Devoutly to be wished.

He invested those five lines with a yearning that was chilling.

Deirdre got through the scene on automatic pilot. She could barely bring herself to look Sebastian in the face. He knew she was pulling back. At one stage he put his hand under her chin and tilted it up, forcing her to look at him, but she kept her eyes lowered. It was with relief that she watched him finally make his exit. Her delivery of the next speech was extremely shaky, and the words rang in her ears with awful irony as she pronounced them: 'O, what a noble mind is here o'erthrown!'

During the interval Deirdre took her coffee back to the dressing-room. Neither Sebastian nor Eva had been in the green room, and the atmosphere there was heavy with tension, as if an electric storm was brewing. Deirdre knew that she would be unable to sit there and listen to the whispering as the actors speculated on what was wrong with Sebastian. Their ears had become so finely tuned to the performance during the course of the five week run, that any unusual pause or inflection that came over the tannoy attracted attention. All of them had noticed that there was something dodgy in the air, and because there was still no sign of David, the company was feeling very insecure. Deirdre remembered that Eva had said that David wouldn't arrive until after the interval. She wondered if he would make it in time for the bedchamber scene.

Stacking together all her old good luck cards, she settled herself down on the chaise longue to leaf through them one last time. Her place looked rather forlorn now. She had taken down her cards and packed her stuff away before the show had gone up that evening, so that it would all be ready to take home with her. Then she noticed that there was an envelope propped up against her make-up case. She went back to her dressing-table and picked it up, stiffening when she recognized Sebastian's handwriting on the front. It was with a cautious hand that she opened it, uncertain as to whether she wanted to read the contents. Inside was folded a sheet of paper on which he had written: 'Not you as well! Please do not abandon me. Sebastian.'

What on earth did it mean? The 'Do not abandon me' must refer to the fact that he'd realized that there was a sea-change in her attitude towards him – her reluctance to meet his eyes on stage would have told him that. But what about 'Not you as well!' That implied that he'd been abandoned by someone else. It was as puzzling as the note Eva had received on the opening night of *Macbeth* – the note she was certain he had sent.

After the interval, as she stood in the wings before the start of the Mousetrap scene, she watched the exchange of dialogue between Sebastian and Jonathan Hughes, who was playing Horatio. He delivered the line 'And my imaginations are as foul as Vulcan's stithy' so vehemently that he spat right into Jonathan's face. The other actor reacted despite himself and then made an effort to control his startled expression. The actors in the wings waiting to go on exchanged looks of alarm, and beside her Deirdre became aware that Eva was shaking. As she walked out onto the stage, Deirdre suddenly thought of Rory's duel with Sebastian in the final scene of the play and felt scared. Sebastian was dangerous tonight.

In fact, he was unexpectedly gentle in his treatment of her onstage. Instead of manhandling her during the scene as David Lawless had directed him, he behaved in a tender and considerate fashion. She was reminded of the way he had made love to her on the Sunday night of her dinner party. It seemed to her that years had passed since then.

However, when he directed his lines towards Eva, the venom started to emerge. 'Look you,' he said, with blatant bitterness, 'how cheerfully my mother looks, and my father died within two hours.' He ran an abstracted hand along Deirdre's thigh and she felt herself recoil.

The tension on stage was palpable. Deirdre was sure the audience must feel it too, for she could hear the noise of people shifting in their seats in the auditorium, and there was a flurry of embarrassed-sounding coughs when Sebastian threw back his head and roared:

The croaking raven doth bellow for revenge!

The cue for all but Hamlet and Horatio to exit finally came, and the cast practically jostled one another in their haste to get off the stage. Deirdre realized she would not be the only member of the company watching the bedchamber scene from the sanctuary of the wings tonight. Nobody made a move towards the green room. They all stood rooted to the spot, watching Sebastian in horrified fascination as he ranged the stage like some angry beast.

On the opposite side of the stage, Eva stood quite alone, waiting to make her entrance. The light that spilled over into the wings made her look like a figure carved from alabaster. She didn't flinch when Sebastian moved downstage and shouted into the wings directly at her:

O wonderful son, that can so astonish a mother!

Out of the corner of her eye Deirdre saw Nick McCarthy make a move towards the control panel, as if to bring down the curtain. Then he hesitated. Sebastian seemed quite suddenly to have regained control of himself. Nick let his hand drop to his side, but his stance was vigilant.

Sebastian played the rest of the scene precisely as he had been directed. There was not an unplotted move or inflection in his performance. The cast relaxed and began to wander away. Only Deirdre remained behind. She had a suspicion that things were suddenly running *too* smoothly.

She found herself wondering why Rory hadn't materialized, and then remembered that he usually listened to jazz on his Discman in his dressing-room during his long wait between scenes. He'd be deaf to the tannoy and wouldn't be aware that there had been anything out of order. He had nearly two consecutive hours off stage, and it drove him mad with boredom.

Sebastian had left the stage and was standing in the wings, waiting for his next cue to enter. Nick McCarthy made an immediate beeline for him. Deirdre could tell from the stage director's body language that he was seriously irate. The pair talked together in an undertone for a minute or two, with Nick pointing his finger a lot, and Sebastian nodding his head. Sebastian spread his hands in an expressive gesture of contrition as he prepared to make his entrance, and Nick strolled back to the prompt corner, seemingly reassured.

'Mother. Mother. Mother.' Sebastian walked out onto the stage where Eva was waiting for him. Her involuntary tensing would be imperceptible from out front, but Deirdre saw it at once. She knew that the actress was going through agony.

Sebastian strolled through the first part of the scene in a curiously detached manner. His emotional level remained steady even when he started to prowl around Eva, delivering the lines that Deirdre knew the actress had come to dread, and scrutinizing her with glittering eyes. He looked like a wounded panther.

You shall not budge;
You go not till I set you up a glass
Where you may see the inmost part of
you.

Eva was beginning to look confused, and Deirdre suddenly registered what Sebastian was doing. He was tormenting the actress the way a cat torments a mouse. He was playing with her.

What have I done . . . ?

Eva's words were barely audible.

. . . What act
That roars so loud, and thunders in the index?

There was a long silence. Sebastian was standing over the actress, looking down at her where she sat on the edge of her bed. There was an odd smile playing around his mouth. Eva stared up at him as if mesmerized. The silence dragged on. There was not a sound from the auditorium. Deirdre was aware that other cast members had started to drift into the wings again, alerted to danger by silence on the tannoy.

Sebastian continued to smile as, very slowly, he sank to his knees by Eva's side. He took her face between his hands and Deirdre's heart stopped. There were tears coursing silently down Eva Lavery's face. 'It's you, isn't it?' Her voice was so hoarse that she barely managed to articulate the words.

Suddenly Sebastian slid his right hand down over her throat and took hold of the locket which hung on a chain around her neck. He gave a tug, and the chain broke, wrenching Eva's head forward. Sebastian sprang to his feet, holding the locket high.

As he did so he knocked against a small table which stood by Gertrude's bed. An elaborately carved antique music box fell to the floor and 'Au Clair de la Lune' tinkled out of tune.

Look here, upon this picture, and on this,

Sebastian instructed, looking down at Eva. He had the liberated air of an animal whose cage door has just been opened.

The counterfeit presentment of two brothers!

He thrust the locket in Eva's face. 'Mother,' he said quietly. The actress tried to rise to her feet, but stumbled and fell back upon the bed. Sebastian made no move to help her, but instead turned his back on her and stood quite still.

Eva tried to move again, but this time she fell to the floor. Suddenly Nick McCarthy was there beside her. He gathered the actress in his arms and carried her off stage. The crowd of actors in the wings parted to let them through. At a signal from Nick as he passed her, Jessica ran to the prompt corner and pressed the button that would bring down the curtain.

Sebastian watched as the blood-red velvet slowly descended. The chain still swung from his hand and the locket glittered in the half-light. There was no sound apart from the discordant jangle of the music box as it wound down and stopped. Then a murmuring started from behind the curtain. It quickly built to a crescendo as the punters began to speculate on the significance of what they'd just witnessed on the stage of the Phoenix theatre. Sebastian bowed his head and stood quite still for a moment. He looked incredibly solitary. Then, raising a hand and pushing his hair back from his face, he turned and moved towards the wings. Once offstage he quickened his pace to a purposeful stride. Not one member of the cast made a move to stop him as he cut a swathe through them. It was as if they had all frozen. On his way past Deirdre he grabbed her wrist without looking at her and said: 'Come with me.' An image flashed across her mind's eye. He had done exactly the same thing once before – that time in Juliet Rathbone-Lyon's office. Except that Sebastian bore no relation to the Sebastian who was manhandling her now. They were two completely different people.

Sebastian proceeded up the stairs, dragging Deirdre behind him. Nobody had dared to follow him. She tried to break free, but his grip was like a vice. He still held Eva's locket in his hand and the chain was digging into her flesh. He was heading in the direction of the dressing-rooms when he suddenly appeared to change his mind and veered off down a flight of steps and along a narrow corridor which led to the prop room. Deirdre had rarely had occasion to visit the place – it was Stage Management's territory, and the actors were discouraged from going in. Once inside Sebastian let go of her wrist and shut the door behind him. Deirdre made for the opposite wall and pressed her back against it. The room was crammed with exotic debris and bric-à-brac, and was dominated by an immense golden throne. A gargoyle leered at her from a shelf. To her intense alarm, Sebastian turned the key in the lock. He registered the expression on her face.

'It's OK, Deirdre. I'm not going to hurt you.' His voice sounded tired and there was a defeated air about him suddenly. All that manic energy had drained from him. He leant against the door and regarded her with sad golden eyes. 'I'm sorry. You're the only person I felt I could explain things to.' He slid into a sitting position on the concrete floor with his legs bent at the knees and his back slumped against the door. For some reason Deirdre was reminded of the photograph of David Lawless as a young man – the one that now hung framed on Eva's dressing-room wall. 'Come and sit beside me.' Deirdre didn't move. 'Please, Deirdre.'

She looked down at him. She had never seen Sebastian stripped of his habitual guardedness before. He looked very vulnerable. She moved slowly towards him and sat down in front of him, still keeping some distance between them.

'She's my mother.'

Deirdre didn't have to ask who he meant. 'You're Eva Lavery's son?'

He nodded. 'Let me tell you a story, Deirdre,' he said. 'You know some of it already.' He took a deep breath, and then let it out in a sigh. 'When Eva left David and ran away to London she became pregnant shortly before the car accident that killed my father, Richard Lawless.' He had some difficulty in articulating the word 'father'. 'She had the baby in London and put him up for adoption. I was adopted by a childless couple called Hardy.' Sebastian wrapped his arms round his legs and rested his chin on his knees. He seemed quite calm all of a sudden, as if he found the mere mention of his adoptive parents soothing. 'They were great parents – very kind. They made no secret of the fact that I was adopted, and they knew that some day I would want and need to know about my birth parents.' He rubbed his chin with a hand. 'Unfortunately, my adoptive father was a workaholic accountant with a bad heart and my mother had cancer. They died within a year of one another when I was nineteen.' He sounded quite matter-of-fact.

Instantly Deirdre felt sympathy flood through her. 'Oh Sebastian – I'm so sorry.' She felt tears rising to her eyes. 'What can I say?'

Sebastian smiled at her. He leaned over and stroked her cheek. 'I was devastated, of course. I was at RADA at the time and I was really fucked up emotionally, but I'm OK now.' He laughed. 'That is, if you can consider what I did tonight to be OK behaviour. Which of course it wasn't.'

Deirdre looked at him in wonder, comparing the Sebastian of earlier in the evening with the Sebastian who was sitting facing her now. They were like two completely different people.

'Why did you do it, Sebastian?' she asked in a careful voice. 'Why did you do it in such a cruel way?'

He shut his eyes for a moment. Deirdre could see him swallow hard. 'I knew it would take time to get over the deaths of my adoptive parents. I didn't want the additional emotional burden of learning the identity of my birth parents until I'd gone through all my grieving. But time went by and I became curious. I needed to know. I suppose when Eva gave me up, she thought I'd never be able to trace her, but since the Adoption Laws changed it's not difficult to locate a birth parent. A visit to the Citizen's Advice Bureau is all it takes.' He smiled at her again, but Deirdre could see a pulse throbbing in his neck, and his knuckles were very white. He looked down at his hands which were clenched around his knees. He didn't speak again for some time and then he said: 'You can imagine that I was – surprised' – he chose the word with care – 'when I found out that my father was a dead rock musician and my mother was a famous actress. I'd been reading interviews she'd given to papers since I was fourteen years old for fuck's sake! I felt like I *knew* her already. Andrew Lloyd Webber could have adapted my life story for a musical!' He lifted his head and laughed again.

For a split second Deirdre felt scared, and then she listened. There was no madness in Sebastian's laugh – there was not even any bitterness. It was as if what he had gone through on stage tonight had had some kind of cathartic effect on him. He glanced down at his hands again and looked slightly surprised when he realized that the chain of the locket was still twisted around his fingers. He unwound it and let it slide to the floor. 'For a long time I wondered what to do – how I should approach her. I'd left RADA at this stage and was doing OK as an actor. I decided that what I wanted to do more than anything else in the world was to come to Eva Lavery as a successful actor in my own right and with my career in the ascendant. I wanted to be able to say: "Look at me! You are a lucky woman. Not only have you achieved fame and fortune, you are also the mother of one of the most up-and-coming young actors in the UK!"' He looked up at her with wounded eyes, and Deirdre felt immeasurably sorry for him. 'Of course I'm not fooling myself that there wasn't a bit of me that wasn't looking for revenge.'

'Like Hamlet,' Deirdre found herself saying.

'Just like Hamlet. Except *he* was solely bent on avenging his dead father. I didn't just have a dead father to avenge. I had a score to settle with a mother who'd given me away at birth.' He fell silent.

'When sorrows come, they come not single spies, but in battalions,' thought Deirdre. How had Sebastian kept it together for so long? She could not conceive of a human being guarding such secrets, or cherishing such dreams as he had. She thought of the extraordinary control he had exerted over his performances to date. No wonder he had finally cracked.

'Poor, poor Sebastian,' she said. He wasn't listening.

'My original plan had been to wait until I had

finished work on the Australian film. I was going to go to her then. But then I met you quite by chance that day in Juliet's office, and when you told me about *Hamlet* I knew I had to do it. I *had* to. I knew I could manipulate events in a way that would allow me to go to Eva and reveal to her that her son was actually playing Hamlet to her Gertrude!' He spread his hands. 'It all fell into place at once, as if it had been fated to happen this way.'

Deirdre was tempted to believe him. Although Fate had certainly had a helping hand from Sebastian Hardy. Sebastian Lawless. He must have worked like a demon during that week in London when he'd put into motion the wheels that would send Mark Llewellyn to Australia and take him to Eva Lavery. His mother. There was nothing demonic about the way he looked now. He looked like a lost little boy. Deirdre's heart went out to him. She took his hand in hers. 'You didn't realize that Eva and David were lovers again, did you? That can't have helped.'

'The first time I heard about it was in the pub that night when Sophie dropped it into the conversation. That was when life started imitating art too closely for comfort and I began to have serious doubts as to whether I could handle the whole thing. I felt like I'd created something uncontrollable that had taken on a life of its own, like Frankenstein's monster. You know something? Revenge doesn't heal anything, Deirdre. It really hurts. I set out to hurt my mother, but I've only succeeded in hurting myself.' Sebastian rubbed his eyes. They were the colour of dark honey now, the colour that David Lawless's eyes were when he was tired. What was the name of that television series Sebastian had done? She knew it was apt, somehow. *Hurting People* – that had been it. The title worked both ways. Sebastian Hardy had been hurt and was determined to hurt back.

'That's why I switched the pictures in Eva's locket tonight,' he continued. 'I'd seen it lying on the prop table before I went on stage every night and it was practically *inviting* me to insert pictures of my own uncle and my father.'

Deirdre picked up the broken locket from where Sebastian had let it fall on the floor and looked at it. One half contained a photograph of David Lawless which had been cut out from the programme for *Hamlet*. The other half contained a photograph of a young man who was indubitably his brother Richard. They could almost have been twins. He faced the camera unsmilingly, a challenging expression on his face. The photograph had been carefully cut from a newspaper.

'It's the only photograph of my father I have. My adoptive parents had kept it for me in an envelope along with a letter explaining the circumstances of my adoption, and my birth certificate. I suppose they got the photograph from an obituary. I saw it for the first time when I went to the social services.' He let his head drop back and rubbed the muscles in his neck with his fingers, as if trying to rid himself of a knot of tension.

Deirdre handed the locket back to Sebastian in

silence. He looked at it once more and then shut it with a little click. 'What will you do about Eva, Sebastian?' she asked quietly. 'You have injured her dreadfully.'

Sebastian let his head drop into his hands. 'I know,' he said. There was an awful sense of hopelessness about him now. 'I didn't mean it to happen this way Deirdre, honestly. My original plan was to produce a definitive Hamlet and present it to her as a gift. Then I found out about her and David.' He raised his head and shook it violently, as if trying to free himself of demons. Deirdre was reminded of the way Eva had shaken her head earlier on that evening in her dressing-room, when she'd confessed that she was in terror of Sebastian Hardy. 'I just wanted to be able to step forward at the curtain call on the last night of the show and make a public announcement. I wanted to have Eva embrace me in front of all the world. I don't know how I could have been so blind and stupid – I was projecting some kind of Hollywood-movie scenario onto my own life. I should have known that things like that don't happen in the real world. I should have known that I wouldn't be able to stay in control.'

'You'd need to be superhuman to stay in control of a scenario like that, Sebastian.' For some time now Deirdre had been aware of noises in the backstage corridors and on the stairs – noises of running feet and people shouting. 'Hey,' she added gently. 'They're looking for us, you know. You're going to have to face them some time.' She paused. She felt very emotional. 'You're going to have to face Eva.'

Sebastian closed his fingers round hers. 'I'm going to have to face my mother,' he said.

'Oh, shit, Sebastian.' Deirdre felt a tear roll down her cheek.

'Don't cry, Deirdre O'Dare. There should be a law against making you unhappy. You need to be cherished.' A second tear followed the first. 'Look at me – I'm not crying.' Sebastian's eyes were indeed dry, but there was an infinite sadness in them. 'Come here for a minute. I could do with a hug before we say goodbye.'

Deirdre was crying in earnest now. She slid herself nearer to him, and he put an arm around her.

'I'm sorry things didn't work out between us.' He kissed her gently on the lips.

The image of the way he had looked down at her before kissing her for the very first time came into her mind. 'Why did you take me to bed, Sebastian?' she said through her sobs. This was something which had always puzzled her. 'Was it just a way of getting access to Eva? I thought that the only reason you came to my flat that night was because you thought she'd be there.' Deirdre gave a great sniff and wiped her nose with the hem of Ophelia's gown. Then she realized that it was the last time she would ever wear it, and she started to cry even harder.

'Oh no, Deirdre. Don't think that! Though I did use you consciously to begin with – of course I did. When you obliged me the very first time we met by informing me that you were working with my uncle and my long-lost mother – well! I mean, what else could I do but try and extract as much information out of you as I possibly could? Only a saint could have resisted the temptation to use you, Deirdre O'Dare. You were so beautifully compliant!'

Sebastian gave a sad smile and pulled her closer to him. She cast her mind back to the first time she'd met him, that day when he'd taken her for coffee. He'd reminded her of a dark angel. How was she to know that he'd turn out to be an avenging angel as well?

'And then,' he went on, 'I began to realize that I wanted to go to bed with you in spite of everything. I really didn't think it was a good idea to trammel myself with more emotional baggage than I was carrying already, but I liked you so much and I was in so much need of comfort and you were so desirable that I couldn't stop myself.'

'So why did you only go to bed with me once?'

'Because I knew you didn't want me.'

'Sebastian! I *did* want you!'

'No you didn't.'

He was right, of course.

There was a noise of approaching footsteps in the corridor outside. The footsteps continued past the door of the prop room and receded. The shouting in the distance was growing louder, and Deirdre could hear her name being called. 'We should go, Sebastian.' She didn't move.

'Yes, we should.' He put a hand up to her face and held it against her cheek. She looked into his beautiful eyes and they smiled at each other. Their smiles were full of mutual regret, mutual hope, and a strange kind of understanding. Suddenly someone was pounding at the door of the prop room. Deirdre leaned forward and kissed Sebastian very gently.

'Will you come with me?' he asked.

'Yes, I will,' she replied. She rose to her feet and reached out a hand to help him stand too. He swayed a little, and she put an arm around his waist to support him as she struggled to turn the key in the lock.

'Deirdre? Are you in there?' It was Rory's voice.

She opened the door and saw him standing in front of her. 'Dear Jesus, Deirdre – are you all right?' he demanded.

'I'm fine, Rory.' She was amazed at how calm she sounded.

Rory looked from her to Sebastian and there was something in his eyes she could not read. His right fist was clenched in the palm of his left hand, and for a moment she thought he was going to hit the other actor. Then he drew himself up. 'I think Ms Lavery deserves an apology,' he said to Sebastian.

'I'm on my way,' said Sebastian, turning to Deirdre and gesturing for her to go ahead of him through the door. Before preceding him along the corridor she turned to find Rory watching her. She couldn't catch the expression in his eyes because he turned his back at once and started travelling in the opposite direction.

They walked together to Eva's dressing-room,

Sebastian running the gamut of curious looks and hostile stares from members of the company. It was David's voice who told them to come in when Sebastian knocked on the door. Deirdre noticed that her sunflowers still lay where she'd left them on Eva's dressing-table.

Eva was sitting hunched in a corner of the couch looking very small and vulnerable. She looked just the way she did in the photograph of her which had been taken on a beach more than two decades ago and which now hung above her on the wall. David was leaning over her. He straightened when Sebastian and Deirdre entered the room. There was total silence. Deirdre didn't know what to do. She looked from one face to another. 'I'll go,' she whispered.

'No,' said Sebastian, taking hold of her hand. Deirdre felt even more uncomfortable.

David's face was carven. He wore the expression of someone just emerging from profound shock. 'Sebastian,' he said. 'I have never wanted to hit anyone as badly as I wanted to hit you when I heard what you'd done to – your mother out there tonight. But Eva asked me not to hit you, and she asked me for a very good reason.' Eva was staring at Sebastian. She still looked completely dazed. David put a hand on her shoulder. It looked as if he was partly trying to reassure the actress and partly trying to steady himself. 'Richard Lawless was the name she gave as your father when your birth was registered. She put a false name on the birth certificate because she felt she could not reveal the real identity of your father, who was a married man. My brother Richard was not your father, Sebastian.' Deirdre could hear him take a very deep, rather shaky breath before he finished what he had to say. 'Eva has just told me that I am.'

Sebastian didn't notice as Deirdre slid her hand out of his. The three leading players in the drama stood quite still, gazing at each other with completely expressionless faces. Then Eva held out a shaky hand. There were tears in her eyes, but there was no longer any trace of anguish in them.

'Mother,' said Sebastian. He walked towards her with an uncertain tread, and then took her hand and lowered himself rather awkwardly to his knees. Eva stood up shakily. 'Mother,' said Sebastian again, looking up at her. He put his arms around her waist and pressed his cheek to her belly. Eva laid both her hands on his head in a tentative gesture, but the beginnings of a slightly incredulous smile were forming around her mouth. 'Mother.' Sebastian closed his eyes like someone who has finally found the longed-for relief of dreamless sleep after being plagued by incessant nightmares.

Then Eva knelt down in front of him and wrapped him in her arms. She looked up at David where he stood watching them and smiled. Her smile was redolent with nostalgia and love.

Deirdre turned her back on the occupants of Eva Lavery's dressing-room and made her exit on soundless feet. The last thing she saw as she closed the door gently behind her was David brushing his hair back from his forehead and looking strangely helpless as he gazed down at his lover and their grown-up son with his almond-shaped, amber eyes.

* * *

She went to the pub. She didn't go to party, she went because she badly needed to talk to Maeve.

Meagher's was much emptier than usual. Most of the punters had already had their post-show drink and cleared off, and there were no last-night liggers hanging around. The atmosphere was hushed and subdued, as if somebody had died. It was pretty obvious that there'd be no celebrations tonight.

It wasn't late – only a quarter to eleven, Deirdre saw from the clock above the bar. On a normal evening the show would only just have come down by now. There were several cast members in a cluster at the far end of the room who looked up eagerly when she walked in. Sophie Burke actually waved her over. Deirdre pretended she hadn't seen her, and was glad when she spotted Maeve and Rory sitting by themselves at a separate table. She got herself a drink and went over to join them.

'You look knackered, Deirdre,' said Maeve.

'Yeah. It's been a hell of a day,' she said as she sank into her chair. 'Oh – shit!' she added. There was despair in her voice.

'Did Sebastian give you a hard time, sweetheart?' Maeve looked concerned.

'No. I've just remembered that I'm due on location tomorrow. I'd forgotten all about that bloody film.' She sat back in her chair and rubbed her eyes.

'What time?' asked Maeve.

'I'm due out in the Vale of Clara at two o'clock. There's a car picking me up at twelve-thirty.' Deirdre looked glum. 'And they're starting with a riding scene, so knowing my luck it'll be freezing cold and raining.'

'Well, at least you don't have to be up at the crack of dawn. Come on, Deirdre – stay for a while. You can't go without filling us in on what went on with Sebastian, for goodness' sake.'

Deirdre proceeded to do exactly that. By the time she had finished her story, Maeve was open-mouthed with astonishment. 'Wow! What an amazing saga! And to think that those jammy punters got their tickets refunded after the show! They should have been charged double the price – what they saw on stage tonight will go down in theatre history.'

'Told you there was something strange about that geezer, didn't I, Deirdre?' said Rory. He looked completely unimpressed by Deirdre's story and she was a bit put out by his indifference. He looked at his watch and drained the last of his pint. 'Time to hit MacNamara's,' he said, getting to his feet.

'Oh, not that bloody shebeen of yours, Rory. I suppose that means you'll be dead to the world all morning.' Maeve gave him a cross look. 'I was hoping you'd do the Sunday paper run this week.'

'Sure I'll do it. I've to be up early tomorrow. I've got shit to do.' He slung his coat over his shoulder. 'Catch you later, Maeve.' He leaned down and kissed Deirdre lightly on the cheek. It took her off guard and she flinched. 'Nice working with you, sweetheart. See you around some time.'

'Yeah.' Deirdre was staring intently at the pattern on the worn, dralon covered arm of her chair.

Then he was gone.

'Great guy.' Maeve leant back in her seat and looked at Deirdre with interest.

Deirdre nodded, still studying the swirly pattern on the shabby fabric. She couldn't trust herself to speak.

Then Maeve said something unexpected. 'Who do you dream about at night, Deirdre?'

Deirdre looked up, startled. Maeve raised her eyebrows at her. 'Well? I suspect you've never dreamt about Sebastian Hardy in your life. You dream about Rory McDonagh, don't you?'

Deirdre swallowed. She still couldn't say anything.

'You're crazy about him,' Maeve continued. 'And he's besotted with you. I don't understand why the pair of you can't just admit it and get your act together at last.'

'What?' Deirdre looked at Maeve in bewilderment. She had finally found her voice again. 'Rory doesn't fancy me, Maeve. He thinks I'm a total airhead.'

'Think what you like. I happen to know different.'

'Why?' Deirdre leant forward suddenly. 'He hasn't said anything to you, has he?'

'Not a dicky-bird, darling. He doesn't need to. But I can tell that he finds you an incredible turn-on, and he laughs more with you than with any other woman I've ever seen him with. You don't see the way he looks at you when your back's turned, Deirdre.' Maeve's smile was knowing.

Just then Sophie arrived at the table, carrying two pints and a bottle of Sol. 'Mind if I join you?' she asked with a bright smile, and sat down before waiting for a reply. 'I thought it might be a nice idea to buy you girls a drink on the last night of the show.'

'Thanks for the thought, Sophie, but I've got to run,' said Maeve, collecting her things. 'Jacqueline's cooking something special for supper and she'll throw a wobbly if I'm late.'

Deirdre looked at Maeve in panic as she rose to her feet. 'Remember what I said to you, Deirdre,' she said. 'It's up to you now. Do the right thing.' She gave Deirdre a big smile, shouldered her bag and moved away from the table.

'So,' said Sophie, leaning forward with an intimate smile. 'What's the low-down on Sebastian, Deirdre?'

Deirdre looked towards the door. Maeve gave her a final wave and swung through it, laughing.

* * *

That night Deirdre dreamt about Rory again.

Chapter Twenty-One

The following afternoon she was picked up by a gleaming black Merc. She felt a bit intimidated as she slid into the back of the car, but the driver was very friendly. Too friendly, thought Deirdre after more than an hour of non-stop stories about the cute antics of his four-year old son and two-year old daughter. She wanted time to herself to go over in her mind what had happened last night. She wondered how Eva was – how all three of them were – and what they were doing. Were they together right now, or apart? She imagined them in Eva's house, sitting at the long table, making plans for the future, and realized that Sebastian would have a half-sister now. A whole new family, a rather unorthodox one, had been hatched overnight. She wondered if the papers had got wind of it yet. Poor Eva would have to barricade her door against the piranhas of the tabloid press.

She also wanted to go over her dialogue. After her riding sequence she had a scene with her screen father where he gives out to her about going around giving food to the starving peasants. She wondered what starving actor had been cast in the role of the evil landlord.

It was a cold day, but fine, and thankfully there

was no hint of rain. As the car travelled through the countryside, Deirdre remembered the last time she'd driven along the Wicklow roads. She'd been sitting beside Rory in his battered orange Saab eating apples. She wondered when she'd see him again. She wasn't sure that she'd be able to hack watching him on the Abbey stage in *Les Liaisons Dangereuses* snogging other actresses.

By the time they got to the Vale of Clara her driver was telling her how his son's teacher had never had such a bright four-year-old in his class and as Deirdre unfastened her seat-belt he was repeating for the third time some mildly amusing remark the child had made that morning. Deirdre forced a last laugh and got out of the car with relief.

The location that had been chosen for the first scene was extremely beautiful. At least Big TP had got something right. The sparks were setting up lights on the banks of a river flanked by grassy meadows on either side. The river flowed down a little valley to a glade of trees where a willow trailed its branches in the water like a mermaid's hair. The air felt crisp and fresh in Deirdre's lungs after the exhaust fumes of the city, and the sky was all-over azure with only one small cloud in it. It looked like a sheep with no legs drifting idly by. There was a pathway running alongside the river which led to a five-bar gate. Deirdre felt a flurry of nerves when she clocked the gate. She hoped they wouldn't expect her to jump it.

The location trucks and caravans were all parked in convoy along a grassy expanse to the left of the little copse. Feeling a bit uncertain, Deirdre made her way towards the trucks. There were an awful lot of people milling around looking as if they knew exactly what they were doing. She supposed she should find the wardrobe van first.

'Hey! Miss Deirdre O'Dare!' came a shout from behind her. She turned to find Big TP O'Reilly bearing down on her. 'Welcome to *The Revenge of Irish Bob*!' He wrapped his arms around her and gave her an enthusiastic hug. 'It's dandy to see you again, little lady! You're looking lovely as ever! Hey – Simon' – TP addressed a lanky man who was passing by – 'how long before we're set up? I'm champing at the bit to get this show on the road!'

Big TP still had his arms wrapped tightly around Deirdre and her head was pressed uncomfortably against his chest. The man called Simon looked at his watch. 'It'll be another hour and a half at least, Big TP,' he said. 'We're having the same problem with the genny as we had earlier over at the big house.'

'Goddarn,' said Big TP with a passion which made him inadvertently bang Deirdre's head off his chest, before adding 'Pardon my French, Miss Deirdre.'

Simon looked curiously at Deirdre, whose head was still held at an awkward angle in Big TP's vice-like embrace. She shifted her eyes away from his, feeling utterly ridiculous.

'Oh – this here's Miss Deirdre O'Dare,' said Big TP, finally releasing her. 'Deirdre O'Dare – Simon Doorley, our lighting cameraman.

Deirdre's our star, Simon. She's playing the part of Tracey!'

Simon gave her a smile. Deirdre thought she detected a touch of sympathy in it. 'Nice to meet you, Deirdre,' he said, shaking her hand. 'Sorry I can't stop to talk – we're running behind schedule already.' He saluted Big TP and loped off in the direction of one of the big trucks.

'Have they kitted you out yet?' asked Big TP. He kept a proprietorial arm over her shoulder. The physical contact made Deirdre feel even more uneasy.

'No. I've only just arrived,' she said.

'Well, let's find AB. Our AD.' TP started striding across the field. Deirdre had no alternative but to trot along with him, welded as she was to his side.

Deirdre knew that AD stood for Assistant Director – but who or what on earth was AB? She didn't have to ask to find out. 'AB's AKA Anthony Brian. He's my cousin. AB O'Reilly'll take care of you, Miss Deirdre.'

Just then a stout man came out of a nearby caravan and negotiated the steps with difficulty. 'Hey – AB!' Big TP waved at him. 'Come and meet our leading lady!' The large man waddled over with a broad smile on his face. He could have been Big TP's twin. 'AB, this is Miss Deirdre O'Dare – star of *The Revenge of Irish Bob*!'

'Nice to meet you, Deirdre.' AB took her hand and shook it with gusto. He didn't release it for a good thirty seconds, Deirdre calculated. She'd taken a severe pummelling in the last five minutes, what with being clamped to TP's side and having her hand nearly pumped off by his clone. 'You must be looking forward to your scene this morning. That horse you'll be riding is a magnificent beast.' His smile became even broader.

'Quiet, AB.' TP O'Reilly nudged him in the ribs in a jocular fashion. 'I'm saving the Lady Tara as a surprise for Miss Deirdre! She hasn't met her yet.' Big TP looked across the field to where a state-of-the-art horse-box was parked. There was a pleased grin on his face. Deirdre followed his gaze reluctantly and with a slight sense of foreboding. Then TP turned back to Deirdre. 'Now, you run along with AB, Miss Deirdre. He'll show you where the wardrobe van is.' He finally removed his arm from her shoulders and Deirdre felt as if she was levitating.

'Come with me, Deirdre,' said AB, draping his left arm around her. Deirdre felt her shoulders sink again along with her heart as they trundled towards one of the caravans.

'Hey! Miss Deirdre!' They paused and turned in tandem. It wasn't easy.

'Yes, Big TP?' She made her tone bright and obliging.

'Maybe we could have dinner together after the shoot this evening?'

The invitation had taken her off guard. Deirdre couldn't think of an excuse fast enough. 'Maybe,' she said. Her attempt at injecting her voice with enthusiasm wasn't very successful, she realized. She wasn't *that* good an actress.

'Better not let Charlene hear you say that, Big TP!' AB called back at him.

'Ha ha ha!' went Big TP O'Reilly.

'Is Charlene Big TP's wife?' she enquired as she and AB swivelled about and resumed their trek towards the wardrobe van.

AB O'Reilly looked down at Deirdre and gave her a big wink. 'No. Big TP left his wife back in Texas. Let's just say that Charlene is a lady friend of Big TP's, Deirdre! Ha ha ha!' And AB O'Reilly rubbed the side of his nose with one finger and gave her a knowing look.

In wardrobe she was kitted out in a Victorian riding habit by a frowning wardrobe mistress. The bodice was very tight and rather constricting. 'Why didn't you phone to say you'd put on weight?' the wardrobe mistress asked crossly. 'You've gone up a whole size – from a ten to a twelve, by the look of it. I'll have to find another wedding dress for you – the one we have is nearer an eight than a ten. It won't go near you now.'

'Sorry,' said Deirdre apologetically.

Just then a bored-looking face poked round the door. 'Can you tell me how long you're going to be, honey?' The voice had a pronounced Texan twang.

'She'll be with you as soon as I'm finished with her, Charlene, OK?'

Two startlingly blue eyes rimmed with navy-blue kohl and fringed with thick black lashes turned their gaze on Deirdre. 'I've been waiting for you in make-up for the longest time. Be as quick as you can, honey.' There was no warmth in the 'honey'.

* * *

'Do you mind going a bit easier on the hair-spray, Charlene?' Deirdre asked half an hour later. 'I suffer from awful asthma, I'm afraid.' She gave an unconvincing cough. 'And I hate having sticky hair.' Charlene had tonged her hair into stiff ringlets, managing to burn her neck twice during the operation, and was wielding a tin of hair-spray the way the conductor of an orchestra wields his baton during a particularly passionate piece of music.

'It's OK, honey. This spray has a very light, gentle hold. Here, read for yourself. It says it right there on the can. It's soft and gentle.'

Deirdre looked at the blurb on the can. '"Soft and Gentle' she read 'is an effective anti-perspirant"'. 'It's deodorant, Charlene.'

'Is it? Oops – silly me! And me a qualified beautician!' giggled Charlene.

She may be a qualified beautician, but she knows bugger all about film make-up, concluded Deirdre. Or the Victorian era, she thought glumly as she stared at her turquoise eye-shadow, stiff hair and orange face in the mirror. Her mouth was an even brighter orange than her face and it was painted bigger than Julia Roberts'. In the mirror she saw that Charlene was examining what looked like a collection of dead spiders on a plastic tray. They were false eyelashes. She wanted to cry, but she took a deep breath and remembered what Maeve had said. Take the money and run.

She descended the steps of the make-up van an hour later as one might descend the steps of a torture chamber, thanking God that none of her friends were working on the film. Her face felt stiff with the amount of slap Charlene had applied, and her eyelids were practically closing under the weight of the lashes that had been laboriously glued on. Her hair had been sprayed with half a can of hair-spray as well as the deodorant, and the burns on her neck were throbbing.

'Hey! You look sensational!' shouted Big TP when he saw her. 'We'll be ready for you in about ten minutes, little lady. Why don't you get yourself a coffee while you're waiting?'

Deirdre trailed off in the direction of the catering truck feeling miserable. The last time anyone had told her she looked sensational had been when she'd been sitting on a bed stark naked, fastening the straps on her high-heeled sandals. It had been Rory McDonagh who'd said it, and the next thing he'd said had been 'Stand up and come over here at once.'

She poured herself a cup of coffee from an enormous thermos and was about to help herself to a chocolate muffin when she saw the tight-lipped wardrobe mistress looking at her and she decided against it.

Big TP's ten minutes dragged on into well over an hour. At this rate they'd be lucky to get the scene in the can before it started to get dark. She was just about to pour herself a third cup of coffee when a greasy-haired youth came up and informed her that she was required on the set. Deirdre followed him down the hill to where the cameras had been positioned, feeling more self-conscious than she had ever felt in her life, and convinced that everyone she passed by was going into fits of giggles behind her back.

'How do you feel, Deirdre?' hollered Big TP when he saw her. He was standing beside his cousin and they looked like Tweedledum and Tweedledee.

Deirdre didn't say anything. She was looking at the horse that was being led on to the set.

'This here's The Lady Tara,' said Big TP O'Reilly. His voice was booming with pride. 'She's my horse, little lady. Flew her over especially. Couldn't leave The Lady Tara out of my own film, could I? Ha ha ha.'

The Lady Tara was a stunningly beautiful palomino, standing about sixteen hands high. She looked a lot bigger than Minerva, who'd stood at just fifteen hands. Her golden coat was glossy with good health, and her mane and tail wouldn't have looked out of place in a shampoo commercial.

She was dancing a little, and her handler was having some difficulty restraining her. Deirdre stared at The Lady Tara frozen in horror and cursing herself. She had been careful to volunteer as little information as possible to Rory McDonagh about *The Revenge of Irish Bob* in case it gave him more ammunition to be scathing to her about. In her endeavours to keep him in the dark she had completely neglected to tell him that the film was set in the Victorian era. The very title would have bumsteered him, since 'Bob' was such an anachronistic name. The Lady Tara was wearing a side-saddle.

She started to sweat. She could feel the sleeves of her tight bodice cutting into her underarms.

'Well, Deirdre, what do you think?'

'She's magnificent, Big TP,' she said in a small voice.

'We don't want you to do much on her today – we just want a shot of you ambling along by the river, revelling in the glories of nature.'

Deirdre thought fast. Maybe she could wing it. Walking shouldn't be too much of a problem. She wasn't too sure about the acting side of things, though. It wouldn't be easy to look as if she was 'revelling in the glories of nature' while sitting side-saddle for the first time on a strange horse. Hell, she'd give it a go and if it proved impossible she'd just come clean, tell them she'd never ridden side-saddle before and give them the option to replace her. She tried hard to remember the shooting schedule. 'When will you need me to ride her again, Big TP?' she asked, as casually as she could.

'Ha ha ha! You're mighty keen to put that horse through her paces, aren't you, little lady? Well, I'm sorry to have to disappoint you, but you won't get a chance for another week. We've nothing but interiors scheduled till next Saturday.'

Deirdre breathed a sigh of relief. She knew she had three days off next week – she'd phone Tommy

Connors and beg him to give her a crash course in riding side-saddle.

'Well, Miss Deirdre O'Dare. How do you feel about a little rehearsal?'

'Just fine, Big TP.' She hoped that her nervousness wasn't too obvious. She didn't want The Lady Tara to sense it. She knew from Rory that thoroughbreds, especially palominos, could be temperamental, even though the horse in 'Paloma's Palomino' in *Bunty* had behaved like a pussycat.

She walked towards the horse wishing she'd remembered to bring an apple. She put out a hand and stroked the soft, cappuccino-coloured nose, and The Lady Tara tossed her head. Deirdre remembered what Rory had told her at her first riding lesson. She started talking to the horse in a reassuring way, pitching her voice low so that nobody else could hear what she was saying. Her soothing tone belied the words. 'OK, you big blond bimbo,' she said. 'I'm going to get up on your back and you're going to behave, OK? Because if you don't I am going to mess up your hairstyle big time and give you a good kick in the leg when nobody's looking. Now,' she took a deep breath. 'Let's go for it. And you be good, Tara, darling.'

She was unsure how to mount side-saddle, so she asked the handler to help her up, claiming that she was hampered by her voluminous skirts. She succeeded in somehow twisting herself around so that her rear end landed with a bump square on the saddle. She was very uncomfortable and deeply insecure as she clung to The Lady Tara's mane with one hand and to the pommel of the saddle with the other. The Lady Tara took a couple of steps sideways and Deirdre felt as if she was about to topple off a mountain. She took more deep breaths and tried to steady herself, knowing that in spite of the classy rig-out, she looked far from elegant. She couldn't bring herself to meet the handler's eyes as he looked up at her uncertainly from where he was standing holding onto the bridle. 'Please God let me get away with it,' she prayed, shutting her eyes for a minute.

'Get off the horse, Deirdre.' It was Rory McDonagh's voice. She opened her eyes with a start. What was *he* doing here?

Rory was striding down the hill towards them. His dirty-blond hair was blown back by the wind and his long, black leather coat was flapping out behind him. 'Get off the horse,' he repeated. People were turning round and exchanging curious looks. 'You fucking irresponsible buffoon,' he said to TP O'Reilly as he drew abreast of him. 'Why didn't you tell her she was going to have to ride side-saddle?'

'Who the heck are you?' said Big TP. 'What darn business is it of yours, pal?' Big TP had gone red in the face.

'What's the name of this set-up?' Rory asked. 'Mickey Mouse Productions?' He looked back at Deirdre. 'Get off the horse, Deirdre,' he said again, in a dangerously calm voice. The crew was silent and uneasy-looking. Deirdre dithered on The Lady Tara's back. The horse took a few more dance steps. Her ears were laid back on her head.

'You get off my film set!' Big TP was shouting now. 'I remember you now, pal. You're a real smart-ass! You think you're God's gift to horses!'

Just then there was a loud popping noise. A bulb had gone in one of the arc-lamps. The Lady Tara shied in alarm and reared up. Deirdre clung tightly onto her mane, but it was no use. Her fingers slid through the horse's hair and she fell heavily to the ground, rolling down the bank and over the roots of the willow tree straight into the river. The last thing she was aware of was Rory's shout and a splash as he dived in after her.

Then the blue sky came crashing down on Deirdre O'Dare.

* * *

When she opened her eyes again she thought she must be in Eva Lavery's dressing-room. There were flowers everywhere. She tried to move and then realized that she was aching all over. She was in a bed and there was something attached to her arm.

'Hello, my love.' It was her mother's voice. Deirdre turned her head on the pillow and saw Rosaleen looking down at her. 'You're OK. You're OK, Deirdre. You're in the Blackrock Clinic, but there's very little to worry about. You've been concussed for quite a while, that's all, and you got a nasty gash on your shoulder from where you fell against a rock, but you've been stitched up nicely.

You're going to be all right.' She pressed a bell on the wall at the side of the bed.

Deirdre looked at her arm. There was a tube coming out of it.

'You're on a drip, my love. You lost rather a lot of blood before the ambulance got to you. The Vale of Clara isn't the most accessible place in the world for the emergency services, you know.' Rosaleen stroked her daughter's face. 'Do you want me to tell you about it?'

Deirdre nodded. Her mouth was very dry and her lips felt sore and cracked. 'Can I have something to drink, Mum?' she asked. Her voice sounded rusty.

'Sure. Here – let me help you sit up.' Rosaleen adjusted the pillows and supported Deirdre as she eased herself into a sitting position, and then poured some water from a carafe into a glass. The door opened and a nurse came into the room.

'Hey – you're back in the land of the living!' she said, crossing the room and looking down at Deirdre with an appraising look on her face. 'How are you feeling?'

Deirdre wasn't really sure how she felt. She was still very confused. All she knew was that she was in pretty serious pain. 'I'm very sore,' she said. She was feeling drowsy, too.

'I'll give you a painkiller for that in a minute,' said the nurse, taking a clipboard from the foot of the bed and running her eyes over it. She gave Deirdre a big smile.

'What's the last thing you remember, Deirdre?' asked the nurse.

Deirdre cast her mind back. Thinking was a bit of an effort, and made her head hurt worse than ever. The only image she could focus on with any clarity was that of Rory McDonagh carrying her dripping wet across the stage of the Phoenix theatre. Then some lines of Eva's from *Hamlet* came to her:

There is a willow grows aslant a brook . . .

'I fell off The Lady Tara into a river. That's the last thing I remember.'

'Do you know where you are now?'

'Yes. I'm in the Blackrock Clinic.'

'That's right.' The nurse jotted something down on the clipboard and hung it back on the end of Deirdre's bed. 'There's nothing to worry about – we won't keep you in long. I'll just go and fetch the doctor – she'll need to have a look at you. Then you could probably do with some rest. I'll be back in a minute,' she said, and disappeared back out through the door.

'What happened, Mum?'

'I don't want to go into too much detail, darling. I'll do that tomorrow when you're feeling a bit better. Right now you need to take it easy.'

'What time is it?' Deirdre suddenly realized that she wasn't even sure what day it was. 'Is it still Sunday?' she asked.

'Yes – only just. It's nearly midnight.' Rosaleen

checked her watch and got to her feet. 'I'm sorry, my love – I can't talk right now. I promised I'd let your father know how you were as soon as there was any news. He'll be sick with worry.'

'Is he at home?'

'No – he's on his way back from Westport. He should be hitting Longford around now. Luckily he has the mobile with him.' Rosaleen picked up the phone.

'Tell me what happened, Mum. Please.' Suddenly it was really important to Deirdre that she knew.

Her mother looked at her and relented. She put the phone back down. 'Well, in a nutshell, your friend Rory McDonagh saved your life. He got you out of that river and held your wound together until the bleeding stopped.' Rosaleen sat down again, and took Deirdre's hand. 'The ambulance got to you as soon as it could. Your cut was stitched while you were unconscious and you were given a cat scan just to make sure that there was no damage done.' Rosaleen stroked Deirdre's hair. 'The film company have asked that you stay here for a couple of days for observation. They're not taking any chances.'

Deirdre looked around the hospital room. It was like a bedroom in a luxury hotel. The walls were papered in muted pastel shades and the carpet was a tasteful grey. There was a television in the corner, a phone by the bed and a door leading to what Deirdre presumed was an en suite bathroom. 'But how can we afford it, Mum? This place must cost the earth! And where did all the flowers come from?'

'Everything's courtesy of Big TP Productions, my love. You've given them a hell of a fright. They immediately smelt litigation in the air, and the production's in abeyance till things have been sorted out.' Rosaleen leaned forward and smiled down at her daughter. 'You *are* an eejit, Deirdre. What on earth possessed you to get up on that horse? I've never had such a scare in my life as when Rory McDonagh broke the news to me on the phone.'

Deirdre had a new thought. 'What was Rory doing there, Mum? He wasn't even *on* the film, you know.'

'He wanted to see that you were OK. He knew you had a scene on a horse and he wanted to be there to check things out and make sure nothing could go wrong. He's a good friend to you, Deirdre.' Rosaleen leaned back in her chair and looked at her daughter shrewdly with her head on one side. 'Apparently he went for TP O'Reilly and would have broken his nose if the crew hadn't held him back.'

The sound of approaching voices came from the corridor. 'Here's the doctor now. I'd better nip down and phone your dad from the foyer. I won't do it from here while she's with you.' Rosaleen stroked Deirdre's hair and then stood up. 'I love you, you precious little dingbat. I'm so glad you're going to be all right.' And as Rosaleen slipped out of the room, Deirdre started to cry.

* * *

Two days later she packed up the few things that her mother had brought in for her. Her father was due to pick her up around midday to drive her home to Kilmacanogue.

Deirdre was feeling better now, although she was still on painkillers for the gash on her shoulder. Her room was more like a posh hotel room than ever. As well as the lavish bouquets from Big TP Productions there had been deliveries of flowers from Eva and David, Sebastian, Maeve and Sally Ruane.

The production company had run into serious difficulties after the accident. One of the backers – another cousin of Big TP's – had been spooked by the news and had withdrawn finance for the project. Sally said that she thought it was extremely unlikely that the film would ever be made, or that Deirdre would ever get paid. She had tried to let her down gently, and had made reassuring noises about the upcoming part in *Ardmore Grove*, but Deirdre was feeling too low to really care about anything much, even when Sally told her that she'd been availability checked for Irina in *Three Sisters* at the Abbey.

As she stuffed her pyjamas into a plastic carrier bag there was a knock on the door. 'Come in,' she said. The door opened and Rory walked into the room. He was carrying a huge bouquet of orchids so perfect that they looked artificial.

'Ba ba black sheep,' he said.

Deirdre sat down on the bed very suddenly. 'What on earth are you talking about, Rory?' was all she could say. She knew she had gone very red.

'That very sexy little nurse down the corridor told me you'd had three bags of saline solution while you were on your drip.'

He threw the flowers onto a chair.

'They're beautiful, Rory. Thank you,' she said.

'They're not from me,' he said. 'The nurse asked me to bring them in to you. These are from me.' He handed her a box of dolly mixtures. The attached card was a reproduction of the Millais painting she'd once told him she loved, and written on the back was:

Too much of water hast thou, poor Ophelia.

'Oh thank you Rory – they're my favourite sweets.' She hid her face behind the card, pretending to be studying it so that he wouldn't see her starting to cry.

He sat down beside her on the bed and pushed her hair back behind her ear. 'What are you blubbing about?' he asked.

'I don't know,' she sobbed.

'I'd like to dissolve you, Deirdre O'Dare, and take you intravenously.' Rory kissed the place on her neck which had been exposed when he'd pushed back her hair. The sound she made could have been a sob or it could have been a gasp. He put a finger under her chin and turned her face so that she was looking into his eyes.

'You saved my life, Rory,' she said.

'Oh, shut up, Deirdre,' he said, and kissed her for a long time. Then he stood up and moved towards the door.

'Where are you going?' she asked in a sudden panic.

'I'm looking for the "Do Not Disturb" sign to put on the door.'

Deirdre laughed with relief. 'Rory – we're in a hospital, not a hotel.'

'Oh yeah. Shit. I forgot.'

He detached the envelope from the cellophane wrapping on the bouquet of orchids. 'Don't you want to know who these are from?' he asked, dropping the envelope on to her lap. Deirdre didn't really care who the flowers were from, but reading the note might be a good way of avoiding looking at Rory. She didn't want him to see her expression until she'd had a chance to control it. She knew she had never looked more like a pathetic, lovesick adolescent.

She slid the card out of the envelope and then burst out laughing.

'What does it say?' asked Rory. 'It must be a pretty good joke.'

'It is.' Deirdre handed it to Rory.

'"Dear Deirdre,"' he read aloud. '"I was sorry to hear about your accident. I hope you are feeling better now. I just thought I should let you know that I won't be able to see you for a while because I'll be up to my eyes for the next couple of months. Jools Rathbone-Lyon has cast me as the young Grace

O'Malley in the film we went up for. Get well soon. Love from Sophie."'

Rory screwed the card up and chucked it across the room. Then Deirdre couldn't laugh any more because he was kissing her too hard. He started to undo the buttons on her shirt and then he slipped his hand inside.

'Rory,' she said finally with what little breath she had left. 'Don't you think you'd better stop? Someone might come in.'

'I told the nurse to knock,' said Rory McDonagh as he lay her down on the hospital bed.

Deirdre O'Dare blossomed like a flower.

THE END